THE HIGHLAND HENS

JUDY LEIGH

B

Boldwood

First published in Great Britain in 2022 by Boldwood Books Ltd.

Cover Design by Debbie Clement Design

Cover Photography: Shutterstock

A CIP catalogue record for this book is available from the British Library.

Paperback ISBN 978-1-80162-354-4

Large Print ISBN 978-1-80162-355-1

Harback ISBN 978-1-80162-353-7

Ebook ISBN 978-1-80162-357-5

Kindle ISBN 978-1-80162-356-8

Audio CD ISBN 978-1-80162-348-3

MP3 CD ISBN 978-1-80162-349-0

Digital audio download ISBN 978-1-80162-351-3

Boldwood Books Ltd
23 Bowerdean Street
London SW6 3TN
www.boldwoodbooks.com

To the many women who inspire me. You know who you are.

1

Mimi tottered over to the stereo system on wobbly heels, bending over the record player, letting the needle drop on the revolving grooves. Immediately, a dusty crackling spat through the speakers and a razzle-dazzle trumpet blasted out.

She twirled in the crumpled costume and the years fell away. The dress was loose now, but the silk was still creamy and soft, the skirt with the long, feathered tail a blaze of scarlet. With her hair piled high, diamanté jewellery glinting, eyelashes fixed like fluttering fans, she was twenty-one again; she could hear the trumpets fizzing from the speakers, the sleazy slur of the saxophone, the rattle of drums. And she was there, kicking high, smiling into blinding lights. She was Mimi Solitaire.

The scent of Scottish pines drifted through the upstairs window, a sharp tang of citrus. The warm July air hung heavily, no breath of wind as Loch Ness shimmered, beaten gold, the blinding light of a vast mirror. Arrow-headed fir trees clung to the banks, rising in clusters to a steep summit beneath a sky stuccoed with clouds, as fat and fluffy as curled lambs.

It was too early for Chardonnay Show Time: that was always

after six o'clock, and it wasn't yet one, but Mimi poured herself a glass of golden wine anyway. The taste was sweet and sharp on her tongue, and she laughed out loud. Such was life, both sweet and bitter.

Mimi felt suddenly alive, her skin tingling with excitement; the melody infused itself like oxygen through her soul, as it always did, and she couldn't help the way her body responded, each muscle and sinew performing a swing, a lunge. It was who she was.

She threw out her arms and smiled; a dancer had to show her most alluring smile. It was the first thing she had been taught in the 1950s when she'd clambered on stage and stood in a huddled line with all the other chorus girls: someone had barked, 'Stand straight, chest out, head back, and *smile*.'

Mimi felt tall and elegant, the spray of crimson feathers bristling on her headdress, the tail of red plumes swinging behind. She smiled, tangy Chardonnay droplets on her tongue.

The tune resounded, the singer began to croon, and Mimi sang along. 'I'm just a girl in a man's world, I'm young and sweet and shy; so treat me like a lady, mister, or I'll have to say goodbye.'

Mimi raised one arm, then the other. It wasn't so easy nowadays to keep the dance going. Her heel hurt, her legs ached too. Her voice was still strong, but it had developed a reedy quality. She launched a toe in a high kick, followed by another, wincing, catching her breath, tumbling into the chair and reaching for wine. She swallowed a reassuring slug and closed her eyes, allowing her body to relax as the music thumped. There were so many memories, creaking wooden boards beneath her feet, the scent of greasepaint and sweat in her nostrils; for a moment, she could feel the flutter of feathers and the synchronised sway of warm bodies in a chorus line. Mimi lifted her glass recklessly and drank again.

'To the good times.'

Crossing her legs, she felt the electric swish of nylon and moved to the window, to the cluster of fir trees and the Highland road that led to Skye, north to the sea and the Orkney islands. Outside, the air was hot and still, the water shimmering through a yellow haze.

She glanced at the two gilt-edged screens behind which she changed into her costumes, the hat stands and the wardrobes bulging with silks, feathers, gaudy finery; she ought to dress for lunch. Mimi sipped her wine, aware of the soft sweep of false lashes against her cheek. She wondered if she should stretch out on the bed and doze; she could miss lunch altogether. That would be no bad thing: Finlay would be at the head of the table, dominating the conversation. Hamish wasn't staying for lunch – he had to get back to Inverness. Hamish had always been her favourite. Angus would eat in his own room; often distant and self-absorbed, he had become worse since the accident. Now he had every excuse to be antisocial.

An aroma oozed through the floorboards from the kitchen below: Ailsa was cooking chicken. The smell carried her back to London, to late breakfasts in boarding houses in the 1950s. It didn't take much to drag her back to the days when she slept in late and sang and danced most evenings into the early hours, filling the middle position in a well-drilled chorus line, kicking her legs high and singing at the top of her lungs.

As the record finished, the memory of an old tune came to her and Mimi hummed softly, adding a few words as she remembered them: 'Rain or shine... laughter and tears... you'll always be mine... through the passing years...' She shook her head, the feathers on the headdress leaning to one side. The song seemed familiar but distant now, long gone. It reminded her of a man she had known too briefly: he'd promised to love her forever.

There was a sharp knock on the landing door that led to her apartment. Mimi opened one eye and called, 'Come in.' Her voice drifted thinly and the knock came again, persistent. She pushed the words from her diaphragm, authoritative and strong. 'Come in.' The effort made her feel suddenly tired.

Ailsa stood in the door space leading to the stairs. She spoke in her small voice. 'Lunch will be served in ten minutes, Mrs McKinlay.'

Mimi staggered towards her, waving her hand, pushing the name away like an irritating fly. 'I'm Mimi Solitaire.'

Ailsa didn't move. 'You can't go downstairs dressed like that.'

'Why not?' Mimi raised her glass. 'Join me in a glass of Chardonnay, Ailsa. Come on, sit down, relax, take the weight off your feet.'

'Drinking wine before lunch?' Ailsa still hadn't budged. She was a small, dark-haired woman, staring through thick-rimmed spectacles. 'Mr Finlay says you've to come down. Mr Hamish has just left – he has work to do.' She paused and, when Mimi didn't reply, she added, 'Shall I help you to get changed?'

Mimi drained the last of the wine. 'I might just eat up here if Hamish has gone home, Ailsa. Could you just bring me a small plate of something – salmon?'

'Mr Finlay says you've to—'

'I don't care what Finlay says.' Mimi raised the empty glass defiantly.

Ailsa took a step forward. 'Shall I get your dress, the brown one with the flowers on?'

Mimi pulled a face. 'Oh, no, please, it's horrible. Such a plain dress. I'd look like I was wearing a sack.'

'The red lace dress, then, Mrs McKinlay?' Ailsa tried harder. 'That's a pretty dress.'

'But it swamps me. I've lost so much weight...' Mimi said

sadly. 'Do you know, I used to fill a dress, I mean, really carry one off...' She reached for the bottle of Chardonnay.

Ailsa was alarmed. 'Please don't drink any more.' She edged forward. 'Mr Finlay says you've not to drink...'

'Finlay?' A laugh burst from Mimi's lips. 'He's like his father – he has no sense of fun.' She recalled a man with red hair and broad shoulders who had captured her heart well over sixty-five years ago, given her a job, two children and a home. She pushed the memory away. 'Oh, very well. I'll come down.' As she stretched her legs, she felt a twinge in her calves. 'I'll just put on a wrap...'

'You should wear proper clothes to come down to lunch.' Ailsa took a breath. 'We could just opt for blouse and slacks?'

'We?' Mimi raised an eyebrow. 'Slacks?'

'Let's get you dressed, shall we?' Ailsa approached, her arms outstretched. Mimi smiled widely and flung her arms around her neck.

'Have you ever been on stage, Ailsa?'

'On the stage? Oh, no,' Ailsa replied. 'Why ever would I want to do that?'

'Oh, it's the most marvellous feeling.' Mimi considered her words for a moment, hugging Ailsa closer. 'More marvellous than a glass of wine – even more marvellous than making love.'

'I wouldn't know, Mrs McKinlay,' Ailsa panted. 'Not nowadays...'

'I do like Chardonnay,' Mimi said. 'And love, love is wonderful, with the right man. I'm not sure Finlay's father was the right man for love, though. But he was rich, and once he made my heart beat so fast. Now, Angus's father – poor as a church mouse but oh, my goodness, that man was special.'

'Mrs McKinlay...'

Mimi patted Ailsa's arm affectionately. 'Shall I teach you to dance? You're small and you have good strong legs – I'm sure we could make you a great burlesque dancer – oh, you should be a cancan girl.'

'I don't want to be a cancan girl.'

'But you will once you start, I promise you – it was the same with me, a high kick and I was hooked.' She wrapped an arm around Ailsa's neck. 'Come on – join in with me. You just lift one leg in the air – whoosh, then the other – whoosh—'

'Whoosh?' Ailsa gargled beneath Mimi's arm.

'Feel the air under your skirts and smile, Ailsa – then magically you're filled with joy. And kick those legs higher – one, two, one, two.'

'I can't keep up...'

Mimi couldn't hear. She was hanging onto Ailsa, who was slowly sinking towards the floor. At that moment, Mimi was on stage again, smiling for all she was worth and belting out a song. 'We're the songbirds of the chorus line and we all get on just fine—'

'No, no, we don't get on fine.' Ailsa's knees buckled.

'We kick our legs so high and make our feathers fly...'

'I can't breathe...' Ailsa's legs gave way and she tumbled down. Mimi collapsed on top of her, an arm trailing in the air as she fell.

'Well, that was fun,' Mimi said. 'Oh, dear. I'm not sure I can get up.'

'Just stay there, darling... I'm here now, don't worry.' A low, drawling voice, heavily accented, came from the doorway and Mimi gazed up at Isabella Ballantyne, who was leaning against the doorpost in a long yellow dress. Her dark hair was piled high, and diamonds sparkled in her ears.

'Isabella – thank goodness,' Mimi gasped.

Ailsa scrabbled to her feet. 'Mrs Ballantyne – does Mr Finlay know you're here?'

Isabella waved a hand. 'I don't announce myself to Fin. I just let myself in.'

Mimi's face lit up. 'Oh, I'm so glad you're here.'

'Your costume is fabulous,' Isabella drawled. 'And now I'm going to take you to lunch.'

'Lunch is downstairs, already prepared...' Ailsa stopped as Isabella raised a commanding hand.

'I'm talking about lunch outdoors, al fresco, in a little place by the loch. Seafood, not chicken fried to within an inch of its life. I'm talking about prawns, oysters, mussels in white wine.'

'Heaven,' Mimi breathed. 'But I can't go out like this.'

'Of course you can. Overdressed is best, I always say. It commands attention. The car's outside.' Isabella sauntered across to Mimi, holding a hand, tugging her gently to her feet. 'Your chariot awaits, darling. Just leave the headdress and tail on the bed, throw a light coat over your costume and we'll go, shall we? Mimi Solitaire and Isabella Giannelli, two single ladies out on the town together.'

Mimi flung the feathered headdress to one side and patted her hair. 'Fabulous. I love my lunches with you, Isabella.'

'Mr Finlay won't like it,' Ailsa said.

'I don't give a hoot what Finlay likes,' Mimi said gleefully. She threaded an arm through Isabella's. 'Where are we dining?'

'Grimaldi's, where else? The best little Italian ristorante this side of Inverness.' Isabella hooted with laughter. 'You and I, darling, we both picked rich Scottish husbands who brought us to the Highlands to live in their big houses. But they are both long gone and we're still here, glamorous women in our eighties who do just as we please.' She flashed dark eyes in Ailsa's direction. 'We haven't changed a bit from the young women we were in the 1960s. I was a fashion model in London then, Ailsa, and Mimi was the star of the stage. It's kept us alive.'

'It has,' Mimi agreed, clutching Isabella's arm for support. The two women tottered towards the stairs on high heels, and Mimi called over her shoulder. 'Tell Finlay not to wait up. Isabella and I are going out to have some fun. And that means lunch and wine...'

'And flirting, and reminiscing about the good old days...' Isabella added.

They cackled as they launched themselves down the steps, heels tapping unsteadily.

Ailsa shuddered. 'Women of their age, driving too fast in that old red sports car. Oh, dearie me – Mr Finlay won't be happy.'

2

Fin took a deep breath, a hand pressed against his forehead. Then his face was composed again, still arrestingly handsome at sixty-four. 'Ailsa... you know how important you are to this household. I value everything you do here.' He ran a hand through thick curly hair, once red, now snow white. His eyes, blue as ice water, met Ailsa's. 'We need you here at Glen Carrick House.'

Ailsa shrugged, undecided now beneath the gaze of this tall, confident man. She said, 'I know you value what I do, Mr Finlay. That's never been in dispute. But...' She gave a small cough.

'Perhaps if I paid you a little more?' Fin's hand went to the breast pocket of his jacket, even though there was no wallet there. He knew this was his checkmate move. 'Perhaps if we raised your hourly rate...?'

'I don't know. Money isn't everything—'

'It can't be easy for John, you being away now he's retired. Perhaps if you came in just for a couple of hours a day...?'

'It's not about the hours I do, it's...' Ailsa put a finger to her lip, a confidential gesture. 'It's Mrs McKinlay. She's so...' Her expression was troubled. 'She's so difficult.' Ailsa's voice was hushed, despite the fact that Mimi was no longer in the house. 'Difficult, Mr Finlay. And her Italian friend, Isabella. She's a bad influence. Well, they are both as bad as each other.'

Fin instantly felt protective towards his mother. She was frail now, a scrap of frills and bones who lived her life in the past, but he admired her determination, her resolve. 'We all love my mother, Ailsa. She's a treasure.'

Ailsa shook her head. 'She wouldn't come down for lunch. She's away now with that mad woman in her fast car. I made far too much food for the both of you. There's a lot left over.'

'The chicken is delicious.' Fin gazed at his plate: the meal was still warm, half-eaten.

'It's overcooked.' Ailsa's lip curled. 'And I hate wasting food.'

Fin said, 'Take the leftovers home – put the meat in a pie for John.'

'Mrs McKinlay never eats what I cook. She picks away at morsels and drinks wine up there in the attic by herself.'

'My mother's eighty-eight. She doesn't have much of an appetite nowadays.' Fin's gaze swept to the ceiling, even though he knew Mimi was out. He tried again. 'She appreciates your cooking but she's never eaten much. I'm sure when she was on the stage, she lived off scraps every day.'

'On the stage?' Ailsa's voice was hushed but the derision was clear in her tone. 'I don't believe she's ever been on the stage, Mr Finlay. People round here say that your father met her in London at a theatre and she was just an usherette. I wouldn't be surprised if it was all fantasy and she's never been on the stage at all. She sits in the attic day after day, drinking and imagining the past, and it's probably just all...' Ailsa's eyes widened, 'in her head.'

Fin pressed his lips together. 'You do a fine job looking after my mother. I'm very grateful...'

'She needs a proper companion. Someone who will live in

and look after her. I've reached the end of my tether. I'm handing in my notice.'

'Ailsa, won't you reconsider?'

'My mind's made up.'

'Just the cleaning? Or the cooking? Both?'

'I can't work with your mother any more. And as for your brother, Mr Finlay—'

'Angus? He's surely no bother.'

'No, but he's always in his room playing strange music and I can't get in there to clean. He won't let me in. If I knock, he tells me to go away – but not in polite terms.' She rolled her eyes. 'And he doesn't eat the food I cook either...'

'He's very particular.'

'Particular? There's nothing wrong with my cooking.'

'Angus eats macrobiotic food. He likes raw vegetables, grains, plants.' Fin sighed. He was becoming a little irritated with Ailsa's comments about his family.

Ailsa shook her head. 'It's not natural.'

'He's in recovery,' Fin said quickly. 'Ailsa – we need you here. Think about it overnight – give it twenty-four hours.' Fin reached out a hand, pressing Ailsa's fingers. He offered a gaze that could melt a heart. 'I'm not sure we could manage here without you.'

Ailsa was transfixed by the power of his eyes for a moment. 'I'll consider what you've said...'

'Thank you.'

'But I can't take much more of Mrs McKinlay. It's gone on for too long.'

'All right.' Fin squeezed her fingers one more time, then gently dropped her hand. 'We'll talk about it some more tomorrow. Come in at twelve.' He placed a palm against her back. 'Shall I see you to the door? It's a hot day – there's not even a breeze coming off the loch. You take care now.'

'It's only five minutes' walk, ten at the most.'

'Give my best wishes to John. Have a lovely afternoon.'

Fin stood up, tall and lean, gesturing towards the door. He was sure Ailsa would be back tomorrow. Hamish would be in Inverness by now, and Angus was just Angus – he'd be in his room for the rest of the evening. It fell to Fin to keep the family on an even keel. He needed a drink before he picked up the paperwork in the snug. His solicitor had sent him some documents that needed immediate attention. Karen was making more demands.

Fin passed the room Angus was using as a bedroom. Music blared from inside. Fin knocked gently. 'All okay in there, Angus?'

A soft grunt came from behind the door, a mumbled word or two that sounded like, 'I'm fine – don't trouble yourself.'

Fin stood still for a moment, then he took his mobile phone from his jacket pocket and pushed a hand through his hair. He pressed a button and, in a swift movement, held the phone to his ear. A voice sounded softly in the speaker and Fin said, 'Hamish? We need to talk. Ailsa has threatened to leave again.' He raised his eyebrows, furrowing his forehead. 'Can you come round tomorrow? We need to be together on this.' He sighed. 'Yes, come round first thing. We'll sort it out over eggs and coffee. Mother's out drinking cheap-shit Chardonnay with Isabella again, bless her heart... Angus? Well, he's going nowhere now, is he? Yes, okay, Hamish. Tomorrow, first thing.'

Fin replaced the phone in his pocket. He thought about calling Karen, asking her to talk to him. The demands from her solicitor were unreasonable: Karen was being deliberately awkward now. They had stopped loving each other long ago and revenge was all she had left. Fin shook his head. He'd pour himself a large whisky and sort out the paperwork. It had been a tough day.

He reached into the cupboard for the bottle of single malt, his eyes icy: every day was tough now.

* * *

Mimi held up her glass and Isabella refilled it from a cool bottle, a cigarette pressed between her fingers. Mimi sipped as Isabella took a drag and blew out a plume of smoke; their eyes met and they smiled at the same time. Their table was sheltered beneath a parasol, looking onto the loch, a gleaming opal between rising mountains. Birds twittered from the high trees. Mimi breathed warm earth and fresh pine. 'This is heaven,' she said.

'We deserve it. I just wish I could have more than half a glass of wine… but we'll push the boat out later.' Isabella blew more smoke through her nostrils, glancing across to where the red Triumph Stag was parked on the gravel. She was thoughtful for a moment. 'It's still going strong, my sports car. It was made in 1973, and it's raring to go, thanks to my mechanic, Greg.' She gave a small laugh, low and layered with mischief. 'Mind you, if Greg laid his hands on me, I'd be raring to go too.'

Mimi poked a fork at her seafood pasta. 'I can't eat all this – I have no appetite.'

'*Frutti di Mare*,' Isabella trilled. 'Fruits of the sea. It will keep you healthy. I don't care. I'm almost eighty-three, I hardly eat, I don't sleep, I chain smoke. I know I won't last much longer, but I'll enjoy every moment I have left.'

Mimi took a glug of wine. 'But I'm eighty-*eight*,' she replied. 'When I was younger, I used to be able to dance for hours. I still put on my costumes and go through the moves but, in truth, I'm tired after just a few minutes.'

'You have the stamina of someone twenty years younger – dancing keeps you alive,' Isabella insisted. 'And I refuse to change who I am for anyone. When I was a fashion model in the sixties, I had to be glamorous and fight for my place. It made me tough. Then I married Archie Ballantyne and I just kept on fighting. It's a habit.' Her eyes blazed. 'I'll be fighting until they take me out in a box.'

Mimi shook her head. 'Donald believed that if he bought things for me, I'd be a good wife. I suppose I was.' She gulped more wine. 'I love my boys, but every single day I wanted to be back on the stage. I kept my career in London as long as I could, even after Hamish was born. But once I came to Scotland, I missed dancing so much.'

'Thank goodness we have each other.' Isabella puffed on her cigarette. Neither she nor Mimi had eaten much; the food was still piled on their plates, cold. 'Of course, I should have had children, but I was worried it would ruin my figure. Yours is still perfect and you had three...'

'I'm all skin and bones now. I used to fill my dresses. Oh, what great days they were, Isabella.' Mimi lifted her glass.

'No regrets, Mimi. We are here and we are alive. We should drink to that.'

'I am drinking,' Mimi laughed. 'Every day.' She gazed at her glass; the wine gleamed like honey. 'Don't you have any regrets?'

'I have no time for them, darling.' Isabella raised her cigarette and watched smoke curl between her fingers.

Mimi sighed. 'I regret leaving London. And then there was the sad business with Angus's father...'

'Rejoice in everything you do, don't regret it,' Isabella announced. 'You were happy for a while, even if the time was too short.'

'You're right, he was the one.' Mimi agreed. 'So, what shall we do after lunch?'

Isabella smiled. 'You're still in costume – so, you and I are going shopping. I think we need a smart new dress each. And there's a little antiques shop that I know of: it's quaint, it even hires out old theatre costumes. The owner, Lionel, is a pleasant man: he's around our age, beautiful manners, a lovely voice. I think he is a little bit in love with me. We will get a good price on anything we want.' She winked. 'And then we'll go to the hotel in Beauly. We can drink champagne all night long and find some young men to flirt with.'

'Wonderful,' Mimi agreed. 'I'm so glad you came round today, Isabella. You always cheer me up.'

'Mimi, you have such *joie de vivre*.' Isabella glanced up at the young man who had positioned himself at her elbow. She raised an eyebrow, her lips pursing in a smile. 'So, Leonardo?'

The young waiter inclined his head. 'Isabella, I will take your plates?' He leaned closer, his voice low. 'I must remind you we have a no-smoking policy here.'

Isabella threw her cigarette to the ground and crushed it with the pointed toe of her shoe. 'Your aftershave smells good, darling. What is it? Dior?'

'It is.' The young man's face remained impassive. 'Two cappuccinos, as usual?'

Mimi clapped her hands. 'Oh, yes, please.' She watched as the waiter began to clear the table. 'Leave the bottle, though, Leonardo – I haven't finished with it.'

'Of course, Mimi,' the waiter said, a slight smile twitching across his lips. 'You are my two favourite ladies.'

'I always tip him well.' Isabella watched the waiter walk away with the dishes and she sighed. 'I love the movement of that young man, the way his trousers fit so snugly.' Her eyes twinkled. 'Ah, if I was twenty again.'

Mimi followed her gaze. 'Do you think we are too old for love?'

Isabella raised her hands, palms up. 'I am not too old for anything. I defy old age to stop me.'

Mimi swallowed the last of the wine. 'It would be nice to have someone to love, who would love me back. Someone to talk to when the sun sets, to chase away the loneliness. I was adored twice in my life, you know. Angus's father – and Charlie, a lovely young man who used to stand at the theatre door and blush whenever he saw me... I wonder if he's still alive...' She gazed at her empty glass. 'All I have now is Monsieur Chardonnay or Signor Pinot Grigio.' She gave a single laugh. 'I'm glad you're driving, Isabella. That means more wine for me. Cheers!'

'*Saluti*, Mimi!' Isabella reached into her expensive handbag for a packet of cigarettes and a gold lighter. She laughed softly. 'Now let's enjoy our coffee, then we'll go and spend some of my late husband's money. As they say, we're only here once.'

3

Mimi opened her eyes and for a moment she was still on the stage: white light from the window streamed onto the soft tartan quilted cover, dust particles twirling in the spotlight. She exhaled and stretched her limbs. Her mouth was dry; her tongue was thick and tasted bitter. As she eased herself upright, she realised that she was still wearing the pink dress Isabella had bought her. Mimi threw back her head and laughed with the careless abandon she'd felt as a young woman, rising from her bed in the early afternoon, late for a luncheon appointment with a particular Scottish gentleman.

Yesterday had been a long day. Mimi had ended the evening in a hotel in Beauly, the village near Inverness where Isabella lived. She'd serenaded the barman, singing songs from *Thoroughly Modern Millie*, dancing the Charleston, trying not to spill the glass of bubbly she clutched in her hand. Isabella was busy telling a portly, middle-aged gentleman about her days as a fashion model in London in the sixties, how she had been photographed with Twiggy, how she had dated one of the Rolling Stones. Mimi's head had been a little fuzzy at that point, but she was sure the Stones didn't write 'Ruby Tuesday' just for Isabella. Then Isabella had staggered home and Mimi had taken a taxi back to Glen Carrick House. Finlay had been watching through the window anxiously; he had paid the driver before helping his mother indoors. She sang to him, her voice dry as dust, and kissed his cheek. 'So sweet of you to wait up for me.'

'You forgot to take your keys,' he muttered.

'I almost didn't come home at all,' Mimi laughed in response. 'Isabella suggested I crash at her place.'

Fin smiled, muttering 'Crash?' Mimi was worse than any teenager.

Mimi moved to the window and gazed out at the view. Beyond the pines, the loch shimmered. She moved towards the bathroom, ignoring her tired legs, taking in the antique Victorian bath with gold taps, the embossed tiles, the gold trim. She had to admit, Finlay had been thoughtful, refurbishing the attic for her five years ago. He'd been unhappy about her living at the top of two flights of stairs, but Mimi had insisted that she was fit beyond her years and it was worth it for the spectacular view of the loch. Besides, she relished the idea of a private apartment at the top of the house. Hamish had chosen the décor; he had exquisite taste and wasn't afraid of spending money, especially when it was Finlay's.

Her sons still had their own rooms downstairs, as they came and went. Hamish often stayed overnight, although his own home was in Inverness. Finlay had a big house there too where Karen still lived, and a flat in London that Donald had left him, and the villa in Spain. Angus had been travelling, living abroad, but he'd been home for a long time now, after the accident on the Inverness road.

Mimi paused to gaze in the mirror. She pulled the silver clip from her hair and it tumbled around her shoulders. Once she'd had the golden locks of Rapunzel, but now it hung in strands. She wondered if Gavin would come today and sort it out. He came every two weeks, or every four, she wasn't sure. She liked Gavin: he told her she was beautiful and showed such interest in her career on the stage. Or perhaps Isabella would visit. Life was always better when Isabella called round.

Languidly, she filled the bath with steaming water, adding perfumed oil from pretty glass bottles, making the air sweet and delicious. She clambered steadily over the edge and slid into the foam, gasping as her skin tingled with the sudden heat. Mimi reached for a sponge and began to lather herself, enjoying the frothy suds that slid over her skin, singing, her voice a little crackly. 'Each day is new, the sun above, a chance for laughter, a chance for love.' Her eyes closed: she was at the stage door; it was 1956 again. She wore a pretty felt hat pinned to her curls and a sweeping fur coat hung around her shoulders.

Mimi's reverie stopped sharply as she remembered Angus, in his early twenties, heaving the coat from its hook, shouting about fur traders, how animals were slaughtered for profit to pamper rich people with trophies, animal skins and ivory. He had sworn he'd deal with such people himself: he'd have them locked in jail and the key thrown away. Then he threw the coat in the dustbin. Mimi had been proud of his passion, enjoying her son's flashing eyes, the absolute certainty that he was right. She laughed out loud. That was Angus; that was how he was then.

Dipping her shoulders beneath perfumed water, Mimi tugged her thoughts back to the theatre. She was swathed in the fur coat, feeling like a princess. A young man stood at the stage door, several years her junior, wearing his smart little uniform, greeting everyone as they came in with his chirpy voice. Mimi remembered a Cockney accent and the way he used to look at her with embarrassment, harbouring an awkward crush, and she'd say,

'Good evening, Charlie,' and he'd blush and reply, 'Wotcha, Miss Mimi.'

Mimi smiled. Charlie, that was his name: Charlie Gosling. He couldn't have been more than nineteen. She'd known him from the first day she'd arrived at the theatre in Bermondsey as an usher – he'd been the door boy until not long after Hamish's birth, then he'd left, married, found another job – she'd heard he'd taken up window cleaning. For the years they worked together, he'd followed her everywhere, chattering his happy banter, offering her sweets, chewing gum, compliments. But in the early days, her mind had been on her career. She'd be backstage, pulling on silks, laughing with the other chorus girls, her fingers smoothing stockings, applying powder, and then she'd rush on stage, blinded by the lights, kicking her legs high, aware that the audience was holding its breath. And she'd smile so widely and wonder if a certain man was out there watching her, waiting for the moment when the curtain fell, then he'd be backstage with flowers, ready to whisk her off to dinner.

Donald McKinlay: handsome, rich, influential. She was young and naïve, and he had swept her off her feet in those early days, bought her a fur coat. Donald had enjoyed showering her with presents simply to watch the expression of joy on her face. That was all so long ago. Mimi sank into the scented suds and let the warm water seep into her eye sockets as she held her breath for a while. Then she sat up, the water splashing over the side of the bath onto the wooden floorboards. All of a sudden, her reverie was over. She eased herself out and reached for a dressing gown, swathing her damp body in the comfort of soft material. She had forgotten about the bath, filled to the brim with cooling grey water. She was thinking about what to wear.

The lilac linen suit with the lace collar would be perfect, pearls at her throat, the blue butterfly brooch, the jewels shaped like open wings: she would go downstairs looking elegant and request a light lunch. Asparagus would be nice, a lemon sauce, a glass of crisp white wine. She'd ask Ailsa, who adored her really, although she found it difficult to show her feelings. She had a heart of gold: Ailsa would do anything for Mimi – freshly made sauce wouldn't be too much trouble. Mimi lifted the lilac suit from its hanger. She'd need to dry her hair, find some stockings, put on some lipstick. Then she'd be ready for anything.

* * *

Downstairs, Fin filled three coffee cups from the large jug. 'So, it's agreed, Ailsa?'

Ailsa picked up her cup. Hamish copied her movements and sipped sweet black coffee, slim fingers reaching for another biscuit. His blue eyes crinkled. He was neat in his dark jacket, shirt and jeans, his face handsome, with Mimi's straight nose, her full lips, arched eyebrows. His hair was pale, grey around the temples now. He offered a biscuit to Ailsa, who shook her head, then he leaned back in his seat. 'Fin and I are so pleased you're staying on.'

'Three mornings a week, two afternoons. Reduced hours, we agreed.'

Fin smiled. 'And an extra pound an hour.'

'I'll just cook and clean. No interaction with...' Ailsa rolled her eyes to the ceiling. 'Just the basics from now on.'

Ailsa picked up a can of polish and a duster, scuttling towards the hallway. Fin watched her go.

Hamish's brow was furrowed. 'Mum could do with more company, not less, Fin.' He toyed with the handle of his coffee cup. 'Isabella only comes round once or twice a week. The mad hairdresser calls by appointment. Mum has no one else, bless her. She's lonely – she just sits up there...'

Fin agreed. 'Drinking Chardonnay, dressing up and singing. We have to do something. We should think about getting her some professional help.' He noticed Hamish's frown deepen. 'Perhaps we could find her a companion. Pay someone.'

'They could live in, be on call,' Hamish added hopefully. 'My old flat in the basement isn't too bad – we could throw that in with the deal.'

'And maybe the person could help out with Angus, get into his room and give it a clean.'

'It probably needs cleaning, Fin. He keeps that dog in there all night,' Hamish grinned.

Ailsa was suddenly back in the kitchen. She had been listening. 'No one from around here will work with Mrs McKinlay.'

'Oh, Mum's totally gorgeous.' Hamish's laugh was a throwaway trill just like Mimi's. Then he frowned. 'Why, do people talk about her, Ailsa?'

'Some do.' Ailsa sounded bitter. 'Most of the people in Drumnadrochit have heard the stories – that she and her friend Isabella behave like a couple of ageing film stars.' Ailsa lowered her voice. 'It's said locally that she's a little mad in the head.'

'She's not mad,' Hamish said fondly. 'She's lovely and sweet and a little bit old...'

'Who's old?'

Hamish and Fin turned to look at their mother, her damp hair pinned askew on her head, leaning against the door jamb, a jaunty crimson smile on her mouth. She wore a purple suit of crumpled linen that hung loose from her slight frame. There was a brooch on her lapel and a string of pearls around her neck. Her lipstick was smudged.

Hamish leaped from his seat and hugged her. 'Mum, you look stunning.'

A slight noise came from Ailsa's mouth as Mimi sat down and crossed her legs. Fin smiled. 'Coffee, Mother? Shall I make us all a fresh pot?'

Mimi smiled. 'Ailsa, darling, I was rather hoping you'd whip up one of your lemon sauces and steam some asparagus for me. Or salmon might be nice. And a cool glass of wine.'

Ailsa was suddenly troubled. She gestured towards Fin, who said, 'Ailsa's just arrived, Mother.'

'Don't worry, Mum.' Hamish leaped up, busying himself in the kitchen. 'You sit down and I'll rustle you up something nice. How about some muffins and fried bacon, hot coffee?'

Mimi settled herself in Hamish's seat. 'I wanted asparagus and lemon...'

'Just think of New York, Mum – of Broadway, an all-day breakfast with the stars.' Hamish rushed over to hug Mimi and then went back to the range, lifting a frying pan. He pressed a button, and a kettle began to rattle. 'Eggs and bacon coming up, ma'am – and sweet black coffee.'

Fin took the hint. 'I'm on it, Hamish, brunch is on its way.' He tried an American intonation, too loud and unauthentic. 'Eggs over easy for Miss Solitaire.'

Mimi sighed. 'That would be delightful.'

'On its way, honey pie.' Hamish continued the game, throwing bacon in the frying pan, crooning 'Food, Glorious Food' in an enthusiastic falsetto voice. Mimi picked up a knife and fork, clicking them together like castanets and joined in the song, her voice faltering on the high notes. Fin, who was no singer, lifted a wooden spoon and began to shake it in the air and kick his legs, wiggling his bottom provocatively. Ailsa watched Mimi and her boys, her expression aghast, and said, 'They're right in Drumnadrochit. What everyone says about the whole family is completely right...'

Hamish was in full swing, singing about custard and mustard, pushing burning bacon around a pan, lifting a muffin from the toaster with a flourish and buttering the charred surface as Fin poured coffee and offered Ailsa his most charming expression. Mimi threw her head back and began to sing 'Tea for Two' from *No, No, Nanette*: she knew all the words. She launched herself towards Ailsa, pressing her face against the other woman's cheek so that she could smell the thick powder and waxy lipstick. Mimi tugged her with remarkable new strength. 'Come on, Ailsa – vamp it up with me. Let's get a high kick or two in for the finale.'

Fin placed a hot jug of coffee and four clean cups on the table as Mimi attempted to heave Ailsa forward. A cup rolled to the floor and smashed. Hamish turned from the frying pan, surrounded by smoke and the stench of burned bacon.

'Dance with me, someone,' Mimi implored, turning to Hamish.

'I'll dance with you, Mother.' Fin was at Mimi's side, gently taking her in his arms, twirling her round. Hamish began to sing louder, his voice exaggeratedly deep and strong.

Ailsa gaped. 'You're all mad...'

Suddenly, the back door that led to the garden banged open and a black Labrador bounded in, dashing to the table and sniffing Mimi's ankles before it leaped up at Ailsa, then it hurled itself towards Hamish, who was ladling bacon from the frying pan onto charred muffins. The air was blue with smoke. The dog barked excitedly, almost knocking the pan from Hamish's hand in a desperate lurch for the bacon. The Labrador snapped at the bread, snaffled the meat and wolfed it down as Ailsa screamed that she loathed all dogs.

'Thor. Come here.' A man appeared at the doorway and the

black dog rushed over to him obediently and sat quietly by the side of his wheelchair. The man's dark eyes blazed as he looked at each face. Hamish and Fin met his gaze, both smiling. Mimi threw out her arms and cooed, 'Angus, darling.'

The man wheeled his chair into the room and stopped abruptly. His skin was weather-beaten, tanned leather, and his curly hair, once dark, was flecked with grey. Both legs were encased in plaster below denim shorts. He sniffed the air disapprovingly. 'I take the dog out into the garden so that he can piss and I come back in here and the whole place stinks like some sort of trucker's dive.' He stared at his brothers. 'What the bloody hell is going on?'

Fin grinned. 'We were making breakfast for Mum – Brooklyn style.'

'It was Breakfast Musical Theatre, like we used to do...' Hamish spluttered.

'Do you remember the old song and dance routines?' Mimi said dreamily.

'Well, why didn't you say?' Angus was in the centre of the room. 'What do the McKinlay boys always make their mother for breakfast?'

A smile spread across his face as he and his brothers chorused, 'Real Scottish porridge.'

The four of them launched into a song, so well-rehearsed: they had been singing it since childhood. Hamish sprang into action, collecting saucepans, clanging them together. Angus wheeled himself to a low cupboard, tugging out a box of oats that he shook like a rattle and Fin began drumming on the table with his fingers while Mimi raised her arms above her head and kicked out a leg. At the top of their voices, they sang a rousing chorus of 'Scotland the Brave' in perfect harmony, Hamish whirling his mother in a dance, Angus propelling his wheelchair in a circle followed by an excited Thor, Fin clapping his hands together and stamping his foot to keep time.

Ailsa watched, horrified, as Mimi and her three sons performed the Highland Fling around the kitchen, smiling and laughing together as they had done for years.

'They are all mad...' she breathed, rolling her eyes. 'Every one of the McKinlays is completely mad.'

4

Jess Oliver swung her car to the left and pulled in at the side of the road where the grassy verge became a tarmac parking space. She leaped out of her beloved classic purple VW Beetle, letting the door slam behind her, and wriggled her phone from her jacket pocket. The view was just as breath-taking through the camera lens: sharp shafts of light reflecting a glare on the water, smooth and bright as silver foil. The wind tugged strands of tawny hair from Jess's ponytail and blew them across the lens. She tucked the tendrils behind her ears, framed her picture and took several snaps: the dappled water, hulking mountains, grand as watching gods. There was a stone castle nestling above the loch, the outline grey and jagged against the vast sky. Jess surveyed her work. They were good photos: she'd always had an eye for detail. They'd look perfect, framed in her new home. She sighed at the beauty of it all.

'A woman needs to do more than go on diets and pay bills,' she reminded herself with a smile. She felt the lightest breeze against her cheeks. This holiday was doing her good; she could sense something in her soul becoming charged with a new energy. She wondered if she should drive into Drumnadrochit and buy a fridge magnet that proclaimed 'I Heart Scotland' to take home with her: it was her first visit to the Highlands and she was already planning her second, maybe driving north, taking in the islands, the Hebrides or the Orkneys.

Jess grinned – her home wasn't ready yet: she was considering fridge magnets before she had a fridge. Her brother probably hadn't even started to fit the kitchen; Paul had said floor first, then he'd install the rest and it would be done by the sixth. Today was August the first: for the next five days, she could do as she pleased. She hugged her jacket against a sudden gust of wind funnelling down from the mountains and strode back to the VW. It was almost five o'clock. She'd drive back to the B & B, have a shower, then it would be takeaway pizza and an early night. Tomorrow she was going to Cawdor Castle near Inverness. She remembered reading *Macbeth* at school: she was sure the old castle would be atmospheric, steeped in history.

Once in the driving seat, Jess delved into the glove compartment and found a packet of mints, unwrapping the foil. Fleetingly, she thought of Andy, her ex, whose love of old things was much greater than his love for her. He'd become obsessed with his metal detector, finding all sorts of fascinating things, including a coin he'd claimed to be Roman on a piece of waste ground. Andy was still handsome in his late fifties, always good-natured. Jess had fond memories of their marriage, but she was happier now.

She'd lived in Greece in her twenties as a holiday rep, working for Sunspot Summers until she was twenty-nine, then she'd come back home to Worcester to start anew. She and Andy were married by the time she was thirty-one; they bought a little hotel, she'd had Saffy at thirty-four, and the years had flown by. Now she was fifty-nine and divorced.

Andy had been the first to admit that things weren't right between them; he'd told her over his breakfast cereal one morning that he wanted to start a new life by himself. He said that he still loved her, but they'd grown apart, and Jess had to concede that she understood: in all honesty, she felt the same way. They worked all week, running a thriving business, often doing separate shifts, and they had no time left for each other, for fun. Andy had said sadly that the hotel was a great little business, but their marriage was a shell, then he packed a case, hugged her, wished her the best and left.

Jess had run the hotel alone for two more years. She had sold it several months earlier, dividing the money. Andy was in Colchester now, the organiser of a busy metal detector club; he was happily retired, going out treasure hunting every day, enjoying every minute. They still kept in touch because they had history together. They were Saffy's parents; their daughter was in London now, in her twenties, independent, living in a flat with three other girls, studying for a PhD at Goldsmiths. Jess and Andy had good memories; they were still friends.

Jess had her own life now. As she started the VW engine, she was thankful that being single had made her independent, financially and in terms of her outlook on life. She'd bought a lovely old cottage just down the road from where her brother lived in Badsey and when she returned next week, she'd start again in a new home. What could be better?

Jess drove steadily, following a large white van with the sign 'Harry's Highland Haggis', a giant cartoon of a haggis in a tam-o'-shanter with legs, a kilt and a sporran. Scotland was such a welcoming place. She'd been staying at the B & B, a small, terraced house called Beraghaig, for four days, and already she was on first-name terms with Heather, the owner, who was incredibly kind. This morning, Heather had plonked herself down at the table, shared coffee and chatted eagerly about the best places to visit; it had been Heather's idea to seek out Macbeth's castle tomorrow and to go to Culloden, where she had been earlier, to visit the battle site.

The phone buzzed in her pocket and Jess pulled over into a gateway. The call was from her brother. She held the phone to her ear. 'Paul. How's it all going?'

'Not too bad,' he replied. 'I'm in the house now. The new floor's looking nice.'

'Thanks.' She was already excited by the prospect of a place she could call her own. She imagined her brother, stocky and strong, surrounded by plasterboard and a workbench covered in nails and drills, his hands on his hips and a pencil lodged behind his ear. 'I've got a couple of bottles of Scotch for you for when I'm back. And Jodie likes a nice Scotch too, doesn't she – the smoky one?'

'Jodie sends her best.' Paul's voice was hesitant for a moment. 'Er, I think we might have hit a snag, Jessie.'

'A snag?' Jess echoed. 'Nothing big, I hope?'

'It might be. It's not ideal.' Paul was being cryptic.

'What's happened?' Jess pressed her mobile closer to her ear.

'I noticed some of the skirting boards in the corner of the living room are damaged – they looked rotten, so I had a closer look.'

Jess raised an eyebrow. It was typical of Paul to be evasive. 'And? Come on – tell me the worst. It can't be that bad, can it? We looked at it together and you said there was nothing you couldn't fix—'

'Rising damp.' Paul sounded irritated. 'It'll be quite a job. It needs a damp-proof course. And I'm not sure the drainage system is helping.'

'Oh, dear,' Jess said. 'Can you sort it out?'

'It's a big project.' She heard Paul pause, thinking. 'I'm due to start a barn conversion over in Evesham next week.'

Jess exhaled. 'I'm sorry, Paul.'

He was suddenly cheery. 'Don't worry, sis. I'll throw a bit of time at it over the weekend. Perhaps it won't be too bad.' He paused. 'How's Nessie? Have you seen the monster yet?'

'The Loch is incredible – it goes on for miles. I love Scotland. I can't believe I've only ever been up as far as Edinburgh before. The Highlands are beautiful – strange and wild and a bit secluded.'

'Just like my big sis,' Paul chortled. 'No, seriously, leave this with me. You just enjoy your trip.'

'Are you sure that's okay?'

'Of course it's fine, Jessie – you've helped Jodie and me out often enough. It's the least I can do. What are you up to tonight?'

Jess shrugged. 'Pizza and maybe a film in my room.'

'Me too – Jodie's working late tonight so I'm having a take-away and a few beers.'

'Paul…' Jess's voice was soft with emotion. 'Thanks for everything you're doing…'

'No worries, it'll be the smartest place you've ever seen when it's finished.' He paused. 'It'll be great when it's all done.'

'I'm so grateful.'

'I'll call you tomorrow or the day after. Don't worry – I'll sort it.'

'Thanks, Paul.' Jess heard the phone click at the other end. She hadn't bargained for problems with the house. She pulled her ponytail free of its elastic scrunchie and tugged her fingers through the strands, looking forward to being back at the hotel and having a shower. Jess started the engine and checked the traffic before swinging the car back onto the road for Drumnadrochit.

When she arrived at Beraghaig, the front door was ajar. She rushed inside, heading for the staircase: her room was on the first floor, a comfortable double overlooking the road. She had only climbed a couple of stairs when she heard a light voice call her name. 'Jess – is that you?'

A slim woman with spiky hair and dark-framed glasses stood in the hallway. Her voice was soft and welcoming. 'I hoped I'd catch you.'

'Hi, Heather,' Jess replied. 'I had a great time at Culloden. I'm doing Cawdor Castle tomorrow.'

'The forecast is a bit grim. It might rain, hen.'

Jess was delighted. 'Thunder and lightning too, I hope. Maybe I'll see the three witches.'

It took Heather a few seconds to work out what Jess meant, then she shrugged. 'Oh, most of the witches live in Inverness now.'

'Anyone in particular?' Jess asked.

'My ex's mother, for one,' Heather grinned. 'No, I wanted to catch you when you came in. Do you have any plans for tonight?'

'A shower.' Jess wafted a hand. 'Then I thought I'd get a pizza.'

'I have a friend coming round, Amy. We were planning to get takeaway food. We've got a couple of chick flicks, a romance with Cate Blanchett, and Les Misérables. I thought we could watch one.' Heather waved a hand in welcome. 'Why don't you join us?'

'That would be lovely – thanks.' Jess was warming to the idea of spending the evening in company. 'I'll bring a bottle. What time?'

'Shall we say seven?' Heather suggested. 'Amy's great fun – you'll like her. Shall I get pizzas? What's your favourite topping?'

'Margherita – or mushrooms.' Jess swung her bag over her shoulder and started to climb the stairs. 'I'll see you at seven.'

'That's great,' Heather called. 'Which film, the romance or the musical, hen? I love romances best – I'm so sad, I have no romance in my life. But then *Les Mis* has Hugh Jackman in it – what's not to like?' She waved a hand. 'You're the guest – you choose.'

'The romance,' Jess yelled, diving for the door of her room. 'Anything other than *Les Mis*. I've never been able to sit through it all without falling asleep. I'm not a fan of musicals.'

5

Jess was eating porridge, her eyes on a guidebook as Heather poured coffee. 'Shall I get you toast? Eggs?'

'Just toast, please.' Jess reached for her cup. 'How are you feeling this morning?'

'Still pie-eyed from last night, to tell you the truth.' Heather gave a wry smile. 'Amy was the worse for wear after drinking red wine then going on to whisky. She stayed over and there's not a peep from her yet. You didn't drink much, though.'

'I'm not a big drinker,' Jess admitted. 'One glass is usually enough to send me to sleep. I liked the first film, *Carol* – it was sad, though.'

'I just adore films about thwarted love. Cate Blanchett's costumes, though – I imagine myself wearing all those fifties clothes, the hats and the suits.' Heather rolled her eyes. 'Talking of clothes, you'll need a raincoat today if you're driving to Cawdor. The weather's going to be filthy.'

'It might blow over.'

'I wouldn't be so sure, hen.' Heather gave her a warning look. 'Do you have plans for tonight?'

Jess shrugged. 'Not really.'

Heather turned to go. 'I might make one of my famous curries. You're welcome to share.'

'Thanks, that's great,' Jess said as Heather scuttled back to the kitchen. She returned to the Highland guidebook and a photo of Cawdor Castle in the sunshine.

Outside, the rain bounced on the tarmac drive as Jess rushed to her car. As she drove along the road to Inverness with wipers swishing and the sound of water squelching beneath her tyres, she wondered if she should have waited for the weather to improve. But she'd promised herself that she would revel in every opportunity: that was why she was here in Scotland. She'd organised the trip without giving a thought for what someone else might want and it had been so liberating. It would be second nature now to please herself.

She turned the radio on and recognised the song: Adele was singing 'Set Fire to the Rain'. The car in front sprayed water from its back wheels as she listened to the strong, soulful voice. Jess wondered what the lyrics meant: perhaps it was saying that passion made a person weak, open to being hurt. Jess had felt like that once, in Corfu where she had met Yiannis; she'd lived with him for five years. It had not ended well. When Jess returned home and met Andy, she'd decided that love was something that should be sensible, not passion then heartbreak, as it had been with Yiannis.

Being sensible saved a lot of misery: Jess had a lovely, brilliant, opinionated daughter, a kind-hearted ex-husband who was a friend, a good-natured, supportive brother and his cheerful wife. She wouldn't change a thing.

The clouds drooped heavily as she drove at a crawl through Cawdor village, bright with blooms and pretty cottages. Her eyes were constantly busy, searching for signs to the castle. She turned down a narrow lane towards a sprawling grey stone building with turrets and tiny windows. Jess stopped the car as water spattered in huge droplets and rain pounded on the roof. She gazed at the bulky grey shape of Cawdor Castle and smiled at the thought of the Macbeths watching rainwater pooling in buckets before emptying them out of the turret window.

The sound of thunder rumbled all around as lightning flickered and cracked the sky. Jess felt snug inside the VW Beetle; as the storm raged, she peered through the driver's window into the wing mirror, just to see if three crazy women in grey rags were leaping around a bubbling cauldron brewing a spell. She'd sit the storm out in the car, then, when the rain stopped, she'd visit the castle, make for the little café and treat herself to a cup of tea.

The rain was still beating on the roof of the car as she drove back to Drumnadrochit. Headlights were switched on, making the greasy roads shine yellow. Jess was looking forward to being back at the B & B, stepping into the hot steam of a shower, sharing a meal with Heather. She'd ask her about places to visit: the Isle of Skye would be lovely when the weather perked up. And perhaps she could find out if there was a nice restaurant locally; she'd treat Heather as a way of saying thanks for being a great host.

Jess pressed the brake pedal gently, slowing the car as she approached a roundabout, waiting in a line behind three vans. The castle had been interesting, but Jess had been a little disappointed to discover that it hadn't been built until well after Macbeth's time. Macbeth had probably killed King Duncan in Inverness castle. She wondered if she should have gone there instead.

To the right, the road was clear; Jess moved her hand to the gearstick. A sudden jolt made the Beetle shudder, jerking it forwards: someone had bumped into her. She glanced around, her heart beating fast, and wondered what to do, then she noticed a grass verge to the left and drove steadily onto the small parking area. Through the mirror, she saw another vehicle following her. She slid from the seat and stood outside, beneath a clump of fir trees. The rain was pelting so hard that her hair was immediately drenched. Behind her, a sleek black car stopped and a man in a dark jacket pushed the door open and ran towards her, leaning against the downpour. Jess wondered if he was going to shout at her.

A slim man around her age stood on the grass verge smiling apologetically. 'I'm so sorry. It was all my fault. I hope you're all right,' he said. His face shone; he was soaked with rain. 'I don't think there's much damage to the cars.'

Jess took in the damp pale hair, the china-blue eyes, the smart jacket. 'What happened?'

The man spoke softly, a hint of a local accent. 'I thought you'd already moved off. I was a bit...' He exhaled. 'A bit keen.' He strolled round to the back of her car. 'This is a lovely old VW. I used to have one just like it in yellow when I was a teenager.' He bent over and inspected the back. 'Ah, no real damage, thank goodness. It seems that I've put a bit of a dent in the bumper, that's all. I can get someone in the garage in Drumnadrochit to sort it out.'

Jess pushed wet strands of hair that had escaped from her ponytail behind her ears and inspected the old chrome bumper. 'It's fine. Please don't worry about it.' She stood up straight, meeting the man's blue eyes. He was a few inches taller than her, with a kind face and a ready smile. She glanced over his shoulder at his black car. 'That's nice. What is it?'

'It's a Saab 900 Turbo.' He shrugged. 'It's just a car. Cars don't matter. I wanted to check you were all right.'

'Oh, yes. I'm fine,' Jess replied.

'Do you have a long journey home?'

'I'm staying at a B & B. I'm not local.' Jess was aware of the rivulets of rainwater running down her face.

'Not far, I hope?' the man asked.

'Ten minutes, tops.'

The man held out his hand. 'Then I wish you a safe journey. And I'm sorry – again – for the bump. I'm glad you're okay.'

Jess shook his hand and then indicated the sky. The rain was still lashing down as they stood there, facing each other. 'I'd better go.'

The man looked back. 'Of course. Yes.' Jess turned, rushing back to the car, and heard the man call after her. 'Enjoy your stay. I hope the weather improves.'

She clambered in, putting a hand to her face. It came away damp – her hair was soaked. She recalled how she had pointed to the sky and said, 'I'd better go,' and the foolishness of her words made her smile.

There was a low rumble of an engine as the black Saab slithered past her, merging with the traffic, the man raising a hand in greeting as he passed. She pushed her key in the ignition and felt her phone buzz in her pocket. She held it to her ear. 'Paul. Hi. What news?'

'Just thought I'd give you an update.' She heard him take a breath. 'How's Scotland? Have you sampled the haggis yet?'

'Scotland's great, but I haven't summoned the courage to try haggis. I might,' she replied. 'It's been teeming with rain here.'

'Oh.' Paul paused. 'It's been bright sunshine here all day. Er – I've come up against a few snags today.'

Jess pressed the phone against her ear. 'My cottage?'

'I'm afraid so. The damp is going to be a problem. The drainage too.'

'Oh, no. Can you sort it out, Paul?'

He made a soft sound and Jess knew that the news wasn't good. 'I can't do it by myself, but I can call in a few favours. It won't be cheap but I'm sure we can sort something out. I'm afraid it isn't a quick job, though.'

Jess was suddenly serious. 'What are we talking about, Paul?'

'I don't know – materials are expensive right now. I'll get some quotes and get back to you.'

'I'm on a budget – I hope it won't be too bad.' She exhaled. 'And is it a difficult job?'

'Specialist.' He sighed. 'I think we're taking about four months before it can be completed, all told.'

'That long?' Jess was surprised.

'It's August. Think positively. You'll be in a nice dry cottage by the winter.'

'Winter?' Jess gasped. 'What am I going to do until then?'

Paul spoke softly. 'Jodie's going to clear out Luke's old room. You're home in, what – five days? We'll have it ready by then. It'll be great fun, Jessie, having you to stay. And Jodie said it would be good to have the company.'

Jess frowned. 'Four months, really?'

'It could be a bit longer. The cottage has to stay empty until all the work's finished,' Paul replied. 'Meanwhile, your things are in storage, Jessie. You're coming to stay with us.'

6

Mimi watched through the window as Hamish parked his Saab in the driveway, rushing up the steps to the front door, fumbling with his keys. The rain lashed the back of his jacket. The drive was spattered with puddles. She peered forward as he disappeared into the house. Hamish: he was hers and hers alone. Finlay was like Donald, a McKinlay through and through. Angus was something else: he was born from a single night of passion. But Hamish, although he was Donald's son, was nothing like his father. He wasn't like Finlay either, selling property, organising people: he was a free spirit, independent, carefree. Mimi wiped the window with thin fingers and gazed towards a haze of mist, the sky now rumpled like a grey blanket. Mimi recalled she was once like her youngest son, full of life, chasing dreams, unafraid of the future. At first, she was hopeful Miriam Solomons; she became Mimi Solitaire, then she was Mrs McKinlay, the boys' mother, Donald's wife. Nowadays, she wasn't sure who she was any more. Perhaps she was just a ghost.

She wandered from the bedroom to the living space. Yesterday's bottle of wine was on the table, a quarter full, and an empty glass. The light through the window was a thin shaft of brightness, contrasting with the dark of the room, like a gleam of hope. Mimi walked over to the table, picked up the glass and lifted it to her lips. The bitter tang of Chardonnay was still there, but no wine, nothing to taste. She wondered if Isabella would call.

Voices came from two flights below, the gentle rattle of conversation. She moved to the top of the stairs to listen, but the sound was just a low mumble. Slowly, gripping the banister, she descended, pace by pace, until she was on the ground floor. The door to Angus's room was closed; no sound came from inside. But the kitchen door was ajar and she leaned forward, taking in every word.

Hamish was laughing. He was glad that the bump hadn't been anything major and that the woman had been so accommodating and friendly. 'She was a tourist, so I don't suppose she'll be on the roads around here again. She had a lovely purple VW Beetle. Thankfully I only dented the bumper.'

'I'm glad it wasn't serious.' Fin knitted his brow at the thought of yet another brother in a road accident. 'We've had enough trouble to last us for a long time.'

Hamish nodded knowingly. 'Where is Angus?'

'Sleeping, I'm guessing. He tends to stay awake most of the night; he won't take painkillers. He's trying to stand on the legs and it's too early.'

'Can we get him to a physio?' Hamish asked. 'He'll do himself some permanent harm.'

'I've tried. I've offered to take him to a physiotherapist or hire one to come here but he's stubborn,' Fin said. 'The doctors have said he won't walk normally again.'

Hamish shook his head. 'Angus, incapacitated, stuck inside four walls? I don't know what he'll do if he can't get outside soon.'

'He thinks he's going to Cameroon in the autumn. We

exchanged words. I told him I thought he was being optimistic in terms of his recovery, and he said he'd do as he bloody well liked.'

'He probably will, Fin.' Hamish moved towards the stainless steel fridge. 'Do we have anything to eat?' He tugged the door open. 'Oh, no.'

'What's the matter?' Fin gazed at the wine in the fridge door. 'Ah, the six bottles of Chardonnay. Mother's well stocked.'

'I am, thank goodness.' A voice behind him made Fin turn. Mimi wandered into the kitchen. 'Yes, please, Hamish – a glass of wine would be delightful. And what did Ailsa leave for us to eat?'

'She said there are some cuts of meat in here.' Hamish lifted out a bowl piled with a concoction of seeds and fruit. 'Oh, what on earth is this?'

Fin laughed. 'It's Angus's food. Oats and nuts and something else – pumpkin seeds? God knows what he's got in here. He made it yesterday.'

'By himself?'

'You know Angus, Hamish. He won't be told. He was here in the kitchen earlier, stretching and lifting. He didn't look happy.'

Hamish took out a plate of sliced ham and some cold potatoes. 'I might stay over again tonight. Will you eat with us down here, Mum?'

Mimi was disappointed. 'Isn't Isabella coming to take me out?'

Hamish wrapped an affectionate arm around his mother. 'Come on, have supper with us. A nice piece of quiche, salad...'

'I'd prefer seafood with Isabella...' Mimi wriggled from his grasp. She gave him a hopeful look. 'You could come up to my room and we could share a bottle, just you and me.'

'And me?' Fin made a face, pretending to be piqued: his mother always claimed that Hamish was her favourite son in the hope that Fin would be jealous. It had never worked. He grinned. 'Let's all eat together, Mother. We could fetch Angus and all four of us could sit down together.' He tried harder. 'You could tell us about when you were in *The King and I*?'

Mimi rushed to the fridge and tugged out a bottle, then retreated to the doorway. 'I'm not hungry. But I will...' She cradled the wine, then laid the cool glass against her cheek. 'I will have a fresh one of these.' She was determined. 'We keep good company together, Monsieur Chardonnay and I.' Mimi twirled away, then popped her head back around the door jamb. 'I'll see you both tomorrow, though, boys. Maybe we can spend time together then.'

She disappeared. Hamish sighed and glanced at Fin, who shook his head and indicated the cold cuts of ham. 'Looks like it's just me and you for supper, Hamish. Shall I get us a bottle?'

Hamish looked towards the fridge. 'Mum's wine?'

Fin's nose wrinkled. 'Ah, no.' He opened a tall cupboard and produced a bottle. 'I prefer this stuff. A nice burgundy.' He met his brother's eyes and smiled. He was determined to be cheerful. His solicitor Hugh had been on the phone today. They had discussed the terms of the divorce and how to placate Karen. Fin was ready to fight back. He thrust out his chin. 'I'm very particular about what I drink. It's the best for me now, or nothing at all.'

*　*　*

Jess held out her glass as Amy filled it up. 'Just a small amount, please.'

Heather spooned curry onto Jess's plate. Amy topped up her own glass. 'I've plenty more bottles in the kitchen. It was on offer in the supermarket, so I bought six.'

Heather grinned. 'I think Jess needs that glass of wine. She's had a hard day.'

Amy was suddenly interested. 'What happened? You went to Cawdor, didn't you?'

'It bucketed down.' Heather offered a plate of poppadums to Amy. 'But that wasn't all...'

'Oh?' Amy raised a fork. 'Do tell all.'

Jess shrugged. 'Not much to tell – a man in a Saab bumped into me. There was only a tiny dent to the bumper – nothing serious.'

Amy swigged wine. 'Was he good-looking, this dangerous driver?'

'He was all right,' Jess replied. 'He had a lovely car.'

'That's a good sign – a rich man is always a smart move,' Heather said between mouthfuls. 'How's the curry, hen?'

'Delicious,' Jess said.

'Tell me more about this mystery man.' Amy offered an exaggeratedly comic nudge to Heather. 'Was he tall, dark and handsome?'

'Not tall – light hair. He seemed pleasant...'

'Pleasant?' Amy reached for the wine. 'I hope you took his phone number, Jess.'

'Why would I do that?'

Heather's eyebrows shot up. 'So that he could pay for the car to be fixed.'

'The car's fine...' Jess protested.

'Of course the car's fine,' Amy insisted. 'But you pretend it isn't. You let on that it's your prized possession and say you'll only be happy if he fixes the bumper...'

'And then he apologises, takes you out to dinner...' Heather added.

'Oh...' Jess smiled ruefully. 'I didn't think of that...'

'Never mind.' Heather sipped more wine. 'We have this lovely food and a glass or two of plonk. Who needs rich, handsome, charming guys in Saabs?'

'I do...' Amy said, and Heather laughed.

Jess was mystified. 'He was nice enough, but it was pouring down with rain – I was glad to get back here.'

'So,' Heather began. 'Tell us about your cottage – you're having a few problems with it?'

Jess nodded. 'A bit of damp. My brother Paul said it could take months.'

'Months? That's terrible,' Amy gasped. 'Is it going to be expensive?'

'I hope not.' Jess was thoughtful.

Heather frowned. 'What will you do? You can't live in a damp cottage...'

'Paul's invited me to stay with him.' Jess sipped her first mouthful of wine. 'His son has left home, so there's a spare room.'

'Is that going to be okay?' Amy asked. 'Do you all get on? I mean, my brother and I fight all the time – and I loathe his wife.'

'Paul and Jodie are lovely.' Jess sat back in her seat.

'Stay in Scotland,' Amy said emphatically. 'I came here ten years ago, found a job and never went back to England.'

'I can see why. It's so beautiful...' Jess was thinking of the view she'd enjoyed as she drove back to the B & B, the creeping mist hanging low over the water.

Heather helped herself to more food. 'Your room here is booked until the fifth of August, but it'll be free until Sunday the eighth. I have someone arriving on the ninth, but you could stay on until then if you want.'

'It might give you time to sort out your options,' Amy suggested. 'You could always go abroad until your cottage is ready. I would.'

Jess was thoughtful. 'I suppose so.'

'I'd go to Turkey,' Heather said. 'It's so hot and welcoming.'

'Greece.' Amy's eyes widened. 'I'd stay on a Greek island, an apartment on the beach. The men there are gorgeous.'

Jess closed her eyes, the memories imprinted behind them like a photograph: handsome Yiannis in denim shorts on a sun-soaked beach in Corfu, holding her hand, telling her that their relationship was over.

'Maybe not Greece.' She thought for a moment. 'But I could travel first. Thanks, Heather – I'd love to stay on here for a few more days. I want to explore more of the Highlands. I feel so at home here.'

'I'd hire a Chevrolet – drive along Route 66.' Heather raised her glass.

'What about going to Hawaii?' Amy suggested. 'A luxury hotel, cocktails – you might meet a film star.'

'It would be an adventure,' Jess agreed.

'Just think, hen,' Heather said. 'You'd come home at Christmas time with a tan and your cottage would be ready...'

Amy added. 'And if you're going to be here for three more days, we can do another movie night.'

'There are tons of films I want to see,' Heather announced. 'Some chick flicks and a whole series about zombies. I can't watch the scary ones by myself.'

'That's decided, then,' Amy said. 'I love a well-built zombie.'

Heather held up her glass. 'To zombies and handsome men in Saabs and good times.'

'Good times,' Jess repeated, feeling a warm glow as she took another gulp of wine. As she stared into the depths of the glass, she imagined herself spending a week or two in the Alps, or haggling for jewellery in a souk in Algeria.

She nodded. 'Yes, I'd love to stay on until the eighth. And after that – who knows? The world is my oyster.'

7

Isabella and Mimi drove along the open road, the wind funnelling in from the Orkneys, a blustery northwester tugging Mimi's hair from beneath the firm hold of the scarf, slapping strands against her skin. Both women wore stylish sunglasses, Isabella frowning furiously, her brown legs bare beneath a short dress that lifted in the breeze as they sped towards the west coast. She overtook Transit vans and trucks, the road twisting upwards through slithering mists hanging between mountain crags. The road to their left became grassland, then there was another length of loch, turquoise melting into azure sky. They drove through Fort William, arriving at the base of Ben Nevis, and gazed up at the craggy mountain, purple and green, disappearing into white clouds that sat on top like piled snow. Isabella accelerated up a bumpy road, the tyres spattering dust and stones, finally stopping in a car park full of vehicles where people stood around in sturdy boots, pulling on jackets, preparing to climb to the summit.

Isabella turned to Mimi, an unlit cigarette in her mouth. 'Ben

Nevis, the highest mountain in the whole of the UK. I have never climbed it.'

'Nor will you,' Mimi said. 'We'll never get up there now.'

'But I have a clever plan, darling...' She reached into the back seat and handed her a carrier bag. Mimi delved in and pulled out a feather boa and a headband with black and crimson plumes. Isabella arched a brow. 'It is much sexier than a nun's habit.'

'Nun's habit?' Mimi was confused. 'What do I do?'

'Put them on. I bought them from Lionel, the antiques dealer.' Isabella took a breath. 'We'll both be dead soon. Let's live a little first.'

Mimi was unsure, but she replaced the headscarf with the feather headdress, wrapping the pink boa around her neck. 'So?'

'So, stand up on the seat and give it your all.'

Mimi smiled slowly: she knew what was coming now. 'I'm ready. Roll the music.'

Isabella fiddled with the cassette player, pushing something into the ancient machine as Mimi, the feathers around her neck shivering in the breeze, eased herself slowly to a standing position on the leather seat, hands on hips as if ready to take on the world. Sweet music began to play, the sway of strings, the rising crescendo of voices. Isabella turned the volume to full and sat back, a cigarette in her mouth, as people turned to watch. Mimi's face lit up; she threw her arms in the air and began to sing, 'Climb Ev'ry Mountain'. Her voice was tremulous, but she closed her eyes, crooning each word as if she was performing in a spotlight. Then she clasped her hands in prayer, a singing nun in fancy feathers that furled in the breeze. People turned from their cars where they were lacing up boots to stare. Several listeners approached the Stag and gazed at Mimi, whose voice swelled with the final strains. Someone took a photo on their phone.

Others applauded and, as Mimi bowed and blew kisses,

Isabella lifted an arm with a flourish and yelled, 'Mimi Solitaire, star of the stage, darling of the West End.' Cigarette clamped in her mouth; she held a hand up to Mimi. 'Now let's go and get an extravagant lunch and find ourselves some handsome men to impress.'

* * *

That night, Mimi couldn't sleep. She rolled over in bed, easing herself out, conscious of the numbing ache in her legs. The pins and needles sometimes plagued her when she moved. As a chorus girl, she'd dance for hours, her young muscles supple and strong. Now her legs were frail and she moved more slowly, the long white nightdress trailing on the floor behind her bare feet. She padded softly downstairs, hearing a clock strike twice: Donald's old grandfather clock stood tall on the first floor. She paused next to it on the landing, staring at the sturdy oak case and the high round face, listening to the steady tock, tock that had been in the McKinlay family for several generations. Everything was still: Finlay would be asleep in the room that used to be the master suite; there was no sound from the bedroom Hamish was staying in and the far rooms, Angus's old bedroom and the guest room, were empty, the doors ajar.

Mimi stepped softly on the flight of stairs to the ground floor. The next set of stairs led to the basement. She turned in the other direction, the deft steps of a ghost. Someone had left a light on in the kitchen. The door to Angus's bedroom, the room that used to be the library and Donald's office that had become a space for Angus to convalesce, was open. She walked down the hallway, past the array of family photos that had been on the wall for over forty years, past the living room and the small snug. She stood by the front door and pressed her fingers against the lighter patch of wallpaper where the antlers used to be from the stag Donald had shot on a weekend trip away. Mimi remembered Angus's anger several years later, as he tore the antlers down. He had been sixteen: there had been a lot of shouting, Donald red-faced and furious, Angus coldly calm, explaining his views. Hamish, then only twelve, had moved to Mimi's side and reached for her hand. Finlay had been away at university in Edinburgh; he was nineteen and, as Mimi recalled in a sudden moment of clarity, during the first year of his studies he had been living with a beautiful woman some ten years older than him.

She drew back the bolt on the large oak door, sliding it back with two hands, twisting the knob as the door creaked open, the cold air shifting around her feet.

It was not raining; the steps were cold under her bare heels as Mimi gazed up into the darkness. Suddenly she could breathe easily: she took two gulps of sharp air, refreshing as new life, staring into the night sky spattered with tiny silver stars. Mimi reached her arms towards the moon that hung like an ancient medallion, stretching her fingers as if to touch it, listening for every sound. An owl rustled its wings and Mimi pretended that it whispered a story about a dancer who found love three times in her life, a rich husband, a passionate lover and finally a third man, a faithful companion who would be with her until the end.

The brief love affair with Angus's father had ended badly. Mimi remembered Donald's anger as he'd visited her at the hospital in London and gazed with disbelief at his second child, dark-skinned with huge brown eyes. Mimi didn't care now: she threw back her head and sang the song she had performed at Ben Nevis, 'Climb Ev'ry Mountain', at the top of her lungs. It felt liberating as she swung her arms vigorously, then she stumbled and fell back against the door. A soft voice came from behind her. 'Come in, Mum – you'll catch cold.'

She turned to stare into the darkness, the outline of a man in a wheelchair holding out a hand. She placed her cold fingers in his warm palm. 'Angus.'

'Can't you sleep?' She shook her head and he murmured, 'Let's go into the kitchen. It's warm there. I'll put the kettle on, make some tea.'

She slithered past Angus while he locked the door. In the kitchen, he manoeuvred himself to the sink, found a cup and made her a hot drink while she slumped in a chair. Mimi sipped warm liquid, cinnamon and fruit, breathing in steam. Angus resumed his place at the table, staring at a laptop, moving a mouse. Thor slipped like a shadow from under the table and settled at Angus's feet.

Mimi held the cup in both hands. 'What are you doing?'

He didn't look up. 'Flicking through photographs.'

'Pictures of Augustine and Fabrice?'

Angus shook his head. 'Pictures of the black colobus monkey, the long-tailed pangolin, the clawless otter – and a few hump-backed whales.'

He smiled and Mimi was reminded of how beautiful he was as a child, how his laughter had brought constant lightness to her life, how his determination had warmed her heart. She put her cup down. 'Did you take those photographs in Cameroon?'

'Some of them: the giraffes were in Namibia, and there's a Savanna elephant or two.' He sighed. 'I've taken some good pictures over the years.'

'You must be very bored in Scotland,' Mimi said.

He lowered his hand to where the Labrador was curled and waited while Thor licked his fingers, then he patted the dog's head. 'There's nowhere else I can go for a while, Mum, but it's always good to spend time with you...' He indicated his plastered legs below the shorts. 'When I'm up and running again, there's plenty of work waiting for me out there.' He ruffled his hair. 'A guy I know wants me to go out to photograph some orangutans in Sabah, Borneo next year for his magazine. I've told him to count me in.' He gazed down at Thor. 'It's just me and you for a while here, boy. I've broken legs and you're a rescued mutt, but we'll both be all right...'

Mimi was trying to remember what she was going to ask him. Then it popped into her head. 'And Fabrice?'

'I'll visit him in Toulouse at Christmas.' Angus thought briefly about his softly-spoken, serious son, researching organic chemistry. They had talked on the phone in French just days ago. Fabrice had been happy enough, but hard at work in the laboratory.

They were quiet, Mimi sipping tea, Angus shaking the mouse and gazing at photos. Then Mimi said. 'I liked Augustine, you know.' She paused for a moment, and then added, 'TB, wasn't it?'

'You know it was.' Angus nodded once. Then he met Mimi's eyes. 'How's the tea? Do you want another?'

'I haven't finished this one.' She lifted the cup. 'Sometimes, you know, Angus, I feel really tired. I mean, tired of life.'

Angus put his hands to his forehead and when he brought them away, his eyes were sad. 'We've had some tough times. Living with Dad all those years was hard for you.'

'Everybody loved Donald, but I knew the real man.' Mimi pressed her lips together. 'He was very controlling. He was a pig.'

'He was certainly an autocrat, Mum.'

'He was a pig,' Mimi insisted. 'And Finlay is the image of him.'

'Fin has a soft side,' Angus suggested. 'He's struggling. Karen's solicitor is having a field day.'

'Finlay is resilient – he'll be all right.'

'He thinks the world of you,' Angus said kindly. 'It's hit him hard, the divorce.' He tried again. 'Hamish is doing okay, though. Did he tell you he has a new commission?'

Mimi tried to remember. 'Was it the advert for funerals?'

'The jingle for Cordial Cremations?' He smiled. 'No, it's a collaboration, composing a score for a stage musical. He's fallen on his feet this time.'

Mimi moved her arms in the air, as if she was doing a little dance. 'He is so like me, Hamish. We understand each other. We're born to be on the stage.'

'You're two peas in a pod, Mum. It's time for bed. It's past three.'

'Angus – do you think I'm crazy?' Mimi's face was suddenly sad. 'People think I'm a little bit mad.'

'Who cares what people think?' Angus frowned. 'You're wonderful.'

'Finlay thinks I'm crazy.'

'Fin thinks you drink too much – that's not the same thing.'

'Hamish loves me.'

'We all love you, Mum. You know we do.' He exhaled slowly. 'Come on – up you go to bed. I'd carry you up dancing and singing but, at the minute, I can't do it,' he joked. 'I don't have a leg to stand on.'

Mimi pushed back her chair and wandered slowly towards the door. Angus wiggled the mouse and stared at the screen, flicking through photographs he'd taken on location; as he skimmed through the images, he paused to stare at one he'd taken over ten years ago in Cameroon: a man, a woman and a young boy, a happy family, standing closely together in the sunshine. Augustine's eyes gleamed with love, his arm around her, his hand on Fabrice's curls. He glanced at it for a moment longer, then clicked the mouse and saw the silver head of a hump-backed whale emerging from the blue depths of an

ocean. When he looked up, Mimi had gone. He sat back in his
chair and rubbed his eyes. He probably ought to go to bed but
for now he was happier with Thor at his feet, thinking about
Cameroon and the woman he'd loved more than words could
express.

* * *

Jess was seated at a table in a charming little café in
Drumnadrochit, flicking through travel websites on her phone,
her coffee cup almost empty. She glanced up through the window
to where her VW Beetle was parked across the road, watching a
man and woman stop to stare at the deep purple colour. It was
late afternoon, the sky overhead a deep burst of blue. She
returned her gaze to a photograph of a cottage in Brittany near
the sea. She'd been considering her finances; August in a pretty
house a short stroll from the ocean might be possible, then when
she returned to Badsey, she could throw herself into life at Paul's
house, helping Jodie with the chores.

She toyed with the idea of asking Paul if she could help him
work on the cottage. She was strong: she could swing a sledge-
hammer, bang in a few nails. Jess sat back in her seat, thinking
that it would be nice to breathe life into her home. By October,
she'd be painting walls in her living room and, in December,
she'd be hanging up Christmas decorations. Last night, Heather
had invited her to come up to Scotland for the Hogmanay celebrations and Jess almost accepted there and then, but instead she
wondered if it might not be nicer to spend her first New Year's Eve
in her own home. Saffy would come back from London – Jess
hadn't seen her for several months and she missed her independent daughter every day.

Jess wondered about going on a boat trip; she'd glide past

ruined castles, birds swooping overhead in an open sky spattered with sparse clouds. She'd take some more photographs.

Her phone buzzed and Paul's voice rattled in her ear. 'Jessie...'

'Hi, Paul.' She was conscious how deliberately breezy she sounded.

'I'll be honest – it's not good news.'

'What isn't good news?' For a moment, she wondered if he or Jodie had been in an accident.

'I've called in a few quotes for the work and it's going to be expensive.'

Jess blinked. 'How expensive?'

'Really expensive.' Paul's voice became louder, then she heard a loud intake of breath before he named the figure.

'Oh...' Jess's thoughts moved quickly. It was much more than she had anticipated. The holiday plans would have to go. She blurted the first words she could think of. 'It'll be fine, Paul. Once the cottage is finished, I'll find a job.'

Paul's voice was louder in her ear. 'I'll do my best to get everything done as quickly as possible, Jessie. But we're talking months...'

'I should have had a survey. I just went with my heart.' Jess exhaled. 'Thank goodness I can stay with you...'

There was a pause then Jess heard Paul swallow. 'Jessie – I'm sorry – Luke came back home last night.'

Jess was confused. 'I thought he was working in Birmingham. You said his room was free...'

'Things have changed.' Paul sounded anxious. 'Kids, eh? Twenty-four years old and they still bring their problems home.'

'What happened?'

'He's split up with Cathy; he gave up his job and came back home to live.' He exhaled loudly. 'I told him he can do a bit of labouring with me, help with the work on the cottage.'

'I see...'

Paul said, 'Do you have some friends you can stay with? Or, if you're stuck, the box room's my office now but I could put you up on a camper bed in the lounge...'

'No, I can find somewhere.' Jess was surprised by her own voice, which sounded far too confident.

'If you're sure...'

'I'll be fine.'

'Right, well...' He took a breath. 'I won't spoil your holiday any more than I have done already. What are you up to now?'

Jess wriggled in her seat. 'I might go on a boat trip.'

'Well, you enjoy yourself.'

'I will.' Jess sighed without meaning to.

'I'm sorry, Jessie.' Paul's voice was filled with regret. 'It's a risk you take with these lovely old houses – I suppose we just have to bite the bullet now and get the work done.'

'No, it'll be fine. I'll be inviting you and Jodie – and Luke – round for Christmas dinner before we know it. And I'm really grateful for everything you're doing – you're a star...'

'Thanks,' Paul said. 'Well, I suppose I'd better get back to work – the sooner it's started, the sooner it's done, eh?' He paused, then he added, 'Well, enjoy the rest of your stay in Scotland. Don't let all this spoil your fun, will you?'

The phone clicked and Jess's thoughts buzzed like flies: the work on the house was going to be very costly, she'd need a job and a place to stay. The glossy brochure of the pretty cottage by the sea in Brittany caught her eye. She would have to make other plans now.

Jess rested her head in her hands: in all honesty, she had no idea what to do.

8

Jess walked across the road towards her car almost in a trance, pausing by the driver's door, thinking. Today was Friday the sixth: she would be leaving on Monday but she had no home to go to. Her belongings were in storage in Worcester; her brother lived twenty miles away in Badsey; her cottage was uninhabitable. Paul had dug up the floors, drilled huge holes in the walls and there would be rubble everywhere. She pictured herself arriving at Badsey on Tuesday afternoon with two cases, a laptop and a handbag to her name. She would be homeless.

She could rent a flat in Worcester, find a job. Slowly a desperate plan was forming; she'd find work and a place to live to keep her going until the cottage was habitable. She'd be fine.

A cyclist whizzed past on the road, then another, and Jess was roused from her thoughts. She glanced over the roof of the Beetle and saw the little Post Office: she'd buy some mints before taking a boat trip. It would be good to have small souvenirs too, to remind her of her stay in Scotland. The Highlands had already etched a special place in her heart. She wandered over to the little shop and gazed into the window.

Several advertisements caught her eye. One was a photograph of a pretty house to rent on the edge of the loch. It was picturesque but it was beyond her means. There was a dog-walking job: the owner of three Dalmatians wanted them walked daily. It wouldn't pay anywhere near enough for a rented room somewhere. A third advert was for a companion for a lady in her eighties in a house two miles outside Drumnadrochit. There would be light duties, accommodation was available, rates were negotiable: there was a mobile phone number at the bottom. On impulse, Jess reached into her handbag for a pen and wrote the number on the back of her hand. She'd transfer it to paper when she was back in the car: there was a little notepad in the glove compartment.

Inside the shop, she picked up mints, a fridge magnet proclaiming, 'I Heart Scotland' and, for some reason she couldn't explain, a cute fluffy Loch Ness monster on a key ring. She took her purchases to the till, where an older man held out thin fingers. As Jess paid for the items, she asked, 'Can you tell me anything about the job advertised in the window? The one for a companion for an older lady?'

The man's eyes glittered beneath curling brows. 'That'll be Mrs McKinlay.'

'I suppose so.' Jess was hopeful.

His expression remained unchanged. 'You're not from round here?'

'No.' Jess took the change he handed her. 'But I used to own a hotel – I can cook and I'd be good company.' She stopped herself; there was no reason for her to explain her skills as if she was already being interviewed. She put her items into her handbag. 'I'm going to apply.'

The man eyed her critically. 'And I'm sure you're likely to get the job.' He gave a little cough. 'Mrs McKinlay's son brought the advertisement in. I can't imagine there will be many applicants. Ailsa Chambers works there several days a week. I know her well, and her husband, John.'

'Oh, that's nice,' Jess said cheerfully.

'Aye, well good luck,' the man mumbled.

Jess left the shop, the little bell tinkling, and clambered into her car. She put her purchases in the glove box, took out the notepad and transferred the phone number to a blank page, writing the words 'Companion job' next to it. She chewed her lip thoughtfully: calling the number wouldn't commit her to anything, there was nothing to lose. Scotland was beautiful – she loved the Highlands and she'd already made friends in Heather and Amy. Besides, it couldn't be too difficult to be a companion to an older lady, to fix her a sandwich and a cup of tea, maybe take her on a few rides to interesting places.

Jess wondered if she could take on the job just for a few months; she'd have somewhere to live, a modest income, while Paul fixed up her house. The idea was growing on her; it would be an adventure. She'd be living in the Highlands through the autumn and into winter. Jess imagined herself gazing through a bedroom window as soft flakes of snow twirled in the sky and fell onto pine branches. It would be perfect. On her days off, she'd meet Heather and Amy. She'd wanted to visit the Isle of Skye, the Hebrides: there would be time to do that if she stayed on.

Suddenly, the idea of taking a job locally really appealed to her: everything was falling into place. She wouldn't be a burden to Paul and Jodie, sleeping on the sofa. Jess took a deep breath and pulled out her mobile phone, carefully pressing buttons, listening for the purr of the dialling tone.

Then a voice spoke in her ear, a low, well-modulated, gravelly tone of a confident man. 'Fin McKinlay.'

'Ah,' Jess said, taking a deep breath and trying not to garble.

'I'm ringing about the job in the Post Office window – the companion for a senior lady. I was wondering if it was still available?'

* * *

'Pastries. How I love pastries!' Mimi clapped her hands together as she sat at the kitchen table, dressed in a satin negligée that reached her bare toes.

'You always used to say that a Sunday breakfast wasn't the same without pastries, Mother.' Fin was over by the stove, filling two cups with coffee. 'Enjoy.'

Mimi plucked the flaky layers from a croissant and shredded them across her plate, the tiny crumbs spreading onto the table. 'Pastries remind me of breakfast when I was a dancer. We girls used to go out for breakfast on a Sunday. We were often invited to a gentleman's club – your father had a friend who owned the Gatzby – or was it the Gallant? Anyway, the lounge lizards in their smoking jackets used to gather together and eye all the young girls as we'd sit round a table drinking sweet coffee and eating pastries...'

Angus said something about exploitation as he poured green liquid from a huge blender jug into a glass. Fin met his eyes. 'What do you have there, Angus?'

'Kale. Apple. Ginger. Spinach.'

Mimi suddenly looked around the table. 'Where's Hamish?'

'He went back to Inverness yesterday, Mother.' Fin placed a small cup of coffee in front of Mimi, taking the other to a chair and sitting down. 'It's just the three of us for breakfast.'

Mimi was sad. 'I miss Hamish.'

'We all do.' Fin patted her hand. 'I wanted us to have breakfast together this morning because I need to discuss something. There's a woman coming at eleven.'

Angus reached down and rubbed Thor's head with his fingers. 'Who?'

Mimi patted her hair, her face filled with mischief. 'Do you have another new girlfriend, Finlay? You haven't got rid of Karen yet...'

'No, I don't – one ex-wife trying to bleed me dry is plenty.' Fin frowned. Mimi had hit a nerve. 'No, there's someone coming for an interview. I put an advert in for a live-in person to spend some time with you, Mother. She's applied for the job.'

Angus murmured, 'The only applicant, I'm guessing?'

'There was another, but halfway through the call, she pulled out. I think she realised who we were.'

'So, you're interviewing?'

'I thought we'd meet her together, Angus. I was hoping I could persuade her to do a few things for you, clean your room...'

'I don't need a cleaner.'

'She could be useful.'

Angus sighed. 'You can hire someone to spend time with Mum – it might be good for her – but I don't want anything from anyone, thanks.'

'Can I meet her, Finlay?' Mimi raised her arms over her head in a flourish. 'She has to be someone I'll like. I want someone who will dance with me, who will learn some steps and join in...'

'I'll take her through the duties – after that, of course you can say hello. It's best to stay upstairs in case she's not suitable, Mother – I'll bring her up to meet you if she is.'

Angus smiled. 'Good luck with that.'

Fin's eyes were briefly anxious. 'I'd have preferred it if you or Hamish were here – to be honest, the idea of interviewing someone fills me with horror – she'll probably be completely unsuitable...'

Angus replied, 'Then again, she might be perfect – she might meet Mum and love her as much as we do and want the job.'

Fin sighed. 'I've thrown in the basement too as part of the package. I asked Ailsa to clean the flat out. She'd be living in.'

'The basement flat?' Angus raised an eyebrow. 'It hasn't been used in years.'

'I've put some flowers in there,' Fin said. 'At least it smells better now.'

'She can spend every day in the attic with me.' Mimi was hopeful. 'I'd like a new friend. We could talk about the old times.'

Fin and Angus exchanged glances. Then Angus said, 'So, Fin, maybe we'd better ask Mum what sort of companion she'd ideally like.'

'We should...' Fin turned to Mimi, made a gallant bow and showed her a mock-serious face. 'So, Ms Mimi Solitaire, ex-chorus-girl...'

Angus pretended to take photographs. 'Star of the stage...'

'Beauty and socialite...' Fin added.

Angus clicked away, his fingers forming the square of a camera. 'And sweetheart of all the revolting lounge lizards of the London Gatzby...'

'...what sort of companion are you looking for?' Fin winked at Angus and held out a spoon towards his mother as if it was a microphone.

Mimi was delighted, pursing her lips, patting her hair. 'Well, gentlemen, I'd like someone nice – someone who'd dress up with me and we could sing a few numbers and I could teach her some dance moves.'

'She'd be one in a million.' Angus raised his eyebrows and Fin smiled. They both leaned forward at the same time, as Mimi continued.

'She'd be like a backstage girl, doing my make-up. She could meet Gavin and he could show her how I like my hair done, piled up, with flowers in it. We could share a bottle of wine...'

'I don't think the wine's a good idea, Mother,' Fin said.

'She could come out with me and Isabella – we'd have such fun.'

Angus grinned. 'I can just imagine the three of you on the town, Mum.'

'We'd go out shopping together – I could buy a nice new fur coat for winter...' Mimi caught Angus's frown. 'I mean, one of those fake ones they make now that look almost real.' She clapped her hands excitedly.

There was a rap at the front door that could be heard in the kitchen. Fin glanced at his watch. 'If that's her, she's ten minutes early.'

Angus sat up straight in his wheelchair. 'Right, Thor – you and I are going into the garden.' He indicated the detritus on the table – plates, pastry crumbs, half-empty cups, the blender jug smeared with green smoothie. 'We'll clean up after the applicant has gone – she may as well know what she's letting herself in for. Good luck...' He grinned, manoeuvring the chair towards the back door, and gave a low whistle. Thor leaped up from beneath the table and bounded after him.

Fin reached for his jacket, suddenly professional. 'Come on, Mother – let's get you upstairs and you can have a lie down. Then I'll meet your potential companion. If she's nice, I'll bring her up briefly to say hello.'

Mimi allowed Fin to usher her to the bottom of the stairs; he watched as she pulled herself up, one step at a time, towards the first-floor landing. Then he straightened his jacket, pushed a hand through thick white hair and strode towards the front door. As he put his hand on the bolt to open it, he muttered to himself, 'Right, Jessica Oliver, let's see what you've got to offer, shall we?' He glanced at himself in a mirror and noticed that his mouth was tight and cynical. 'In truth, I can't say I'm expecting very much.'

9

Mimi wore her favourite headdress – red plumes, silver diamantés sewn to a band: she was so excited about meeting a new friend. She touched the jewels, the silky feathers. It made her much taller; she'd need to walk upright or it would tumble. She moved precariously towards the wardrobe and opened the door, staring at the colourful costumes crammed inside. A glittering silver bodice with a matching voile skirt caught her eye, long at the back and short at the front. She held the costume up and gazed in the mirror, dipping and swaying a little to show it off: it was perfect. She pulled the headdress off and struggled into the costume, which was now too big around the bust and sagged around the hips, but Mimi thought it suited her well enough. She pushed the headdress back on her head, reached for a crimson lipstick and moved closer to the mirror. She would make an entrance.

* * *

Jess knocked again. The Glen Carrick House sign appeared below a wooden carving of a deer's head. The door opened and a tall man wearing a smart dark jacket stood inside, his piercing blue eyes assessing her. He pushed fingers through thick white hair and his initial scowl immediately became professionally pleasant. 'Jessica Oliver?' He held out a hand.

She took it and returned his firm squeeze. 'Jess.'

'Nice to meet you. I'm Fin McKinlay. We spoke on the phone. Do come in.'

His eyes met hers. Jess decided he was the sort of man who was confident around women, sure of his good looks: she was immediately on her guard. As she followed him into the house, she wondered if the veneer of friendliness hid a cool scrutiny. The hallway was vast, the walls covered with antique gold-embossed wallpaper. There were several photographs placed at intervals; from the colours and the ageing tarnish on the frames, they were probably taken in the 1960s or 1970s: spirited boys at play, a glamorous woman surrounded by three happy children; a tall red-haired man wearing a kilt, with a strong chin and a serious face. There were other, later photos, smiling young men, graduations, wedding groups. Jess's eyes slid over the pictures quickly. Fin McKinlay was talking to her.

'I'm hiring a companion for my mother. She's eighty-eight, but quite mobile. As I said on the phone, she seldom goes out, except with one friend.'

He led the way into the kitchen and indicated that Jess should sit. The table was untidy; breakfast dishes hadn't been cleared away and there were crumbs and empty cups and plates left untended. Jess sat down awkwardly as Fin asked, 'Can I get you a coffee?'

'Please.' Jess was gazing around the kitchen: the Aga stove was a modern design in shiny red. The chrome sparkled: it was clean.

The table was solid oak; the cabinets were attractive reclaimed wood, probably handmade. The family seemed well-off and the house well cared for, apart from the residual breakfast mess. Fin poured coffee from a jug. 'Milk? Sugar?'

'No, thanks.' She met his gaze as he passed a cup. 'So, does your mother live here alone, Mr McKinlay?'

'Fin.' He smiled but his eyes were assessing her. Jess noticed he hadn't made coffee for himself. 'My mother has an apartment upstairs, at the top. She loves the views from there. I'm staying temporarily while I sort out some business. My brother has a room here while he's convalescing. We have a housekeeper who pops in as and when, keeps the place tidy.' He sat down opposite her. 'So – let's talk about you, shall we, Jess? What experience do you have of caring for older people?'

Jess took a breath. It was best to be completely honest. 'My background is in the hotel business. I ran my own place for a long time, so I'm used to looking after the wellbeing and comfort of guests. I have a website – I can show you reviews. Years before that, I was a holiday rep abroad in the Greek islands.' She paused, watching his face; it was expressionless. 'My experience is limited in terms of one-to-one daily care.' He was still scrutinising her, his eyes impassive. 'But I'm personable, patient; I think I could take care of Mrs McKinlay's everyday needs – companionship and basic safety.'

Fin brightened. 'I wouldn't expect you to be responsible for anything other than spending time with her, maybe making sure she has a cup of tea, a sandwich, that she doesn't drink too much.' He winced. 'She's partial to a glass of wine every now and then. Do you drink, Jess?'

'No, not really.'

'Good.' Fin was relieved. Jess Oliver initially seemed pleasant, calm – too good to be true. He took a breath. 'One thing – you're clearly not local. Why do you want to stay in Scotland?'

'Who wouldn't want to?' Jess's eyes shone. 'In truth, I've spent two weeks here and I'm in love with the place.' She was aware of his discerning gaze, trying to read more into her answers. She tried again. 'I'm from Worcestershire. I have a house there that my brother is renovating. It will take months to sort out, so – I'm at a loose end.' She paused, aware that she was giving the impression that she had nowhere else to live, but it was the truth.

Fin narrowed his eyes; the woman just wanted somewhere temporary to stay. He was on his guard: his mother was vulnerable. 'So, you're looking for somewhere to call home for a few months?'

'Yes.' Jess noticed that he was frowning. She said, 'Can I meet Mrs McKinlay?'

'In good time.' Fin rose from the table; he wanted to trust this woman, but he was unsure. 'I'll show you the flat that comes with the job. It's quite… basic, but comfortable.'

He led her down a flight of stone steps and flicked on a light switch. The basement flat was small but tidy with an en suite bathroom. The main room was dark, only one bulb overhead. Jess looked around: the floor was carpeted in shaggy beige; there was a cream armchair by a woodburning stove, a television, a map of the Highlands on the wall. Adjoining the room was a small kitchenette, clean and perfectly serviceable with a kettle and a toaster and there was a low table with a bunch of bright flowers in a vase. In the far corner, a double bed had a black and grey cover; there was a simple wooden wardrobe. Jess had the impression of being underground and realised that it was, in fact, the case, as there were no windows, just a strong whiff of something that might have been damp earth.

Fin explained. 'My youngest brother moved in here when he

was a teenager – he used to love it. We had friends round, parties. We used to call it Laird Hamish's lair.' Jess noticed an expression she hadn't seen before: he seemed wistful, almost sentimental. He faced her and his expression was business-like again. 'It's what it is... but it comes with the job.'

For a moment, Jess was conscious that she was in a strange place with a strange man, and neither of them was speaking. She felt uneasy. Her thoughts raced; she wanted to break the silence. 'Well, it's functional, but I'm sure it'll be fine.'

Fin smiled. 'Shall we go back to the kitchen?'

Jess followed him up the steps to the first floor, back into the warmth of the kitchen. They faced each other across the table. Fin gave a small cough. 'So, there you have it. Your job would be five days a week, flexible but based around my mother's waking hours; she tends not to rise until noon, and she sometimes sleeps in the afternoon. The duties would entail making light meals, monitoring her – her wine intake, keeping her company. That's the most important thing; she can feel a bit lonely, and it would be good to establish a routine where she sleeps at night.' He pushed hands into his jeans' pockets. 'My mother used to be a dancer many years ago. She loves to talk about the stage and her time in London when she was in the chorus line. That's where she met my father.' He sighed. 'He's deceased now.'

'I see.' Jess was thoughtful. 'And what about taking her out – you know, for an occasional coffee?'

'I suppose we could discuss it.' He wondered for a moment if appointing Jess might make Mimi less reliant on Isabella: they were good friends, but a bad influence on each other. Adding Jess to the mix might calm them both.

'Right – Jess. Do you want to meet Mimi then go away and think about the job? If you're still interested, phone me later and we can firm up on hours and rates of pay. What about we say you'd work here until the end of December, to see how you get on...' He chose his words carefully. 'And perhaps we'll see how my mother settles...'

'Okay, that would be perfect,' Jess agreed. 'To be honest, I'm not sure I can work beyond that. My house should be ready to move into.'

'The end of December, then,' Fin sighed. Beggars couldn't be choosers, there were no other applicants.

'It's a huge house,' Jess remarked, changing the subject. 'Did you say that other people are living here?'

'My brother Angus can't go far at the moment – he's in a wheelchair.'

'Oh—'

'He was involved in a road accident back in the spring – he'd come home to visit for the week, the roads were wet. It will take some time...' He paused. It was best to say no more about Angus. 'I'm staying on for a while. I have properties elsewhere, but I'm based here for the time being. My youngest brother lives in Inverness – he often visits. But we keep ourselves to ourselves and, as I said, Ailsa keeps the place tidy.'

'Did you say your mother's name was Mimi?' Jess asked.

There was a rustle in the doorway, a swish of silk fabric, and a soft voice, the same hushed crackle. 'Hello. I'm Mimi – I think you must be looking for me...'

Jess turned to see a figure standing in the doorway, a spectre with a pale face, glittering eyes and the most inviting smile. The figure tottered into the room on high heels. A glitter-covered bodice with a matching skirt hung from her tiny frame; her legs were clad in fishnet tights. A feather headdress wobbled as she extended a slender arm. 'Please allow me to introduce myself. I am Mimi Solitaire.' Her face was enthusiastic, charming. 'I am so pleased to meet you.'

Jess took her hand. The nails were painted orange, still sticky. 'I'm pleased to meet you too, Mimi – I'm Jess.'

'Jess.' Mimi spoke slowly. 'That's a nice name. And I understand you are going to be my friend?'

Jess scrutinised the old lady's face, eyes shining with delight, pink powder clumped in the creases of her sockets, her lipstick smudged. Then she became aware of Fin watching, assessing her response. Jess noticed the hope in Mimi's expression and said the first words that came into her head.

'Were you a dancer, Mrs McKinlay? I – I'm afraid I know nothing at all about dancing or musicals.'

'Oh, dear.' Mimi's lip trembled. Fin looked on anxiously.

Jess kept the soft hand in hers and tried again. 'But your son said you'd been on the stage, and I'd love to find out all about it. I'm sure you have lots of fascinating stories.'

Mimi's cheeks flushed with pride. 'Oh yes,' she breathed. 'I have so many stories. And do you know, Jess...' Mimi glanced at Fin for approval and then patted her hair. 'I am so looking forward to telling you all about my time in London when I was a chorus girl. Such happy times.'

Fin had a slight smile on his face. Jess thought he looked relieved.

Mimi took the younger woman's hands in her slim fingers: she thought that she had a kind face; her hair, a light reddish colour under the light, was tied back in a ponytail; her soft brown eyes were calm and steady; there were small freckles on her nose. She seemed genuinely interested, and Mimi felt her heartbeat quicken.

'Jess,' Mimi repeated, thinking that she must be about the same age as Hamish; she could be like a daughter, the daughter she'd always wanted. Mimi was suddenly breathless with excitement. 'Oh, I can't tell you how delighted I am. And Finlay says you're coming here to stay. It will be so nice to have another woman around with all these men. My friend Isabella says that too much testosterone in a house is a dangerous thing, and I'm sure she's right. You must meet Isabella. She used to be a model in the sixties. We have wonderful days out together and now you can come with us. Oh, we are all going to have such a fabulous time.'

10

Isabella was leaning out of the open window as she blew smoke in a thin stream. A 1920s show tune on a jangly piano was blaring from the attic apartment. Mimi was playing a record of songs from *The Boyfriend*, rummaging in her top drawer, pulling out pieces of jewellery, holding them up to the light for inspection. She sang along to 'Won't You Charleston with Me', wearing a loose beaded dress in black and gold, the fringed hem skimming her calves, and a thin headband with a small black feather.

It was early Monday morning, a light breeze coming through the window. Outside, the sun shone bright as runny honey, the loch smooth as a silver spoon.

Isabella said, 'I hope this woman is a free spirit. I hope she has a sense of humour.'

'Oh, she does,' Mimi replied dreamily, holding up an expensive necklace. 'You'll love her. She'll fit in so well.'

'Then we'll have to plan a girls' evening together – cocktails in a hotel, perhaps. Or maybe we could go away for a weekend – Mimi, we should all go to London. What a time we'd have of it. *Tante risate* – so much fun!'

'Yes, that would be wonderful.' Mimi's eyes shone. 'You, me and our new friend Jess. We could have lunch at the Ritz, take in a show.'

'Night clubs, shopping. Oh, the times we'll have.' Isabella stubbed out her cigarette in a saucer. 'I can't wait, darling.'

Fin emerged from the shadows and strode smoothly towards his mother, a light skip in his step, before taking both her hands in his and raising them as they swayed together in time to the music. They danced, Mimi singing along, and Fin joined in, a deep rumble: he knew all the songs from his childhood. Mimi lifted a leg, trying a deft move, and slipped, falling against Fin's chest, her expression delighted as he deposited her gently on the edge of the bed.

Isabella held up her arms. 'Me too, Fin – I want a dance with a handsome young man.'

Fin moved to Isabella, sweeping her round in a circle. She put her mouth close to his ear. 'I hope you've chosen someone suitable as Mimi's house companion...'

'Trust me,' Fin smiled.

Mimi clapped her hands. 'She's coming today, Finlay.' She held up a charm bracelet, her eyes bright. 'I want to give her a present.'

'My father gave you all those things, Mother. Some of them were expensive.'

'Money! Who cares about money?' Mimi's lip curled. 'Donald gave me presents so that I'd forgive him every time he did something wrong.'

Fin nodded sadly. 'I suppose he did.'

'He definitely did. I remember,' Isabella snorted. 'He was like my husband, Archie. They were both chauvinist pigs.'

'It's true,' Mimi insisted, lips pursed. 'Donald would go drinking, gambling, and I'd get a nice bracelet when he came home.

Then there were the affairs – so he'd buy me a diamond and tell me he loved me best in the whole world.' Her face showed no sign of regret. 'He bought me a car once, Finlay – a sporty thing. I never even learned to drive it. We sold it years later.'

'It was an Alfa Romeo, a beautiful, sexy Italian car. I'd have loved it,' Isabella sighed.

Fin took his mother's hand. 'You'll need a nap first, Mother. Would you like me to help you choose a nice brooch to give her later?'

'Oh no, no, not a brooch.' Mimi's brow crumpled. 'A brooch has a pin in it – that's bad luck – it means the friendship will be pierced. And I do want Jess to be my friend.'

'Give her something with a diamond in it, darling,' Isabella said. 'Everyone likes diamonds.'

'Let's pick something out together,' Fin offered hopefully.

Mimi's eyes were wide. 'Oh, Finlay, I'm so grateful that you've found me a friend. I do hope she'll like me.'

Fin wrapped his arms around his mother. 'How could anyone not love you?'

'Everyone loves Mimi. She has the voice of an angel. After all these years, she can still turn heads.' Isabella rummaged in her handbag for more cigarettes.

Mimi stepped back, suddenly horrified. 'Oh, I can't wear this dress. I look so old-fashioned.'

'Why don't you find something casual?' Fin asked.

Isabella made a low sound. 'Silk. I always find it's a reliable choice.'

Fin offered his mother a winning smile. 'Do you remember, Jess was wearing a blouse and jeans when she came here – you could wear something in the same style?' Fin had no idea what he was talking about, but he desperately wanted his mother to appear normal. He sighed. Mimi was Mimi; he hoped Jess would take to her, that she would be able to do something, however small, to make his mother's life better.

'Isabella, will you help me choose something to wear?' Mimi was fretful. 'I don't want to make a bad impression.'

'You won't, it's not possible,' Isabella reassured her. 'She'll love you, darling.'

Fin watched sadly as Isabella pulled out bright purple trousers from the wardrobe and held them towards Mimi. 'Here, lots of colour. You'll look a million dollars…'

An hour later, Fin sat at the kitchen table with Angus, drinking coffee, a frown on his face as he pushed a hand through his hair. 'Isabella has only just left, and Mother's up there, wearing a pink cashmere jumper and purple silk trousers, wrapping an expensive gold bracelet in tissue paper. I hope this woman I'm employing is going to be worth the trouble.'

Angus poured green liquid from the blender jug into a glass. 'You said she seemed all right.'

'Jess, yes – she seems pleasant enough. My overriding impression was that she just needed somewhere to live for a few months.'

Angus shrugged. 'If that's the case, she won't last the week.'

'Oh, I hope she does. She said she'd stay until the end of the year. I mean, she's not local. She won't know any of the stories.'

Angus laughed once. 'Like the incident at Christmas last year when Mum and Isabella danced to the Bing Crosby song in the aisles of the Co-op in Drumnadrochit? The young lad who was stocking the shelves ended up with his face covered in lipstick. The manager said he'd never be the same again.'

Fin exhaled slowly. 'Then she accosted the man in the street outside the Post Office and kissed him too. Bless her, she thought he was Fred Astaire.'

'She was in a ballgown,' Angus smiled. 'She and Isabella are eccentric but...' He shrugged expansively. 'Mum is incredible. A bit of eccentricity is a good thing.'

'Jess Oliver doesn't seem eccentric. She seems – well, quite ordinary.'

'That's a shame.' Angus drank from his glass. 'Well, things are what they are, Fin.'

Fin was suddenly sad. He glanced at the wheelchair. 'How are the legs now, Angus?'

'I'm getting there.'

'You need a physio.'

'I can do it by myself.'

Fin was exasperated. 'You need specialist medical help.'

'I broke the legs – I'll fix them.'

'In actual fact, Angus, it was the other driver who broke them – the car that hit you.'

Angus shook his head. 'The woman didn't see me – it was misty, wet – I was going too fast.'

Fin's face froze as he recalled the image of the motorbike, twisted metal. 'I saw the remains of the Gold Wing before I saw you, Angus.'

'The motorbike was a write-off.'

'It was unrecognisable.' Fin put a hand to his face, the memory still with him. 'When I saw you in the hospital, you were unrecognisable too. I hadn't the heart to tell Mother for two days. Both legs broken, busted ribs, bruises. You looked awful. I thought you wouldn't make it.'

'I'm here now.' Angus gave a low whistle and Thor emerged from beneath the table. He ruffled the dog's head. 'I'll mend.'

'Let me get someone to come in, a physio, once a week.'

Angus was feeling tired. 'The muscles are the problem – I'll have to work hard to make them strong again. I'm trying the crutches out in my room later, so if you hear a loud crash, don't worry yourself. I'll get the legs back to normal, as normal as they can be. Time is a healer.'

Angus moved his wheelchair back as if to leave, but Fin lifted a hand, a practised way of gaining attention. 'I'm meeting Hugh later. He's the best solicitor there is, but I don't think even he can save my skin.'

'Karen's taking you to the cleaners?'

'She is. She can.' Fin sighed. 'I don't pick women well, Angus.' He thought for a moment. 'You know, Karen always hated our mother.' He rubbed his chin. 'And now Karen hates me.'

'Mum's a good judge of character.' Angus had no further observations to make; his legs were aching. Thor leaped towards the back door and wagged his tail, eager to go outside. But Fin was keen to talk.

'The next woman I fall in love with will have to love my mother.' His voice was determined. 'Perhaps if she loves my mother, then maybe she'll love me too.'

'Maybe.' Angus swivelled his chair around.

'My first wife and Mother didn't get on too well either.'

'You were in your twenties, Fin. Fiona was young too.'

'That's true.' Fin reached for his cup. 'But Augustine was young, and she and Mother adored each other.'

Angus gave a brief nod. 'Yes, Mum loved Augustine.' He paused for a moment, remembering, then he moved his gaze to the Labrador, who was leaping up at the door. 'Come on then, Thor, let's get you outside and around the garden.' He wheeled his chair away from the table. 'Good luck with this new woman you've employed, Fin. She's coming today, you say?'

'She is. Do you want to meet her when she arrives, Angus?'

Angus shook his head. 'I'll leave her to you. I'm assuming she'll eat and sleep in the basement and spend her free time with Mum, so I don't expect to see much of her.' He reached the door and turned back. 'Maybe it's best to warn her about Ailsa, though. No doubt everyone's favourite housekeeper will have to put in her ten pence worth about how difficult Mum is. We don't want Ailsa to spoil things.'

'No, you're right.' Fin's face was troubled. 'Mother already thinks that she, Jess and Isabella are going to be the Brontë sisters. I hope she won't be disappointed. She's frail nowadays.'

Angus had reached the door. 'Mum's lonely, Fin. Let's just hope this Jess woman can cheer her up.'

Fin watched as Angus pulled open the back door and manoeuvred the chair into the garden, following the dog. He exhaled slowly. 'I hope so,' he said. 'Goodness knows what we'll do if it all goes wrong.'

* * *

Jess stood outside the little terraced bed and breakfast. Her two cases and her laptop were stowed in the back of the Beetle. Heather gave her a warm hug. 'Good luck, Jess.'

Jess squeezed Heather's shoulders. 'I have to admit, I'm a bit nervous now.'

'Nervous about Mrs McKinlay or her suave son?' Heather's voice was mischievous.

'Both...' Jess took a breath. 'Of not getting it right. I mean, Mimi is sweet. Fin, however, seems quite exacting. I hardly got a smile from him when he was interviewing me.'

'But he is handsome...' Heather's eyes sparkled. 'A good looker. You said it yourself, hen.'

'I said he was nice.'

'When you've settled in, invite me round. I'll give him the once-over. Maybe he's just what one of us needs...' Heather suggested. 'And on Friday, you're coming round here for a film and a meal. Amy's bringing wine.'

'I'll look forward to that.' Jess gazed up at the sky. The air was already warm and it was only just past eleven. 'I suppose they'll allow me Friday night off – Fin said hours were negotiable.'

'Fin. You're on first-name terms already. I am so pleased you're staying. It'll be lovely having you living so close.' Heather smiled. 'I bet your brother's glad he'll have more time to fix the cottage too.'

Jess nodded. 'He was so relieved – I could hear it in his voice. Now he has a houseful, he was worried about having to put me up. We'd have all bumped into each other.' She was thoughtful for a moment, glad that she had somewhere else to stay for a few months, determined to make things work with Mimi McKinlay. She turned to Heather, her face shining with optimism. 'Do you know, I spoke to my daughter about the McKinlays on the phone this morning.'

Heather remembered. 'Your daughter's at university in London?'

'Yes – Saffy was delighted when I told her I was going to work with Mimi.'

'Is she a fan of musicals?' Heather was interested. 'Wasn't Mimi a chorus girl in the fifties?'

'Saffy is doing a thesis on feminist gerontology for her PhD.'

Heather spluttered. 'What on earth is that when it's at home?'

'It's the study of how gender affects the status and treatment of older people, and the disadvantages experienced by many women. She has strong views on how some older women lose privilege and are treated differently.'

'Oh, she's so right, hen.' Heather waved a finger. 'I'm fifty-two and some kiddie pushed in front of me in the supermarket only two days ago and claimed he hadn't seen me, as if it was my fault.'

'We all know how that feels,' Jess agreed. 'But my daughter Saffy's very enthusiastic about her studies – she has opinions and she doesn't care who hears them.' Jess's face flushed with pride. 'So, she was pleased to hear that I was going look after Mimi – she was saying how alienated Mimi must feel, living alone in the attic flat with only a few visitors. She's even recommended some reading for me.' Jess pushed her hands into her pockets. 'Oh, I'd better get going – it must be half eleven, Heather. I said I'd be there for twelve to move into the flat.'

'Ugh, a basement, though, hen...' Heather pulled a face. 'Is it damp and cold?'

'It's all right.' Jess pushed her car keys into the lock. 'To tell you the truth, I'm looking forward to this job now. It'll be a challenge. I'll enjoy it.'

'Oh, it will have its compensations, I'm sure...' Heather said with a wink, as Jess slid into the VW and started the engine. She waved an arm as the purple Beetle moved slowly down the drive and out into the road, joining the flow of traffic.

Heather watched the car disappear into the distance. She hoped Jess would be all right working with Mad Mimi McKinlay. She'd been talking to a woman in the baker's only two days ago, a friend of the McKinlays' housekeeper. By all accounts, Jess would have her work cut out tending to the strange old woman who was apparently a 'wee bampot' and 'completely mad in the heed'. The woman in the shop had declared that despite Mrs McKinlay's dusty hoard of old costumes, all the stories of her life as a chorus girl were from her imagination: she'd met her rich husband when she'd been an usher on the door of a London theatre. What was worse, the woman said, she and her crazy Italian friend tore around the Highlands in an old open-topped car dressed to the nines and behaving like teenagers: it had to be seen to be believed.

Heather wasn't too worried: Jess could take care of herself. And apparently, Mimi had three good-looking sons and the eldest had recently split up with his wife. The family was not short of a bob or two, either. Jess was pretty, warm-hearted, and most importantly single, Heather thought excitedly, so surely one of the sons would notice her before too long. Although Jess didn't realise it, she definitely needed passion in her life. In Heather's opinion, this was far too good an opportunity to be missed.

11

Mimi was lying on the bed wearing the pink cashmere jumper and purple trousers, her eyes closed. Yellow hair tumbled across her face, a film of perspiration on her brow. The gold bangle wrapped in tissue paper was still firmly clenched in her hand as she dreamed about dancing alone in a spotlight to the whirling tune of a violin, played offstage by a dark handsome man. In the audience, a woman with tawny hair in a ponytail was gazing up, her hands poised to applaud.

Outside Glen Carrick House, the air was glue-sticky, still as an oil painting. The loch blazed, vermillion in the amber sunlight, as if on fire. Jess exhaled in the heat and was about to knock when the door was suddenly thrown wide and Fin appeared, wearing a white shirt, carrying a jacket and a briefcase. He stared: for some reason, he'd thought she was arriving later. He recovered his composure and offered her a charming smile, moving past her to the bottom step.

'Jess. Can you help yourself? You know where everything is. Mother's asleep in her room so you'll have plenty of time to move in and Ailsa's around somewhere, cleaning.' He took two steps forward. 'I'm afraid I'm away to a meeting... it's unfortunate timing.'

'That's all right,' Jess replied. 'I only have two bags and a laptop.'

'Right – if there's anything you need...'

'I'll be fine – thanks.' Jess was looking forward to shopping for the things she didn't have. It might be fun making the little flat her own.

'Okay. Well. Good luck.' Fin seemed distracted. 'And can you park the car round the side of the house when you're done? Everyone leaves their car there to keep the drive free for visitors.' His face was suddenly welcoming. 'You're no visitor now, Jess.'

'Thank you.' Jess watched him go, wondering if she had changed her opinion of him: she'd initially thought him distant. But the Fin she had just spoken to was preoccupied, off his guard. She thought he'd seemed troubled.

It was becoming increasingly hot outside. Jess thought that the basement flat might be humid – there was no ventilation. She'd buy herself a nice fan to cool the air. She turned back to the car; she'd take both cases inside in one go. As she opened the Beetle, she felt a surge of optimism.

Jess was greeted in the hall by a small dark-haired woman observing her through thick-rimmed spectacles. The woman waved a hand. 'Hello. You must be Jessica. I'm Ailsa, the house-keeper.' Jess put her cases down and held out a hand, but Ailsa was walking away, her voice trailing behind her. 'When you've put your things in the basement, come up to the kitchen and I'll have a cup of tea ready for you. You'll be in need of some refreshment, no doubt.'

'Thanks,' Jess called after her, lugging both cases towards the steps that led to the basement.

Half an hour later, her bags unpacked and her car moved to

the neatly gravelled area at the side of the house, Jess peeked into the kitchen but there was no one there. She moved quietly towards the stove; the kettle was cool and no teacups had been laid out. Jess assumed Ailsa was busy, so she decided to find her.

Jess wandered into the little snug where there was a television, heavy velvet drapes at the window, and then she peeked into the enormous lounge opposite, with its vast stone fireplace and curved sofas, bookcases. It was a spacious room where banquets might have been held years ago; in one corner was a grand piano. Heavy drapes hung at three tall windows and light streamed in, illuminating a Persian rug on the wooden floor. Huge gilt-framed pictures hung from the wall: a blue leaf-shaped loch, a majestic reindeer with high antlers, snow-capped mountains.

The hall was cool and comfortable. Jess stood still, listening; a soft sound came from another room. It came again, a bumping noise. She assumed Ailsa must be dusting, so she knocked at the door lightly, pushed it open and stepped inside. The room was large, the bed in the centre covered by a striped pale grey duvet; the curtains were silver-grey. On the walls were several framed photographs – gorillas at play, a tiger stalking through grass, a giraffe with a twig in its mouth, leaping dolphins in the ocean. There was a desk by the window, a laptop. In the corner of the room was a static exercise bicycle, a set of dumb-bells and an acoustic guitar. Ailsa was nowhere to be seen. Then Jess saw the source of the noise: a black dog, a Labrador, was in the corner, resting in a spacious dog bed, twitching its tail. Jess walked over, a hand out, and bent down.

'Well, you're a sweetie, aren't you?'

The dog wagged its tail harder. As Jess rubbed the soft ears, she noticed framed photographs by the bedside and moved closer to observe one. She stared at a beautiful African woman, her hair braided and beaded. The second photo was of the woman again, her arm around a young man in his early teens; Jess assumed he was the woman's son: she looked proud and happy.

Jess was fascinated by the people in the photos: the woman's face was placid and sweet, the young man's more questioning and thoughtful.

She was tugged from her thoughts by an angry voice behind her. 'What the hell do you think you're doing?'

Jess glanced towards the door and saw a broad-shouldered man in a wheelchair, his legs in plaster beneath shorts. His eyes glowed like coals. She stepped back and caught her breath. 'I'm so sorry... I was looking for Ailsa.'

He glared. 'She's not here, clearly.'

'I – I saw the dog and...' Jess shook her head. 'I didn't mean to pry...' His eyes were fixed on her, and Jess took a breath. 'I'm Jess. I'm here to—'

'I know who you are.'

Jess exhaled. The man held her in his gaze. There was nothing more to be said. She stood as tall as she could and said, 'I'm sorry – I didn't mean to disturb you.' She moved past him quickly and out into the hall, then she rushed to the security of the kitchen. Ailsa was in there, boiling the kettle and setting out cups.

'Tea with or without milk or sugar?' Ailsa looked pleased to see her.

'A little milk...' Jess stood by a chair, then sank onto hard wood, her face still flushed. 'I think I've just upset the man in the wheelchair. I went into his room because I thought you were there and he came in and was cross with me.'

'That would be Mr Angus,' Ailsa said knowledgeably. 'Don't pay any mind to him. He can be a carnaptious devil.'

Jess frowned. 'Carnaptious?'

'Bad-tempered.' Ailsa poured tea into two cups. 'He was bad enough before his motorbike accident, but at least he was mostly away working. Now he's stuck here, he has a rage on him most of the time.'

'Oh.' Jess sipped her tea. It was scalding hot; the air in the room was warm and humid too and she dabbed perspiration from her cheeks.

'It's warm today – I'll open the back door.' Ailsa heaved open the door and then sat down, picking up her tea. 'Have you been around the garden yet?'

'No, not yet.'

'Oh, it's beautiful, fir trees and plants and flowers, and a most spectacular view of the loch. You're not Scots, Jessica?'

'Please call me Jess,' Jess replied. 'No, I'm from Worcestershire.'

Ailsa nodded, as if that explained everything. Jess leaned forward enthusiastically. 'I'm going to spend time with Mimi. I'm looking forward to getting to know her.'

Ailsa's brow clouded. 'You be very careful with that one. She's a little bit mad.'

'Mad?' Jess was astonished.

'Oh, yes,' Ailsa said. 'She tried to teach me a dance one time. She had me by the neck – I almost suffocated. She and her Italian friend are not safe together in that sports car. Everyone thinks so around here.' Ailsa saw her surprised expression and continued. 'My husband John keeps telling me I shouldn't work for them. The McKinlays are a strange bunch. But I don't know how they'd manage without me. Mr Finlay always says the family couldn't cope...'

'He seems nice, Fin,' Jess suggested amiably.

'Ah, he's a troubled man,' Ailsa confided. 'He has marital

problems. His wife wants to take everything she can. Mr Finlay is seeing his solicitor in Inverness...'

'Perhaps that's where he was going when I arrived?'

'But she's furious with him, his wife – she's divorcing him.'

'Oh.' Jess felt immediately sorry, remembering Fin's anxious expression as he had rushed off.

'Mr Hamish is the nicest one – he lives in Inverness.' Ailsa's eyes shone in admiration. 'He's a composer.'

'I haven't met him yet.'

'Oh, he's a sweet-natured man. The most normal of them all, if you ask me.' Ailsa rolled her eyes. 'Everyone likes Mr Hamish. He calls in all the time – he often stays over. And he's devoted to his mother, goodness knows, he thinks the sun shines...'

Jess understood. 'Talking of Mimi, I should go up and say hello...'

'I'd let sleeping dogs lie, as they say.'

Jess was still wishing she'd left the dog to lie in Angus's bedroom and not gone in there. She felt awkward about the incident: she had no right to be in his bedroom and the excuse about looking for Ailsa had sounded weak. She thought of the photos on the walls, the animals, and the framed pictures of the beautiful woman and her son.

Ailsa was saying something to her, in a kindly voice. '...could make you a sandwich, if you like? There's some cheese, or cold cuts in the fridge...'

'Oh, cheese would be nice.' Jess felt suddenly hungry. 'Would it be okay to have a sandwich for Mimi too? I could take it up to her.'

'She rarely eats much,' Ailsa said. 'She'll nibble at things sometimes and make a mess all over the table.'

'What does she like?'

'Prawns.' Ailsa's face suddenly lit up, pleased with the idea. 'I have some in the fridge. I could put some on a plate with a wee bit of dressing and you could take those upstairs to her in the attic.'

'Great,' Jess enthused. 'I'll eat my sandwich with her up there, if that's okay.'

'Oh, it's fine by me,' Ailsa replied, her brow clouding with the familiar foreboding. 'But don't be surprised if she hurls the prawns – and you – down the stairs.'

Twenty minutes later, a plate in each hand, Jess made her way up to the attic. The door was open and Jess crept inside, through the small sitting room area, past the kitchenette to the bedroom, where Mimi was asleep, fully clothed, on the bed. Jess positioned the plates on the bedside table and leaned over the sleeping woman. Mimi had something clutched in one hand, tissue paper with something wrapped inside, so Jess lifted her other hand and whispered softly. 'Mimi... it's Jess. Would you like something to eat?'

'Isabella?' Mimi murmured, turning her head to one side, then her eyelids flickered open. She stared at Jess for a moment, with a look of confusion.

'It's me, Jess.'

Mimi struggled to sit upright. Her head was still full of the dream, the dancing, the heady lift of wild applause. 'Did you enjoy my dance?'

Jess didn't miss a beat as she eased a pillow behind Mimi's back. 'You were on stage, Mimi?'

'Dancing, and someone I used to know was playing violin. You were clapping.'

'You must have been magnificent.' Jess assumed Mimi wasn't yet fully awake.

'Oh, I was.' Mimi paused for a moment, then she said, 'I've been asleep – I've been dreaming.'

Jess nodded encouragingly. 'I've brought you some lunch.'

'Oh, yes, please.' Mimi stretched her legs. 'A glass of white wine. That would be perfect.'

Jess lifted the plate of prawns. 'I always think prawns go well with everything.'

Mimi was delighted. 'Prawns? Well, I could—' She plucked a prawn from the plate and popped it between her lips. 'Delicious. How thoughtful of you.'

'Have one more.' Jess held the plate within Mimi's reach. 'Then we can decide what to do this afternoon. It's warm, but it's a bit cooler downstairs. I noticed a television there. Shall we go and watch something together?'

Mimi pushed the plate away. 'I don't like television.'

Jess tried again. 'What about musicals? Maybe there's one that we could watch?'

'Do you like musicals, Jess?'

'I don't know much about them. But I'm going to learn.'

'I love musicals, especially the old ones. I was in *My Fair Lady* – and *The Boyfriend,* in the 1950s. Oh, the songs are just dreamy... and the costumes I used to wear were so glamorous.'

'Do you have either of those musicals downstairs on film that we could watch on the television?'

'Not those...' Mimi was confused for a moment, then the tension in her brow relaxed. 'I think there are a couple of modern films – there's the one about the young boy who becomes a ballet dancer and his father wants to stop him – and the other one about the King Lion and his son. Angus bought them for Fabrice when he was here and we watched them together, years ago...' She thought for a moment. 'I haven't seen Fabrice for a while. He's grown now, he's doing something... chemistry, I think, in Toulouse...'

'Shall we take our lunch downstairs and watch *The Lion King*?'

'With a nice glass of wine?'

'I seldom drink in the day, Mimi. I find I'm useless afterwards if I drink at lunchtime.'

'Surely that's the whole point?' Mimi protested. 'Isabella says the world is always so much nicer when you feel a little soft around the edges...'

Jess offered a hand. 'Let's go. Lunch and a movie...'

Mimi reached out with one hand and realised that she had something held tightly in the other. She proffered the tissue paper with the bangle inside. 'Oh, I almost forgot – this is for you.'

Jess took the package anxiously. 'For me?'

Mimi met her eyes earnestly. 'It's a special present for you, Jess. I want you to have it and for it to remind you of me always. I want us to be good friends.'

12

The night air crackled with heat as Mimi slid beneath the duvet and closed her eyes. She had enjoyed the day immensely: they'd watched *The Lion King*, then Jess had shown her pictures on the laptop of how the dancers' puppet costumes were made. Mimi was stunned by the sophistication of the modern dancers, imagining herself dressed as a gazelle, moving gracefully with a pack of other prancing animals to the tune of 'The Circle of Life'.

Jess was so friendly; every time Mimi spoke about being a dancer, her eyes were bright, fascinated. Mimi was thrilled: Jess was genuinely keen to listen. Then she had researched pictures of Julie Andrews in *The Boyfriend* in the early 1950s on her laptop. Mimi clutched Jess's arm, chatting about how she had been in that show, peering at every picture, her face frozen in an expression of joy, examining each dancer wearing a cloche hat and a short white dress to see if she could recognise herself.

She and Jess had sat at the window in her attic room eating supper, a bowl of soup each, discussing the fashions that women wore long ago, Mimi explaining how liberating it had been to dress how you wanted, and not in the same style of clothes your mother had always worn. Jess had understood exactly how Mimi felt; although she was born in 1963 and not 1934, like Mimi, Jess had been a rebel of sorts: she'd explained to Mimi that, as a thir-teen-year-old, she had been in love with the Bay City Rollers, wearing baggy red tartan trousers which her father had thought ridiculous, and a scarf emblazoned with the name Eric, which her mother had finally ruined in a hot wash, making all the colours run. Mimi smiled more than she had in a while.

Mimi said that when her three boys were lively youngsters, Donald had moved the family back to his parents' house, the one they now shared. She recalled dancing with her sons around the kitchen to the Sex Pistols' song, 'Pretty Vacant', Angus playing a thrashing guitar, Finlay drumming hard against the worktop with wooden spoons and Mimi and Hamish pogoing, singing raucously into a banana. Tears of amusement welled in her eyes. Donald had arrived home early and was livid that she encouraged his sons to participate in unruly behaviour when they should be studying quietly in their rooms. Mimi told Jess that she and her three boys always sang and danced together. Donald had two left feet and was tone deaf.

At 8.30, Mimi felt suddenly tired. Jess promised she wouldn't be too far away when she woke up. Once in bed, Mimi closed her eyes and began to doze.

Jess went downstairs, slipping quietly into the kitchen, carrying the empty soup bowls. Fin was sitting at the table, glancing through papers, a bottle of wine and a half-filled glass next to him. He looked up. 'How's it going with Mother?'

'I think it's going well.'

He waved a hand, indicating that she should sit down. She lowered herself into the hard wooden chair opposite him, her eyes resting unintentionally on his paperwork: legal documents from a solicitor in Inverness. Jess pulled her gaze back and noticed he was watching her.

'So, I hope Mother is behaving herself?'

'She's charming – we talked about musicals.'

'Oh, musicals.' Fin gave a short laugh. 'She'll be your biggest fan if that's the topic of conversation.' Jess couldn't tell if he was joking or being sarcastic. He lifted the bottle. 'Can I offer you a glass of burgundy?'

'No, thanks.' Jess shook her head. 'I don't drink much.' She watched Fin refill his glass and said, 'So what is the situation with your mother having a glass of wine? She's asked me several times if she can have one and I've managed to sidestep it because you asked me to.'

Fin shrugged. 'She'll sit in her room all day, swilling cheap Chardonnay, going through a whole bottle if we don't put the brakes on her.'

Jess watched him drain his glass. 'So, is it just the price of the wine that's the problem?'

He gave her a sharp look. Jess wondered if she'd overstepped the mark but she didn't care: already she felt loyal towards Mimi. Then, suddenly, his face relaxed.

'I take your point,' Fin sighed. 'Look, Jess, my mother drinks too much because she's lonely and it gives her comfort. If you and she want to share a glass with a meal, then that's fine, but I don't want her boozing alone.' He was watching her expression. 'Do you think I am being controlling?'

'No – you're just concerned.'

'I'm anxious about my mother.' The tension drained from his face. 'I hope this works out, having you here.'

'I hope so, too.'

'That's good.' Fin glanced at his paperwork and then back to

Jess. 'Well, it's a hot night – we need a good downpour to cool things off.'

Jess nodded, feeling awkward. He was talking to her about the weather because they had nothing in common. She decided to bring the conversation back to business. 'Fin, can we discuss my working schedule? I have a dinner invitation on Friday evening and I've said I'll go. I'd like to know what days I'll be free. I'm happy to swap around occasionally to suit you, but I need a bit of clarity.'

'Of course.' Fin pushed his papers to one side. He was being rude: the divorce was filling his thoughts. He made an effort to be sociable. 'Dinner dates already and you've only just arrived...'

'It's just a takeaway and a film with Heather at the B & B where I stayed.'

'Ah – I'm glad you're settling here. How about we say you take weekends off, and we can alternate as you wish, start early or finish late. I'm happy to be flexible and work around what suits you, as long as you give me a bit of notice. My mother isn't a nine-to-five person. But if you can do six hours a day, five days a week, I'll cover the rest.'

'Sounds fair.' A thought occurred to Jess and she thrust out a hand. 'Also, Mimi gave me this.'

Fin looked at the bangle on her wrist. 'I know about that.'

'It's gold. I can't accept it,' Jess said. 'I've only just met her.'

'It's her jewellery,' Fin replied simply. 'She can give it away to whoever she pleases.'

'Well, I'll wear it now because it's a present, but I can't keep it.' Jess met his eyes directly. 'When I leave, I'll give it back to you.'

'As you wish. My father gave it to her and clearly she wants you to have it.' Fin was suddenly apologetic. 'Oh, goodness me – I haven't offered you a drink – coffee, tea...?'

'I have the kitchenette downstairs – I'll stock up at the weekend, but thanks – I'm fine.'

'This kitchen is the heart of our home.' Fin offered a charming smile; he appeared to be warming to Jess. 'Please do treat it as such – you're welcome to eat in here any time.'

'Thanks.' Jess thought it might be nice to spend time in the kitchen. Ailsa had been welcoming earlier and Fin's company was pleasant enough. But she certainly wasn't keen to bump into his temperamental brother. She sighed.

'I think I'll call it a day now – it's been a busy one.'

Fin stood up. 'You must be tired. It's humid in here – that doesn't help. The kitchen gets very warm this time of year.' He moved to the back door and opened it wide. 'I'll let some cool air in. It's almost too hot to breathe.' A blast of oven-warm air swirled into the room. He sat down again and lifted a pen, indicating his paperwork. 'I've this to keep me busy for a while...'

'I won't disturb you then,' Jess said and stood up.

In the hallway, as she approached the steps to her basement flat, she glanced at the door to Angus's room, which was closed. She could hear the lilt of soft music inside, an instrument like a harp, a high melodic voice. She considered whether she should knock and apologise for being in his room earlier. But she had already said sorry, and he'd been rude. Jess decided the best plan was to avoid him. Fin seemed agreeable enough, if a little too suave and formal; Ailsa had been welcoming and Mimi was adorable: she didn't need to interact with Angus. She had a roof over her head, a job she might find very rewarding, and she'd take each day as it came.

* * *

Angus was lying on his bed, his eyes closed. He was listening to Ayub Ogada singing and playing the nyatiti lyre. The music was relaxing, but he felt his shoulders tense: his legs ached. He was using crutches now; soon the plaster would come off and he'd see his legs again for the first time in months. Angus knew what they'd be like: wasted muscle, thinner, weaker. He'd joked he'd have the legs of a Hollywood actress. But it made him even more determined: he'd run, cycle, exercise to build himself back up and then he'd be away again, off to Cameroon. Fabrice would want to go with him, to see his grandparents. In Yaoundé it would be hot, but Angus always felt comfortable there. He'd take his camera, photograph some gorillas, elephants. The thought of working again made his heart beat faster. Here in the Highlands, although it had been his home for so many years, he felt like a sleepwalker. But once he was travelling again, taking photographs, he'd come alive.

* * *

Jess was more tired than she had thought; it couldn't have been much past 10.30, but she was ready to fall asleep as soon as she curled up beneath the duvet. She decided she'd buy some new bedding at the weekend: the covers were heavy, so she flung out a leg to allow some cooler air to touch her skin. It was humid in the basement but the flowers on the table gave off a sweet aroma. Jess imagined how nice it would be to have her own place but until then, she'd do the best she could to make Mimi happy, she'd enjoy the changing seasons in the Highlands, perhaps explore to the west and the north. Jess thought about Saffy in her little flat in London, energetically discussing opinions, going to galleries and theatres, meeting friends in wine bars and eating in trendy bistros. She hugged the pillow, smiled and drifted into a contented sleep.

Much later, Jess opened her eyes with the distinct feeling that someone was in the room. She wasn't afraid. Her first thought was that perhaps the dog she'd seen in Angus's room had padded down to investigate. She blinked. There was a figure huddled in the corner, not moving. Jess held her breath and stared harder: the dark shape was wearing a thin light-coloured nightgown and had yellow hair. A soft voice whispered her name. 'Jess?'

'Mimi, are you all right?'

Mimi approached the bed tentatively. 'It's so noisy.'

'Noisy?' Jess sat up and stretched her arms.

'Upstairs. Outside. There's a storm.'

Jess picked up her phone on the little cabinet next to her bed. It was past three o'clock. She pushed her feet out of bed. 'Shall we go up to your apartment?' Mimi nodded. Jess took in the bare feet, the uncombed hair, the thin nightgown. 'We'll watch the storm from your room.'

'It's loud – thunder crashing, lightning.'

Jess was suddenly excited. 'Can we see the lightning over the loch from your window, Mimi?'

'Oh, yes.'

Jess took her hand. 'Come on, then. Let's go and watch the storm play out over the water.'

Jess led Mimi up the steps, going deliberately slowly, at her pace. 'We'll make a hot chocolate in your kitchen, shall we?'

'Oh, yes – what fun.' Mimi grasped Jess's hand tightly and suddenly felt safe. Alone, in the darkness, the thunder rumbling outside her window, the lightning illuminating the whole room and then plunging into shadow, she had been nervous. But Jess wasn't scared of anything and suddenly, Mimi was no longer afraid.

13

Mimi sat close to the window, listening to the grumble of thunder as the lightning brightened the sky. The trees illuminated and the light reflected on inky water. Then there was sudden blackness again. She was enjoying the storm raging outside and the warmth of being safely indoors, her nose close to the windowpane and a mug of hot chocolate in her hands. She watched Jess drink from her mug, noticing the gold bangle on her wrist, and she smiled. 'I like thunder now.'

'It's exciting...' Jess wiped a smudge of chocolate from her upper lip. 'Scotland is beautiful. Even in the middle of a storm.'

Mimi sighed, a soft sound of contentment. 'I remember being a child in London. My parents lived in Stamford Hill. I must have been about six years old – I woke up one night to hear the most incredible storm. My mother came to the room where my sister and I slept, and she wrapped us in blankets and took us down to the basement. Thunder boomed so hard the house seemed to shake. I'd never felt so afraid.' Mimi took a breath. 'We stayed in the basement all night, huddled together, listening to the clatter above us. In the morning, we crept upstairs and peered into the street. Several houses were just rubble, the school was completely flattened. I remember looking at all the dust and bricks. I've never liked storms since that day.'

Jess made a quick calculation in her head, Mimi's age now, the dates she'd have been a child. 'That was the bombing during the war – the Blitz?'

'It was, yes.' There was a loud crash outside, the windowpane was briefly white, and Mimi closed her eyes.

'The wartime must have been terrifying to a child. Were you and your sister evacuees?'

'My father refused to allow the family to be parted from each other. Rachel and I stayed in London.'

'Were you a close family?'

'I suppose so. My father was strict.' Mimi clucked her tongue softly. 'He wouldn't let me go on the stage. I was desperate to sing and dance. "Miriam," he said to me, "Your mother didn't bring you up to be a floozy – you take a nice job in a good department store, sell hats, then find yourself a husband." Of course, I didn't listen to him. I left home at eighteen.'

The room was still humid, the air heavy. Outside, the thunder rolled in the distance. Jess opened the window slightly and the room was flooded with a cool breeze. 'So, how did you become a dancer?'

'Oh, it was hard at first.' Mimi gazed into the distance. 'I moved into a flat with another girl and found myself a job on the stage door in a little theatre in Bermondsey. There were dancers there and I watched them. I begged the theatre manager to let me try. I knew I could dance.'

'What happened?'

'One night, one of the dancers didn't turn up. The others said she wasn't coming back. I persuaded them to let me have her costume and I took her place.'

'That was brave.'

'I was terrified. But I knew all the words of every song, all the moves – I had watched night after night. And once I was on stage, once my heart had stopped knocking so hard and my jelly legs held me upright, do you know, Jess, I never looked back. Those were the best times. I had friends, I had fun. Then I met Donald.'

'Your husband?'

'He co-owned the theatre in Bermondsey. He came to see a show one night and saw me dance in the chorus. I was told I had to have a drink with him afterwards. He was twenty-eight and I was only nineteen. We went to a swanky bar up west. At first, I just sat at the table with an orange juice, too nervous to speak. He was tall, red-haired, broad-shouldered – Finlay is the image of him. He had a deep voice, booming in his chest, and an accent I'd never heard before and, oh, he was so sophisticated. He wore an expensive jacket with a tartan lining – he was a proud Scotsman, smoked cigarettes, drank whisky: I'd never seen a man so self-assured and handsome.'

Jess grimaced. 'I'm not sure I'd go for the cigarettes and whisky...'

'Oh, but in those days, Jess, that was glamorous. I was completely bowled over by him. He spoke as if the world belonged to him and he could have anything he wanted.' Mimi arched an eyebrow. 'And the thing he seemed to want most was me.'

Jess watched as Mimi's expression became sad. 'And what did you want, Mimi?'

'I didn't know – I was swept up on a cloud of emotion. He had influence, contacts. My career blossomed: I was in *The Boyfriend* as one of the leading chorus girls. I couldn't believe my luck. But it was all down to Donald.'

'So, you were an item, you and Donald?'

'Item?' Mimi was confused. 'Oh, Jess, I knew nothing about men or the world Donald lived in, or about courting. But...' She took a little breath. 'He bought me presents, jewellery, furs – he took me to expensive restaurants. I was whisked off my feet. Oh, Donald knew how to romance a girl.' Her face took on a dream-like expression and she was lost in thought.

'And you fell in love?'

'Love?' Mimi snapped from her reverie. 'Do you know, he never once told me he loved me.'

'Never?' Jess offered a sympathetic face.

'But he got me a solo spot on the stage, a song and dance. He had influence.' Mimi's expression hardened. 'I sang a song he said he'd written specially for me.'

'Do you remember the song?'

'Oh, yes.' Mimi's mouth was firm. 'I remember it well. I sang that song every night for a month. I wore a long dirndl skirt and I danced as I carried a basket of flowers. Some of the audience sobbed at the end. I never had such applause as when I performed that song.'

'Sing it for me,' Jess said, her voice a whisper.

Mimi gave a little cough and then began to sing, her voice wavering.

> A traveller boy knocked at my door
> With his pretty horse and cart
> He asked me for a single coin
> I gave him all my heart.
>
> That night we talked, he held my hand
> He told me of his life
> I said that I would follow him
> He said he had a wife.

And then the soldiers came for him
And put him behind the wire
Where white ash falls like snow from smoke
That billows from the chimney fire.

Now many years have passed me by
As I am growing old
The traveller boy, he fills my dreams
But my heart is icy cold.

The growl of thunder drifted into the distance. Mimi turned her face to Jess, her cheeks damp, surprised that Jess too had tears in her eyes.

'That's a lovely song, Mimi. And Donald wrote that, just for you to sing?'

'That's what he told me then,' Mimi whispered. 'Much later, I found out he'd got it from a Hungarian woman, one of his mistresses. He had been seeing her at the same time as he was courting me, the same time that he put a diamond ring on my finger and told me we were getting married.'

Jess was quiet for a while. Then she said, 'You've had an interesting life.'

'Oh, that was just the start...' Mimi's lids were heavy as she yawned.

'We'd better get you into bed – you're tired.' Jess helped her to her feet.

Fifteen minutes later, Jess crept down to the basement. The house was still, every corner a shadow. She slid into bed and closed her eyes. It was almost five o'clock.

* * *

Jess woke, her limbs heavy with sleep. She glanced at her phone: it was past ten. She'd missed a call from Paul and one from Saffy. She texted both, pulling on her dressing gown. As she wandered upstairs bleary-eyed, Ailsa called out a cheery greeting from the hallway, pushing a vacuum cleaner around. The kitchen smelled of toast; there was a simmering pot of coffee on the stove and Jess poured some into a mug, then flopped on a chair. She would wake up properly in a moment – her hair wasn't properly brushed – then she'd organise herself, drive into Drumnadrochit and buy food to stock the kitchenette. Mimi wouldn't wake for a while and anyway, Jess had agreed with Fin that she'd start work at two. Jess glanced at the bangle at her wrist and wondered if she could buy something for Mimi that would be a gesture of friendship.

It was cooler in the kitchen since the storm; Jess stretched out her legs beneath the dressing gown, wriggled her toes and sipped coffee, feeling the bitterness on her tongue jolt her awake. Briefly, she wondered if Mimi was still asleep. Jess recalled the sad song Mimi had sung, about lost love and loneliness in later years. She and Mimi were in a similar situation: single women on their own, unlikely to find love again. Jess shrugged. Being alone didn't affect her now. Her phone buzzed on the table and she picked it up, thumbing a reply to a text from Saffy, who was asking how she was settling in the new job.

A voice came from behind her, a light, friendly tone, a hint of a local accent. 'Hello?'

Jess swung round. A man was standing behind her in the doorway. He was wearing a dark jacket, a T-shirt and jeans. His china-blue eyes and disarming smile were familiar. She was suddenly conscious that she was wearing a dressing gown and her hair was unbrushed. She smiled to cover her awkwardness. 'Hello.'

The man extended a hand. 'You must be here to look after Mum. Fin told me he'd hired someone. I'm Hamish.'

'Pleased to meet you. I'm Jess.' As she took his hand in hers, she realised that they had shaken hands before. 'I know you from somewhere...'

Hamish hadn't recognised her at first. Then he remembered the shining face, wet hair dripping. 'I'm so sorry – I didn't know it was you. When we last met, we were standing in a lay-by.' His eyes danced with the memory as he released her hand. 'You have a purple Volkswagen Beetle.'

Jess recalled where she had seen him before. 'And you have a Saab.'

'Well, it's nice to meet you under drier circumstances.' Hamish shoved his hands into his pockets. 'I hope the bumper is all right.'

'It's fine...'

'I thought you were a tourist.'

'I like it here,' Jess replied by way of explanation. 'I stayed on.'

'Well, I'm pleased you did,' Hamish said. 'And Mum's pleased too.'

'Mimi is really nice.'

Jess noticed Hamish's eyes stray to the bangle on her arm. He poured coffee, his movements easy and relaxed as he turned his blue gaze on her. 'Well, hopefully we'll bump into each other more often. Not in our cars—' he smiled at his joke, '—just around the house. I visit whenever I can. Mum's special and we all like to make her feel that way as much as we can.'

Hamish drew up a chair as if settling down for a long chat. Jess decided that Hamish was certainly the nicest of all the three brothers, the most comfortable to be around, but she had plenty to do. 'I must be on my way – I'm off into Drumnadrochit to buy a few things...'

'Of course – don't let me keep you.' Hamish sat up quickly.

'Nice to meet you, Hamish.'

'Likewise...'

Jess was on her feet. Ailsa was vacuuming near the front door; a loud buzzing filled the air. She made for the steps to the basement and found herself facing a scowling man in a wheelchair. She caught her breath and muttered, 'Good morning.'

He nodded once. 'You're my mother's companion.'

Jess hesitated, then she held out her hand. 'Jess...'

He didn't extend his own. 'I know.' She looked around intending to bolt, then he added, 'When I found you in my room – I was rude to you. I'm sorry for that.'

Jess was suddenly apologetic. 'Oh, no, it was my fault.'

He was staring at her. 'I should have been more understanding.'

'Yes...' Jess wasn't sure what to say. She felt suddenly awkward.

Angus's dark eyes gleamed and Jess wondered why she felt so unnerved. 'It'll make a big difference to Mum, having you here.'

'Oh, I'm glad to help...'

'She deserves a bit of happiness in her life.'

Jess nodded. 'I'll do my best.'

He gave a soft grunt, turning his wheelchair around, and Jess fled to the basement, her heart thumping, glad to be running from the feeling of embarrassment that seemed to weigh on her shoulders as she spoke to Angus.

14

Several days later, Mimi and Isabella sat on a wrought-iron bench on soft cushions in the garden, sipping white wine. Isabella blew smoke upwards from her cigarette towards puffball clouds overhead, straggles of white skeins in a grey sky. Mimi said, 'Jess doesn't approve of smoking.'

Isabella laughed. 'I think it's sexy to smoke.' She inhaled deeply and gave a throaty cough. 'It won't be so sexy when it kills me, though. My doctor says it will catch up with me one day. But my lungs are clear as a bell.'

'Donald smoked. It was sexy at first, but I hated what the smoke did to my voice.' Mimi wrinkled her nose. Then she caught the mischief in Isabella's eyes and she smiled. 'We have to die from something. At least it won't be boredom.'

'So where is she, this Jess? I want to meet her.'

'You'll love her,' Mimi enthused. 'I already do. And we must plan to do something together soon. She's such good fun. She has a wicked sense of humour. And she's so independent, living alone and doing what she likes. She told me that diets and bills aren't important. I thought that was wonderful.'

'I like her already.' Isabella raised an eyebrow. 'Let's take her out for lunch.'

Mimi gazed towards the loch. 'I always feel better when I'm up here, looking at the view. It's like a piece of my soul is hovering over the water. It makes me feel calm.'

'But you love the spark, the vibrations of London. So do I.'

Mimi reached out and grasped Isabella's hand. 'And we'll go there again soon, the two of us. We'll take Jess.' Her face glowed with happiness. 'She'll be here in a moment. She had some phone calls to make. She has a daughter and a brother.'

'But no man.' Isabella grinned wickedly. 'Fin will be free soon. Do you think they'd hit it off?'

'Finlay? I can't imagine...' Mimi stretched out her arms. 'Where shall we go for lunch? Grimaldi's?' She gazed towards the loch, where a treacle-dark cloud huddled between the mountains. 'You can always tell when the bad weather will come creeping in.' Mimi shrugged. 'There's often rain looming behind the brightness, just waiting.' Then she grabbed Isabella's arm, her face brightening. 'Oh, look who it is!'

A figure she recognised instantly was walking towards her and Mimi felt a familiar happiness rising in her chest. Although her sight wasn't as sharp as it had been, she knew Hamish by his easy gait, his light hair, his wave as he raised his hand to greet her. Mimi called out, 'Hamish – it's so lovely to see you.'

'Hello, gorgeous.' Hamish kissed her soft cheek. 'Isabella – you're looking stunning as ever.' He sat between them on the bench. He was wearing a light scarf over his jacket against the cool breeze, the familiar shirt and blue jeans. He gazed at the sunshine reflecting blinding light on the loch and said, 'You're not cold here, are you, Mum?'

She leaned her head against his shoulder. 'I have this cardie.'

He wrapped an arm around her. 'And you have me too now.'

'Where have you been, Hamish? Have you been too busy to visit me?'

'You have the lovely Jess to take care of you now.' Hamish pulled her closer, aware of the brittleness of her bones. 'I've been co-writing a musical.'

'Ooooh, tell me.' Mimi was immediately impressed.

Isabella tapped his knee. 'Are you taking it around the world on a tour, darling? America?' She smiled mischievously. 'Can I come?'

'We're going to take it to London first. Its working title is *The Flower of the Highlands.*'

Mimi wrinkled her nose. 'Is it about botany, Hamish? That's not very exciting.'

'No, Mum, it's about a beautiful Scottish lassie, Flora, who lives a rural life and sings all day long, then she's discovered and put on the stage by an ambitious manager.'

'Romance, sex, betrayal,' Isabella gasped. 'I'll love it.'

'Oh.' Mimi thought for a moment. 'So, I expect she's young and naïve and the manager takes advantage…'

'That sort of thing.' Hamish's expression was boyish.

'I want to see it.' Isabella's hand was still on Hamish's knee. 'I hope it will make me cry. Love stories should always make you weep…'

'So,' Mimi leaned closer. 'Where's Fin? And Angus?'

'Angus has gone to the hospital in Inverness – he has an appointment with the specialist. Fin took him in his car. Angus wasn't happy.'

'I'm sure he wasn't.'

'So…' Hamish winked. 'I wondered if you'd like to come to Inverness with me and I could play a few of the tunes from my musical for you both.'

'Will we take your sexy black car, Hamish?' Isabella asked.

'Definitely. Would you like to hear all the songs, Mum? Shall we go? I'll make you both the most delicious lunch.'

'Two conditions.' Mimi pressed her lips together.

Hamish's face shone. He winked at Isabella. 'My lovely mother is setting conditions to visit her son.'

'First of all, I want Jess to come.'

'I don't see why not,' Hamish smiled. 'There's room for the three of you in the Saab.'

'And secondly, I'd like a glass of cool white wine with lunch.'

'Done.' Hamish was delighted. 'Let's go and find Jess and then we can get going.'

'I can't wait. Lunch with handsome Hamish.' Isabella clapped her hands.

'And you must drive steadily, Hamish – I know you drive that car too fast.'

Hamish protested. 'That's three conditions, but all right, Mum – anything for you.'

* * *

A light rain was falling in Inverness as the Saab slowed down. Hamish's home was a Georgian terrace, situated at the end of a short gravel drive. To the left was a sweeping willow tree, branches bending under the weight of densely woven leaves. The door was dark blue and, behind huge casement windows upstairs and downstairs, lights blazed. Hamish helped Mimi and Isabella out of the car and Jess followed them to the door.

Hamish led them through a narrow hallway to a room that contained a huge grand piano. He immediately seated himself on the stool and Mimi leaned against the piano, the practised stance of a singer. Jess and Isabella moved to a sofa on the other side of the room, next to the window, and listened as Hamish swept his fingers across the keys. He played whirling notes, from high to low and then high again, the keys tinkling, ending in a flourish, and Jess leaned forward, clapping her hands.

'You're very good,' Isabella purred.

Hamish peered over the piano. 'I was just warming up.'

'He takes after me,' Mimi said proudly. 'Hamish is just like me. And Finlay is just like his father.'

'And Angus?' Jess asked.

'I guess he's like his father too,' Hamish grinned, and Isabella clapped her hands.

'Bravo, darling!'

Mimi moved behind him, patting his hair affectionately. 'So, let's hear some of this musical you've written.'

'Right.' Hamish shrugged with an air of mock-modesty. 'It may all change, but this is the beginning of the overture – four of the songs I've co-written are incorporated in it – it's designed for an orchestra, but obviously this is the bare bones...'

Hamish began to play. The melody was light and playful, reminiscent of a pastoral setting: lochs, pines, mist, fawns frolicking, mountains. Then the volume rose, a minor key, the sense of passion, longing, sadness. The music became spirited again, then suddenly poignant, evoking loneliness, and finally there was a flourish of triumph, bold notes banging from the piano, an urgency, then silence.

Mimi gasped. 'Oh, Hamish. How I wish I could be in this musical. It is so dramatic.'

'It's meant to be,' Hamish said. 'Flora hits the big time, and yet behind the mask of her success are sorrow and loneliness.'

'A role for the wonderful Mimi Solitaire,' Isabella breathed and Mimi's face was suddenly sad.

'Not now. As I used to be, long ago...'

Hamish gave her a tender look. 'To be honest, Mum, you were

in my mind when I wrote it. You were the inspiration – you are with everything I do.'

Mimi ruffled his hair, tears in her eyes. 'Oh, Hamish, I'm quite overcome...' Her voice was small. 'May I have lunch now? And a glass of wine.'

Hamish leaped from the piano stool. 'Of course. Anything for you, gorgeous. Then, after lunch, shall I play you one of Flora's songs? There's one you'd really like, called "Alone in a Crowd".'

Mimi closed her eyes. 'I'm quite exhausted now. I think I'll just have a few minutes...'

'And I'll step outside. I need to smoke,' Isabella announced.

Hamish winked at Jess. 'Come and help me make lunch – let Mum have a rest.'

Jess was on her feet. She followed Hamish into a well-equipped kitchen, everything coordinated in grey and stainless steel, with granite worktops. A wooden table and four chairs stood solidly in the centre of the room. Hamish opened a fridge and produced pâté and cheese and handed Jess a bottle of wine. 'You could open this. Glasses are in the top cupboard. Of course, I won't have any as I'm driving you all back.'

Jess busied herself with glasses as Hamish assembled bread, grapes, olives, tomatoes and salad. 'This is a lovely house.'

Hamish agreed. 'I've been here for three years now. Before that, I lived in Edinburgh.'

'It must be a great life, being a composer.'

Hamish offered a rueful smile. 'It is when the work is good. Right now, I'm in clover.'

Jess poured wine into three glasses. 'Your mother adores you.'

'I adore her – we all do.' Hamish's eyes twinkled. 'It's always been that way: ever since we were kids, I've been the favourite.' He waved a hand to dismiss the thought. 'I don't think Fin cares and Angus probably never even noticed.'

Jess thought about asking questions about Hamish's brothers. Fin was going through a difficult divorce; Angus was alone, his legs broken. She was surprised how concerned she felt. Instead, she said, 'I'm really enjoying working with Mimi.'

Hamish stopped slicing bread and came over to Jess, his expression earnest. 'Mum seems so much better, healthier, happy.'

'Mimi is wonderful...'

'She's lonely. She has no one except Isabella and her memories. But now you're here, you are filling so many empty spaces.'

Jess shrugged. 'To be honest, it's filling my spaces too.'

'I'd like to say thank you properly,' Hamish said. 'I'll take everyone to dinner soon...'

'That would be lovely,' Jess replied cheerfully. She exhaled slowly: a thought had just come to her. 'Hamish, I'll just check on Mimi. She might have fallen asleep...'

'Yes, of course...'

'I'll tell them both that lunch is ready, shall I?' Jess disappeared through the kitchen door, rushing into the room where the piano was, glancing towards the sofa. 'Mimi...'

The sofa was empty. Jess blinked and stared around her. She hurried back into the hall: the front door was ajar. She called out, 'Hamish.'

She flung the door wide and gazed down the drive into the street. Rain was falling heavily, pounding on wet gravel. Hamish was at her side.

'Where's Mum?'

Jess was uneasy. 'I don't know. The door was open – there's no sign of Mimi or Isabella.' She took a deep breath. 'She's gone.'

They rushed into the street, along the road, past other terraced houses. Rain was splashing from a pewter sky, funnelling through gutters, gurgling down drains. A car flashed by, its tyres squelching through water. Hamish called out, 'Mum? Mum?'

He turned to Jess: both of them were drenched. Jess was reminded of the time he had bumped into the back of her car, their first meeting, then she whirled round and yelled, 'Mimi? Isabella?'

Hamish's voice was anxious as they hurried forward past more houses, shouting. Another car crashed through puddles of rain. The tarmac shone with grease, a rainbow film of oil. Jess pushed wet hair from her face. 'Where can she be?'

Hamish shook his head, water flying from damp hair. 'Maybe I should ring the police?'

'Do you think she could have gone back to your house? Could she be upstairs?'

'What if she's lost, out here in all this rain?'

'Why would she wander away?'

'I've no idea.'

They turned the corner into another street, rain blinding their vision. Then they saw Isabella, drenched, clapping her hands in a rhythm, smoke curling from the cigarette between her lips. Mimi was holding onto a lamp post, leaning away in a pose. As Jess approached just behind Hamish, she noticed that Mimi was smiling for all she was worth and singing. She flung out an arm and twirled around the lamp post. Jess recognised the song – 'Singing in the Rain'. Two people had stopped to listen, huddled beneath an umbrella while Mimi, oblivious of the downpour, continued to smile and sing. She whirled around the lamp post twice and launched herself, feet first, into a puddle, water splashing upwards, drenching her clothes.

Hamish yelled, 'Mum...'

Isabella shot him a triumphant look. 'Come and watch, darling. She's performing like a goddess.'

Another person had arrived, a teenager in a parka jacket, hood up, filming on a phone. Mimi strutted across the pavement, still singing, and made a pirouette. She turned a wet, shining face to the heavens and continued her song, a broad smile on her face.

'Mum...' Hamish tried again.

Mimi was oblivious, in the zone, giving her all.

Jess stared at Mimi's wet feet and ankles, the damp cardigan, rain dripping from her hair onto her face, making her skin shine. Mimi skipped towards a puddle, heaving herself forward, singing for all she was worth. Hamish turned to Jess. 'We can't stop her – she'll have to get to the end of the song.'

Jess smiled at exactly the same time as the grin appeared on his face: they'd had the same idea. Without a word, he took her hand and they leaped onto the pavement next to Mimi, throwing out an arm, lifting a leg, dancing and joining in, 'Singing... and dancing... in the rain.'

In truth, Jess wasn't sure of the words: while Hamish was a

perfect Gene Kelly, tap-dancing and waving an imaginary umbrella, she simply stuck out her hands from straight arms and splashed in the water, a flat-footed river dance. She smiled energetically, performing her best. Then Hamish whirled towards her, lifted her in the air, and they finished the song either side of Mimi, kicking up their legs in a chorus line. The teenager in the parka pushed the phone into a deep pocket and shuffled away as Isabella clapped furiously and the couple beneath the umbrella rolled their eyes and said something inaudible. Then Hamish hugged his mother and whispered, 'Let's get you home now – you're freezing.'

Mimi and Isabella sat on Hamish's sofa wrapped in blankets, their hair dripping, sipping white wine. Mimi was exhausted, shivering and Hamish was concerned. 'You'll catch a cold, Mum – we were worried...'

Mimi laughed. 'I saw the rain and the puddles and the lamp post and I just couldn't resist it.'

'You can't stop a woman when she's in the throes of creative passion...' Isabella said into her wine glass.

Mimi's eyes sparkled. 'I saw the film with my sister in 1952. It was one of the films that made me determined to dance. I wanted to be Debbie Reynolds. I looked a little like her, you know, in those days. But Gene Kelly – there's so much abandon in his dance, not caring at all about being soaked to the skin.'

Isabella laughed. 'Who cares about pneumonia and death when you can sing and dance?'

Mimi spoke to Jess. 'When you're in love, all you care about is that happy feeling making your heart soar and you just want to celebrate, splashing in puddles and enjoying the sensation of being drenched through. Jess, have you ever felt like that?'

Jess was unsure. 'Once, perhaps.'

'Yes, once – it was the same for me too. Perhaps twice... I loved

Donald, at first, although I was dazzled and foolish then.' Mimi shook droplets from her hair. 'It doesn't last though, that feeling of being hopelessly in love. When I first met Donald, I felt like Gene Kelly did when he had no choice but to dance and sing. And then there was real love, Angus's father... oh, how nice it would be to feel like that, just one more time.' She paused, thoughtful, then her eyes fell on Hamish. 'I'm so sorry I worried you. I was being a bit silly but, you know how it is, Hamish,' Mimi explained. 'When the urge takes you.' She glanced at Isabella.

'I know what you mean, darling.' Isabella held out her glass for a refill and Hamish splashed more wine. 'In the 1960s, I was always in love. So many men – it was so nice to be worshipped, adored.' She snorted. 'Then I met Archie Ballantyne and married him. That was the end of love forever for me.'

Hamish turned to Mimi. 'Have some pâté, Mum? An olive?'

'Oh, I couldn't eat a thing, Hamish...' Mimi protested. 'I'm cold to my bones and my legs ache now, like pins and needles. But this wine is so delicious, thank you.'

'We should probably get you home, Mimi.' Jess glanced at Hamish. 'She needs a warm bath.'

'I'm fine,' Mimi protested. 'Isabella and I towel-dried ourselves.'

'And we haven't finished the bottle yet,' Isabella added.

'No, Jess is right,' Hamish said. 'Come on, Mum – let's get you on your way.'

Mimi smiled, acquiescent. 'Oh, if I must. But do you know, Hamish, I've had such a lovely time. We must all do it again next time it rains.'

* * *

Back at Glen Carrick House, Jess and Hamish ushered Mimi and Isabella inside, still wrapped in a blanket. Fin met them at the door, his face anxious. He turned to Jess sharply. 'What on earth were you doing, letting my mother get into this state?'

'I had such fun, Finlay. I was Gene Kelly, dancing in the rain.' Mimi's face glowed although her hair was still damp. 'I had a wonderful time. Don't be so cross.'

'It was my fault.' Hamish raised a hand. 'We only let her out of our sight for a few minutes...'

'You can't let her out of your sight at all.' Fin looked at Jess.

Jess exhaled. 'You're right – I'm sorry.'

'My legs ache...' Mimi was shivering.

'We should get Mum dry first and argue about whose fault it is later, Fin.' Hamish threw a protective look towards Jess.

Fin did not miss the glance exchanged between them and his frown deepened. 'Can you take Mother up to her apartment please Jess, and help her to warm up?'

'Of course,' Jess said.

'I'll come – is there anything warming to drink up there? Whisky?' Isabella put a hand to her wet face. Her mascara was smudged.

'Finlay.' Mimi raised a hand, her voice quiet but firm. 'I don't want you to blame Jess just because I wanted to sing. I don't want you to blame Hamish either.' She gave him a withering look. 'In fact, I don't want you to blame anybody at all.'

'I worry about you, Mother.' Fin turned to his brother. 'Hamish, you and I need to talk.'

Hamish shrugged expansively, as if he was impervious to Fin's bad mood, and followed his older brother into the kitchen. Jess and Isabella hugged Mimi close as they moved towards the steps, Isabella saying that she needed a cigarette and Mimi muttering that Finlay was just like his father. As they ascended slowly, Ailsa emerged from the snug and watched them, a duster in her hand.

Half an hour later Jess came downstairs, Mimi having bathed and settled for a nap, Isabella resting beside her, her hair wrapped in a towel, her eyes closed. Jess stopped in the hallway hearing raised voices, unsure about whether to go into the kitchen and apologise again. Ailsa emerged from the lounge and mouthed, 'They've been at it for a while now.'

A black Labrador scuttled from the kitchen and Jess knelt down, allowing Thor to sniff her hand with his wet nose. She heard Fin speak, his voice tense. 'Mother is old now, Hamish. She's frail.'

'She's better than she was,' Hamish answered quietly. 'Jess is marvellous. She even joined in with the dancing!'

'I've seen the performance.' Fin sounded sad. 'It's all over social media. Mum, singing in the rain, splashing in puddles, soaking wet. You and Jess are both crazy. People online are finding it hilarious. It shouldn't have happened.'

A third voice, deeper, more resigned, replied. 'Mum's happier than she's been in a while. She's being well cared for, and we should all be grateful for that. Leave things as they are, Fin.'

'And we need to resolve your situation, Angus. You know what the doctor said.'

'There's nothing to resolve.' The low voice rumbled again. 'The doctor said I'm doing fine on the crutches.'

'You need more help.'

'I'll manage.'

Hamish intervened quietly. 'Look, we all agree, Jess is a gem. She's got Mum eating out of her hand.'

'And she's leaving in December,' Fin said. 'What will happen to Mother when she goes?'

'We'll get someone else,' Angus suggested.

'I like her.' Hamish's voice rose in appreciation. 'She's perfect.'

'Mother's not getting any younger,' Fin countered. 'You're in Inverness, Hamish, working all hours. Angus wants to get off on his travels as soon as he can. Karen seems hell-bent on taking everything I've worked for. But we have to decide what's best for Mother.'

Hamish spoke up. 'She's not going into a home, Fin. It'd kill her.'

'Don't be melodramatic, Hamish,' Fin said rapidly. 'What else can we do?'

'I'm with Hamish. She's happy here, in her own home.' Angus's voice rumbled. 'It's all right, Fin – we'll sort something out between us – she's our mum and it's down to us all to care for her.'

Jess heard Fin sigh. 'As usual, you two will leave it with me to find a solution while you go off and do your own thing. Don't worry yourselves – I'll make sure Mother is all right.'

Jess rubbed the Labrador's brow as a low whistle came from the kitchen. Thor pricked up his ears, then turned around, his tail wagging and ran back to Angus. Jess glanced at her damp hands and heard a soft rustle of fabric over her shoulder. Ailsa was standing behind her, hands on her hips, shaking her head. She leaned towards Jess and said under her voice, 'There's a lot of misery under this roof. There always has been. They're not a happy family, the McKinlays. Not at all happy, not one of them.'

* * *

It was early morning, a Friday, several days later. Loud music boomed from Mimi's room, a scratchy record of a man crooning over the strains of an orchestra playing 'A Woman is a Sometime Thing' from Gershwin's *Porgy and Bess*. There was a huge open box of chocolates on the coffee table, empty wrappers from the sweets eaten already: Fin had bought them for his mother, a gift, hoping she hadn't suffered too much in the rain in Inverness.

Mimi was singing along to the music, dressed in a rose-gold lamé pantsuit, swaying to the music, waving an empty cigarette holder. Jess was seated on a rug on the floorboards, a mug of tea between her hands, smiling. Gavin, dressed in faded jeans with bright braces and a white T-shirt, was holding up scissors, explaining what he was going to do to make Mimi beautiful. His own hair was a thick black tuft on top of his head, shorn at the sides, gravitating towards a neat dark beard. When he spoke, his accent had a thick Scots inflection.

'So, I'm going to soften the colour, Mimi, add a bit of balayage, and then accentuate the curl. I'm thinking all the Bettys – Bette Davis, Betty Grable.'

'All the Jeans – Jean Harlowe, Jeanette McDonald.' Mimi waved the cigarette holder. 'I know just the look I want, Gavin.'

'Of course you do.' Gavin whirled around the room to face Jess. 'And what about you? I can see you do your own hair. You could do with a refresh or – I'm thinking a complete restyle.'

Jess was suddenly horrified. 'Me? Oh, no.'

'The colour needs attention.' Gavin persisted. 'That ponytail – it's doing you no favours. I'm thinking – curls, a redder colour, Kate Winslet in *Titanic*, or smooth and straight, Jennifer Aniston in *Friends*...'

Jess clutched her ponytail defensively. 'Oh, please just concentrate on Mimi. It's her day.'

'Or Nicole Kidman, her early style.' Gavin hovered around Jess, his fingers spread wide over her head like a crown. 'What do you think, Mimi – make more of these natural highlights, get rid of the grey...?'

'Grey?' Jess hadn't noticed.

The music swelled and Mimi joined in, her voice rising high as she paraded up and down in the shiny pantsuit. 'He can make us both look a million dollars, Jess.'

Gavin squatted down next to Jess, the braces on his jeans stretching tight over the curve of his back. He whispered, 'I'll keep it subtle – a light trim and just a little colour?' He offered a conspiratorial wink. 'And then we'll glam Mimi up so she's ready for the spotlight again.'

Jess nodded, unsure. She hadn't been to a hairdresser in a long time. It might be perfect timing: she was meeting Heather and Amy for a meal and a film later.

She thought about the three McKinlay brothers for a moment. She liked Hamish instinctively – he was Mimi's favourite and he could do no wrong. He was open, friendly. However, Fin was changeable, professional, mostly pleasant, but he had personal difficulties that made him detached and distant. And as for Angus, he terrified her. Jess wasn't sure about him at all: he was unpredictable and troubled and probably best avoided.

16

Mimi pushed the window open to let fresh air filter into the room. The moon slid behind a smoky cloud and the loch shimmered, a silver pathway reflected across the water. She sighed and closed the window and the cool rush of air stopped.

She glanced at the clock on the wall: it was late, past ten. Her hair was piled in soft curls; she smoothed the material of her pantsuit and stared into the darkness, thinking about playing a record, listening to *My Fair Lady*. Mimi frowned: hadn't Julie Andrews performed as Eliza Doolittle? Mimi had always wanted that role for herself. She'd always seen herself as the character, determined, a London flower girl who is transformed into a woman of poise and polish. It was a romantic idea in a musical but, in real life, it would involve sacrifice, something of Eliza would be lost in transition: she'd lose the person she really was. Mimi knew all about that. She recalled her twenties, transformed in silks and furs, no longer dark-haired Miriam Solomons but Donald's girl, a sophisticated blonde. She remembered the cheeky door boy, Charlie Gosling, staring, mouth open, winking and calling, 'Wotcher, Miss Mimi. Well, take a butcher's at you!'

She pressed her cheek against the glass of the window and began to sing softly: 'Wouldn't it be lovely...' Her breath made a mist on the pane. She sang louder, wandering around the room. She'd go to the kitchen and find some wine. She trod lightly on the stairs, moving stealthily. On the ground floor, she stopped to listen. The television was blaring from the snug; she peered into the room. Fin was sitting on the sofa, paperwork strewn on the coffee table, a glass of Scotch in front of him. He was sifting through correspondence, oblivious of the noise around him.

Music came from Angus's room: a CD, the soft sound of a male voice, an African harp, percussion, the flighty notes of a flute. Mimi moved quietly towards the kitchen and opened the fridge. She lifted out a full bottle of Chardonnay, cool droplets on the glass, and held it to her face, closing her eyes for a moment. There was an empty glass on the table; she picked it up and shuffled towards the front door, the words of the song still fizzing in her brain: 'Wouldn't it be lovely...'

* * *

Jess relaxed into the softness of the sofa. Amy and Heather were sitting closely on either side, drinks in their hands, leaning forward to stare at the television as the credits to the film rolled: they resembled three smiling statues. Amy moved first to lift her glass. Heather glanced at Jess. 'Your hair looks wonderful – I never noticed the highlights before.'

Jess made a mock-grimace. 'Mimi's hairdresser insisted on giving me the once-over.'

'She's very good,' Amy said, her mouth full.

'*He*. He's called Gavin.'

Both women gaped at Jess at the same time. Heather's jaw dropped. 'Not Gavin Gillespie?'

Jess nodded. 'I think so...'

'He's the best hairdresser in the area.' Heather's eyes were wide. 'He has a salon in Inverness.'

'He comes to Mimi's home once a month.' Jess placed her glass on the floor. 'Mimi won't have anyone else. He's very nice.'

'Your hair looks lovely, the way he's shaped it so that it hangs just right.' Heather suddenly became suspicious. 'So – you aren't telling me you've had your hair done for just this evening?'

Jess said, 'I just had it done.'

Heather smiled. 'I bet you've had it done for someone special, hen – what's he called?'

'The man who bumped into your car and just turned out to be Mimi's handsome son...' Amy was quick to pick up on Heather's lead.

'He's just a nice man.' Jess was enjoying the teasing.

'So – which one is first on your list?' Amy asked, wide-eyed.

'Three gorgeous brothers under one roof,' Heather sighed. 'That's one each.'

'Mmm.' Amy held up three fingers and counted them, one by one. 'Handsome Hamish for you, Jess, and Fabulous Finlay for me.' She gave a raucous laugh. 'That leaves Angry Angus for you, Heather.'

Heather laughed again. 'I'll have Handsome Hamish if you don't want him, Jess.'

'I'm not sure any of Mimi's sons are looking for a partner,' Jess said. 'Fin's going through a nasty divorce, Angus has broken legs and Hamish – well, he's a professional, a workaholic, he plays the piano beautifully and lives in a lovely house.'

'You've been to his house?' Heather asked.

'Yes. He's very talented.'

'You need to make a swift move, lassie,' Heather coaxed. 'Before someone else snaps him up.'

'We'll be your romance coaches,' Amy offered.

'That's very kind,' Jess replied. 'But I definitely don't want anyone...'

'You're crazy,' Amy protested. 'I've spent forever trying to find a decent man – you have three of them, and you're not interested.'

'She's playing it cool,' Heather teased.

'I'll let you know if I change my mind, I promise,' Jess said. 'So, what shall we watch next? What have we got?'

'*Warm Bodies*.' Heather groaned in delight and waved the DVD box with relish: the cover depicted a morose young man in casual clothes holding a yellow flower out to a blonde woman. '*Romeo and Juliet* reinvented with a paranormal twist.'

'It's a zombie classic. Girl meets zombie, zombie meets girl, and they fall in love against all odds.' Amy rolled her eyes with pleasure.

'Shall I whack it on, hen? It might give you some clues about how to seduce your favourite McKinlay.' Heather leaned forward and placed her wine glass on the floor. 'We'll watch this, and then we'll put our heads together and make some real plans... starting with Jess and the Handsome Hamish...'

* * *

Several hours later, Jess drove along a dark road lined with shadows of trees, the film still buzzing in her mind: leaping zombies, macabre romance. She thought of Heather and Amy: both women had been married, both had been hurt more than once, but they remained so positive, good-humoured and optimistic. She liked them: they were good fun and she sensed that they were looking out for her happiness. The constant teasing about Hamish was an opportunity to bond. Jess knew their rowdy humour hid a deep longing for romance. Jess wondered why she didn't feel the same need to be loved.

A car passed her, going in the other direction, its lights too bright. She blinked, staring at the road ahead, thinking that the dark drive to Drumnadrochit was a perfect setting for zombies. She tugged her thoughts back to the McKinlay brothers. She was warming to them. They were devoted to Mimi and Jess respected that. Hamish was the easiest to talk to; Fin was pleasant and Angus simply made her feel nervous.

Her thoughts drifted to her last chat with Saffy over the phone. Her daughter was very keen to hear about Mimi's past: in Saffy's opinion, poor Mimi had never known anything but exploitation, her husband being the worst offender. Then Jess thought about Paul and his family problems, Luke drinking heavily, Jodie defending her son.

A car whizzed past on her right-hand side, overtaking too fast, and Jess tugged her thoughts back to concentrate on driving. She would be back soon at Glen Carrick House, in the warm. It was past eleven. Fin might be in the kitchen, poring over paperwork. Jess wondered if they could share a coffee; if she could cheer him up. He had been very apologetic for snapping at her over Mimi's disappearance and Jess felt they were both keen to build bridges. Fin was an unhappy man, but she liked him.

Suddenly a shadow dark as a zombie leaped in front of Jess and her feet slammed down hard on the brakes. A stag bounded away from the Beetle, antlers high, the muscles in its thighs quivering as it rushed across the road into the forest. She was thankful that no other cars were behind her and accelerated away steadily. Half a mile later, she turned into the drive of Glen Carrick House, parking the car next to a black Jaguar and slid out, locking the door, picking her way over the gravel. Above, the moon was covered in grey cloud; the night sky was starless, infinite. In a nearby tree, an owl ruffled its feathers and hooted softly.

A rustling noise in the bushes behind her made her heart leap: she was still partly in the world of zombie films. But as she whirled round, she saw a figure standing in the garden. Jess took several speedy steps forward towards the front door, then turned sharply, taking a breath, door key in her hand. 'Who's there?'

The figure moved towards her, a shining pale shape, ethereal. It made a soft noise as it moved, the sound of dead leaves drifting in the wind. 'Jess...'

Jess watched the figure approach, a glass in one hand, a half-empty bottle in the other. She recognised the halting gait, the outstretched arms. 'Mimi?'

'Jess – I wanted to tell you about a musical... I waited for you.'

Jess wrapped Mimi in her arms. Her hands were cold as stone. She held her tightly to share her own warmth. 'Let's get you inside.'

Mimi waved the bottle; wine sloshed against the glass. 'It was Chardonnay Show Time tonight. I was Eliza Doolittle singing "Wouldn't It Be Loverly". Do you know the song?'

'Not very well, but you can teach me.' Jess urged Mimi forwards, up the steps towards the front door, pushing her keys into the lock.

Mimi started to sing, her voice a high pipe. Jess could smell the bitterness of the wine on her breath. She hugged the small woman, noticing that the soft blonde hair that had been so carefully piled was dampened and dishevelled by the night air. Beneath the thin lamé material, Mimi was shivering. Jess pushed the door open wide and guided her inside.

Then Fin was in the hallway, his hands on his hips, a frown between his eyes. 'Mother – where have you been?'

Mimi flourished the half-empty bottle. 'I was waiting for Jess.

It was show time tonight and I've been practising my steps in the garden.'

Fin's face was a mask of shock. 'I'd no idea you'd gone out.'

Jess propelled Mimi forward, pushing past Fin. 'Let's go to the kitchen, Mimi, and make you a warm drink.'

'Oh yes, please...' Mimi replied. Then she started singing 'Wouldn't It Be Loverly?'

In the kitchen, Jess pulled out a wooden chair for Mimi and sat her down, then bustled around, filling the kettle. She turned to Fin. 'Can you find a blanket, wrap it around Mimi, keep her warm? You were supposed to be looking after her tonight...'

Fin moved quickly, covering Mimi snugly in a tartan rug, then he faced Jess, his eyes sad. 'You're right, I've been too immersed in my own problems,' he said. He gazed at Mimi. 'I'm sorry, Mother.'

Mimi took his hand and held it to her cheek, her eyes misty. 'You were my first baby, Finlay. I remember when I used to dance and sing and you'd be backstage in a little Moses basket, blowing kisses with the girls in the chorus. They used to love looking after you. You were the sweetest, best behaved of all my boys...' She gazed at the table, looking for her bottle of wine, reached out, lifted it towards her lips and took a delicate swig.

Fin gave a deep sigh. 'I've spent too long obsessing over this damned divorce, and it just isn't good enough...' He shook his head. 'Jess – you're right, I should have been more vigilant. I'm going to have to make some changes. Mother comes first.' He moved to a cupboard and brought out a bottle and a glass, pouring himself a Scotch and draining the contents. 'From now on, things will be very different.'

17

Over the next few days, true to his word, Fin made every effort to be cheerful and attentive. Each day he took Mimi breakfast in bed, complete with a flower in a vase; he offered to make Jess coffee whenever they bumped into each other in the kitchen, and he seemed to be going out of his way to show her his most affable side. On Wednesday, when a smartly dressed man arrived at the door and introduced himself to Jess as Hugh Bishop, Fin's solicitor, Fin was all smiles, hand extended, as if he was about to receive some good news, which Jess doubted very much.

On Thursday, Fin insisted on making Jess lunch by way of thanks. And Jess had to admit, despite her recent late-night antics in the garden, Mimi was blossoming. Nowadays, her eyes shone; she threw herself into spending time with Jess with enthusiasm, listening to music, dressing in her wildest costumes and teaching her new friend the words and the dance moves of her favourite musical hits. Jess was almost of the opinion that Fin was paying her to enjoy herself.

On Friday, Jess bumped into Angus again. She caught her breath as a tall man on crutches with dark grey hair and scowling eyes emerged from the kitchen as she was on her way in. He swung his way past her, grunting disinterestedly. Jess took a breath; she'd build bridges, start polite conversation. She made her voice as confident as she could. 'Good morning.'

Angus paused, then he muttered, 'Jess.' He had used her name.

Jess tried again. 'I'm about to make coffee. Do you want one?'

'No...' Angus was about to limp away. Ailsa, watching from the vantage point of polishing the front doorknob, shook her head in disbelief. He glared in her direction, then he added, 'Ah, let me make your drink, by way of an apology for my rudeness the other day.'

'All right...' Jess was unsure what to say.

He raised eyebrows, speaking loudly for Ailsa's benefit. 'We'll take it in my room where we won't be overheard—'

Ailsa's mouth was open as Angus pushed open his door and ushered Jess inside. She stood awkwardly, nervous, then Angus grinned.

'Sorry about that. Ailsa can be a gossip. I don't want her listening to every word...'

Jess was momentarily taken aback by his smile. He limped to the desk by the window, poured two drinks from a jug and handed one to Jess. She sipped a mouthful of sweet liquid.

'Coconut water,' Angus explained. 'I have no coffee, I'm afraid. But I wanted to tell you that I appreciate how you've transformed Mum. She's been lonely and you've brought a new lease of life to her. That's a big deal to me and my brothers.'

'Thanks.' Jess sipped, gazing around the room at the exercise bicycle, the static weights; then her eyes fell on the pictures on the wall. She approached a colourful picture of a tiger, examining the definition of whiskers, the white strands of fur on the face. 'I love these photographs.'

He seemed genuinely pleased. 'The gorillas were taken in one of the national parks in Uganda. The tiger was in Sumatra. They are protected. Every part of the tiger, from whisker to tail, is traded in illegal wildlife markets.' Angus frowned. 'It makes me furious.'

'Did you take them?'

'These and plenty more,' he nodded. 'Over many years. It was my job. It will be again.'

'They are incredible.'

He came to stand behind her. 'I remember that tiger well. On the same day, I got some great shots of orangutans, rhinos and elephants too.'

'Did you never feel afraid? Being close to such wild animals is a risk.'

Angus laughed softly. 'There are worse risks. And this tigress was special. I was privileged to be there, to take her photo. Who knows how much longer these species will last?'

Jess sighed. She was moved by the tiger's beauty and majesty, but she was also conscious of how close Angus was standing, so close that the warmth from him was tangible. He said softly, 'It gives life meaning, being among these animals. I miss it.'

Jess met his eyes and he smiled for the second time, and Jess was aware of a passion she hadn't glimpsed before. She took in the handsome face, the glimmer in his eyes, then she finished the contents of her glass in a gulp. 'Well, thanks for the drink. I ought to go up to Mimi now.'

'Of course.' Angus took the glass from her hand.

'I love the photos.'

'Thanks.'

'And the drink.'

'My pleasure.' He was staring at her again.

'I'd better go...' Jess turned quickly, gratefully making for the stairs to the attic, aware that Ailsa was still hovering in the hall. She wondered why Angus made her feel so nervous. He certainly troubled her.

* * *

On Saturday morning, as Jess was in the hallway about to leave to do a little shopping, Hamish arrived, declaring that he had come to take Jess, Mimi and Isabella out to lunch, as he had promised. Mimi appeared, clad in a white pleated dress not unlike the one Marilyn Monroe wore in *The Seven Year Itch*, complete with crimson lipstick. Jess, in jeans, T-shirt and jacket, wondered if she was too casual. Hamish offered them an arm each and escorted them to the Saab. As they drove away, Fin waved from the doorway.

They met Isabella outside the Royal Cedar Lodge and a waiter showed them to a table with a pristine white cloth, crystal glasses and silver cutlery. The restaurant was half full, mostly couples sitting quietly at various tables in the spacious banqueting room. There was a piano in the corner and Hamish eyed it with interest. Mimi waved a gloved hand in thanks to the waiter as he pulled out a chair for her to be seated, as if fine dining was an everyday occurrence in her life. After she had studied the menu, Mimi waved a finger. 'Your finest white wine, please.'

'The same for me, darling,' Isabella smiled.

'Right...' Hamish glanced at the wine menu. 'The ladies will have a bottle of Vermentino di Gallura.'

'Just sparkling water, please,' Jess said.

'I do enjoy being taken out to lunch.' Mimi waved her arms as if conducting an orchestra. 'This is such a treat.'

'It is,' Isabella replied, tapping Hamish's arm. 'But we deserve to be pampered from time to time by a handsome man or two.'

Hamish said, 'Order whatever you want, Mum.' He glanced at the waiter. 'I'll have salmon.' He turned to Jess. 'I recommend the haggis, though – it's exceptional.'

'Oak-smoked salmon for me,' Mimi decided.

'For all three of us,' Isabella agreed, placing her cigarettes on the table.

Jess shook her head. 'I'll have the ravioli.'

Mimi's eyes sparkled wickedly. 'Of course, if we were here with Angus, he'd have us all eating salad.' She looked around for the wine waiter. 'It is nice to be naughty.'

'It is,' Hamish agreed, his eyes dancing.

'Isabella and I have so much fun,' Mimi said confidentially. 'We break the rules a bit. In the old days, we chorus girls were taken out to lunch all the time. Oh, we lived the high life.' She watched the waiter fill her glass. 'Thank you so much.'

'It must have been fun.'

'It was, Hamish.' Mimi's face shone. 'I miss it. But I'm determined that the fun won't stop, just because I'm a little older.' She was thoughtful. 'Do you know the musical *High Society* by Cole Porter?'

Jess shook her head as Hamish nodded.

'There's a song called "Let's Misbehave".' Mimi rubbed her hands together.

'And my favourite…' Hamish leaned forward. '"Who Wants To Be a Millionaire?"'

'Oh yes, it's heavenly.' Mimi was off. She threw her hands in the air and started to warble, 'Who wants to be a millionaire?'

Hamish grinned, singing the response, 'I don't!' They joined hands across the table and began to chirp to each other, enjoying the musical banter of the song. Jess looked from Mimi to Hamish: they were two peas in a pod.

Mimi topped up her drink and Isabella's. Hamish appeared not to notice, so Jess resolved to keep an eye on the wine intake. Mimi waved her glass; a little of the wine spilled onto the white cloth. Jess noticed that the diners at the next table were watching.

Hamish leaned forward. 'This is a bit of a celebration, Mum – I have some good news.' He smiled. '*The Flower of the Highlands* is in rehearsal. I'm going to be in London for the next few weeks. Fin says I can stay at his flat.'

'I hope it still is his flat...' Mimi said. 'I've heard Finlay talking to Hugh – Karen wants the flat or the villa in Spain.'

'Fin told me that he'll keep the flat.' Hamish waved his fork.

'I don't really like Karen,' Isabella whispered loudly. 'She's a greedy little gold digger – and she has a nasty temper.'

Mimi's eyes shone with mischief. 'It's the menopause, you know.'

Jess covered her smile with her hand. Mimi was enjoying holding court. 'I liked Angus's wife, Augustine. She was really sweet. I didn't care for Fin's first wife, Fiona. Donald liked her, of course...'

Isabella snorted. 'But he would, darling – she was a woman.' She burst out laughing.

Mimi immediately refilled her glass to the brim. 'A good Chardonnay is like a good man,' she said, taking a swig as the diners on the next table turned to listen.

Isabella agreed. 'Both are best if they are transparent and expensive. A refreshing clear wine. And a refreshing clear man. A woman should always be able to trust her husband. But some of them can be deceitful pigs.'

'I know what you mean.' Mimi turned all her attention to Jess. 'You know, Hamish is a good catch, don't you think, Jess?' She raised an eyebrow. 'Of all my sons, Finlay is the richest, Angus is the most handsome, but Hamish – he's sweet and considerate and the most fun.'

Hamish smiled. 'Mum's been trying for years to match me up.'

'I can't have everything I want.' Mimi sighed dramatically. 'Do you know, one role I really wanted was Calamity Jane. I'd have loved to play Calamity – she's so dynamic, she stands up against all the macho cowboys and she's so glamorous...' Mimi reached over and patted Jess's hand. 'I was very like Doris Day when I was in my thirties. Do you know the film *Calamity Jane*?'

'No...' Jess said, filled with fondness for Mimi; she admired her passion.

Mimi grabbed a linen napkin from the table, whirling it above her head like a lasso, launching into the words of 'Whip-crack-away!' at the top of her voice.

The waiter was at her shoulder, his arms behind his back, speaking quietly. 'Madam, I'd be grateful if you'd keep your voice down a little.'

'Oh, I'm so sorry...' Mimi reached for the wine, suddenly awkward. 'I didn't mean to...'

'My fault completely – I'll keep the noise down...' Hamish began, apologetically.

'No, let the lassie sing if she wants to...' A man at a nearby table who had overheard called out cheerily.

'You sing, hennie,' a woman added. 'She has a lovely voice on her.'

Isabella lifted her glass in reply. 'Mimi Solitaire was the star of the West End stage in the sixties...'

'Aye, then give us a sing-song or two...' another man said.

'Do you know "I'm Getting Married in the Morning"?' a different woman called out. 'Because I'm getting married tomorrow. It would be lovely if you could sing it for me.'

The waiter hovered at the table, unsure. Isabella stood up and addressed the people in the dining room. 'Would you all like Mimi to sing?'

Mimi feigned modesty. 'I couldn't... oh, it's been so long...'

There was a round of applause from the diners. Someone called out in encouragement, 'Gie it laldy, Mimi.'

Hamish glanced at the waiter. 'You've a nice piano over there...'

The waiter looked around for support; the other guests began to cheer. He inclined his head towards Mimi. 'If you would be so kind, madam – the bottle of wine would be on the house, naturally.'

Isabella was quick as lightning. 'And a second bottle, of course.'

Jess leaned towards Mimi and whispered, 'Do you want to sing?'

'I always want to sing,' Mimi said, taking a large swig of wine and standing up too quickly. Jess supported her arm.

'Come on, Mum,' Hamish said eagerly. He was already striding towards the piano, sitting down, stretching his fingers.

Jess held Mimi's elbow as she staggered after him. Hamish was already seated, rattling out a lively sequence of notes. Mimi leaned against the piano, her face flushed by the wine, and she began to sing 'I'm Getting Married in the Morning' in her high voice. Jess stayed close at her side; Mimi swayed as she sang, and her voice faltered. She had clearly drunk too much already, throwing her arms in the air to accompany the high notes.

Back at the table, Isabella was on her feet, conducting the diners as everyone joined in. Jess could hardly hear Mimi singing for the bawling chorus of happy customers, and the waiters seemed delighted, busily rushing around as orders for drinks increased. The applause was loud as Mimi finished her song and

Hamish immediately launched into another. He played 'Some Enchanted Evening' and 'Ol' Man River'. Mimi sang both songs animatedly, Jess close by to steady her as she tottered on her heels. Mimi whirled the pleated skirt of her white Marilyn Monroe dress and sang from the heart as Hamish accompanied her and everyone else in the restaurant to 'Diamonds Are a Girl's Best Friend'. Isabella was on her feet, joining in.

Then, at Hamish's suggestion, Mimi sang 'The Bonnie, Bonnie Banks of Loch Lomond' and every voice in the room swelled to join her. Some diners raised their arms above their heads, their eyes closed in rapturous expressions of happiness, as Mimi gave her all, her small face tight with effort, beads of sweat on her brow, determined to thrill her audience.

When they'd finished, Jess led Mimi back to her seat amongst loud cheers and tumultuous applause. Isabella hugged her friend and thrust a glass of wine into her hand as Mimi sat down in her seat and the delighted waiter brought the food. Mimi pushed her plate away and took a gulp of wine, her eyes half closed. She was exhausted. Still at the piano, Hamish had started to play 'Over the Sea to Skye', making each phrase of notes ripple like water. Jess glanced at him: he was in a world of his own.

* * *

Two hours later, Mimi was tucked up in bed, sleeping off the effects of lunch. Hamish had dropped off Isabella and then driven Jess and Mimi home. While Mimi was asleep, Jess and Hamish sat in the kitchen, discussing the episode with a concerned Fin over coffee. Ailsa, who had seen Mimi staggering up the steps to the door on weak legs and being helped into the house, was dusting the stairs in the hallway just outside the kitchen, listening carefully.

'I have to say, Mum has some spirit,' Hamish said. 'She still hasn't lost the sparkle. The audience loved her.'

'Maybe.' Fin shook his head. 'But I think she must have drunk too much cheap-shit Chardonnay.'

'Actually, the wine was forty quid a bottle, although we had two bottles on the house.' Hamish leaned back in his seat. 'It was all great fun.'

In the silence that followed, Ailsa could be heard moving about softly in the hallway.

'Mimi was wonderful,' Jess said. 'In fairness, she probably didn't have more than a couple of glasses. Isabella drank most of it while Mimi was singing.'

'Lunch was a huge success,' Hamish protested. 'You know how Isabella encourages her. They are as bad as each other. Mum enjoyed herself.'

'I'm sure she did, but she's not twenty-five. She looked dog-tired when she came in,' Fin replied, pouring water from the kettle. 'I just wonder – perhaps it's time we thought carefully about some professional care?'

'You're not suggesting she goes to a residential home again, Fin?' Hamish said, shocked.

Fin shrugged. 'I'm just saying...'

Jess took the mug of coffee Fin handed her. 'Mimi's doing fine – she loved having the chance to sing.' She met Fin's eyes, then Hamish's. 'She loves her family and her home. She thrives here.'

'I'm with Jess on that one. She's exactly right.'

Jess turned to see Angus, tall on crutches, leaning against a post in the doorway. Again, the glow of his eyes beneath dark brows unnerved her a little. He shook his head. 'Mum's eighty-eight, but she's no trouble, not if we all keep an eye on her. It does her the world of good to have a little fun.'

Jess stared. Not only was Angus on her side, but he had actually used her name for the second time. She was full of gratitude. His glance held hers for a moment, a smile momentarily on his lips. Then a frown crossed his brow.

'Things aren't helped by Ailsa eavesdropping. She was in the hall, taking in every word. She tells everyone who'll listen that Mum's a drunk.' He shrugged. 'I've just told her to bugger off home.'

Fin was appalled. 'You did what?'

Angus almost smiled. 'She's running away to get her coat now like a scalded hen. She won't be back tomorrow, unless it's for her wages.'

'Ah.' Hamish coughed. 'Was that wise?'

'I don't care if it's wise or not – she's gone.'

Fin put a hand to his brow. 'She keeps this place ship-shape, Angus. Who'll clean up after us?'

Angus laughed. 'We'll do it, Fin. When these legs work again, I'll get down on all fours and scrub the bloody place from top to bottom myself.' He glanced down at his legs, dangling beneath him. Thor had arrived and was seated by his feet, gazing up with round eyes.

'Right. I need to find a new cleaner. I'll make sure everything's fine for Mother, just like I usually do.' Fin slumped down at the table. 'Here we go, Jess – Hamish is off to London next week. Angus will be gone the moment he's able to travel again. It's just you and me looking out for Mother.' Then he brightened, smiling, a moment of acceptance. 'But you're right, she's best off with her own family who love her, even if the responsibility is all down to me. I'll manage just fine, of course, like I always do.'

18

In late September, the garden was strewn with damp leaves, crumpled gold, furled amber. Mimi was huddled on a bench, wearing a long coat and a silk scarf, a blanket over her knees, watching the pale sun dip behind the hills. Isabella sat one side of her, smoking furiously, warm in a smart coat and boots. On the other side, Jess hunched, hands in pockets, wrapped in a warm jacket, jeans and boots. They both tucked an arm through Mimi's.

'I love it out here.' Isabella blew smoke slowly through her nostrils. 'It makes me feel free and alive.'

'It's my favourite view,' Mimi whispered. 'I'm always calm and at peace out here in the garden.'

Jess agreed. 'Scotland is so beautiful.'

There was the soft sound of tyres on gravel in the drive, just beyond the garden. Mimi narrowed her eyes. 'We have a visitor. Someone for Finlay, probably.'

'He's a nice man, very handsome,' Isabella observed. She wriggled round to gaze solemnly at Jess. 'You like Finlay, don't you, darling?'

Jess was thoughtful. 'I wasn't sure about him at first but, yes, he's lovely.'

Mimi patted her hand. 'That's good. I hope you two will become friends. Finlay needs a friend like you.' She was lost in her thoughts for a moment, then she asked, 'And how are the renovations going on the cottage?'

'Slowly,' Jess sighed. 'It should be finished in December.'

Isabella made a face. 'You should sell it and buy a cottage in Scotland. You should stay here.'

Jess gazed over the loch, the breeze cool against her forehead.

'Jess...' Mimi raised an eyebrow. 'I don't think I apologised properly for being too loud in the hotel restaurant with Hamish – I forgot where I was for a moment. But it all worked out so well. I so enjoyed singing for all those people – and they loved it. It was just like old times.'

'Please don't apologise...'

'I enjoy a drink or two. It makes me relax, then I get the urge to perform.' Mimi sighed. 'I've always been a performer. I love being the centre of attention...' Her expression clouded. 'You know, I'm quite shy really. But being on stage, I can forget about the girl I was. Miriam Solomons is in the past and suddenly I'm transformed, I'm someone else and, you know, I'm not just a nobody any more – I'm talented and I feel loved.' Her blue eyes were piercing. 'But of course, it's all a lie, a big act, Jess – because inside I'm still the frightened little girl putting on a big show.'

'I can understand that, Mimi.'

'I thought you were wonderful at the hotel, darling,' Isabella said.

Mimi continued to stare ahead. 'I paid a high price for my ambition. I was a show piece, a trophy wife.'

Jess frowned. 'Did he treat you badly?'

'Neglect, Jess – he neglected me,' Mimi said. 'Men in those days ruled the roost.'

'They did, or at least they thought they did,' Isabella agreed.

'But of course, I fought back.' Mimi sighed. 'You were the same, Isabella. That's why we're such good friends.'

'Pigs, both of them, darling,' Isabella said. 'Boars.'

'What did you do?' Jess asked.

'I threw things,' Isabella laughed. 'Expensive objects. At his head. Then I spent his money.'

Mimi took her hand. 'Donald couldn't take what I did or my performing away from me – I would always retreat upstairs into the attic, put on my costumes, sing and dance – Chardonnay Show Time. At first, I'd dance with my boys. Then, after they'd all left home, I danced alone – it was all I had. In our spare time, Isabella and I would go out, we'd flirt outrageously with every man we saw – we'd put on a good show. But in the evenings, Donald would come home, and I'd be the good wife. He thought he'd turned me into meek little Mrs McKinlay. But I was always Mimi Solitaire.'

'She's right.' Isabella ground her cigarette beneath her toe. 'And I am Isabella Giannelli. I was never Mrs Ballantyne. Who wants to be a Ballantyne? He couldn't take away from me the person I am.'

'I think you're both great.' Jess hugged Mimi's arm.

'You were married once, weren't you, Jess?'

'I was, Mimi. Andy is a nice man.'

'So, what was wrong with him?' Isabella folded her arms. 'Why would anyone let a nice man go?'

Jess stared into the distance, at the fading sunlight on the loch streaking the water silver, the sparkle of rhinestones. 'I suppose I loved him in a way, but I was never really *in* love with him. We had a quiet marriage, but in the end we both realised it was a bit lonely. So, we went our separate ways.'

'Quite right too. Love is no good without passion,' Isabella agreed. 'Archie was passionate, I'll give him that much.'

'It was passion that kept me with Donald – you know, Jess, I was besotted with that man at first. And, despite his affairs and his floozies, he always came home to me – he couldn't resist me.' She leaned a head against Jess's shoulder. 'A relationship is an empty shell without passion.'

'I think you're right, Mimi.' Jess closed her eyes. 'When Andy and I decided to separate, it was easy – as if we'd already separated. I suppose we had – we were just business partners.'

Isabella raised an eyebrow. 'You give the impression of being someone who's so calm, Jess, in control. But I think inside there's a hot-blooded woman who needs to be loved.'

'Oh, yes,' Mimi agreed. 'When I first met you, you seemed confident and able to take everything in your stride. I was in awe, a bit – you're very independent. But...'

'But?' Jess wondered.

'I know you better now.' Mimi's eyes twinkled. 'Yes, you are all of those things, but there is something missing, deep down – I can see it. Something you've been trying to avoid in your life...'

'I've no idea...' Jess began.

'I know what it is, darling.' Isabella held up a finger. 'Passion. Love. *Amore.* You are too cautious because you don't want to be hurt. So, you won't take a risk and let anyone into your life.'

'Passion has done me no favours in the past,' Jess insisted. 'I'm single and happy.'

'No – you mustn't say that!' Mimi was appalled. 'I haven't given up on passion. I'm eighty-eight years old and, do you know, if the right man came along and whisked me off my feet, I'd be only too willing to drop my guard – and that's not all I'd drop.'

'Mimi!'

Mimi took both of Jess's hands, squeezing them earnestly. 'That's what keeps us alive.' She gazed up at the sky, mottled blues and purple clouds. 'What I'd give for one more chance at love.'

'You're just so impressive, Mimi, Isabella – both of you have such enthusiasm.' Despite their age, Mimi and Isabella had more confidence and passion than she had. Jess sighed. 'I wonder if we should go in – it's getting dark.'

'It must be half seven...' Isabella said. 'I should drive home.'

She stopped, listening to footsteps approaching. Fin turned the corner, striding briskly over the grass towards them. 'I thought I'd find you here.' He was smiling. 'I've got some good news.'

Mimi clapped her hands. 'Champagne on ice?'

'With caviar?' Isabella added.

Fin shook his head. 'I've just taken on a new housekeeper. She can only do a couple of afternoons a week because she has other commitments, but—'

He held out a hand and a woman peered around the corner of the house. She had spiky hair, dark-framed glasses and a wide smile. Jess noticed that she was wearing a smart black dress with a plunge neckline and stiletto heels. She ran over and Jess grinned. 'Heather?'

Heather hugged Jess, and then spontaneously she embraced Mimi and Isabella. Her face was bright with excitement. 'I heard in Drumnadrochit that Ailsa Campbell had stopped working here, so I phoned...' she glanced over her shoulder, 'Fin... and offered to do a couple of afternoons a week. The B & B is quiet this time of year so I can fit it in no problem.'

'That's great,' Jess smiled.

Heather was almost bouncing on the spot. 'So, we'll see more of each other and...' She peeped at Fin again and then back at Jess. 'It couldn't be a more perfect arrangement.'

Fin was pleased with himself. 'I feel a lot happier now I know we have a little more help here around the house.' He offered an arm to Mimi. 'Let's take you inside, Mother. It's getting cold out here.'

'Thank you, Finlay.' Mimi slid her wrist neatly through the crook of his elbow. 'A small glass of something warming might be pleasant too...'

'I can manage one drink, although I have the car.' Isabella tucked her hand through Fin's other arm.

Heather hugged Jess as they followed close behind, her voice a low whisper. 'What a fantastic house, Jess.'

'It's lovely...'

'But not as lovely as Fin. My goodness me – he's so handsome and charming.' Heather breathed excitedly. 'I'm going to enjoy working here.'

'Heather...?' Jess put her mouth close to Heather's ear. 'You're not telling me that you've taken a job just so that you can meet Fin?'

'Who wouldn't want to bag a McKinlay, hen?' Heather suggested. 'Just look at him... unless you've got designs on him for yourself, Jess?'

'Me? No, not at all,' Jess said, watching Fin ahead of her, his arm affectionately wrapped around Mimi.

Heather asked, 'Who was it who said, "the lady doth protest too much"?' She was so loud that Fin turned round. He looked suddenly younger, happier.

'I think I'm going to enjoy having you two working together here...' He raised an eyebrow. 'It's been a long time since we've had so much fun in the house.'

* * *

Angus sat on the edge of the bed, the door ajar, listening to the low chatter. He could hear Fin's voice drifting from the kitchen, his lazy contented drawl. It was the tone he used when he was cheerful: Angus hadn't heard Fin sound so cheerful in a long time. Karen, the divorce, the anxiety about Mimi, these things had been strangling Fin, making his voice tense and strained. Hopefully, things were improving.

He knew he hadn't been the best brother over the years: he'd always promised to be there if Fin had a problem. But he'd lived away, in Cameroon, in Paris with Augustine and Fabrice, or working all over the globe. He'd missed Fin's wedding to Karen. He and Augustine had enjoyed life far away from Drumnadrochit; they'd been so happy together living in France, and he'd always been working, photographing wildlife across continents. Those had been the best times, times when he'd never considered a future world where he'd be unhappy. Now he was miserable.

Angus could hear Mimi and Isabella in the kitchen, their voices pealing with laughter. His mother seemed much calmer and happier now. Jess was nice, but she'd be leaving before Christmas. Angus gazed down at his legs: the plaster would come off soon, and he'd be ready to get his muscles working again, so that he could leave too. He'd need the crutches for a while, but he'd do it, despite the doctor telling him there was a good chance he'd never walk normally. What did doctors know? One had promised him that Augustine was getting better three days before she'd died. Angus sighed. It had not been the doctor's fault.

He listened to the voices rising and falling, taking turns: Fin's soft words, Isabella's smooth loud tones, his mother's excited, shrill pipe. She was singing now. Angus wasn't surprised he knew all the words to 'Getting to Know You': he had joined in all the songs with his mother – all the boys had – when he was a kid and his father had been alive.

Angus frowned. Donald was not his father – he'd never let Mimi forget that. Donald had made sure that Angus knew he was the son of another man whose name he would never utter. Angus had put equal energy into letting Donald know that he didn't care. He had never particularly respected Donald, mostly because of his father's inflated view of himself, and how at times he had treated his mother so badly. Some days, he'd shower her with compliments and gifts; some days, he'd disapprove; other days, he simply wouldn't be home.

He heard Jess's soft voice. He was glad she'd arrived; she seemed really nice. At least for now, Mimi had someone to talk to each day who respected her, who was genuinely good-natured, who wouldn't spread rumours like Ailsa had. Ailsa was gone and there was a new voice, full of energy and enthusiasm: the new cleaner. Angus had seen her arrive – a friend of Jess's. He couldn't remember what Fin had said she was called.

He pressed his feet to the ground and wondered if he could stand upright. He reached for a crutch, using it to lever himself up. Thor was immediately by his side, gazing up at him. Angus closed his eyes, feeling the pain spread through his legs as he rocked forward. But the hurt wasn't so bad now, not as bad as it had been when he had been in hospital, bruised, battered and broken, believing as the morphine kicked in that he'd simply close his eyes and drift, then never wake.

He dragged himself across the room, to the CD player, finding music and turning up the volume. Les Têtes Brulées: one of his and Augustine's favourites. He limped back to the bed and fell onto the soft surface, closing his eyes. He breathed in the music, allowed it to wash over him and, for a moment, he was back in Paris, his wife in his arms, his son close by. He exhaled deeply and wished with all his being that nothing had changed.

19

'What shall we do today, Mimi?' Jess held out a plate of eggs Florentine she had just cooked, arranged on a dainty china plate: Mimi's breakfast. It was well past one o'clock.

Mimi sat up in bed in her flouncy nightdress. 'I want to take brunch outside, please.'

'It's October the first,' Jess said. She moved to the window, opening it slightly. Gauzy mist, like a light chiffon scarf, draped itself between the fir trees. 'There's a haze over the water. It's stunning but the air's cold.'

Mimi reached for the plate of food. 'Eggs, spinach, creamy sauce. My favourite, Jess.'

'Eat it up.'

Mimi's eyebrows shot up. 'Oh, I can't, not all that. The cream, the calories – I'm a dancer!'

'A woman needs to do more than go on diets and pay the bills, Mimi.'

'What does that mean?' Mimi stuck a fork into an egg.

'When I came to Scotland all by myself, I decided that was my new motto. I was determined that I wouldn't think about all the ridiculous things I'd worried about before – carbohydrates, paying for utilities.'

'And did it work, Jess?' Mimi licked a prong of her fork, pretending to eat. 'Are you carefree?'

Jess sighed. She had been talking to Paul earlier that morning. The damp-proof work at the cottage was well under-way, but it was expensive. 'I will be, when my house is finished.'

'Where's Fin?' Mimi's eyes shone with a sudden idea. 'Where's Heather?'

'Fin's taken Angus to hospital – he has an appointment this afternoon. Heather's probably cleaning the kitchen – she's just arrived.'

'That's perfect.' Mimi's eyes gleamed. 'So, what did you just say about diets? A woman needs to do more than go on a diet?'

'Indeed,' Jess grinned. 'My daughter has a T-shirt that says *Riots not Diets*. I'm with her on that one, too.'

'Right. Then we're going out for cakes.'

'We are?' Jess repeated.

'Yes. Light airy sponges topped with strawberries. And wine. Help me get ready. We are going out for afternoon tea – me, you, Isabella and Heather. My treat.'

The plate of food was cooling on the top of the duvet, as Mimi pulled out dresses from her wardrobe, holding them up, discarding them on the floor. 'This one is too dull – I should throw it away...'

'Mimi, it's silk...'

'This one doesn't fit me. And I hate this one. Oh – this dress isn't fashionable any more but—' She held out a green polka-dot dress with a full skirt. 'Donald loved me in this.'

'It's gorgeous, but it's a summer dress.'

Mimi was sad. 'Pick something for me, Jess. I can't choose –

there are too many memories.' She watched as Jess lifted out a smart salmon-pink suit with matching buttons.

'You'd be sophisticated in this...'

'I wore that suit for Donald's funeral,' Mimi said. 'I haven't worn it since.'

A cheerful voice came from the doorway. 'It's about time you wore it again, then.' Heather was standing next to a vacuum cleaner, a bright bow in her hair, smiling.

Mimi hesitated. 'The pink suit?'

'It's beautiful, Mimi.' Jess held it up. 'You'll look a million dollars.'

Heather was next to them. 'Wear it with a bright scarf, earrings, some lippy and you'll knock them dead. Where are you going, Mimi?'

'We're all going – all four of us.' Mimi caught her breath. 'Fin's not here. I'll call Isabella and tell her to join us. So, we're going out – for afternoon tea.'

Heather waved a hand. 'I was just going to give your room the once-over – then I'm free. What about that great place in Drumnadrochit that sells cream cakes to die for?'

'I'm not sure...' Mimi was suddenly flustered. 'I overheard Ailsa saying that people talk about me in Drumnadrochit.'

'It's probably Ailsa spreading the gossip herself.' Heather pulled a face. 'I'd pay no mind to her now.'

Jess said, 'Then we've got a point to prove. We're just four ladies having tea.'

Mimi's eyes shone. 'Oh, I'm looking forward to this. Yes, we are single ladies who drink afternoon tea together and don't care at all about bills or calories. How wonderful.'

* * *

Four figures sat around a table in the little teashop at the back of the village store, studying the menu. The sunshine filtered through the window, illuminating a square on the wooden floor, brightening the white walls. Isabella crossed elegant legs, leaning back against cheerful cushions, muttering something about biscotti and cannoli filled with cream. Mimi glanced up from the menu. 'I'll have salmon finger rolls.'

Isabella asked loudly, 'Do you have fine wine? *Vino rosso*?'

The young waitress in the black dress and short white apron shook her head. 'I'm sorry, madam – I've only started work here this week. But we don't do wine.'

Isabella tried again. 'Whisky, then? There must be whisky – this is Scotland, for goodness' sake.'

The waitress shrugged. 'No, sorry.'

Mimi frowned. 'Tea will be wonderful for us all.'

Jess had already decided. 'Oolong and a slice of drizzle cake for me.'

'A pot of Ceylon.' Heather sat up straight. 'A cinnamon scone and some finger rolls with cream cheese and dill.'

'Yes, I'll have cake, darling,' Isabella said. 'Do you have tiramisu with amaretto?'

'Let us all eat cake.' Mimi waved an arm. 'Just bring everything you have.'

The waitress gripped her pad and pencil tightly. 'Everything?'

Mimi leaned forward; her voice low. 'I was a dancer on the stage and in those days, I had to count calories. But now I'm giving a banquet for my friends.' She offered her sweetest smile. 'Bring a selection of everything, my dear – the more calories the better. Today, we're breaking all the rules.'

Isabella smiled. 'My friend here is a famous music hall dancer. Retired now, of course. And today, she'd like a cream tea.'

The waitress said, 'Yes, madam, of course,' and scuttled away.

Heather rubbed her hands. 'This is wonderful.'

'Four single ladies,' Isabella announced. 'On the town. Who don't care a bit about calories or bills or rules – or men – *non mi interessano gli uomini*!'

Mimi waved a hand in agreement. 'All together, sharing our love of freedom and independence and *joie de vivre*.'

'And cups of tea,' Jess added.

'But what if we weren't single?' Heather leaned forward, suddenly excited. 'I mean, if we were here sharing romantic scones and whipped cream with an ideal man, who would it be?'

Jess pushed any contenders from her mind. 'I'm not sure I know an ideal man...'

'There's no such thing.' Isabella's nostrils flared.

'But what about...' Heather's enthusiasm was brimming. 'Brad Pitt – Antonio Banderas – or George Clooney? All of them and me, hen, sharing scones together, one plate...'

Isabella laughed. 'I'd have chosen Gianni Versace for his money and fashion.' She brightened. 'Italians are the most handsome. I don't know why I picked Archie. He had skinny legs.'

Jess leaned back in her seat. 'I'm happy with peace and quiet.'

'No, I know who I'd choose.' Mimi lifted a finger. 'I used to think that Cary Grant was the most dashing man alive, but if I could pick one man to share tea with right now it would be... a man I remember as Emile Lavergne.'

'Was he in *Breakfast at Tiffany's*?' Heather breathed.

'No. He was Angus's father.' Mimi patted her hair, a practised gesture of nonchalance. 'I fled into his arms one night.' She sighed. 'And, for that one wonderful night, we were the whole world to each other.'

Isabella spoke quietly. 'You fell for that man in a big, big way, darling.'

'I did.' Mimi cleared her throat. 'Little Finlay was in our flat in

Islington with his nanny. Donald was somewhere else...' A mistiness filled her eyes. 'Emile played the violin and I danced and danced. After the show, we went to a bar and talked. We had so much in common. And then attraction, like the tugging of a powerful magnet, pulled us together...'

Jess nodded. Heather rested a hand on her arm, a gentle prompt. 'And then what...?'

'We went back to his room for a nightcap. I didn't intend to sleep with him, of course, but then...'

'Then?' Isabella asked, her eyebrow arched.

'Before I knew it, he was telling me I was the only woman he would ever love, and I was swept away with the passion of his words. Do you know he promised me then that we'd be together for eternity?'

'*Che bello!*' Isabella purred. 'He loved you, darling.'

Jess asked, 'Were you showing Donald that you didn't care?'

'Donald was the farthest thing from my mind that night.' Mimi turned ice-blue eyes towards Jess. 'For once, I was loved for who I was. I was complete.'

'Then what happened, Mimi?' Heather was enthralled.

Mimi took a breath. 'The next morning, I went back to our flat, to Finlay, to Donald. I had no choice.'

'And Donald would never have known,' Isabella reminded her. 'But you were pregnant with a love child.'

'Oh, yes. I fully intended Donald to think that the baby was his. It was the easiest way out. And he bragged to everyone how he intended to fill the world with McKinlay sons. Yes, he was very proud of himself.'

Heather's eyes were round. 'But he found out...'

'He came to the hospital to visit me when Angus was born. He took one look at the baby and there was an awful row. Angus was dark-skinned – Donald and I were both very pale. He knew the baby was not his – he accused me of cheating in front of the nurses and all the new mothers…'

Jess rested an arm on Mimi's hand. 'What did you say?'

'I hugged Angus and burst into tears. I thought Donald might try to take my baby away. Angus was mine and not Donald's – he would never be Donald's. Finlay was undeniably his and I'm sure Donald had other children by various women – but I stood up to him that time and, after that, things changed.'

'You should have left him, darling,' Isabella sighed. 'You should have found Angus's father and stayed with him. Love is everything.'

'I'd have been penniless, the children too. In those days, divorce was a terrible thing for a woman.'

Jess said, 'So is a lonely marriage.'

'I gave him respectability: I was the little wife at home. And then I gave him Hamish – although Hamish was truly mine. But, after Angus was born, things were never the same. Donald knew I was no longer his property. And he never really accepted Angus. After Hamish, we moved back to Scotland, to the big house, and I lost everything – my career, my friends, my passion…'

'You had your boys, hen,' Heather whispered.

'Yes, your beloved boys. And the memory of a brief but perfect love,' Isabella said in a low voice.

Jess squeezed Mimi's hand. 'It must have been hard.'

'It was.' Mimi closed her eyes. 'Of course, I could have taken up with Charlie Gosling.'

'The boy at the theatre door who blushed whenever he saw you?' Isabella remembered.

'I often find myself thinking about him, wondering where he is now. I'd love to meet him again,' Mimi smiled. 'Charlie adored me and he was so sweet. Being loved is priceless, worth more than all Donald's money. But I was young then and foolish.'

A figure in a black dress with a white apron was next to the table, holding a tray, piling pots of tea and plates of sandwiches, displays of cakes onto the table in front of them. Mimi breathed out. 'Wonderful. Afternoon tea. We should spoil ourselves more often.' She smiled at Jess and Heather.

'Madam?' The young waitress stood by the table, her face hopeful. 'Is this everything?'

'It's delightful – thank you so much.' Mimi waved a hand beatifically.

'Then, please...' The waitress fumbled in her apron pocket. 'Would it be all right if I get a selfie with you?'

Mimi was puzzled. Jess spoke softly. 'She wants to take a photo, Mimi – both of you together.'

The waitress's hand shook as she held out the phone. 'You being so famous...'

Isabella was delighted. Mimi patted her hair as the waitress crouched beside her and held out her phone. Mimi's smile dazzled as the flash lit up her face.

'Thank you so much,' the girl said nervously. 'I'll treasure this photo. I know who you are. I saw an old picture of you in one of my grandma's magazines, wearing a bowler hat and black stockings. I was sure it was you. Then when your friend said you were a famous dancer, well, I put two and two together.'

Mimi opened her arms in an expansive gesture. 'You're very welcome, dear.'

'I can't wait to tell my gran that I met a famous singer and dancer.' The waitress lifted up the empty tray as Mimi began to pour tea into a china cup. 'She's a great fan of yours. She loves all the musicals. Thank you so much and – do enjoy your cream tea, Miss Minelli.'

Heather was puzzled. 'Minelli? She thinks you're...?'

Isabella watched the waitress walk away and laughed softly. 'Liza Minelli is in her seventies – I'd take that any day, darling.'

'And she's American. These young ones have no idea, do they, hen?' Heather said. 'Although perhaps you do favour her a bit around the eyes, Mimi.'

'You do,' Jess agreed. 'And it's a compliment.'

'At my age, I'll grab any compliment with both hands,' Mimi smiled, then she reached for a cake.

* * *

Fin drove the Jaguar smoothly through traffic, leaving Inverness behind, taking the road to Drumnadrochit. Angus was slumped in the passenger seat, his legs stretched out, now without the plaster casts. He was staring through the window.

Fin put a hand on his shoulder. 'You can't complain. A few more months of physio and you'll be back to your old self.'

Angus sighed. 'I have legs like Twiggy's. The muscle's gone.'

'The doctor said you should use the crutches and exercise every day...'

'And I will, Fin. I just...' Angus pushed against the seatbelt. 'I just need to get away.'

'I feel the same, but with you gone and Hamish hopping between here and London, I'm stuck,' Fin said. 'As soon as this divorce is through, I want a break.'

'What's the latest?'

'Hugh says he thinks he's got all eventualities covered. Karen will accept the lucrative deal he's offering, and we'll be shot of each other in weeks, not months.'

'You need to go somewhere new when it's over, Fin – go travelling.'

'I'd like to see the girls, get away somewhere,' Fin said. 'But what about Mother?'

Angus shrugged. 'Maybe Jess will stay on? They seem to get on okay...' He noticed Fin's sad expression. 'Mum's our responsibility, mine and Hamish's too, not just yours, Fin. We'll take it in turns. We'll make sure she's fine.' He glanced down at his legs, now in jeans. 'I'll get my strength back. I'll be able to help more. Hamish will too – when is this musical opening?'

'Next year sometime...' Fin's eyes were on the road as he eased the Jaguar comfortably past a lorry. 'But there's a special publicity event before then. Some of the songs, an invited audience, press, that kind of thing. Hamish has asked us all to go down to London.'

Fin turned the corner into the drive to Glen Carrick House, the tyres scrunching on gravel. He brought the Jag to a standstill in the car park. He frowned. 'Where's Jess's car? The Beetle's not here.'

Angus swivelled round, already reaching for his crutches. 'She must be out, I guess.' Then the thought came to him. 'With Mum...'

Fin flopped back in his seat and placed his hands over his forehead. 'Bloody hell. I wonder where they've gone. More to the point, I wonder what heap of trouble they'll bring back with them this time?'

Fin sipped coffee, watching Jess pile grilled asparagus and white sauce on a plate. She had certainly made a difference to Mimi's eating habits. She noticed him observing her and smiled. 'Mimi likes a creamy sauce.' He was still staring, so she added, 'I ran a hotel. I made a lot of breakfasts for... people with refined tastes.'

'For fussy eaters,' Fin suggested. 'Who don't take breakfast until one o'clock.' He leaned back in his seat. 'It has to be said, Jess, you've made such a difference.'

Jess glanced over her shoulder. 'I like Mimi.'

'She likes you,' Fin said. 'The afternoon tea expedition to Drumnadrochit worked so well, she wants to go every week. She's looking so much better – she's put on a little weight; she only drinks a single glass of wine a day. She's visibly happier.'

Jess held up the plate of food. 'Let's hope she enjoys this.'

She collected cutlery and a mug of coffee, placed the breakfast on a tray with a flourish and moved towards the door. Fin was thoughtful. Mimi was going to miss Jess when she left at Christmas. Everyone would miss her. Quietly, but with a strength and confidence he admired, Jess had worked her way into Mimi's heart, into the heart of the household. He sighed again. For a moment, he thought of Karen: she was aloof, she could be selfish. When he had first fallen in love with her, he had taken her arrogance as self-assurance, and now he was paying the price. He'd thought the fact that they looked good together meant that they would be good together. He had been so wrong. In comparison, Jess was kind, honest, devoted to his mother, and she was attractive too. Fin closed his eyes and pushed the thought away. He needed to go out; he had a meeting with Hugh that afternoon.

Jess carried the tray towards the stairs and heard a crash in Angus's room, the low rumble of his voice. He was exercising again and must have fallen. She resisted the strong temptation to call out, to ask if he was all right. She took the stairs towards Mimi's attic apartment. She could hear music coming from above: the effervescent boom and brass of a big orchestra, a woman's mischievous trill.

She turned the corner and heard the music bellow. Then she saw Mimi. She was holding two gigantic feathers as fans, a white one across her body and a pink one in the air. As the female voice crooned 'Diamonds Are a Girl's Best Friend', Mimi swished the feathers in the air, an ecstatic smile on her face, her eyes closed. Jess noticed the high heels, the slim legs, as Mimi twirled around, moving the fans in practised choreography. Then Mimi opened her eyes, threw both feathered fans into the air and rushed to Jess.

'Breakfast. I'm so hungry.' She took the plate, standing in a silk shift. 'Don't you adore *Gentlemen Prefer Blondes*, Jess? It's a wonderful musical. I always thought that Marilyn Monroe and I had so much in common.'

Jess turned the volume down on the record player and guided Mimi to the table, sitting her down. Mimi lifted a forkful of food in the air. 'Did you make this just for me?'

'Eggs, asparagus, parmesan sauce.' Jess was pleased with herself as Mimi tasted the food hungrily.

Mimi licked her lips. 'I never could cook, Jess. I never really cared to.' Her eyes sparkled. 'We were always taken out to dinner, we chorus girls. Then later, Donald always took me to the best places. Of course, a glass of champagne was all I'd allow myself.' She thought for a moment, then looked at Jess, her eyes hopeful as a puppy's. 'A glass of white wine would go down well with this...'

'I'll make you a fennel, crab and orange salad this evening if you like. A small glass of Chardonnay will go well with that.'

'Oh, that would be lovely.'

At that moment, there was a sharp knock at the door, despite it being wide open. Both women turned to see a pale-haired man, smiling in a dark coat and a tartan scarf. Mimi pushed her food to one side, stood up and threw out her arms. 'Hamish!'

Jess turned as Hamish strode over, whirling his mother in his arms. He turned to Jess and kissed her cheek briefly. 'My two favourite ladies,' he cooed.

'Oh, Hamish.' Mimi was breathless. 'I didn't know you were coming.'

'Whirlwind visit from London – I'll be here just for a couple of days.' Hamish kissed his mother's cheek and turned to Jess. 'What are you both doing tomorrow?'

'Tomorrow?' Jess asked. 'We haven't decided.'

'Well, now you have. I'm taking you both to the Isle of Skye.'

'Oh, Skye is beautiful in autumn.' Mimi laid a hand against her heart.

Jess clapped her hands together. 'I've always wanted to visit Skye.'

Hamish's eyes twinkled. 'I'll take us to Skye, we can have lunch, go on the beach at Dunvegan and have a wonderful time.'

'Splendid.' Mimi was excited. 'I can't wait. But Hamish – have you spoken to Finlay? He mightn't be too keen on me going anywhere with you after the *Singing in the Rain* episode...'

'Oh, Fin's fine with the idea,' Hamish replied. 'He's coming too. So, I'll pick you up tomorrow morning at ten. We'll have a lovely day, all four of us together.'

* * *

Mimi and Jess sat together in the back of Hamish's Saab. Fin was in the front, talking in a soft voice to his brother about Karen, about how she'd agreed to the terms of the divorce, how it was expected to happen before Christmas. Hamish was in a good mood, chattering about his musical, *The Flower of the Highlands*. An orchestra was already in rehearsal. He was thrilled that the actress who was playing Flora Fraser, the star role, reminded him of Mimi.

Mimi and Jess stared out of the windows: a dense mist clung to the long straight road that took them west. On the right, trees climbed high: firs, Scots pine, hazel and birch, russet and silver leaves mixed with deep green. A wild boar was ambling by the side of the road, strolling by with a nonchalant roll. Jess was searching for deer in the depths of the forest, keen to spot the slightest movement.

They turned a corner and the mist fell away to reveal tall peaks hugged by low hanging clouds. A river sliced through banks of yellow gorse, green shrubs and spindly brown trees. The sky overhead was an expanse of blue. They passed a craggy cliff, a ruined castle, its grey reflection symmetrical in still water.

Soon they were crossing a long bridge, water either side drifting into the distance, mountains rearing in front of them. The car swung right onto a narrow road rising and Hamish said,

'We're in Skye.' Jess held her breath, taking in the rugged landscape, jagged mountains, brooding castles overhanging sheer drops down to the splashing surf below.

Mimi touched her arm. 'I love Scotland with all my heart,' she whispered. 'You know, I never saw my father or my mother much after I'd married. Of course, they came to our wedding; my father wished me the best and my mother told me to be a good wife and then she cried. I wrote to her when I had Finlay and sent her photographs. Then my parents passed away within a year of each other. They never met my boys. I always wrote to my sister Rachel: she married a nice man called Simon and moved to Highgate. She died a few years ago.' Mimi's eyes were suddenly misty. 'I wanted a daughter so much. I begged Donald for a fourth child. A daughter would have made me so happy.'

Fin turned round from the passenger seat in the front, his face deliberately cheerful. 'So – lunch first, ladies? Or shall we go to the beach?'

'I don't mind – I'm just glad to be here,' Mimi shrugged, small inside a large coat. 'You decide, Jess.'

Jess gazed through the window: to the left, hills swelled, and to the right, the land fell away down to the frothing sea. 'The beach please. Lunch can wait.'

They walked down the path towards the sea, ankles twisting, feet slipping on stones. Mimi leaned against Fin. 'I shouldn't have worn heels, Finlay...' He swept her into his arms, a tiny woman in a huge woollen coat, and forged ahead towards the expanse of smooth yellow sand that stretched below the hills.

Hamish made a face. 'I knew one of us would have to carry her. It's always the same with Mum and her heels.' He shrugged. 'I'll do the return journey.'

The wind blew, a sudden stiff gust, thrashing Jess's face with strands of her hair. She pushed the tendrils back and shivered. 'It's very cold.'

Hamish raised his eyebrows. 'Do you want me to carry you?'

'No...' Jess protested.

Hamish took a tartan scarf from around his neck and wrapped it around Jess's. 'Here, then.' His voice was gallant. 'This will keep you warm.'

'Thanks.'

'It's the least I can do,' Hamish said. He threaded an arm through hers and they wandered onto the sand. Fin deposited Mimi in front of the lapping water and he waved an arm. Hamish joined him and they spoke quietly together. Jess rushed towards Mimi, who was standing in the full force of the sea breeze.

Mimi's face was bright, the wind tugging threads of yellow hair from the pins that held it in place. She grasped both of Jess's hands. 'Isn't this place wonderful?' She heaved Jess towards the water. 'The air is clean; it's so sharp, like the first taste of whisky.'

Jess nodded in agreement, and they moved towards the foaming sea as it writhed towards them, filling damp sandy spaces between small rocks. 'This is beautiful, Mimi. I love Skye.' She gazed at the enormous sky, the ocean curving away, the grey silhouette of another island.

'I feel good here.' Mimi's eyes glittered. 'It's that sense of being alive, that whatever happens tomorrow, no one can take this moment away.'

'I know what you mean,' Jess agreed. 'Like being part of nature.'

'It's the same feeling when you're on stage, giving everything as you dance, it's a true moment of passion. There's nothing like it.' The wind lifted a lock of Mimi's hair, waving it around her face, silky tendrils alive on the air as her eyes shone. 'The power of the sea, the way it rushes in at you and you can't stop it, as if it's trying to possess you. The wind lifts you up and batters you so that you feel as if you are new again. That's the joy, the exhilaration of being alive.'

Jess squeezed Mimi's hand. Mimi tugged her closer to the water's edge, resting against her, the wind pushing both of them back as they leaned into its force. Then Mimi began to sing, her voice tossed away on the gusts. Jess could hear snatches of the song, and she knew some of the words so joined in: 'I could have danced all night...' Mimi threw her arms in the air and twirled around, and Jess copied her. Their fingers met and they were singing aloud, their voices whirling in the wind as they laughed.

At a distance, Hamish and Fin watched the two women dancing together. Fin said softly, 'It does my heart good to see Mother so happy.'

'It certainly does, Fin. We haven't seen her look so well in a long time.'

'It's a shame Angus isn't here with us to see this. I know he's been worried about her too.'

'What's he up to?' Hamish asked.

'Exercising – non-stop,' Fin said. 'He's determined to get back in shape, like he was before the accident.'

A squeal went up in the distance: Mimi had dipped a toe in the frothing icy sea. She was holding a stiletto in one hand. Jess pulled off her trainers and socks, tugged up her jeans and ran into the water, leaping over a rolling wave. Mimi took a step forward and yelped, grasping Jess's arm.

'She's quite something, isn't she, our Jess?' Hamish said.

Fin's eyes shone as he watched the women shrieking and jumping waves. 'She certainly is.'

'We can't let her leave, Fin.' Hamish put a hand on his brother's shoulder. 'One of us should marry her to stop her from going back at the end of December.'

Fin's eyebrows shot up and Hamish winked mischievously. Mimi called from the water's edge, 'What are you two smiling about?'

Hamish waved. 'We're watching you two having fun.'

Mimi called, 'Come on, Hamish – I need to sit down inside a warm restaurant. My feet are wet and cold. You'll have to carry me back to the car.'

Hamish rushed to Mimi and swept her up in his arms.

Jess was next to Fin, her face flushed and bright. 'Right now, Skye is the most beautiful place on earth.'

'Once you've been to Skye, it holds a place in your heart forever,' Fin said. 'I think you've made Mother very happy.'

'It's fun,' Jess smiled. 'I'm having the most wonderful time.'

'I'm glad.' Fin offered her his arm and she pushed a hand through the crook of his elbow. 'From where I was standing, it looked very wonderful indeed.'

* * *

They drove back in the late afternoon, Mimi's head on Jess's shoulder, sleeping. Hamish chatted animatedly from the front of the Saab about his musical, how he'd been talking to the press, and how he'd been interviewed on the radio too; that he'd dedicated the musical and, in particular, one of Flora Fraser's solos to his mother, Mimi Solitaire, the famous dancer. Mimi had slept through the whole conversation; she hadn't heard a word. Nor did she hear Fin whisper that Hamish's comment might have been rash; no one was completely sure that Mimi had ever been a chorus girl.

Back at Glen Carrick House, the sun sank low behind the loch and the water rippled like spun gold. It was past six and Hamish had carried the slumbering Mimi up to her room, laying her gently on her bed before tiptoeing downstairs.

In the kitchen, Fin made coffee. Jess and Hamish leaned back on wooden chairs at the table, tired. Jess exhaled. 'That was a lovely day. Thank you both.'

Hamish stretched his arms over his head. 'Shall we make some food, open a bottle, make a night of it? I could stay here – my place in Inverness can be very lonely...'

'Good idea,' Fin agreed. 'We could cook something together. I haven't had pasta in ages.'

'Mum's out for the count,' Hamish agreed. 'Pasta it is. I'll call Angus... even if he won't eat our pasta, he can make some of that macrobiotic stuff he calls food. Maybe he'll join us in a glass of something nice. What do you say, Jess?'

Jess wasn't ready to go back to her basement apartment yet, although the thought of Angus's company unnerved her a little. She still couldn't explain why he made her feel uncomfortable. It was something in his presence, the searching gaze. She lifted her chin and gave a bold smile. 'I can help cook a mean pasta.'

Hamish was on his feet, moving towards the wine rack, selecting a bottle of red, finding a corkscrew. There was a sudden rapping from the front door, and Hamish put the bottle down. 'That'll be Isabella, I bet. I'll go.'

He disappeared down the hall. Jess caught Fin's eye.

'Jess...' He moved over to sit next to her. 'I wanted to say thanks – we had a great time today.'

'No, thank you,' Jess protested. 'Skye was so lovely.'

'You've done so much for my mother. I'm really grateful.'

'She had a great time,' Jess said.

'So did I.' Fin's voice was low. 'I had a wonderful time.' He put a hand on her arm. 'I'm glad you came here...'

The moment stretched, Fin unsure how to express his feelings of gratitude, new feelings of warmth and respect, Jess wondering what this charming man was about to say. Indecision held them still for a moment longer, then they were jolted apart by the screech of an angry female voice in the room. 'Fin!'

They looked up sharply towards the doorway, where Hamish was standing with a chic, dark-haired woman wearing a smart white coat. She was clearly livid. Hamish's expression was one of troubled surprise.

Fin stood up quickly, moving away from Jess, his hands in front of him, suddenly awkward. 'It's not what you think.'

'I can see exactly what's going on here. I came round to discuss something to do with our agreement, but you're clearly otherwise occupied,' the woman snapped. Then she put her hands on her hips. 'Exactly how long has this affair been going on?'

Jess stared from the woman back to Fin, unsure what was happening. Then Fin said, 'Affair? You've got it all wrong, Karen...' and then it all became very clear.

Jess tensed as the woman turned diamond-hard eyes on her. 'And who are you?'

Jess said, 'I live here.'

'I'm sure you do.' Karen's voice was bitter. She stared at Fin. 'It didn't take you long to find someone to warm your bed. I have to say, Fin, she's not your usual type – you don't normally go for the docile ones...'

Fin's voice was hushed. 'Jess is Mimi's carer.'

'I'll bet she is. And I wonder who else she cares for?'

'Stop it, Karen,' Fin said.

Karen laughed. 'Well, this is wonderful. It's just what my solicitor needs to know. You move out into your mother's house, and you get a woman in under the pretence that she's a carer.' She turned to Jess. 'I bet you don't have a single care qualification to your name, do you?'

'Look, I'm not...' Jess began.

Karen's eyes danced. 'I can't wait to tell Cheryl about this. She'll be talking to Hugh first thing tomorrow. You're an adulterer, Fin, and that changes everything – absolutely everything. You'll get your divorce, but I'll make sure I bleed you dry first.'

21

Several days later, Jess sat on the squashy sofa in the living room in Beraghaig, Heather's B & B, Heather on one side and Amy on the other, their mouths open in astonishment.

'I knew something had happened,' Heather said. 'When I was cleaning the hall the other day, I heard Fin on the phone talking to Hugh; he sounded so agitated...'

'So.' Amy's expression was a mixture of fascination and horror. 'She caught you in a compromising position with Fin? Tell us all the goss...'

'Fantastic. Are you an item now?' Heather asked.

'Not at all,' Jess replied. 'It was just a silly misunderstanding. Fin and I were talking. Karen assumed there was something more going on, so she started shouting. Fin tried to calm her down and she said she'd tell her solicitor and make Fin suffer. Then Hamish tried to help – he said I'd been out with both of them, meaning we'd all just been to Skye, and Karen completely misunderstood...'

Heather wrapped an arm round Jess. 'Are you all right, hen?'

'I suppose so,' Jess said. 'Karen accused me of sleeping with the whole McKinlay family, then Angus rushed in on his crutches and told her to go back to the hole she'd just crawled from...'

Amy smiled, putting a hand over her mouth. 'Good for Angus.'

Jess recalled how Angus had been fiercely protective, how he had asked Jess afterwards in a soft voice if she was all right, how he'd listened intently to her enthusing about the trip to Skye. She almost wished he'd been there with her, imagining him in Mimi's place, splashing in waves. In her reverie, his hand was in hers. She tugged herself away from the thought.

'Poor Jess,' Heather said. 'So – what happens now?'

'Karen is accusing Fin of adultery. Fin, of course, isn't having any of it. Hamish has gone back to London. Meanwhile, Fin and I are tiptoeing around each other, being polite...'

'The question is, do you fancy him, Jess?' Amy asked. 'Be honest...'

'I'm at Glen Carrick House to care for Mimi,' Jess protested. 'Fin's my employer...'

'Then there won't be a problem with you coming to the Hallowe'en ball with us in a couple of weeks. It's in Drumnadrochit. It'll be brilliant,' Heather grinned.

'Fancy dress...' Amy added. 'We could go as the three raunchy witches... fishnet stockings, little skirts, pointed hats. Or we could be cats, complete with tails and whiskers.'

Jess smiled. 'Yes, why not? I could do with a night out. When I rang Saffy yesterday to tell her about the thing with Karen, she told me that if I lived in a house with three sex-starved single men, what did I expect?' She grinned. 'No sympathy from her.'

'It's decided, then,' Heather replied. 'We'll dress up and go to the Hallowe'en ball. We can have a few drinks and dance the night away and forget all about the McKinlays for a while, especially Fin's horrible ex.'

'I'm looking forward to that.' Jess recalled the scene with Fin, his face ashen as Karen screeched at him, Hamish's disbelieving expression as the row had developed and how Angus had swung through the doorway on crutches, his voice like thunder, and calm was restored. She pulled herself back to reality: she was thinking of Angus again. 'So – shall we order a takeaway? What film are we watching tonight?'

Heather waved a DVD in the air. The cover depicted the serious faces of a man and a woman in a photograph torn in half. '*Fatal Attraction.*' She winked at Jess. 'I thought you might need a few tips about bunny boilers.'

* * *

Mimi was playing a record in her apartment, wearing a long, sparkling dress, shuffling her feet and waving her arms. Music was booming from the speakers, a cha-cha-cha rhythm, a woman with a high voice singing 'Shall We Dance?' Jess sat on the floor by the window, watching her. She turned her gaze out of the window. Rain pelted, huge droplets hammering against the pane, slithering downwards. Jess watched Mimi: she swirled as if with an invisible partner, her eyes closed, her face shining and happy. Jess was immediately reminded of Hamish, the same serene expression, the languid movement. The song came to an end and Jess brought her hands together in applause.

Mimi turned off the record player and sashayed towards Jess, draping herself across a chair. Her blue eyes shone. 'Did I ever tell you that I met Yul Brynner? I was in the chorus of *The King and I*. He and Gertrude Lawrence were wonderful.'

Jess nodded. 'You must have so many memories.'

'I loved Rogers and Hammerstein,' Mimi breathed. 'But I adored Binkie Beaumont most. It was Binkie who made musicals so glamorous, you know. Donald and I had dinner with him and his wife Mary several times. He was such a charming man, Binkie.' For several seconds, she was lost in her dreams of the past, a palm across her heart. 'I was in some truly wonderful shows. *Free as Air. My Fair Lady. Chrysanthemum. Fanny.* I wore so many delightful costumes.'

'It must have been incredible, Mimi.'

'The nights on stage, the glamour, the dancing, and in the morning, I'd wake up with my beautiful boys. Oh, Jess, I was the happiest woman.'

Jess gazed out of the window. 'Do you miss London?'

'I cried for a month when Donald brought me here.' She waved a languorous arm. 'This place, Glen Carrick House, was his parents' house – they left it to him.' She sighed. 'Then the boys grew up and left home. Then Donald passed away...' For a moment, her face was sad. 'I was left by myself to wither away to nothing.'

'Oh, that's not true.' Jess took Mimi's soft hands in hers. 'Each day brings something new. What about Hamish's musical in London? You must be looking forward to seeing that.'

'*The Flower of the Highlands.* He's writing it for me, you know.' Mimi's eyes were wide as a child's. 'Will you come to London, Jess?'

'Hamish said there was a publicity event in December, a preview. We could go down for that. It would be exciting.'

'It would.' Mimi clasped her hands. 'Isabella will come too. I'll have to start thinking of what to wear. I'd need a fur coat against the winter cold, but Angus would disapprove of real fur.' She turned to Jess anxiously. 'Could I get one made of pretend fur, like the youngsters wear nowadays? I'm sure Angus would find that acceptable.'

'Of course.'

She put a hand to her yellow curls, pinned securely. 'I do hope Gavin comes soon; I need a complete overhaul.'

'Mimi.' Jess took a breath. She'd just had a wonderful idea. She was unsure that what she was about to say was wise, but Mimi's wide-eyed enthusiasm had moved her, and it seemed suddenly important. She touched the shimmering gold gown, her fingers rubbing the thin fabric. 'You really love dressing up, don't you?'

'It's my life,' Mimi said simply.

'I don't suppose you'd like to come to the Hallowe'en ball?'

'Oh, no. I'd have to be a witch or the Bride of Dracula.' Mimi was anxious. 'That's not glamorous.'

'I was thinking about someone dazzling – the Ice Queen,' Jess suggested. 'Or Maleficent, Cruella De Vil. Or...' Her mind raced and she blurted the first idea that came into her head. 'The ghost of Marie Antoinette.'

Mimi thought for a moment, then she smiled. 'Marie Antoinette – a huge wig and a silk ball gown. Yes, I'd love that.' She clasped her hands. 'Isabella will get me a costume – she knows a man who owns an antiques shop and he hires out fancy dress.'

'Isabella must come too.'

'Oh, yes.' Mimi's face flushed with happiness. 'So, we'll all go to a Hallowe'en ball, Jess, and dance the night away?'

Jess breathed in deeply. Mimi and Isabella might prove a handful, but Heather and Amy would be there: she'd have support. Perhaps all five of them could make a really fun night of it. Mimi had enjoyed the afternoon tea: there was no reason why she shouldn't have a wonderful time at the Hallowe'en ball. Jess was sure she could convince Fin that Mimi would be in safe hands. She exhaled slowly. 'Yes, Mimi. We're dressing up – you, me, Isabella, Heather and her friend Amy – we're all going into Drumnadrochit on the thirty-first to a Hallowe'en ball.'

'Then we must all meet here before we go.' Mimi was delighted. 'We could get ready together. It will be like old times – we'll have wine and canapés and do each other's hair – we'll get in a party mood before we perform to the world. Oh, Jess, I can't wait.'

* * *

Angus was sitting in a chair in the snug, his laptop on his knee, Thor dozing at his feet. He chewed his lip in concentration as he typed an email, a frown between his eyes. Opposite him, Fin was studying Hugh's latest letter, outlining how Karen's demands might now be placated. He sighed from somewhere deep inside his chest and Angus glanced up. 'Are you all right, Fin?'

'Mmm.' Fin waved a sheet of paper and simply said, 'Karen.'

Thor pricked up his ears, gazed up at Angus and settled back to sleep. Angus said, 'She's not still harping on about adultery?'

'Hugh's spoken to her solicitor, Cheryl.' Fin scratched his head. 'I think he's finally managed to convince her that Jess is an employee, that nothing is going on between us.'

'And is there?' Angus raised an eyebrow.

'Is there what?'

'Anything between you and Jess?'

'No, there isn't.' Fin shrugged. 'While this divorce is going on, I can't let anything complicate my life.' He paused. 'Jess is great, though.'

'So – when you're through with Karen, what then?'

'I don't know, Angus.' Fin reached for a glass of whisky on the table. 'I think I need to take some time for myself – I could see Issy and Alice, then go on a long holiday, hire a boat.' He swallowed a deep draught. 'Although it might be better to have some company. Who knows?'

Angus pressed a key on his computer and sent his email. 'I'm going to Sri Lanka.'

'When?' Fin was surprised.

'In the middle of November – for six weeks.'

'What about the legs?'

'Oh.' Angus glanced down as if he'd forgotten about them. 'I'll be up and running by then – I'll make sure I am.'

'The doctor said it would take longer.'

'I'm working on it,' Angus shrugged. 'I'll be fine.'

Fin leaned forward. 'Why Sri Lanka?'

'I've been offered a job. I've just said I'll take it. Some guy has written a book and the publishers want photos of animals in the wild – leopards, elephants.'

'Isn't that dangerous?' Fin took another swig of whisky.

'Some things are, Fin – wild animals, motorbikes, relationships with women.' Angus's eyes glistened. 'You have to die of something.'

Fin smiled. 'I'd prefer to go happily with the love of a good woman.'

Angus reached a hand down to pat Thor, who stuck out a pink tongue. 'I'll be back after Christmas. I want to catch up with Fabrice first. Then I thought I'd spend a couple of months here, so that you can take a break. What do you think?'

Fin closed his eyes. 'The divorce will be over. Yes, that would be good.'

'Great.' Angus closed his laptop. 'That's decided. By the start of next year, Karen will be gone, Jess will be gone, I'll be back here, and you can take a well-deserved holiday.'

Fin reached for the whisky bottle and gestured to Angus, who nodded. Fin splashed amber liquid into two glasses and sighed.

'Next year will be a kinder one, I hope. Hamish has his London musical, Mother's looking well. It's just a shame we can't persuade Jess to stay in Scotland.'

'Jess has her own life, Fin.' Angus took the glass Fin was offering. 'She has a home in England, family there, doesn't she?'

'A brother, I think – and a daughter in London,' Fin said. 'But it would be nice if we could persuade her that she liked it enough here in the Highlands to stay on. Very nice indeed...'

* * *

The following day, Jess wandered into the kitchen early to make coffee. It wasn't quite seven o'clock, but the back door was ajar, cool air drifting in. She was about to close it when Thor bounded in, nuzzling her legs, then rushed out again. Jess followed him outside to see Angus sitting in the garden, his crutches laid flat by his side, a digital camera in his hands. He smiled when he saw her, and Jess felt her breathing quicken. She smiled back. 'You're up early.'

'So are the birds.' He grinned, then his voice was a whisper. 'Look, to the left, by the pine tree – there's a capercaillie.' He patted the space next to him. She moved across the grass silently, sitting down. Angus pointed to a blue-black grouse strutting forward, its tail curved. 'There, look.'

She watched as he took some photos, then he handed her the camera. 'You try...'

Jess leaned forward, adjusting the frame, and snapped away. 'He's beautiful.'

'He's quite rare too,' Angus said. 'When I was a kid, I took a photo here of a lek, a group of them in the mating season, showing off.'

Thor padded silently, sitting at their feet. Jess handed the camera to Angus and he stared at the pictures. 'These are good.'

'I like taking photos, especially scenery.'

'Scenery, animals, places, people,' Angus agreed. 'I love the idea of taking a perfect moment in time and holding it forever.'

Jess was conscious that he was sitting close to her. His arm was against hers and she could smell the sweet warmth of him. She shivered. 'I take lots of photos. I have hundreds of Loch Ness. I'm not so good with people.'

'People are easiest,' Angus smiled. 'They have life and energy and spirit.'

Jess thought of the beautiful photo in Angus's bedroom, the one of his wife, and she said, 'I'm not photogenic. I look awful...'

'Not at all.' He leaned closer. 'It's easy to take a stunning photo if you have an eye for it.' His gaze met hers and Jess felt warmth spread through her body. 'You'd be a great subject – you definitely have a light about you that the camera would capture...'

Jess looked down at her hands. 'I don't know...'

He grinned again. 'I'm waiting for a goshawk or a golden eagle to appear. They sometimes fly low around here...' He held up his camera and gazed through the lens.

Jess watched him. 'It must be lovely, travelling, taking photos of wildlife. I expect you miss it.' She thought for a moment. 'You must feel like time has stood still since – since your accident.'

'I'm thankful I'm alive,' he said softly. 'And being here has its compensations.'

Jess tensed. She was unsure if he had paid her a compliment.

Then he said, 'It's good to spend some time with Mum. We're all very close, me and Hamish and Fin. And we owe her so much – for me, she's the Sumatran tigress in the photo. She protected her cubs and allowed us to become the people we are.'

'She's wonderful,' Jess agreed. 'I'm fond of her.'

'And she's fond of you too.' Angus's voice was hushed. 'We all are.'

'Oh...' Jess breathed. Angus's eyes were dark with golden flecks and for a moment, words would not come.

'I liked the way you spoke about your trip to Skye...' Angus closed his eyes for a moment. 'You love it here, don't you?'

Jess nodded. 'I'd like to explore more of Scotland.'

Angus made a soft sound of agreement. 'You get a real sense of the Highlands on the motorbike. The roads are open and the air is fresh. Going north, you reach the islands, the Orkneys, the Hebrides to the west. The oceans there are full of dolphins, seals. There are puffins, red deer. It's a perfect place.'

'I'd love to go...' Jess sighed.

'I'll take you there, when the legs work properly...' Angus smiled and Jess wondered if he was about to kiss her. She was suddenly nervous.

'Well, I'd better not disturb you any more.' She stood up quietly. 'I'm going to make Mimi's breakfast. Can I get you anything?'

Angus shook his head. 'I'll be here a while.'

'Right, well, thanks for letting me use your camera...'

'Anytime...'

Jess began to walk away, through the garden, towards the house. Her feelings were a jumble. Angus made her feel nervous, troubled, yet he had just paid her a compliment; he might even have been about to kiss her. Jess's frown deepened: she didn't know what to think.

22

Heather was playing the soundtrack of *The Rocky Horror Picture Show* on her phone in Mimi's apartment. She and Amy were dressed as cats, pointed ears, long coiled tails, cute animal noses and whiskers. Jess wore a long crimson dress, small red horns protruding from wild hair. They were sitting on the floor, Mimi sipping slowly from the glass Isabella had given her. Jess had suggested she have only one drink before they went out. Fin had offered to give them all a lift into Drumnadrochit and he'd pick them up at 11.30. Jess thought that he'd volunteered because he wanted to keep an eye on Mimi.

Mimi clasped her hands in excitement; she had a huge box full of soft tissue paper containing a costume from Isabella's contact, Lionel. Isabella was dressed as Death, in a top hat and fitted black tailcoat, a cigarette holder between crimson lips. She watched as Mimi delved into the box, her face set in an expression of excitement. Mimi pulled on the long Rococo gown; a red silk dress edged with gold brocade around the neck. She gazed at her reflection in the mirror as she adjusted the white wig that wobbled like an ice-cream cone and fell around her shoulders in a cascade of ringlets. 'What do you think, girls? Is it me?'

'Gorgeous, darling,' Isabella purred. '*Una bellissima regina.*'

'You look great, Mimi,' Jess said, cradling her full glass.

'Very regal, hen,' Heather agreed.

'I want to look beautiful and rich,' Mimi said.

A lively tune rattled from the phone and Amy shouted out 'Let's do "The Time Warp"!'

Mimi and Isabella watched, mouths open, as Heather and Amy leaped up and danced in synchronised moves, their hands on their hips, thrusting pelvises back and forth, jumping around. Halfway through the dance, a tiny Marie Antoinette with a wobbling wig stood beside them, steadily copying the sequence of moves, a broad smile on her face.

'Maybe they will play this one tonight.' Jess was enjoying Mimi's enthusiasm. 'Perhaps we can all join in.'

Isabella put her hands on her hips. 'Well, my days of dancing like that are way behind me.'

'Oh, teach me, teach me.' Mimi was excited. 'I so want to learn this dance. It's not difficult. But we'll do it together, in a chorus line – it will be perfect.'

Amy panted; her face hot beneath the cat make-up. 'It will.'

'Come on, Mimi.' Heather stood firm, her hands by her sides, a prancing cat in heels and painted whiskers. 'I'll show you how to do "The Time Warp". It's not too demanding if you just raise your arms and shimmy down slowly. You don't want to put a hip out, though. Keep the leaps grounded and you'll be all right.'

The four women stood together, a cavorting cat on either side and Marie Antoinette and a red devil woman in a long dress in the middle. Amy started the track again and Heather explained the moves. Jess found it difficult to pick up the dance, almost bumping into Mimi as she lurched the wrong way, but Mimi had the choreography perfect. After a few minutes she stopped, breathless, her face glowing. 'Oh, it's very energetic – I need to rest and have a drink.'

Mimi swallowed a glug of Chardonnay and performed a little curtsey. 'How exciting – I really think I'm going to have the most glorious time tonight.'

* * *

Fin watched as Heather and her friend sauntered towards the pub, arm in arm. Jess levered Mimi gently from the car, adjusting the tall wig that had become lopsided as she clambered out. Isabella followed, positioning her top hat perfectly, slipping her arm through Mimi's. Fin gazed at his mother, her tiny frame delicate as she moved forwards and for a moment he felt a lump of nostalgia swell in his throat. Mimi had been the best mother she could have been, but she had not been conventional. She had dried his tears and stuck a plaster on his cut knees as a boy but as he'd grown into manhood she'd been less able to patch his problems. His acrimonious split with Fiona when she left and took his two girls to Cornwall had broken his heart. Mimi had poured him a large whisky and told him there were more, prettier fish in the sea. He'd already met one, that had been the problem – a very pretty fish called Karen. Mimi had warned him that she was a vacuous gold digger and anyway, marriage was overrated: Fin would be better advised to lead a bachelor life henceforth and indulge in a penchant for tarts such as Karen which, she added bitterly, was what his father should have done instead of ruining her life.

Fin knew he resembled Donald physically, but he wasn't like his father, to whom he owed his business acumen and his suave charm: that was where the similarities ended. He cared deeply about his mother and, as he watched her move slowly, leaning on Jess's arm, her high wig jiggling, he felt his heart lurch. She was frail now, yet she was stubborn, determined. She had become that way by necessity, bringing up her three sons alone, often neglected by her husband. Fin knew she had worked long hours in theatre when he was first born and through his earlier years; his earliest memory as a two-year-old was waking from a bad dream and calling out for Mimi, his nanny telling him his mother would be home soon and Fin missing her, wanting the comfort of her arms and the scent of her perfume. Then she had arrived in the early hours, whisked him out of deep sleep to kiss his cheeks and hug him, telling him that he was her treasure, the love of her life.

Now he watched her disappear into the pub; she would go downstairs into the basement hall with Isabella, Jess and her two friends who clearly had their sights set on a good time. Fin was worried about Mimi, about how physically vulnerable she was, how emotionally vulnerable. He exhaled slowly. He'd pick her up in three hours. She'd be fine until then: he trusted Jess. He slid the car into gear and drove slowly away, his heart heavy as a stone.

* * *

In the dance hall, the lighting was scarlet, illuminating every face, and the music throbbed, a thumping heartbeat. Isabella was already at the bar, her top hat tipped forwards, talking to a man who was dressed as the Grim Reaper in a hooded cloak, carrying a scythe. The room was molten hot. Mimi wondered if this is how hell was, noise thudding incessantly, lights swirling and flashing. The blood-red colour made her dizzy. She clutched Jess's hand.

'What happens now? Are they going to play "The Time Warp" so we can dance?'

Jess gazed at Mimi, recognising the uncertainty in her eyes. She offered a warm smile. 'Shall we sit down for a minute and get our bearings?'

They moved to a table in the corner and huddled together. Heather and Amy were already dancing; Mimi watched them amid a throng, moving their hips, thrashing their arms, and she exhaled sadly. Their dancing had no panache, demanded no skill; it was a random urgent lurching that lacked style and razzle-dazzle. She glanced around the room; there were witches, green-faced with black hair and pointed hats, women with tattered clothes and mouldy skin, dancing in a similar pitching and tossing style.

Several men were close by: a tall thin vampire leaped up and down, waving his arms as if in flight; a clown wearing a tartan costume whirled round; a man in a face mask had a cushion stuffed up the back of his coat that fell out several times when he wiggled. Mimi put a hand to her wig, smoothed the silk fabric of her dress. These people were much younger than she was; their careless abandon made her feel like an outsider.

Mimi looked for Isabella: she had disappeared. Then she noticed her, seated at a small table, still with the Grim Reaper, sharing a drink. She waved and blew a kiss. Mimi raised a tired hand and turned to Jess. 'Can I have some wine?'

'I'll go to the bar.' Jess patted her hand. 'Would you like to try a spritzer, Mimi?'

Mimi said stubbornly. 'I usually drink white wine – or champagne.'

Jess nodded. 'It's very hot in here though, and a spritzer might be cooling.' What she really meant was that it was diluted and might last longer. She didn't want Mimi wolfing down glass after glass of wine. 'We could both have one.'

Mimi was thoughtful, watching the dancers. The beat was punishingly loud, not like the glorious razzmatazz of an orchestra. She raised her voice above the music. 'When I was in the go-go dancing group in the sixties, Body Magic, we were properly choreographed. There were six of us. We all wore hotpants and huge false eyelashes.'

'Those must have been wonderful times.' Jess put her face close to Mimi's, so that they could hear each other over the vibrating music.

Mimi closed her eyes. 'Oh, yes. Hamish was crawling all around the flat. Angus was naughty – we lost two nannies because of his tantrums – and Fin was so grown up, even though he'd have only been around nine then.' She met Jess's eyes. 'But I felt like I was living three people's lives.'

'Three?'

'I danced in a corset so tight that no one would know I'd had babies.' Mimi patted her wig. 'Then I'd come home, spend time with my boys. I loved being a mum, Jess.' She paused, thinking. 'And Donald would require my presence at social gatherings; I'd be there looking like Jackie Kennedy to his JFK, smiling, being the perfect wife.'

Jess placed a hand on Mimi's. 'He loved you, though, Mimi.'

Her lip quivered. 'It was a sort of love. Not the sort I needed. I haven't given up yet, though, Jess.'

'Given up?'

Mimi nodded. 'On love. There's time. I still might meet someone who will adore me for who I am and promise to love me for ever.'

Jess thought about Mimi's words: someone who'd promise to

love her for ever. That was what love was, just promises. She wouldn't risk broken promises again.

Mimi squeezed her hand, as if reading her thoughts. 'Are you going to leave us at the end of December?'

'It's what I agreed,' Jess sighed. 'My cottage will be ready. I have family in Worcestershire, friends.'

Mimi's eyes twinkled. 'You should stay.' She sat up straight. 'You should marry Hamish and stay with us in Scotland.'

Jess smiled. She raised her voice. 'Monster Mash' was booming through the speakers. 'I'll go and get us a spritzer, Mimi. You'll like it, I promise.'

Mimi watched Jess weave her way towards the bar, taking small steps in her tight red dress. She had desperately wanted a daughter, after Hamish had been born, but Donald had said no.

Mimi gazed at the dancers. Heather and Amy were dancing with partners now, wiggling their hips. One man was tall, wearing tattered clothes, a Frankenstein's monster mask. The other man, Amy's, was shorter in a long black cloak, his hair slicked back, his face pale. A slow song came over the speakers, a whining guitar, and the two men sidled forward, their arms around Heather and Amy, their bodies pressed close. Amy began to kiss the vampire with a sudden passion.

Mimi rested her cheek against her hands and watched. Isabella was still talking to the Grim Reaper, who was leaning forwards, fascinated. She wondered if Isabella had just met the man or if she knew him already. He appeared to be besotted. Mimi wasn't surprised: Isabella was glamorous, gregarious, confident.

For a moment, Mimi thought about true love: for her, it had been one snatched night of passion with a handsome man who had whispered in her ear that they'd be together for eternity. The next day, he had left for... she tried to remember... somewhere, and the beginnings of a new life stayed: Angus, already strong and determined, had taken root. But for several hours, Mimi had known a brief love that would be precious for the rest of her life.

She remembered Charlie Gosling, the young lad who stood at the theatre door, doffing his cap, murmuring, 'Wotcher, Miss Mimi,' his eyes shining. He would have loved her, taken care of her. She hadn't thought about him twice at the time; she'd chosen Donald and missed another opportunity to be cherished. But nowadays, she often wondered what had happened to him, how different her life might have been.

Suddenly Mimi was filled with a sense of emptiness that made her body ache. She was eighty-eight years old: she could no longer cavort like the young ones who shook their hips as if the dance didn't matter.

Mimi realised in an instant that she would never dance again like she used to. She'd never love again or be loved. She was waiting for Isabella to come over, or for Jess to return with a spritzer: she was waiting for the end of her life.

She didn't cry, she couldn't; with glazed eyes, she watched as Isabella flirted with the Grim Reaper, as the dancers enjoyed their moment of recklessness and she knew, her throat swollen with grief, that the moments she had left were meaningless.

23

Mimi stared at the melee on the dance floor. She was Marie Antoinette in her once-finest clothes, waiting in prison for the end to come. It would not be long.

Three young women walked towards her in short, dark, ragged dresses, black wigs, their faces painted white. They approached her table and smiled through purple lips.

'Hello. I thought I recognised you.' The one who spoke had black stitches painted across her mouth.

Mimi was puzzled. 'I'm sorry – do I know you?'

A second girl, taller than the first, spoke excitedly, her words a little slurred. 'I love your costume and make-up. It's really tidy! You're the ghost of Anne Boleyn.'

The first girl moved her face closer to Mimi's. 'You remember me? I'm Claire from the tea shop. You came in a week or two ago with your friends and ordered cakes. You let me take a selfie with you.'

'Oh, I did.' Mimi patted her wig, vaguely remembering.

The third girl spoke excitedly. 'Were you really a famous dancer?'

Mimi blinked for a second. 'Of course.'

'She was, too.' The first girl, Claire, waved a hand. 'Miss Minelli was in *Cabaret*, the best musical ever. She sang that song about money making the world go round. She's Judy Garland's daughter, you know, the lassie who was Dorothy in *The Wizard of Oz* with the red shoes and she's been married four times, my gran says.'

'Aye – all millionaires too, so fair play to you, hen,' the second girl enthused.

The third girl whispered, 'I thought Liza Minelli lived in the USA?'

'No, she's retired here in Drumnadrochit,' Claire insisted.

'We're out on the skite tonight,' the second girl added. 'We've had a bevvie or two and now we're up for a dance.'

'Do you still dance, Miss Minelli?' Claire asked.

The girls' faces reflected pure respect. Mimi smiled. 'Of course I still dance – I dance every day, but I'm waiting for the right song to come on before I take the dancefloor by storm. I haven't heard it yet.'

'Oh, it's no problem, Liza,' the second girl added. 'The DJ's my cousin. What tune do you want?'

'Well, I'll tell you.' Mimi felt a little more cheerful. She inspected the three girls: they were dressed similarly, smiling: they'd make a good chorus line. She waved a finger. 'But only if you promise to come and dance with me...'

Mimi watched the girls walk away, their laughter hooting. Mimi Solitaire, Liza Minelli – it didn't really matter: the girls respected her because she was a dancer, that was the point. She sat up tall in the costume, crossing slender legs. Then Isabella arrived, her hand in the hand of the Grim Reaper. 'Mimi – look who I found,' she breathed. 'I always said Death was just around the corner for me – well, here he is.'

Mimi held out a hand. 'Hello – am I pleased to meet the Grim Reaper?'

'We've met already, I believe...' The Grim Reaper took her hand in his: it was soft, a little damp. He pushed back the hood and his face was familiar: bushy white brows, matching hair. 'I've seen you in my shop. When Isabella hired the costumes and said she was coming here, I just had to make my move.'

'It's Lionel from the antiques shop,' Isabella explained. She plonked herself down next to Mimi and smiled. 'I don't suppose you could get us some champagne, could you, darling?'

Lionel scuttled off to the bar. Isabella leaned forward confidentially. 'I think he's in love with me. I always suspected it, whenever I went in the shop.' She put her lips close to Mimi's ear. 'What do you think, darling? He's incredibly rich.'

Mimi squeezed her hand. 'I think it's hilarious.' She laughed for the first time that evening. 'Death and the Grim Reaper. You suit each other perfectly.'

* * *

Jess queued at the bar for twenty minutes; the poor barman was rushed off his feet. He finally handed her two spritzers, ice clinking in tall glasses and, as she turned to go, she heard familiar music: a piano, a guitar, a frivolous chorus of voices. She carried the cold drinks carefully, shuffling in her tight dress towards the dance floor. 'The Time Warp' was blaring loudly from the speakers. She stopped. Mimi was in the middle of dozens of dancers, leading the synchronised movements. In her red and gold dress and tall white wig, surrounded by monsters in dark rags with ghoulish faces, she was the centre of her own chorus line. As she raised her arms, shaking a leg and smiling, the other dancers copied her. Jess gaped as Mimi led the dance, a whole crowd following her every move. A short distance away, Isabella clapped her hands and tapped her foot as she sipped champagne. Behind her, a man dressed as the Grim Reaper was hovering. Jess placed the drinks on the nearest table, pulled out her phone and took several photos. Mimi danced on, her wig askew, her tiny body weary, but she was determined to perform 'The Time Warp' to the end.

When the dance finished, people crowded around Mimi, clapping and cheering. The dancers were impressed that an elderly woman in a high wig and a silk Rococo dress was leading the moves, tired, smiling, kicking her legs out. Then Mimi gave a low curtsey and a voice from the stage yelled over the microphone. 'Let's hear it for Miss Liza Minelli – she still has what it takes to wow us all.'

Jess smiled. Mimi was revelling in the attention. Dracula and a tartan clown kissed her hand, and she raised a graceful arm in poised gratitude. Isabella rushed over, thrusting a small champagne glass into her hand. Phone cameras were waved and Mimi posed for more selfies, then she saw Jess and rushed forward. 'Oh, I'm absolutely tired out now. That was exhausting. Jess – is there another drink for me?'

She gazed round at her fans and waved. 'Do pardon me. I simply must sit down.' She offered them a radiant smile. 'But if you give me a half an hour to recover, I might come back and do an encore.'

* * *

The next morning at breakfast, Mimi held Jess's phone out towards Fin. 'What do you think?'

Fin poured coffee into his and Jess's cups. Angus was drinking purple liquid, tipping it into a tumbler from the blender jug. Jess watched Fin's expression as he gazed at the photograph of Mimi dancing in her Marie Antoinette costume, leading the troupe. 'Well, Mother, you still have the gift.' He passed the phone to Angus.

Angus studied the picture, smiling broadly. He was impressed and Jess felt her heart flutter. 'You've framed it well, Jess – this one catches the moment perfectly, Mum – the way your wig is leaning over to one side, the happy face.'

Mimi frowned. 'But don't you think I shine like a star in that photo, Angus? I positively shine.' She pushed away a plate of scrambled eggs Jess had placed in front of her moments before. 'Don't you think it shows my passion?'

Fin patted her hand. 'It certainly does.'

'Definitely.' Angus handed the phone back to Jess. 'Great photo.'

Jess sipped her coffee, squirming a little at the praise. A thought came to her. 'I could send it to Hamish. I was talking to Saffy the other day – she's in London. She heard Hamish on the radio, talking about the new musical. Saffy said he talked about you, Mimi, how you'd been his inspiration behind the character of Flora.'

'I'm a star in London again.' Mimi raised both hands above her head. 'I can't wait for the preview in December. Fin, you must book a suite in a hotel for us all, somewhere near the theatre. Angus – you simply can't be off somewhere; you'll have to be back in time for Hamish's evening.'

Fin said, 'I was thinking – it's Bonfire Night soon. We could have a little celebration together in the garden.' His eyes met Jess's. 'A few fireworks, some food, maybe a few drinks.'

'A party!' Mimi was already excited. 'We could invite people – Isabella and the Grim Reaper – we could ask your friends, Jess.'

Angus reached down a hand, rubbing Thor's head with his

fingers. 'I'm not sure Thor would like all the whizzbangs.' The Labrador was seated by his chair, gazing up soulfully. 'I have him calm now. He had a bad time before he was rescued – he doesn't like noise.'

'We could settle him in your room first.' Fin's face was earnest. 'A few sparklers, some gentle fireworks, jacket potatoes...'

'Oh, and wine.' Mimi clapped her hands. 'Yes, we should celebrate everything. I wonder if we could persuade Hamish to come up specially. What do you think? It would be nice if we were all together, one happy family.'

'I'll phone Hamish now,' Fin said. 'After all, Angus, you're off abroad in a week or so – we'll make it a special occasion. We've been through some tough times as a family – let's have some fun for once.'

Angus nodded, glancing towards Jess, an intense moment, a meeting of eyes. 'Yes, it's a good idea. I'm looking forward to being outside, stretching the legs, spending time together.' He grinned warmly in her direction. 'Some fun is just what we all need.'

Jess gazed around the table. Mimi's cheeks were pink with delight. Fin leaned back in his chair, suave, self-assured, pressing buttons on his phone, and Angus was patting his dog. Jess couldn't help smiling. In different ways, she was becoming fond of them all. She imagined them all clustered around a bonfire and her eyes drifted to Angus again: she wondered what the night would bring.

* * *

Jess was busy in the kitchen. She'd volunteered to make some food for the bonfire party, even though Fin had insisted that it wasn't part of her job and he'd sort it all out when he returned. Fin was meeting Hugh; there had been a whispered phone call earlier and Fin had dashed away, his face concerned. Angus was in his bedroom, grunting, lifting weights and exercising on the static cycle: the sound of his efforts was drowned by the sound of the vacuum cleaner as Heather cleaned the downstairs rooms. Mimi was treating herself to what she called a 'long siesta' which would restore her energy for the party. She was asleep in her apartment with an eye mask on her face. Hamish had promised that he would arrive an hour or two later, around six: he was flying into Inverness from London today.

Jess scrubbed potatoes and started to make a salad. She wondered what Angus would eat, whether she could make something special for him. She'd ask him later. She'd make something for Mimi first, a plate of something with prawns, to tempt her appetite. There were several bottles of red wine, and a Chardonnay for Mimi chilling in the fridge.

Heather appeared, dragging a vacuum cleaner. She grinned. 'Shall I do here now or are you only going to muck it up, Jess?'

'I'll clean up when I've finished.' Jess brandished a handful of cherry tomatoes.

'Only – I have a date tonight, well, it's a double-date. '

'Oh?' Jess asked. 'The dancers from the Hallowe'en ball?'

'Yep, Amy and I met these two guys...' Heather leaned on the kitchen worktop, ready to tell her story. 'She's very keen on hers – Kyle, he's called. The one I met is called Davie. I haven't seen him since the ball in Drumnadrochit – I've been putting him off.'

Jess asked, 'Don't you like him?'

'I'm not sure. Amy thinks Kyle is lovely and he and Davie are best friends. She's been out with him twice since the ball, but I don't know if I want a boyfriend.'

'Really?' Jess was surprised.

'Aye,' Heather said. 'I mean, men are great when you don't

have one, all that testosterone gets you going, you know what I mean?'

Jess shook her head, smiling. 'I'm surrounded by it here...'

'But now I've met Davie, I'm thinking – can I honestly be bothered? He's a big sweaty man. I don't want to be stuck again with washing someone's socks and making their dinner... I have enough on my hands with the B & B. I don't need the extra work.'

'But what about love?' Jess was puzzled.

'Love?' Heather squealed. 'Isn't it all just a rush of crazy chemicals taking over our bodies? It's just nature's trickery to get us to set up home and cook and clean and wash...'

Jess winced. 'I'm not sure – you might be right.'

'I think we need a pizza night and some girl talk, hen.' Heather nudged Jess gently. 'And I'm keen to know which of the three McKinlay boys you've set your sights on.'

'Oh...' Jess began, then she stood still, listening. The door clicked and suddenly Fin was in the room. He threw them a miserable look.

'I need a drink.'

Heather watched him rummage in the cupboard for a bottle of whisky. She asked, 'Isn't it a bit early, Fin?'

'Purely medicinal...' He was already filling a glass. 'Karen's come up with something I wasn't expecting – as usual. Where's Angus?'

Jess moved her head, a nod towards the hallway. 'Exercising, I think.'

Fin clutched his glass. 'Ah, well. I need to talk to someone.' He sank into a chair and put his hands to his head. 'I just had a meeting with Hugh. It went badly.'

'Oh?' Heather sat opposite him, offering her most sympathetic expression. 'Do you need a shoulder to cry on?'

Jess asked, 'Would you like me to go and ask Angus to join us?'

'I'm just exhausted...' Fin's eyes shone, his face pale. 'The woman is half-crazy. Karen says she doesn't want a divorce at all any more. She wants us to try again.'

24

'Karen's always been unpredictable.' Angus gazed at his knees, where Thor was resting his chin. 'I'd pay no mind to her, Fin.'

Fin said sadly, 'She likes to play games. She's being her usual controlling self – one day she's angry, then out of the blue she tells me she can't live without me.' He sighed. 'I don't need that now.'

Hamish and Mimi had taken their places round the table. Jess said, 'It's Bonfire Night. Let's all have some fun and concentrate on enjoying ourselves. What do you think?'

'Oh, let's.' Mimi clasped her hands.

Angus rubbed the Labrador's forehead. 'You can stay in my room, Thor. I'll put some treats in there for you and come and check on you every so often. You'll be okay, won't you?'

Thor raised trusting eyes towards Angus.

'Isabella is coming. Why isn't Heather staying for the party?' Mimi touched the newly coiled curls that adorned her head. Gavin had left moments ago.

'She has a date,' Jess said. 'With the monster she met at the Hallowe'en ball.'

'I've met a few of those myself,' Hamish quipped. 'In fact, I'm working with one in London right now. The guy in charge of the choreography, Jasper, is so finnicky. Jomo and Zane and I as the composing team try to stay well out of his way.'

'I could come to London and take over the choreography for you, Hamish,' Mimi offered. 'And we could meet for lunch every day in an expensive restaurant. You could come with us, Jess, and I'd invite Isabella.'

Hamish grinned. 'I'm looking forward to you all coming down in December for the special preview. Just invited guests, friends, family. It will be a wonderful evening.'

'That will be great, Hamish – something to look forward to.' Fin shook himself from his thoughts. 'There will be room in the flat for three of us.'

'Three?' Hamish was surprised. 'Who isn't coming?'

'I can't make it – I'll be in Sri Lanka.' Angus fondled Thor's ears.

Hamish screwed up his face. 'I thought you were going to Borneo?'

'Next year, maybe in April or May.' Angus glanced at Jess, then leaned back in his seat. 'Sri Lanka first. The work is starting to trickle in now my legs are back.'

Fin gazed at the crutches resting against the table next to Angus. 'They're not quite back yet, Angus. I think you should finally give in and get a physio in to help for the next week or two before you're off to Sri Lanka – you know, marginal gains.'

'I'm doing fine,' Angus replied.

Jess gazed at the food she had prepared; her mind was occupied with thoughts of Angus in Sri Lanka. He'd be leaving soon and the thought troubled her more than she'd expected. She took a breath. 'Well, shall we start the festivities? We could go outside and start the bonfire?'

'I'll have a glass of Chardonnay.' Mimi's face brightened.

'I've had a whisky already.' Fin noticed his almost-empty glass. 'I'll light the bonfire before I have another drink.'

'Oh, let's have a quick snifter first.' Hamish stood up and moved around the room, pouring wine, helping himself to a large one. He raised his glass. 'A toast to us all. To the McKinlays – and Jess.'

Fin raised his glass. 'The McKinlays and Jess.'

Jess glanced at Angus, who acknowledged her with an almost imperceptible wink.

Glasses clinked. A sudden harsh rapping came from the front door.

'Isabella!' Mimi announced excitedly.

Hamish, already on his feet, took another glug of wine. 'I'll go.'

Mimi stretched out an arm for her glass and sipped her Chardonnay. The four of them listened, still as a picture, as voices came from the hallway, Hamish's soft and placatory and a woman's voice, harsh and insistent. Then Karen was in the kitchen, her white coat buttoned to her chin, her face frowning and troubled. She sought out Fin with glittering eyes. He leaned back in his seat and said 'Karen' in a tone of resignation.

'We need to talk, Fin...' She looked round at the other faces scornfully. 'In private.'

'Not now – I'm with my family...'

'And I'm not family now, of course,' Karen snapped. 'As if I ever have been. The great McKinlay clan, all together – I've only ever shared the name,' she said melodramatically. 'And now you want to take that away from me, Fin.'

Fin sighed. 'You asked for the divorce, Karen.'

'And now I don't want one.' She put her hands on her hips. 'I want a reconciliation. We can try again. We could go to counselling.'

Fin wiped his brow. His eyes were tired. 'I don't think...'

'We should take a holiday, the Seychelles, and start again, just me and you. Some time away...'

Fin shook his head. Mimi swallowed a sip of wine and turned to Karen. Her voice was level. 'Go home, Karen. Let the solicitors sort it out. That's what they're paid to do.'

Karen whirled towards Mimi, her eyes sharp daggers. 'You mind your own business. You've always pushed your nose into my relationship with Fin.'

'Enough,' Angus said. 'If you can't be civil, Karen, you should leave.'

'I'm trying to save my marriage, for goodness' sake.' Karen's voice became louder. 'And you're all ganging up against me...'

'Karen.' Fin spoke softly, rising from his seat, extending a hand. 'We can talk about this another time. Not now. Please, go home.'

Karen's anger rose. 'Look at you all, the big family together – and your mother in the centre, like butter wouldn't melt, pretending she's been a great dancer on the stage when we all know what she was, nothing more than a common London call-girl—'

'That's just not true.' Mimi was shocked.

Angus's face was thunder but he spoke quietly. 'It's time you left.'

Fin touched Karen's shoulder gently. 'Go home please, Karen.' She grasped his arm, pleading. 'Come back with me, Fin.'

'I'm sorry...'

Karen stabbed a finger towards Jess. 'I suppose you think you've taken my place, lining up to be the next McKinlay wife?'

Jess opened her mouth to reply as Karen's voice became a

screech. 'So, which one are you sleeping with? Fin? Angus? Not Hamish, surely? Maybe you're bedding all of them, maybe you're just like Mimi, maybe you're nothing more than a...'

'No more,' Angus said, his tone protective. Karen froze, then she reached towards the table, her hands connecting with a glass bowl full of salad, and hurled it across the kitchen with a scream. There was a loud crash and glass shattered. Thor yelped, then the Labrador skidded from beside Angus's feet and rushed towards the front door. Angus heaved himself from his chair and reached for his crutches.

'I left the door open...' Hamish gasped.

Hamish hurried into the hallway, followed by Jess, Angus swaying after them and finally, Karen.

Outside, the sky was dark. A stiff breeze was blowing from the loch and a soft mist hung on the air. Karen rushed towards her car, a white sporty Audi, and leaped into the driving seat, revving the engine. Angus hurtled down the drive on crutches, Hamish and Jess next to him, when they heard a screech of brakes from the road.

Hamish stopped dead for a moment, but Angus was still moving. He passed the gates, stopping suddenly by the side of the road where a car had come to halt. A young man opened the door and staggered out, gazing at the curled dog that lay still in the brightness of the headlights.

Thor raised his head slowly and looked around, dazed. He tried to scrabble to his feet, flopping over, then he pulled himself onto his forelegs and dragged the rest of his body painfully towards Angus who stood at the side of the road. Angus threw the crutches to the ground and, with effort, leaned forward and swept the dog into his arms, cradling his hind quarters.

The driver, a very young man, was shaken and confused. 'The dog just ran out in front of me. I couldn't stop.'

Angus gave him a savage look but his voice was soft. 'It's not your fault.' He twisted round. 'Hamish... can you give me a hand back to the house with Thor? You and Fin can stay with Mum. Jess...' He met her eyes. 'Can you drive me to Drumnadrochit? Everyone else has been drinking. I'll get Fin to ring Kelvin the vet, tell him we're coming, that it's an emergency.'

'Yes, of course.' Jess felt her heart thumping. As she turned to Angus and placed a hand against his arm, a white Audi rumbled down the drive, hurtling past them and into the road. Karen joined the traffic and roared away without looking back.

* * *

Jess sat in the corner of the waiting room: there was no one else there, not even a receptionist. The vet's surgery had closed thirty minutes ago but Kelvin, a tall, lean Scot who was a friend of Angus's, had waited behind and now they were both in the treatment room with Thor. Jess had driven to the surgery as fast as she could in the small car, Angus hunched in the cramped space next to her, cradling the Labrador wrapped in a blanket. She'd watched him struggle from the passenger seat, carrying the large, crumpled dog in one arm, a crutch under the other, limping heavily as he held Thor to his chest. Throughout the journey Thor had been quiet, his trusting eyes on Angus. Now Jess was waiting, sitting on a hard chair, her phone in her hand: Angus had been in the treatment room with Kelvin for almost half an hour.

Jess needed to talk to someone. She messaged Saffy and asked if she had time for a chat. Saffy replied straight away: she'd catch up later as she was at a bonfire party. Beyond the window, a rocket exploded, shedding fleeting bright sparks in an ebony sky, then another. Jess texted Paul to ask how things were going and he replied that he and Jodie were out for a meal together; it had been a stressful week but the cottage was coming along well and he'd phone her soon.

Several fireworks burst in the darkness, flaking shards of gold fizzling to nothing. It occurred to her momentarily that love was exactly the same as fireworks: at first you were bursting with happiness but all too soon it was gone. She thought of Yiannis, her first and only love, imagining him now living a peaceful life in the Corfu sunshine with a wife, children, grandchildren. And Andy, Saffy's father, a man she now counted as a friend, was happily doing his own thing in Colchester. She thought about texting him, asking him how he was. Suddenly, Jess felt very alone. Through the window, another firework crackled loudly, spluttering white diamonds.

A door opened and Angus appeared, leaning on a crutch. He looked exhausted. Jess stood up and moved towards him. 'How's Thor?'

Angus shrugged. 'Kelvin is keeping him overnight. He's having an X-ray. It seems that it's a broken pelvis, but we don't know if that's all. If there's more, internal bleeding, other injuries, then – we'll know for certain tomorrow. Kelvin will ring me.'

Jess put a gentle hand on his arm. 'Are you okay?'

'I'll live,' he replied bitterly. 'I just hope Thor will too.'

They began to walk towards the door. Suddenly, Angus stopped. 'I don't suppose you fancy a drink? I'm not ready to go home yet and I could use one...'

'Of course,' Jess replied without thinking.

Angus looked relieved. 'There's an inn across the road. I'll message Fin, tell him how things are with Thor. He and Hamish can look after Mum for an hour or so.' He gave a rueful smile. 'I think you probably deserve a night off.'

25

'Thanks, Jess.' Angus brought the whisky to his lips. 'For driving me to the vet's, for being here.'

She sipped orange juice and looked around. The pub was cosy, a warm fire leaping in the hearth, soft orange lights overhead, just a few customers at tables. 'What did Kelvin say about Thor?'

'He's checking him over – we'll know tomorrow.'

'Has Thor been with you a long time?'

Angus nodded. 'I got him over two years ago. He's four years old now. He'd had a tough life with a previous owner – he was thin and very nervous, all ribs, when I took him.' He met Jess's eyes. 'He's so much better now. He goes with me on photo shoots when he can – he has a passport.' He shrugged. 'A couple of times he's stayed with Fin or Hamish...'

Jess was tempted to put a hand out and cover his, to say that she hoped Thor would pull through. Instead, she said, 'Fingers crossed, eh?' The words sounded too simple and she felt awkward.

Angus cradled his glass in both hands. 'So... you know Fin

and Hamish and I are bowled over by what you're doing for Mum – you've made such a difference.'

'Mimi is lovely...'

'But...' His eyes were suddenly thoughtful. 'It doesn't quite add up. I know your cottage in England is being renovated but – why stay in Scotland? Why not just down the road from your own place?'

'I was on holiday, and I chose to stay on. It's beautiful here. It seemed like an opportunity to experience somewhere different for a while.'

She felt uncomfortable for a moment, as if she was having an interview: he still had the ability to make her feel ill at ease. Then Angus said, 'So – you're rootless?'

Jess frowned, a little offended. 'What does that mean?'

Angus's eyes shone in the firelight. 'I've always felt rootless. Travelling about suits me. It seems you're the same – you stay somewhere for a while, then you move on. I can understand that.'

Jess thought about his words. 'I ran a hotel for a long time in one place. It was quite a responsibility, especially towards the end. Now I feel like I can be more independent, do what I like.'

Angus gazed at her for a while. 'That makes sense. I was wondering about you.'

'What were you wondering?' Jess was alarmed by his frankness.

'At first, when I saw you, I didn't get it. You were kind to Mum, patient, sweet-natured, outgoing. I couldn't understand why you were here alone.'

'You mean without a partner?' Jess bridled a little.

'Just by yourself,' Angus said. 'I won't pry.' He sighed. 'We all have to move forward. I've had my own share of troubles.'

Jess caught his eye and smiled mischievously, repeating his words. 'I won't pry.'

'That's for another time, maybe.' Angus swallowed some whisky. 'So, tell me what it is that you love about this place.'

'Oh, where to start?' Jess placed a hand across her heart. 'The loch, the rising mist in the evening, the sharp air, the smell of pine, the deer running free by the roads.'

'My first photos were of deer in the forests.' Angus smiled. 'I was a teenager – I crept out at night-time and waited for hours. There was nothing for ages and suddenly, I was confronted by a gigantic stag, its antlers aloft, just standing, staring at me. He waited while I took some pictures, as if allowing me the privilege, then he leaped away, all muscle. It was magnificent.'

'I'd love to see that,' Jess breathed. 'Is that why you wanted to take photos of animals?'

'Oh, yes,' Angus replied. 'Fin and Hamish were the perfect sons, always focused on a career. I was a drifter.' His eyes narrowed. 'My father wasn't my real father – I was the result of a fling between Mum and a man called Emile. My dad never let me forget that. I was always the outsider.' He shrugged. 'After a while it became a badge, you know, an excuse to be awkward.'

'You've done well, though.'

'I guess.' Angus finished his drink. 'I lived in Cameroon for a while, then I was based in Paris for several years. Those were the best times. My son lives in Toulouse now. I moved around a lot until I had the accident back in the spring. I need to get my life back on track. That's why I agreed to the job in Sri Lanka.'

'It must be great to travel to so many exciting places.' Jess had hardly touched the orange juice. She felt comfortable, relaxed, close to the warmth of the fire. She noticed the clock on the wall and was surprised that almost an hour had passed.

Angus followed her glance. 'Ah, we should be heading back. You shouldn't have to listen to me going on about my life.' He reached for his jacket. 'I've never been one for dwelling in the past.'

'I know what you mean.' Jess stood up, finding her car keys. They were walking through the pub lounge and someone called out to Angus, who replied, 'Goodnight, Murray,' with a wave of his hand before limping forwards on the crutch. He held the door open for Jess.

'Thanks again for being there, for the lift and the company.'

'I was glad to help,' Jess replied.

'Next time, I hope it'll be happier circumstances,' Angus said. 'Maybe dinner somewhere? I owe you.'

Jess made a soft sound, turning her back and walking towards the car, Angus next to her, moving slowly. She didn't know how to reply. She wanted to be alone, in the privacy of her own space: she needed time to think. Her first reaction to Angus's mention of dinner was a sudden leaping of her heart, an immediate desire to say yes.

* * *

As Jess parked the car at Glen Carrick House, she saw the bonfire beyond, in the garden. Four figures were standing in the red glow of the flames: Fin, wearing a heavy coat, Hamish in a hat and scarf, Isabella swathed in furs and Mimi, who was pointing and laughing as a firework fizzled in the sky. Angus's voice was low. 'I'd almost forgotten about the family bonfire.'

Jess was suddenly enthusiastic. 'It's a party. I've been making food all afternoon. What's not to enjoy?'

'Mum's having fun, I see.' Angus tugged the door open and wrenched himself out. 'Well, we'd better join them. The dancing has started, and we can't miss that.'

'Do you usually dance on Bonfire Night?' Jess asked.

Angus's face shone as he remembered. 'The McKinlay boys dance all the time, whenever they can. And we sing too. Mum loves it. We were like the bloody Von Trapps as kids.' He laughed, and Jess loved the mischief in his eyes. 'If my legs worked right, I'd be flinging you across the garden right now in a reel, singing "The Bonnie Banks of Loch Lomond".'

Jess wondered if he was about to suggest that they attempted a slower dance together, but Fin rushed over to Angus straight away to ask about Thor. Then Mimi and Hamish were next to her, Hamish throwing his arms around her. 'Good to have you back, Jess. You took ages. I hope poor Thor will be okay. He's in safe hands with Kelvin.'

Mimi took over. 'Get Jess a drink, Hamish – and I'll have white wine. We have some fireworks to enjoy. Finlay's doing a marvellous job.' She turned over her shoulder. 'Finlay, I need some music.'

'I have it ready, Mother.' Fin pressed a button; some speakers were wired from inside the house and music began to play loudly.

Mimi brushed a finger against Isabella's coat. 'This is beautiful. Don't let Angus see it. He'll throw it in the fire.'

Isabella laughed. 'It is pure mink, a present from Lionel. From his shop. He's called Lionel Genghis McPherson and he's absolutely charming. And rich. He and I are dating.'

Mimi clapped her hands. 'So where is he now?'

'At home languishing because I told him I wanted to spend quality time with my friend Mimi.' She waved a hand dismissively. 'He does not come first in my life, certainly not yet. He will have to earn that place, darling.'

Staccato voices, then a rousing female chorus boomed from the speakers and Hamish couldn't help the broad smile that spread across his face. 'It's "The Cell Block Tango", from Chicago.' He wrapped his scarf around his neck. 'I made a playlist for Mum

– I thought it was time to introduce her to some up-to-date clas-
sics and a few old ones: Barbra Streisand, *Funny Girl*; "Let It Go",
from *Frozen*; "Take Me or Leave Me", from *Rent*; "Burn", from
Hamilton. All the modern belting songs. She'll love it.'

Mimi took the wine he offered. The loud music filled her with
energy and she was happy, surrounded by her friends and family;
the fireworks were a celebration of life. She felt the urge to dance.
She raised her glass. 'Isn't this glorious, Jess?' She called over to
Fin. 'We need more fireworks.'

Fin and Angus obeyed. Almost immediately, rockets were
whooshing, exploding in the night sky, showering shards of silver,
red and gold. Mimi clapped her hands as music blared, too loud.
'Oh, isn't this dreamy?'

Above, a cacophony of explosions and splutters accompanied
the rousing tune of 'All That Jazz' from *Chicago*. Isabella lit a
cigarette, gazing up at the sky. Mimi immediately kicked off her
shoes and began to twirl barefoot on the grass, throwing her
heavy coat to the ground, grasping Hamish's hand. She threw
back her head and kicked out a leg, Hamish dropping to his knee.
A green star whizzed above and shattered into falling fragments.

Fin picked up Mimi's coat and wrapped it around her shoulders, guiding her to a chair he had placed near the fire. There was
a loud whoosh and a bang, a brief shooting of gold sparks in the
sky: Angus was on firework duty. Mimi gazed into the flames,
then up at her eldest son. 'I do wish you wouldn't fuss, Finlay. I'm
enjoying myself.'

'I don't want you catching cold, Mother.'

'That's nonsense – you just don't like me having fun.'

Fin kissed her cheek. 'You're shivering. We'll all go in and eat
soon.'

'I'll stay here all night long if I want to.' Mimi twisted round to
Hamish. 'I love these modern musicals. They are so – racy.'

Hamish winked. 'When you're in London in December, I'm going to take you to see *Hamilton*, Mum.' He approached Jess and took her hands, dancing to the music, 'I Dreamed a Dream' from *Les Misérables*. 'You too, Jess – I have contacts, I can get great seats.'

'I'm coming to London with you,' Isabella chimed. 'I want to go shopping in Knightsbridge.'

Jess knew *Hamilton* had good reviews, but she knew little else about it. She allowed Hamish to sweep her across the ground, whirling round: he was an accomplished dancer and he sang well, his voice tuneful. Then he put his face closer to her ear. 'I'm really looking forward to you and Mum coming down to London, Jess – Isabella too, we'll have such fun. We'll go to some great places for dinner and you can meet some of the cast of *Flower of the Highlands*.'

'Sounds perfect,' Jess agreed. She noticed Fin watching her, his face serious. Angus was lighting fireworks, placing rockets in bottles, standing back and sending sparks of colour shooting skywards. Isabella opened wine as Mimi warmed damp feet, stretching them out towards the bonfire. She raised both arms, letting the coat fall from her shoulders.

'Oh, I'm having such a lovely time. Will you top up my glass, Isabella?'

'We should get you inside soon,' Fin sighed.

'I'm not cold,' Mimi smiled.

Hamish pretended to be shocked. 'You can be such a party-pooper sometimes, Fin. We can eat at midnight. Right now, Mum wants to dance – *I* want to dance. This is heaven, out here in the cold, stars twinkling in the heavens. Who could possibly want more?'

Jess met his smile. Then, as she stared over Hamish's shoulder, she noticed Angus, his hands in his pockets, staring into the blaze. Fin was joking with Hamish, saying something about him being exactly like his mother, and Isabella was agreeing loudly. Mimi said that Hamish was her boy, her mini-me.

Hamish whirled Mimi into another dance, spinning her round to 'Let It Go' from *Frozen*. He was calling for more drinks as Mimi shrugged off the coat, linking hands with Isabella, dancing in her bare feet again, twirling round and round.

Jess moved over to the bonfire, warming her hands, and she looked around for Angus. He had gone. She stared into the crackling flames, enjoying the heat against her face, the cold bite of the wind from behind, and her mind drifted to thoughts of her new cottage: soon it would be ready, freshly decorated. She sighed: she was happy in Scotland, living with the McKinlays. She was drawn to them all as she was drawn to the comforting heat of the blaze. She didn't want to move.

Something caught her attention and she glanced over her shoulder. Angus was just a few feet away, his camera angled towards her, taking photos. She held out a hand, suddenly awkward, muttering, 'Oh, no, please – I look awful in photos.'

Then he was by her side. 'Not at all. I've some great pictures: Mum dancing, Hamish playing the fool, Fin lighting fireworks. And now I've some beautiful ones of you by the bonfire.' He smiled, resting a hand against her back. 'Jess, Mum's started to get cold and everyone's gone inside for food. I don't want you missing out, especially since you've made it all. Come on, let's go in – it won't be the same without you.'

She glanced up and felt the comforting pressure of his hand. She was tempted to stay, to spend more time outside in the garden in his company talking. The blaze from the fire was dreamy, and the stars above filled the sky like tiny diamonds. It was the perfect place to linger, to be alone with him. His eyes met hers and she was sure he was thinking the same thing. But Mimi was indoors now, and the family party was underway.

'Yes, you're right, we should go in,' Jess sighed. 'And I made a rice salad specially for you.'

Her words sounded awkward as soon as they left her mouth. She caught his smile and she smiled back, took a deep breath, and rushed to the kitchen where there would be safety in numbers, where she'd have time to pause, to think straight: right now, her feelings were beginning to run away with her.

26

As Mimi slept, she felt herself pulled down into boiling depths, as if she was being tugged into the centre of a bonfire. The heat was unbearable, flames grasping, smoke choking her and she heard her own voice groan. She rolled over and the mattress beneath her felt damp. She dreamed that she was in a room packed with cavorting dancers with grotesque faces. Suddenly there was a man in the distance, holding out a hand: Donald, broad-shouldered, beckoning. Her throat was constricted, her voice was dry as ash; her heart thudded, making her body judder again and again. Mimi wondered if he had come to claim her. She whirled around and saw another man; even though he was half in shadow, she recognised the scent of him, the stillness, the strength. It had been sixty years since she'd seen him. In her dream, she called 'Emile?' She gasped and forced her eyes wide open.

Mimi sat up in bed. Her face was wet with perspiration, her chest hurt and the muscles in her legs ached. She eased herself to the edge of the bed and tentatively stood up, her nightgown trailing at her feet. It was hard to catch her breath. Suddenly she was shivering violently. Through the window, the moon hung low, bright as a silver penny, reflecting shimmering light on the water. Mimi leaned against the window ledge and felt herself lurch forward. Her forehead was cool against the glass. Then her body shook, gripping her so hard that her teeth chattered. She needed help. Mimi thought of Fin first and tried to call out his name, but her voice was a croak.

With a mighty effort, she pushed herself upright and turned back to the bed. Four, five steps and she could fall onto the mattress, close her eyes and drift into sleep. She took one pace, slowly, and was overwhelmed by a dizziness that clouded her vision and made her head whirl. In desperation she lunged forward, her arms out, and stumbled onto the wooden floor. Mimi lay still, sprawled out facedown, her legs twisted, and didn't move. The moon slid behind a cloud and as it emerged from the other side, Mimi was flooded with light from the window, an illuminated rag doll, her white nightdress crumpled beneath her.

* * *

Hamish was in the kitchen, cooking and humming to a pop song that was jangling on the radio. He was wearing a T-shirt and jogging bottoms, his feet bare. As he poached eggs and sliced bread for toast, he shuffled his feet in a little dance. He glanced at Jess as she padded into the kitchen, wearing pyjamas and a dressing gown, her hair dishevelled, her eyes bleary.

'Good morning, gorgeous. Aren't we getting dressed today?' he teased as she rubbed her eyes. 'Coffee? Black, I suppose?'

'It's Saturday, so I can wear pyjamas all day,' Jess retorted. 'But yes, please.'

'I'm doing poached eggs, toast.' Hamish brandished a butter knife. 'Would you like to partake?'

'Just a slice of toast, please.' Jess took the mug of coffee he offered.

'Exactly how much wine did you drink last night, Jess?'

She grimaced. 'Two glasses.'

'Lightweight,' Hamish replied. 'I think we managed to restrict Mum to two. The eggs are for her, although I don't suppose she'll eat them.'

Jess glanced at the kitchen clock. 'It's almost ten o'clock. Any news of Thor?'

'Angus and Fin went off to Kelvin's over an hour ago. Angus wanted to get there as soon as the vet's opened.' He made a sad face. 'It's possible the poor dog will have to be put down. There may be internal injuries.'

'I hope he'll be all right,' Jess said anxiously. 'It's tough for Angus.'

Hamish was momentarily angry. 'I blame Karen. I hate to say it, but I'm glad Fin will be rid of her soon. She's always been the same. The things she said about Mum yesterday – seriously, Jess, I was furious.'

'She shouldn't have said what she did.' Jess sipped her coffee thoughtfully. 'Hamish – can I ask you something?'

'Anything, darling.' Hamish wiggled his hips as the radio changed to another lively song. 'But don't expect a sensible reply.'

'Mimi tells such authentic stories of her past, being in a chorus line. So – why did Karen say she hadn't been on stage?'

'Ah, she worked front of house as a teenager – that's how she started out. Then she begged a place on the stage, met Dad, the rest is history.' Hamish placed eggs on a plate. 'She and Dad argued a lot over the years and he often said that he'd dragged her out of obscurity, you know the sort of thing – she'd come from nowhere. I suppose people heard him and made their own story up.'

'What do you think?'

Hamish exhaled. 'Mum loves the theatre. You saw her last night. She's eighty-eight and she still has a spring in her step – she just wants to dance.'

Jess agreed. 'She's marvellous.'

'I owe Mum everything – she brought me up to love playing the piano, singing, composing. Yes, Jess, I believe her.' He arranged china on a tray. 'I suspect Fin doesn't completely believe she was a star of the West End – perhaps that's where Karen got her ideas from. And as for Angus, I can't imagine he cares what she did – he accepts her for who she is.'

Jess's thoughts moved to Angus and she made a soft sound. 'I hope Thor will be all right.'

'Me too.' Hamish picked up the tray. 'I'm fond of the mutt.' He moved towards the door. 'I'm off back to London today, so Mimi's getting breakfast in bed and a kiss on the cheek before I head off. Want to come up with me? She'll be so glad to see you.'

'I'm meeting Heather for lunch later but I have plenty of time.' Jess sipped coffee. 'Of course. I'm right behind you, Hamish.'

Hamish skipped up the stairs, balancing the tray on one hand, his voice resonant as he sang out, 'Oh, what a beautiful morning,' Jess just behind him. He rushed into Mimi's apartment and through to the bedroom, then he stopped. Mimi was stretched out on the floor.

Hamish froze. 'Mum? Mum?' He called to Jess, his heart thudding, unable to move.

Jess was by her side in seconds. 'Mimi?' She placed her fingers on Mimi's neck, on her forehead. 'She is all right, Hamish – but she's really hot. We need to get her into bed.'

Hamish swept her up in his arms with no effort and carried

her tenderly, placing the duvet over her body. 'Mum? Mum, can you hear me?'

Mimi moved her head slowly. 'Donald?'

'It's me, Hamish.'

'Hamish...' Mimi's lips were dry. Jess found a glass of water and, as Hamish lifted her from the pillow, Mimi took a sip. 'Hamish...?'

Then Hamish had his phone in his hand. 'I'm calling Alasdair Harris. I'm sure he'll come out.'

Jess frowned. 'Is he a doctor? Will he come over on a Saturday...?'

Hamish spoke quickly. 'Yes – he's a friend of Fin's – they went to school together.' There was a voice in his ear. 'Ali – it's Hamish McKinlay – Mum's not well. She has a fever – I found her on the floor – I've put her back in bed. Can you come over?'

He listened for a moment then he turned to Jess. 'He's on his way. I'll ring Fin now.'

Jess soaked a flannel in water and pressed it against Mimi's forehead. Her eyelids fluttered, white and waxy. 'Jess?'

Jess grasped the fingers that Mimi held out. They were ice-cold. 'Just lie back and rest. The doctor's coming to check you're all right. Just relax.'

'No...' Mimi opened her eyes; they shone like blue glass. 'I won't go to the hospital...'

'You're safe here, Mum,' Hamish soothed. 'Just rest – you'll be fine.'

Mimi summoned her strength, her fists small balls. 'I won't go...' She leaned back against the pillow and closed her eyes, her fingers still gripping Jess's.

* * *

Alasdair Harris pushed his hands into his jeans' pockets. His eyes met Fin's then he glanced towards Angus and Hamish. Jess sat at the kitchen table, clutching the mug of coffee.

'Your mother has a viral infection – most probably flu, I'd guess.' He ran a hand through dark hair. 'Can you take care of her here? You say she won't take a hospital bed?'

'She won't,' Hamish agreed. 'She was quite clear about it.'

Fin said, 'She'll go if she needs to. I'll make sure of it.' He met the doctor's eyes. 'What are your thoughts, Ali?'

'We can monitor her for the next few days, see how she develops,' Alasdair said. 'I'll prescribe her some antiviral drugs and come in and check on her tomorrow. Meanwhile, if you change your mind, Fin, ring me and I'll get her a bed in Raigmore…'

'I'll make sure she has lots of rest,' Fin agreed. 'Plenty of fluids. If I'm worried, I'll ring you – thanks, Ali.'

Hamish folded his arms. 'We'll all help out – I'm not going back to London until next week now.'

Angus nodded. 'And I'm staying here for a while too.'

'Glad to hear it.' Alasdair gave a dry laugh. 'You need to give those legs a rest.'

Angus rolled his eyes and Fin added, 'You should get some proper physio, Angus – it'll do you good.'

'I've no time for that – I have my own exercises.' Angus's eyes gleamed. 'I have to keep Thor in a cage for six weeks: he's not allowed to move, and he needs to be cared for.' He shook his head. 'We're lucky it's only his pelvis that broke.'

'So, we have three patients in the house?'

Angus glanced at Alasdair. 'We'll take care of Mum. We'll stay with her day and night if that's what she needs.'

'We certainly will,' Hamish added.

'All right,' Alasdair agreed. 'I'll pop round tomorrow.'

Fin clapped him on the shoulder. 'Thanks, Ali.'

Alasdair said softly, 'Come round and see Faye and me some-time soon, stay for dinner. I was sorry to hear about Karen, you know...'

'Of course.' Fin's charming smile covered his emotions. 'I'll see you to the door.'

'I'll check on Thor. He's due some meds.' Angus followed them out of the kitchen.

Hamish turned to Jess, his face mischievous, and whispered, 'I'm surprised Ali Harris invited Fin round, now he's single...'

'Why?'

'His wife, Faye...' Hamish's eyes twinkled with mischief. 'She and Fin were an item for years at school. When he left for uni and dumped her, she fell into a rebound thing with Ali. But I've always thought she never got over her first love for my evil big brother. He is like that with women, of course, Fin – all charm and seduction, wins them over and then he breaks their hearts.'

'Is it me you're gossiping about?' Fin was back in the kitchen. He waved a piece of paper. 'Ali's given me a prescription for Mother – I'll go into Drumnadrochit and get it for her. Do you need a lift to Heather's place, Jess?'

'I think I'll ring her and cancel.' Jess was thoughtful. 'Just while we keep an eye on Mimi.'

'I'll stay on for this week,' Hamish added. 'Hopefully there will be some improvement.'

Fin was anxious. 'Ali was quite concerned, given her age. The first sign of anything not quite right and she's away to hospital.'

'What about Thor's progress? How is the mutt?' Hamish asked.

Fin rolled his eyes. 'Thor's out for the count on painkillers. Poor thing tried to leap up and wag his tail when he saw Angus, but his back legs won't work. Angus has him stowed comfortably in the snug.'

'At least he's all right,' Jess breathed.

'Angus postponed his trip to Sri Lanka,' Fin said thoughtfully. 'I'm glad he's staying. It'll be nice to have him here. He can take time to heal his legs properly and we can share caring for Mother now.'

Hamish glanced in the direction of the hallway. 'Is he in the snug with Thor now?'

'No.' Fin's eyes widened. 'He dragged himself upstairs on crutches to check on Mother, to keep her company. And guess what else he's done?' He met Jess and Fin's eyes, his own round with surprise. 'His insurance money has come through after the accident. He's only gone and bought a new motorbike.'

'He hasn't! This crazy family,' Hamish sighed. He reached out an arm and pressed Fin's shoulder. 'We're not a run-of-the-mill bunch, we McKinlays, but we look out for each other.'

Fin hugged his brother, one sudden strong clasp. 'Yes, and we'll take good care of Mother.'

'Too right,' Jess added, her voice thick with emotion. 'We'll all take shifts and get her better. She's very precious, our Mimi.'

Hamish wrapped an arm around Jess. 'And you're precious too, Jess.' He pressed his cheek against hers. 'You're almost one of the family.'

'I'll second that.' Fin hugged her and suddenly the three of them were bound together, arms linked in a tight squeeze. Jess gazed up from Hamish to Fin and back to Hamish. It felt very nice to be accepted in this way. It was a warm feeling, a feeling of belonging, sharing, comforting each other. Jess's eyes shone: she only needed Angus to complete the embrace. The thought made her skin tingle and her heart thump, a feeling not unlike love.

27

The following day, Jess rushed into the kitchen to make Mimi's breakfast. Angus was there already, limping heavily, leaning against the counter. He had prepared a tray laden with whole-meal toast spread with honey, a glass of green liquid, a steaming cup of tea. He smiled. 'I've made Mum something to eat.'

Jess was impressed. 'What's in the tumbler?'

'Mango, pineapple, strawberries, spinach, kale. It'll do her the world of good if we can get it down her. Mum's been ill and she needs to get her strength back.'

Jess saw the concern in his face and she wanted to hug him. Instead, she said, 'Shall I take the tray up?'

'I was hoping you would.' He looked down at his legs with a shrug. 'It would take so long for me to get up there, the tea would be cold.'

Jess picked up the tray. 'Thanks, Angus.'

He replied with a soft smile and murmured, 'You're welcome. Tell Mum there's a get-well card on the tray for her – and there's a card for you too.'

Jess noticed two envelopes and frowned, puzzled. She hurried towards the stairs, the tray in her hands.

Mimi was sitting up in bed, a cardigan around her shoulders. Jess placed breakfast on her lap.

'What's this?' Mimi wrinkled her nose. 'Can't I have pastries?'

'Angus made it. It's good for you. You're convalescing, Mimi.'

'If Hamish was here, he'd bring me pastries. Angus gives me rabbit food and cardboard bread. Can't you call Isabella? She'd bring me a cappuccino, arancini.' She offered a crafty smile.

Jess perched on the edge of the bed. 'Eat some of this now, Mimi, and I'll bring you an omelette for lunch.' She patted her hand. 'We need to get you well to go to see Hamish in London.'

'Hamish? London?' Mimi's eyes were misty. 'I'm getting so confused with everything, I'd forgotten. When are we going to London?'

'Next week.' Jess pushed the tray closer to Mimi. 'It's the beginning of December already, the second. We're off to London on the tenth for Hamish's preview evening, then it's the run-up to Christmas, which will be really good fun. We can go shopping for presents; we can put up a tree in the lounge.' She watched as Mimi lifted the green liquid to her nose and sniffed it, then replaced the glass on the tray. 'You need to be strong so that you can enjoy Christmas.'

'What do we have here?' Mimi picked up the envelopes. 'A card? There's one each.'

'From Angus...' Jess watched as Mimi tore open the paper eagerly and held up a glossy photo. 'Look. It's me, dancing on Bonfire Night with Hamish. It's wonderful – look at my smile.' She held out the other envelope. 'Open yours now, Jess.'

Jess's fingers trembled as she slid a photograph from the envelope. It was a photo of her staring into the bonfire, her face lit by firelight. Her skin and her hair were illuminated amber and bronze and her expression was one of warmth and love. Angus had captured her perfectly: it was a photograph taken by someone who understood her, who truly cared. Jess swallowed, afraid she would cry.

'It will be Christmas soon.' Mimi was talking to her, interrupting her thoughts. 'Are you staying with us, Jess?'

'My daughter's coming for Christmas Day. Paul says the cottage is almost ready. I'll invite my family to lunch.' Jess took in Mimi's sad expression and was filled with regret. 'But I'll come up here and see you in the New Year.'

'Oh, you should be here for Hogmanay.' Mimi brightened. 'We open up the lounge; there's a roaring fire, feasting and drinking and we have a piper to play bagpipes at midnight. Finlay organises it – all the boys wear their kilts. It's custom.' She sighed, remembering. 'Donald was a proud Scot, very fond of tradition. He'd make it happen every year. I'd wear a ballgown and Hamish and I would dance a reel. Fin, too.' She clapped her hands. 'Angus brought Augustine and Fabrice many times and they loved it. Oh, I can remember Augustine's face when she first saw the boys in their kilts. And Finlay used to bring his family, Fiona and the girls, all dressed up. Hamish would bring a whole group of his friends, many of them were musicians and they'd play and sing and we'd all drink champagne and whisky. We'd all have such a good time. They were good days.' Mimi's face became sad. 'Those times have gone now. What I'd give for a special Hogmanay again...'

'What happened to Fin's children?'

'Fiona took them away to Cornwall, to Truro. They were lovely girls, teenagers then, Alice and Isabelle. They've grown up now – Alice has children of her own. I don't see them much now.

Finlay does: he sends them money, visits and phones them. I think Issy is a midwife...'

'Poor Fin.'

'He made a bad choice.'

'What happened, Mimi?' Jess glanced again at the tray of food; it was still untouched.

'Karen happened. She was determined to take Finlay from Fiona and she got her way. Of course, Finlay was weak where she was concerned and Fiona was very angry when she found out about the affair. She took his girls as far away as she could to punish him. It broke his heart when they left, but Karen wanted him and she got him.' Mimi pressed her lips together. 'I'm glad he'll be rid of her soon.'

'Fin's been through a lot. He must be lonely now...' Jess picked up the tray and sighed.

'No one should be lonely – I'm here now.' A figure stood in the doorway, dark hair piled, a white trouser suit. Isabella held out a huge box wrapped in ribbon and a bouquet of flowers. 'Look, I have Baci truffles. *Baci* means *you kiss* in Italian. Hidden in the foil of each truffle is a love note. Eat these, darling, and you'll be happy.'

Mimi reached out her arms. 'Isabella – thank you for visiting.'

'I phoned Fin every day – he tells me you have been at death's door but now you are well.' Isabella launched herself onto the edge of the bed and rummaged in her designer bag for a packet of cigarettes. 'Oh... I suppose this is not a good idea, is it?' She pushed them away. 'How are you? How is she, Jess? I have been so worried.'

Jess hugged the photo Angus had given her. 'She's on the mend.'

'And we're going to London soon to Hamish's launch.' Mimi smiled. 'You must come with us.'

'I wouldn't miss it for anything.' Isabella kissed the air around Mimi's head.

'And how is Lionel?' Mimi asked, her eyes shining.

'He adores me. I want him to take me to Rome and Florence. He has bought a Maserati, a black one, just to impress me. So now I know he is serious.' She laughed. 'It is good fun, having a man friend who is intoxicated by me.' She patted Jess's arm. 'You should get one yourself.'

'Oh, I wish,' Mimi smiled. 'To love and be truly loved...'

Mimi closed her eyes for a moment. When she opened them, she said, 'I'm tired now. I'll rest for a while. Tomorrow, I'd like to try a walk in the garden, though, if I can. Would you come with me, Jess, Isabella?' Her eyes shone. 'I can wear that new coat Angus got me online, the faux-fur one, and the scarf Hamish sent from London.'

'I'm sure we could go outside tomorrow for a few minutes.' Jess squeezed her hand. 'You relax now. I'll come up later with a cup of green tea.'

Mimi gasped. 'Oh, not green tea – don't tell Angus, but I find it so bitter. A sweet coffee – a small one, two sugars. I'll sleep afterwards, honestly.'

'All right.' Jess put out a hand and touched Mimi's soft hair.

'You have what you want, darling,' Isabella boomed. 'You're the patient...'

Jess lifted the full tray and moved briskly through the apartment towards the stairs, Isabella at her heels. Mimi's voice followed them. 'But patience isn't one of my virtues, is it? I've never been very patient... or very virtuous.'

As they stood on the top step, Mimi's voice called again, a little stronger. 'Come to think of it, I don't think I have any virtues at all.'

* * *

An hour later, Mimi was fast asleep, Isabella had left to have her hair done and Jess was washing the empty plates in the kitchen. The chugging and bumping of a vacuum cleaner came from the hall and Jess set out in search of Heather, who was in the snug, the nozzle in one hand, the other stuck through the bars of the cage where Thor was resting. The Labrador wagged his tail.

Heather switched the machine off. 'Thor seems to be on the mend. He has three more weeks left of life behind bars and look at him – he's raring to get out.'

Jess crouched down next to her. 'Thor's doing well, Mimi too. Three weeks ago, they both looked so poorly.'

'They've been well cared for.' Heather patted Thor's nose. 'Angus has done a great job with both of them. It's a shame he's not doing so well on himself.'

'What do you mean?' Jess was concerned.

'I heard Fin on the phone the other day.' Heather lowered her voice. 'He said one of Angus's legs wasn't healing properly. He sounded worried.'

'Oh?' Jess was suddenly anxious.

'Then he went out in his best bib and tucker – he was quite the dapper chappie. Has Fin got himself another woman?'

Jess shrugged. 'I know he went to dinner with Alasdair and his wife last night. Fin's really grateful to Ali for taking care of Mimi. He said he'd been wonderful to her and he owes him big time...'

Heather's voice was confidential. 'You seem to know a lot about Fin.' She squeezed Jess's arm. 'Do you like him the best?'

'No, not in the way you mean.' Jess changed the subject. 'So, have you seen Davie from the Hallowe'en ball recently?'

'I've double-dated with Amy and Kyle a couple of times. Amy and Kyle are a big thing – she's totally smitten. But I'm thinking – Davie's not for me, Jess.'

'Oh?'

Heather sighed. 'I was so keen on a hot romance and now it's just too much like hard work, getting dressed up to go out and having to be on my best behaviour. I can't be bothered. No...' She shook her head. 'I think I'd be better off with a dog. I'm getting quite attached to this young man.' Heather rubbed Thor's ears. 'He's loyal, no trouble and easy to manage.'

Jess agreed. 'You might be right.'

'How about you, hen?' Heather's eyes met Jess's in a discerning way that made her feel uncomfortable.

She kept her voice light. 'I'm off back to Worcestershire at the end of the month. It'll be nice to be independent and in my own space again.'

'Is the cottage ready?'

'Almost. Paul and Luke have been working hard...' Jess frowned. 'I'm not sure things are going too well, to be honest – I think he and Luke argue a lot.'

'Why?' Heather leaned forward, interested.

'Luke's been drinking too much and Paul isn't happy, especially since he's Luke's employer too now. I'm hoping Christmas will give them the chance to have a really nice family time.'

Heather wasn't sure. 'It sounds like Christmas dinner in your house will be a minefield. Is that going to be any fun for you, Jess?'

'Saffy's coming down for a day or two. We might have a quiet Boxing Day together, just the two of us – it'll be a lovely way to start life in my new cottage...'

Heather frowned. 'Maybe, but you'll miss Mimi and me – and the McKinlay boys...'

Jess forced a smile. 'My stay was only ever going to be until Christmas, and it will be nice to see Saffy...' A loud rap at the front door made her stop mid-sentence, glad of the interruption. 'Shall I just see who that is?'

Thor barked twice as Jess opened the door, Heather at her heels. She saw a tall woman, a case in one hand, scrutinising her with a serious expression. The woman had blonde hair, whisked into a high ponytail, dressed impeccably in a dark jacket, belted at the waist, and tight dark trousers.

'I am looking for Mr McKinlay.' Her accent was mixed, Scottish and something else, Eastern European.

Jess noticed the woman's cool expression, and said, 'Which one?'

The woman cast her eyes over Jess. 'My appointment is with Mr McKinlay.'

Jess and Heather exchanged glances. 'Angus or Fin?' Heather asked, her eyes on the woman's large dark case that she held in a gloved hand.

Then Fin appeared in the hallway, dressed in a smart roll-neck jumper and jeans, cleanly shaven, smelling of an aftershave reminiscent of pine trees. He smiled disarmingly and held out a hand. 'Ms Bortkiewicz?'

'Mila.' She offered him an angelic expression. 'So pleased to meet you, Mr McKinlay.'

'Fin.'

'Fin,' she purred. 'Alasdair said you lived in a beautiful house, but I hadn't imagined one so lovely – what a great view of Loch Ness.'

'My mother has the best view upstairs,' Fin smiled. 'We are very lucky to live here – do come inside.'

Mila smiled politely towards Jess and Heather as she brushed past them. 'I have left the bed in the back of my car...'

'I can help you with that, Mila – but would you like to meet Angus first?'

Heather raised her eyebrows as Mila and Fin waked towards Angus's room. Heather offered a mischievous wink and mouthed, 'She's brought a bed?'

Jess said, 'She must be a physio.'

'Escort,' Heather grinned. 'Did you see her bag of tricks? Fin seemed smitten. And I bet she can help Angus with his recovery.'

'Heather!' Jess gasped. 'She's been referred by Alasdair the GP.'

Heather put her hands on her hips. 'Exactly my point, hen. He's clearly trying to get Angus back on his feet by keeping him off them for a while.'

Jess was about to defend the woman about whom she knew nothing when there was another knock at the door. She met Heather's gaze. 'It's like Euston Station here today.'

'Do you think it's a second woman?' Heather's eyes shone with mischief. 'One for Fin?'

Jess thought about Heather's words and tried to ignore the sudden strange feeling gnawing at her stomach as she opened the door. A man stood facing her, a flat cap on his head, holding out a clipboard and a pen. 'Delivery for McKinlay.'

Jess stared, waiting for the man to hand over the parcel. He sighed and spoke louder. 'Delivery. McKinlay. Gold Wing.'

'I don't understand.' Jess felt her cheeks warming as the man frowned, clearly annoyed.

He thrust out the clipboard. 'Sign here, please, and I'll drop it off and be on my way.'

Jess was puzzled. 'What am I signing for?'

'Look...' Heather pointed over the man's shoulder towards the drive. There was a van and a trailer: mounted on the trailer was a chunky red and black motorbike, shiny and new. The man turned his attention to Heather and pushed the clipboard at her.

'So, will you sign for this now? New Honda Gold Wing motorcycle to be delivered to Mr Angus McKinlay.'

28

Several days later, Mimi sat in the garden in her faux-fur coat as the sun melted into darkness behind the loch. She looked cosy and elegant: Fin had bought her a matching hat and with her hair freshly done, she felt like Catherine the Great surveying her grand estate. Jess was beside her on one side, hands deep in her jacket pockets, Isabella on the other. The air was fresh pine, ice-cold in her lungs. Mimi's eyes glittered.

'Should we go in now?' Jess asked. 'Fin is making a roast for supper.'

'I don't want roast,' Mimi replied. 'I told him I'll have a prawn salad and a glass of Chardonnay.'

Mimi closed her eyes. A stroll in the garden each afternoon was all she could manage nowadays. The illness had taken her energy away. 'I'm tired. And I miss Hamish.' She gazed at Jess sadly. 'All a mother wants for her children is for them to be happy.'

'I know,' Jess answered. Saffy was very contented to be in London, studying, living with friends, but Jess missed her. She hadn't seen her for several months.

Mimi gave a soft sigh. 'I didn't expect two grown-up sons to be living with me at their age...'

Jess said, 'I'm sure they both have plans for the future.'

Mimi's eyes narrowed. 'That woman has been here again. That's three times now.'

Isabella was interested. 'Which woman?'

'The blonde one, Mila,' Mimi replied.

'Fin's girlfriend or Angus's?' Isabella wanted to know.

'She's a kinesiologist and a chiropractor,' Jess explained. 'She's helping Angus get back to normal.'

'So he can go out on that motorbike again.' Mimi's voice was bitter.

'I expect he's quite careful.' Jess made her tone as placatory as she could: she was worried too. 'He took it for a short spin earlier today. Fin said he'd be safe enough.'

'Safe?' Mimi was horrified. 'Finlay wouldn't take me to the hospital when Angus had his accident. I had to wait for him to come home to find out how badly injured he was. I didn't sleep for a week after Finlay brought him back and we turned the library into a big bedroom for him. Jess, he looked awful. I thought he'd never move again.'

'It was horrible,' Isabella said. 'Poor Mimi was worried sick. He shouldn't have another bike. He should get a sensible car, or take a taxi.'

Jess shuddered. 'I can imagine that it was a shock...'

Mimi took a breath. 'It would give me so much peace to know that my boys were happy. I think they are both lonely. Finlay is a charmer, but he's had no luck with women. Neither has Angus, losing Augustine. I worry. I don't want them looking after me for the rest of their days. I'm an old woman now but they still have a life to lead.'

'Things will work out.' Jess took Mimi's hand. It was ice-cold.

'And you, Jess – what will happen to you after you go back to your cottage?'

'Oh, I'll be fine.'

'Do you think so?' Mimi shook her head. 'You're the kindest, warmest, most generous soul who has so much love to give.'

'Thank you, Mimi.'

Isabella's dark gaze turned on Jess. 'And you need someone to love you, darling – someone special in your life to make you smile.'

'Oh, no...' Jess swallowed hard and for a moment she thought she might cry: she was surprised that Isabella's words had hit a soft spot. 'I'm looking forward to going to London. That will be fun.'

Mimi clasped her hands. 'Tomorrow, all of us together.' She hugged her coat tightly. 'We'll have such a good time. I always have most fun when I'm with Hamish.'

'And I am coming down to see you in the Maserati with Lionel.' Isabella pushed a hand through her dark locks. 'He has booked rooms in a very nice hotel. He can explore all the antiques in Old Spitalfields Market while we ladies have a good liquid lunch.'

Mimi tucked her arms through Isabella's and Jess's. 'We'll all be together, won't we?'

'We will.' Jess gazed at the loch. The sky was dark as rumpled velvet, the pine trees tall grey shadows. 'We should go in and have dinner. Fin wants an early start tomorrow morning. We'll have an early night, shall we? It'll be a long day tomorrow.'

* * *

Jess was in her room in the basement, packing clothes into a small case. It was almost ten o'clock. There was a light knock at the door. She looked up, startled. 'Come in.'

Angus was in the doorway. 'Are you ready for London?'

Jess nodded. 'Don't you wish you were coming?'

'I do, but Thor needs me here.' His eyes met hers and held them for a moment. Then he showed her a set of keys. 'It's a beautiful night for spotting some deer.'

'Deer?' Jess asked.

'I thought we could go for a ride into the forest. You could take some photos, maybe.'

'Deer?' Jess repeated and felt foolish.

Angus limped into the room leaning on his stick and threw a jacket and a helmet onto the bed. 'The bike's outside, ready to go.'

Jess's heart lurched with shock: she hadn't expected to ride on his motorbike. He read her thoughts. 'I'll go slowly,' he said. 'I know the forests round here well. There's a full moon. It will be lovely.'

Jess realised she was staring, so she picked up the leather jacket.

'It was Hamish's,' Angus explained. 'And the helmet's a spare, but I think it'll be all right.'

'Oh.' She struggled into the jacket, which was a fairly good fit. She picked up the helmet.

'You can't live in the Highlands and not see deer at nighttime.' Angus turned to go, limping heavily, and Jess followed, feeling a mixture of dread and excitement, clutching her phone, trying to concentrate on the beautiful pictures she'd take.

Her arms around Angus's waist, the helmet fastened tightly and her teeth clamped together, Jess hung on as the motorbike accelerated down the drive and onto the road. It took her a few minutes to open her eyes, to relax her grip and allow the tension to slide from her arms. Pine trees were on either side, everything around her a canopy of darkness except for the yellow light from the headlamp showing the way forward.

Seconds later, Angus swung the motorbike into a side road, and they began to climb. Jess felt calmer: she leaned into the movements of the bike, Angus strong in front of her. Then the terrain became rougher, with stones and bracken, and they were on a path through the forest. Jess held her breath; the only sound was the throaty chugging of the bike. Angus slowed down as a badger scuttled in front of them and disappeared into a hedge. Then he turned towards the woodlands, climbing a bumpy track and Jess pressed her face against his jacket to prevent herself from wobbling. The path twisted and narrowed until they came to a patch of scrubland. Angus stopped the bike, placing his feet firmly on the ground, and Jess climbed off. He took off his helmet, pushing a hand through his hair.

'Is this where the deer are?' Jess asked. There was no light at all. Angus was a dark shadow in front of her.

Angus spoke quietly. 'No, we probably won't see deer here, but – listen.'

Jess listened. At first, the stillness was all around, then she heard a low, rushing sound: moving water. She met Angus's eyes and was sure he was smiling.

'We can walk to the waterfall from here.'

'But it's dark...'

'You won't see the waterfall, Jess – but the sound of it is quite incredible.'

'Oh.' She took a breath. 'Isn't it dangerous?'

'Not at all.' Angus pulled a torch from his pocket and took her hand with the other. 'I know the way.'

He led her expertly down a narrow path and along a wooden bridge. Beneath her feet, Jess could feel the soft soil of the ground, the crisp crunch of leaves, the snap of twigs. The rushing water had become louder, a thunderous roar, and Angus turned to her, his eyes shining. Jess listened; her ears full of the noise. She closed her eyes, her senses tingling, the hammering sound of the waterfall all around. When she opened them, the darkness was so intense she could see nothing at all: everything was obscure, the dense forest, the overhanging sky, and she felt the constant rumble of water falling from a great height. She listened, holding her breath. There was nothing else in the world at that moment except Jess, Angus and the raw power of nature. She inhaled the sharp scent of pine and cold air that filled her nostrils. She sighed. 'This is wonderful.'

He agreed. 'It's so good to be away from everything else.'

Her voice was a whisper. 'Have you been here many times?'

'I had a bike as a teenager. I'd escape to this place, where it was quiet,' he said. 'I liked being here better than being at home.'

She met his eyes. 'It's such a calm place.'

They stood for a while, small in the darkness beside the overwhelming thunder of water, then Angus took her hand again. 'It's time to find some deer now.'

They walked back to the bike; the earth spongy beneath their feet.

Back on the motorbike, her phone ready in her hand, Jess gazed from side to side as they cut through the forest, trees dense on either side. Above, she could see the moon shining through the gaps in the trees, in view then suddenly hidden by branches, emerging a coin of silver again. Angus was driving slowly, the huge machine making a soft chugging noise beneath them. There was no sign of any deer. She gazed upwards at the full moon high in the sky, slipping behind a cloud and sliding out the other side. The forest seemed to be an endless stretch of high pines, grey shadows, an eerie silence except for the cough-cough of the engine.

They turned a corner and drove on. Jess wondered if the splutter of the motorbike was scaring the deer away. Rocks rose on the left-hand side, grey jagged shards; to the right, the trees were dense and tall. Then Angus waved an arm towards the forest and Jess stared: a pair of shining eyes like tiny lamps glowed in the dark, then two more. Jess couldn't help the expression of joy that had spread across her face. 'Deer,' she whispered. 'Look.'

Then she moved her gaze to the left: on top of one of the rocks the silhouette of a huge stag stood tall, his antlers high. Behind him, another one loped forward: there were two, then three, magnificent and statue-still. Angus stopped the bike, the head-lamp a strong yellow beam, and motioned for Jess to slide off. She whisked off her helmet, focused her phone on the rocks and took a photograph. Angus clambered from the bike, pulling off his helmet, and stood behind her. Two more deer emerged from behind a rock and moved slowly on sure feet. Jess held her breath.

Then a huge deer crashed down from the rocks, crossing the path just feet away, its thighs shuddering at each step. It paused in the beam of the headlight for a moment to stare at them, antlers tall, eyes shining, as Jess took several pictures. Then it leaped away and was lost in the darkness of the forest.

Jess gasped. 'That was amazing.'

Angus smiled. 'We'll see more on the drive home. Did you get some good photos?'

'Yes.' Jess's voice was a whisper. 'Thank you, Angus. This is just incredible.'

She glanced towards the rocks where a cluster of four deer watched them from on high. She turned her gaze back to Angus's face. His eyes glowed as they met hers and time seemed to stand still. Then his arms were around her and their mouths met in a kiss. Jess closed her eyes and, despite the cold air on her face, she was immediately enveloped in a feeling of warmth, suddenly wanting nothing more but to hold onto the moment, the tenderness of his lips against hers. Jess leaned against Angus, the darkness surrounding them, and was lifted by a swirl of passion and happiness that she had forgotten existed.

They pulled apart. Jess wasn't sure whether she had dragged herself from the kiss or whether it had been Angus who tugged away. They were staring at each other as if stunned.

Angus said, 'It's late. We should get back.'

Jess had no idea what to say, so she nodded, pushing the helmet over her hair, clambering behind him as he started the engine.

As they drove back, Jess's thoughts raced. She held onto Angus lightly, her arms around his waist; the word *mistake* repeating itself over and over in the chug of the engine. She had kissed him and it had been lovely but she had made an incredible error of judgement, responding to the mood, the moonlight, the beauty of the deer. She was annoyed with herself.

She recalled the last time she'd felt powerless and vulnerable: in her twenties, she'd loved Yiannis with every fibre and it had ended in her being torn apart. She had vowed it would never happen again: her steady, measured marriage had been testament to that.

Now, in a moment, she had thoughtlessly kissed Angus and new, strong feelings were bubbling to the surface. There was no space in her life for a relationship and certainly not one that made her heart thump and her emotions swirl. She would be returning to her cottage in a few weeks – she was going to Hamish's preview with Mimi and Fin tomorrow. She would go to

London, compose her feelings and then keep a polite distance from Angus until she left just before Christmas.

Jess knew it would be so easy to fall in love with Angus: she was a little in love with him already and it made her giddy, out of control. She would not let that happen. Her feelings were spiralling; she had to rein them in.

As the bike swayed onto the main road, Jess felt her grip tighten around his waist. She moved her hands away, her fingers resting lightly on his shoulders. When they arrived at Glen Carrick House, she'd avoid the intensity of his eyes; she'd stay back, far away from his embrace. She would thank him politely for the evening, the waterfall, the deer, and then she'd flee to her room and hide beneath the duvet. She would manage the next two weeks as best as she could. But she would not allow herself to fall in love with Angus.

29

The following morning Mimi was waiting in the hallway, her faux-fur coat draped around her shoulders, a heavy case crammed with clothes at her feet. Fin, looking suave in a smart jacket, was organising everything; he had checked the plane tickets, boarding cards – they'd fly from Inverness and then travel by taxi in London – and he was making sure Mimi had the medication Alasdair had given her to build her strength. It was almost 9.30 and the three of them were ready to go. There was no sign of Angus.

Jess thought briefly about the look in his eyes as she'd whispered goodnight on the doorstep and fled to her room. She had wondered if he'd try to kiss her again: she was almost disappointed that he hadn't, but his expression had been haunted as he leaned heavily on his stick.

'Jess?' Fin's voice pulled her from her thoughts. 'Do you have everything you need?'

'Oh, yes, sorry...' She followed Fin and Mimi out of the door and onto the path, breathing in cold air. Mimi glanced towards the sky.

'We'll get snow today, Finlay.'

'Not where we're going, Mother.'

A blue car, a Tucson, had pulled up in the drive and a woman leaped out, her blonde hair blowing across her face. She smiled at Fin. 'I'm not late?'

'Mila, of course not – the front door is still open, and Angus is in his room.' Fin's voice was syrup-smooth. 'We'll be back in five days – do make sure he gives you a key and you can come and go as you need to.'

Mila said brightly, 'I will. Do you think we'll have snow?'

'I'm sure of it.' Mimi gazed upwards. 'You might get stranded if we have big drifts. That often happens here.'

'If I do, Angus and I will be just fine,' Mila replied. She turned to Jess. 'Have a lovely time in London. I'm so jealous, all the shopping and a musical too, and the fabulous restaurants. I almost wish I was coming.'

Jess nodded; she wished she could swap places with Mila. 'We'll have a great time – we must catch up for a coffee when we're back.'

'Oh, yes.' Mila's smile widened. 'It would be nice to compare notes.' She glanced at Fin. 'Have a wonderful time.'

Fin waved a hand. 'I'm sure we can find something to bring back for you, a souvenir...'

Mila's laughter trailed as she rushed towards Angus's room. 'I love anything from Harrods.'

Fin looked pleased. 'She's a good acquisition. Ali was right – she's doing wonders for Angus. He looks tired – I think he's been overdoing things lately.'

Mimi was arranging herself in the front of the Jaguar as Fin stowed her case in the boot. Jess gazed back at the house. The front door was closed. Angus and Mila were inside. She exhaled sadly: she wanted to avoid seeing him but, at the same time, she wished he'd come out and spoken to her, but it would have been awkward, and Jess was sure she'd have blushed. She stared up at the sky, weighted with the first flurry of snow. She was determined to enjoy her stay in London; she'd have fun with Mimi and Fin and Hamish; she'd buy some Christmas presents and try her best to thoroughly enjoy herself. The break in London was just what she needed.

By the time they were in the taxi to Fin's flat in Islington, Jess felt calmer, even excited by the days that lay ahead. She watched Mimi and Fin. Mimi pointed at landmarks, shrieking, 'Oh, I remember that,' or 'That place has changed – it never used to be so modern...' Fin lay back in his seat, his eyes closed, relaxed and in control, very much at home in the city. Jess hadn't been to London since May: the last time was to visit Saffy. This time was very different. She felt like a guest of honour. She thought fleetingly of Angus, back in Glen Carrick House. She wondered if Mila was still there, if she was massaging his muscles. Jess sighed and gazed through the window as brightly coloured shops slid by.

'There are some lovely restaurants in Islington,' Fin said. 'We could eat out tonight – there's a nice Italian place two minutes' walk from the flat, or a great Turkish restaurant...'

Mimi clapped her hands. 'I love Finlay's apartment. Of course, it used to be Donald's and mine, but the boys make good use of it too now, and it's so modern since the kitchen has been updated. I'm so pleased it's still in the family and Karen didn't get her claws on it.'

'I forgot to say.' Fin's eyes twinkled. 'My decree nisi came through – Karen and I are almost done. By the end of January, I'll be a free man.'

Jess was unsure what to say, so she replied, 'That's good news, Fin.'

'We are here to celebrate so many things – Hamish's music,

Finlay's freedom and now I'm better after my little illness.' Mimi laid a hand on her heart, the fingers heavy with rings.

'What's the schedule?' Jess asked. 'Tomorrow evening is Hamish's preview, but what else do we have lined up?'

'Shopping! I need a brand-new wardrobe,' Mimi exclaimed. 'And we'll have lunch with Hamish. But what I'm looking forward to most is being inside a theatre again, standing on a stage and hearing a proper orchestra play. Oh, I do hope I can get up on the stage – perhaps Hamish will let me sing and dance...'

Fin raised an eyebrow. 'You'll need to take things easy and not get overtired.'

'I'll dance if I want to dance, Finlay – as soon as I smell the theatre, the melting make-up and the sweet scent of perspiration on pretty costumes, it will all come rushing back. Hamish understands how I feel. It's in his blood too.'

Fin squeezed her hand. 'We'll have lunch together tomorrow. On Sunday we can do whatever we like, shopping on Monday, then we fly back on Tuesday.'

'I've arranged to see Saffy tomorrow morning – we're meeting for coffee at half ten,' said Jess. 'That will fit in with everything else, won't it?'

'You do just as you please while you're here, Jess.' Fin offered his charming smile. 'But I've booked lunch for us at Bellaire. Can you be with us for 1.30? Just jump in a cab.'

'Oh, you can't miss lunch at Bellaire.' Mimi grabbed Jess's wrist. 'Isabella's meeting us there. Bring Saffy too – we can book for another person, can't we, Finlay? I'd love to meet Jess's daughter.'

'Of course,' Fin smiled.

Jess imagined her daughter in her torn jeans, ankle boots and cropped red hair meeting sophisticated Fin. Saffy would have a lot to say about the restaurant too: Jess could just hear her ranting about privilege and making a comparison to the families who live on handouts and food banks. Immediately, Jess was filled with admiration for her smart daughter and was thrilled with excitement about seeing her soon. She met Fin's eyes. 'I know Saffy's always busy. She has a group she chairs and there will be a protest on somewhere, I'm sure.'

Mimi brought her hands together in admiration. 'You have such a strong daughter, Jess – I can see she gets it from you.'

Fin smiled at his mother's chatter affectionately as the cab turned into a side street, driving past two rows of magnificent four-storey houses, each with steps leading up to ornate doors and railings around the basements. 'Here we are, we're the ground floor...' Fin raised his voice. 'It's the house at the end on the corner on the right, driver – yes, stop just here, thank you.'

* * *

Mimi threw the sparkly dress on the bed on top of all the others. She had no idea what to wear for lunch. She gazed around in a panic. She'd insisted on packing her own case and everything in it was unsuitable: it was all evening wear, feather boas. She rushed to her bedroom door and called out, 'Jess? Can you help me?' Then she remembered that Jess, happily installed last night in the bedroom next to hers, had left much earlier to meet her daughter. She thought about rushing to Hamish in the master bedroom, but of course he'd be out by now at the theatre. And Isabella was in a hotel somewhere with Lionel.

'Finlay...' she murmured. He'd slept on the sofa bed in the lounge; she knew he'd be there now, probably on the phone arranging some business just as Donald used to do, but she didn't want to ask him for help.

She picked up the clothes again and sorted through the silky heap, trying to choose a dress: the ballgown, the white sweeping diamanté-edged robe, the velvet off-the-shoulder dress that was now far too big. She held up a sparkling silver dress. The last time she had worn that was to a dinner with Donald – she had been in her early fifties.

She put a hand to her chest, and it was suddenly hard to breathe as she caught sight of herself in the wardrobe mirror, a waif in a white nightdress: her recent illness had weakened her. She'd so wanted to dazzle, to be the centre of attention. She picked up the ballgown and thrust out her chin. Fifty years ago, she'd have pulled it off, a ballgown for a lunch date.

She slipped the gown over her head. It skimmed over her skin, the material tumbling to her feet; it was too long: she had shrunk. The sleeveless bodice hung loose, the delicate straps falling from her shoulders onto her elbows. She took a breath and swirled towards the wardrobe, trying her widest smile, the one she used on stage, full of bravado, and opened her eyes. A tiara, she decided, would complete the look. There was one in her case. A smear of lipstick, Donald's diamonds, a necklace and a smile. She could do it. Mimi began to sing 'I Could Have Danced All Night', her voice strong and determined. She'd wear the dress; she'd prove to herself she still had what it takes. She was still Mimi Solitaire.

* * *

Jess slipped her arm through Saffy's. They were sitting close together on a bench in Green Park, their heads touching. Jess clutched a cup of coffee in her hand; Saffy had another in her own bamboo mug. She was huddled inside a thick coat, scarlet boots at the end of ripped jeans matching her vibrant red hair. She leaned against Jess. 'It's been too long, Mum.'

'It has.' Jess was sad. Saffy had a meeting early that afternoon and she'd said she'd be busy for the next few days.

Saffy sipped coffee. 'You should've given me more notice.'

'Next time.'

'Dad came over last week and we went out for a meal.' Saffy turned blue eyes on her mother. 'You should live down here, Mum – you should move to London, get some proper friends, not those men you live with in Scotland who drive expensive cars and own luxury flats and eat in Mayfair.' She took another mouthful of coffee. 'Disgusting.'

Jess wasn't sure if Saffy meant the coffee was disgusting or the McKinlays, so she said, 'I like them.'

'Especially the nice lady who used to be a dancer?'

'All of them.'

Saffy spluttered. 'I think you have a crush on one of her sons, Mum.'

'No, I don't.' Jess answered too quickly.

'You like the lifestyle, a flat in Islington, a house in Loch Ness,' Saffy teased. 'It'd be great for me, though – I could bring my friends up for Hogmanay and have a proper Scottish piss-up.' She linked an arm through Jess's. 'Hamish McKinlay has been on the local radio again, banging on about his musical, *The Flower of the North* or whatever it's called. I feel like I know his mother's entire life history now, from Blitz child to showgirl. He was talking about his bloody musical for almost an hour. I thought you hated musicals, Mum.'

Jess changed the subject. 'How's the research?'

'Great. It's going really well.' Saffy's eyes sparkled. 'And I think I may have a job lined up afterwards: there's an administrator role at Stonewall and it's mine if I want it.'

'Wonderful.' Jess was trying to remember what Stonewall was.

'I heard from Uncle Paul yesterday – would you believe it? Luke thinks he's Heathcliff from *Wuthering Heights*.'

'Paul rang you?' Jess asked.

'Luke's been phoning his ex at midnight and two in the morning, completely pissed, moaning, "Cathy, come home to me." It's so sad.' Saffy snuggled closer to her mother. 'Uncle Paul was asking me if I was back for Christmas and could I meet up with Luke and give him a talking to. It's a shame I won't be able to help.'

Jess suddenly froze. 'Saffy – you are coming home for Christmas, aren't you?'

Saffy's brow crinkled and she showed the 'can't help it but...' face she'd used since childhood. 'I would love to, Mum, but Aoife – you met Aoife last time you came up, didn't you? Anyway, she's invited me to Dublin – her dad has a flat there and he's away over Christmas, so we thought it would be great to spend time...' She took in Jess's expression. 'You don't mind?'

Jess sighed. 'I'd hoped we'd...'

'The new place, I know, your cottage.' Saffy squeezed her arm. 'I'll come up in February, I promise. We can have a whole week together – I told Uncle Paul I'd see him, and Luke too, if he hasn't completely lost it by then.'

Jess took a breath. 'February – that will be lovely.'

'I knew you'd be all right with it, Mum.' Saffy kissed her cheek, then checked her phone. 'Crikey, is that the time? I have a meeting at two...'

'It's not one yet...'

'No, but I walk everywhere, Mum – I'm not like you boomers with your taxis and stuff. Walking keeps me fit and the meeting's an hour from here, or I use e-bikes.' She stood up, running her hand through short fiery hair. 'Next time, we'll catch up properly, have a few drinks. It's been great seeing you, though. I have to dash, Mum – sorry.' Saffy pecked Jess's cheek again. 'Watch out for all those randy Scotsmen. I'll see you soon.'

Jess watched her daughter walk briskly away, striding along the path that cut through the park, turning back once to wave. Jess lifted a tired arm to wave back. Christmas was going to be strange this year. She sighed and wondered what to do. The restaurant was a short walk away. Jess gazed again at Saffy, now a small figure in the distance, and turned towards the main road.

30

Bellaire was an exclusive restaurant with soft gold lighting and white linen. The young waiter gestured a polite welcome as Fin and Hamish arrived, Fin impeccable in a dark suit and Hamish flamboyant in checks. Jess felt quite shabby in long boots and a dress but Mimi was resplendent in her silver ballgown, a diamanté tiara adorning her golden hair, her shoulders swathed in the faux-fur coat. Her face was composed but she gripped Jess's hand. 'I really had nothing else to wear.'

The waiter inclined his head towards Fin, whom he had identified as the person to address. 'Your table is this way, sir.'

Then there was a squeal from behind them as Isabella rushed in, sophisticated in black, hugging Mimi. 'Oh, darling, you look stunning. I wish I'd dressed for dinner now. You look a million dollars.'

Mimi put a hand to her face, temporarily relieved. Isabella clutched one arm and Jess supported her on the other side as they strode into the restaurant.

Fin and Hamish led the way, following the waiter past several tables where guests spoke softly. Mimi thought a portly man in a suit was looking her up and down. A young couple, holding hands across the table, caught each other's eyes and smiled. She heard someone make a soft sound and she was sure it was mockery: people were whispering about her clothes, she was running the gauntlet of their sarcasm. She breathed, 'I don't think I can do this.'

Isabella said. 'You're fabulous, darling.'

Mimi hesitated, gazing around wildly. Everyone was engaged in their own conversation, but she was convinced now that they were talking about her. She saw a smart woman glance at her and quickly look away. Isabella hissed, 'You are Mimi Solitaire. People like us don't wear jeans – we sparkle. Hold your head high.'

Jess noticed Mimi's discomfort. She was fairly sure that no one was paying her much attention, although she had noticed the odd smile and raised eyebrow at her choice of outfit. But she wanted Mimi to feel relaxed, and currently she was noticeably uncomfortable.

Mimi leaned towards Isabella as they sat down. 'I need a glass of wine – several glasses.'

'Of course,' Isabella agreed. 'We'll order a bottle each, darling...'

Jess heard Mimi's comment and thought instantly of Saffy: what would her feisty daughter say in such a potentially awkward situation to save Mimi's feelings and prevent her drinking too much? Her mind raced. Then an idea came to her: it was outrageous, but it would help Mimi feel as important as she looked.

'Excuse me.' Jess touched the young waiter's arm; he immediately turned.

'Madam?'

'I wonder – would it be all right if we sat close to a window, where there's better ventilation?' Jess indicated Mimi. 'Dame Mimi has a gala performance straight after lunch and she needs to look after her voice.' Jess had no idea what she was talking about, but she increased her volume for effect. 'Particularly since she will be singing for royalty.'

Hamish heard Jess's comment and he was immediately onside, a smile breaking on his face. 'As Dame Mimi's Director of Music, I need to make sure that she has the best care possible. She's ready to be whisked off to the opera house immediately after we finish lunch. Fresh air is so important before a concert – no cheese, of course: it's strictly off limits for Dame Mimi.'

'No cheese, Hamish?' Mimi was aghast. 'I'll need a glass of wine...'

'Just the one,' Jess murmured encouragingly.

Isabella's lips twitched in a smile, then she drew herself up to her full height and composed her face. 'I am Dame Mimi's Personal Assistant, and what Dame Mimi wants, she always gets.' She arched an eyebrow, smiling at the waiter flirtatiously. 'I rang ahead of our reservation to explain what Dame Mimi requires. I trust you have received this information, darling?'

'Oh – oh, of course.' The waiter's expression troubled. He was young, new to the post; he clearly had little experience of dealing with customers of such high status. He turned to Mimi. 'Welcome to Bellaire, Dame Mimi.'

Mimi's face flushed with pride. She caught the wink in Isabella's eye and replied, 'Where else would one go for a pre-performance lunch?'

Fin patted his breast pocket to indicate his wallet and lowered his voice so that he was just audible. 'Obviously, we're here because we want the best for Dame Mimi – so could you make sure that she's not pestered – you know the sort of thing – autograph hunters...'

'Paparazzi,' Hamish gasped, fanning himself with his hand as if just recalling a bad memory.

'People wanting selfies,' Jess added with a wink towards Mimi.

'Fans.' Isabella's lip curled in scorn. 'Fanatical admirers can be so difficult. Last time the unwashed hordes followed Dame Mimi, they wrecked the entire hotel. Can you believe they burst in, a group of a hundred, just to tell her how wonderful she was? They caused thousands of pounds of damage.'

'God forbid!' Mimi joined in enthusiastically. 'I just want a quiet lunch with my... entourage this time.'

'Of course.' The waiter gave a little bow, his face serious. 'I had no idea, Dame Mimi. Please, do come this way.' The young waiter led them to a damask-covered table at a distance from the others, the cutlery and glasses shining in the lamplight. 'We're always glad to welcome celebrities.'

Jess noticed to her delight that the nearby diners had overheard their conversation and were watching with interest. She thought she heard a woman murmur, 'I have a CD by her at home...'

Jess caught Hamish's eye and he winked. The waiter fussed around the table, taking Mimi's wrap and holding her chair so that she could sit down comfortably. He was attentive, fretting, moving between Fin and Mimi, eyeing Hamish, Isabella and Jess anxiously.

'So – could I recommend wine or sparkling water?'

'Water, and just one bottle of wine...?' Jess suggested.

The waiter continued intrepidly, speaking to Fin. 'And of course, for a light lunch without cheese for Madame, perhaps she might like to try the...'

'Caviar,' Mimi said, her face flushed with happiness as Isabella clapped her hands. 'Your best caviar, waiter, and a bottle of your best champagne.'

'One bottle of the house champagne between us all, Dame Mimi,' Fin grinned as he winked in Jess's direction.

* * *

Mimi slept for most of the afternoon; lunch had made her feel overwhelmingly happy and tired. They had left Bellaire, joyful and chattering. Hamish and Jess chuckled when a smart man wearing a bow tie and a dinner jacket had approached Mimi by the exit and insisted on kissing her hand, saying he had heard her perform many years ago in the Royal Opera House and she had been, without doubt, the most exquisite contralto he had ever heard. Mimi was utterly charming; she lowered her eyelids and thanked him for the compliment, adding that it was a shame he couldn't be there this afternoon to see her perform to King Knut of Sweden but unfortunately all the tickets in the restricted view areas had sold out long ago. Isabella almost choked with laughter. Fin, fearing imminent discovery at this point, whisked them into a taxi as quickly as he could, back to Islington.

Hamish rushed off to the theatre to prepare for the preview after having drunk two strong black coffees in succession. Isabella kissed everyone and took a taxi back to her hotel. Fin was on the phone in the lounge, and Jess was resting in her bedroom, a beautiful vast Georgian room with a high ceiling and a huge white bed. She was texting Paul. He repeated Saffy's concern about Luke; it appeared that his son was doing his best to win back Cathy each night with little success, particularly since he would sink several cans of beer first to steel himself against inevitable rejection. The good news was that Jess's cottage was almost ready and Paul offered to organise for her furniture to be moved in from storage next week. Jess stared at her phone, about to suggest that they all come round to her new home for Christmas dinner. Then she imagined Luke drunk and tearful, Paul and Jodie in paper hats arguing furiously across the table. Perhaps she'd be better off by herself.

Her phone still in her hand, Jess began flicking through the last few photos she had taken. She gazed at an impressive stag standing tall on the path in front of her, its thighs muscular, its antlers held high. She remembered the journey to the forest, the intense darkness, the ice in the air, and for a moment she imagined Angus's arms around her. She closed her eyes and the emotions came pelting back stronger than ever.

Jess was dragged from her thoughts by a sharp knock on the door. She glanced up, alarmed. 'Mimi?'

'It's Fin,' the voice replied crisply. Jess bounded to the door. He was smiling, casual in jeans and a shirt. 'I made coffee.'

Jess followed him to the kitchen, a large square room where everything was bright white or shiny chrome. The scent of roasted coffee beans filled her nostrils. Fin poured coffee into two cups. 'Lunch was fun.'

'It was the most lavish lunch I've ever had.' Jess's eyes were wide.

'Mother enjoyed it and that's most important.' Fin smiled. 'Now things with Karen are almost sorted out and I've moved a few investments around, I wanted to push the boat out. My father used to be good at doing practical things for my mother – but he seldom made her smile. I so want her to enjoy London.'

'She was the centre of attention,' Jess observed with a wry smile. 'It was great to see her so happy.'

'Thanks to you, we avoided a catastrophe. I'm sure no one was interested in Mother's attire, but she felt awkward. She will insist on wearing the most inappropriate clothes.' Fin smiled. 'Mother is not as tough as she seems. But you saved the day.'

Jess sipped coffee. 'I'm fond of Mimi.'

'She's fond of you, Jess.' Fin's eyes met hers. 'We all are.'

'Thanks,' Jess replied. 'You've all been lovely. Apparently, my cottage is almost finished. I just texted my brother.'

Fin's expression was sad. 'We can't persuade you to stay on?'

'I don't think so.' Jess exhaled, imagining Christmas alone.

'That's a shame. Well, while you're here, we'll make sure we all have some fun. You've been wonderful, Jess. Everyone says that, even Angus.'

Jess's heart leaped. 'Really?'

'I rang him earlier and he sends you his best. Mila was there – she gave him a lift to the vet's so that Thor could get checked out. He's making good progress.'

Jess made her voice light. 'Thor or Angus?'

'Both,' Fin replied. 'But Mila's doing an excellent job – the leg we thought might not ever work properly is improving. She's done a lot for him.'

Jess wasn't sure what to say. Fin drank the last of his coffee. 'Right. We're due at the theatre at six. Do you want to get ready and we'll wake Mother? I'll book a taxi.'

'Okay.' Jess put her cup down. 'I hope Mimi enjoys herself this evening. It's a big deal for her, going to Hamish's musical.'

'I hope she doesn't go on about wanting to sing on stage.' Fin's face was serious for a moment. 'It's Hamish's evening – he has sponsors there, and the press.'

'It'll be fine,' Jess reassured him.

'As long as my mother behaves herself.' A thought occurred to him. 'Jess, can you persuade her to wear something low-key?'

Jess grinned. 'Mimi? Low-key?'

'Not that wedding dress and the bloody crown jewels again,' Fin said. 'Just keep her subtle.'

'Subtle?' Jess raised an eyebrow.

'Just do the best you can – you have far more influence than the rest of us. You have all the McKinlays eating out of your hand.'

Jess grinned. 'I'll do what I can.'

Meanwhile, despite her calm exterior, her thoughts were racing. Fin had said that she had *all* the McKinlays eating out of her hand. The thought thrilled her that Angus might be developing feelings for her: the kiss they'd shared confirmed that. Part of her wanted to push the idea away, to avoid complications. But the other part of her wanted to kiss him again.

* * *

Mimi sat on her bed in her dressing gown, her head in her hands. As Jess walked in, she showed her a forlorn tear-stained face.

'I've been really stupid,' she wailed. 'I've only brought these things...' She held up the silver ballgown and the pink sparkling dress she'd worn over thirty years ago. 'I've nothing to wear. I can't go.'

Her tiny shoulders were hunched. Jess put an arm around her. 'We'll think of something...'

Mimi shook her head. 'I can't spoil Hamish's evening. I'll have to stay here.'

Jess plonked herself down on the bed next to Mimi. 'What else do you have?'

'A white diamanté-edged robe, a fur-edged stole...' Mimi was distraught. 'Isabella is out with Lionel so I can't ask her to lend me something. What can I do?'

'What if we go for a new style of our own?' Jess thought for a moment, then she said, 'I'm thinking a bit quirky, very stylish, maybe a bit androgynous, you know, Garbo, Dietrich?'

'It won't work.' Mimi's hand shook. 'We haven't got any clothes like that...'

'I know someone who has and I'm sure we can borrow them. Come on, Mimi – it'll be fine.' Jess tugged her arm.

Mimi held back, unsure. 'Will I embarrass Hamish? Will people laugh?'

'No, Hamish will really appreciate the gesture,' Jess said emphatically. 'And if people do, they'll laugh at us both...'

'I don't understand.' Mimi's expression was confused.

'Come with me – let's go and take a look in Hamish's room, grab everything you fancy, then we'll dress up.'

Mimi's eyes wide with excitement. 'Dress up?'

'Tonight, Mimi Solitaire,' Jess whispered, 'you and I are going to look stunning. We'll make Hamish so proud.'

31

Mimi was sure reporters were photographing her as she approached the theatre from the taxi, her arm lightly linked through Fin's. Jess was on the other side of him and the three of them strolled in, their chins high, Fin impeccable in a black suit and tie. But Mimi knew that she and Jess were turning heads. They'd raided Hamish's wardrobe and tried on his most ostentatious suits. Jess had found a suit in midnight blue velvet and although it was a little loose, she looked stunning in the long jacket and waistcoat, a cream tie, her own trousers and boots. Mimi was Garbo, Dietrich and Solitaire, rolled into one. She had borrowed a navy, yellow and cream tartan jacket of Hamish's. It swamped her but she cinched the waist with a huge belt and it looked like a dress. She teamed it with a silk scarf and a cream felt fedora. Tiny diamonds sparkled in her ears and, with crimson lipstick and black leggings borrowed from Jess, she was the centre of attention.

A young man showed them discreetly to seats at the front. Mimi caught her breath as she gazed upwards. The ceiling was made of painted golden plaster with delicate blue birds, a canopy illuminated by bright lights. Each level of seating seemed to glow, the lights reflecting on gold rails and red seating. Mimi inhaled the scent and sighed. 'This takes me back... I remember it all so well.' She gazed up at the royal box swathed in plush red velvet and said, 'I wish we were up there.'

Mimi clasped both their hands excitedly. Jess squeezed her fingers, complicit, and Mimi was delighted to see that she still wore the gold bangle on her wrist. She gazed towards the orchestra pit where musicians were tuning up. A grand piano was on the corner of the stage and Mimi's heart leaped: it was the one that Hamish would play. She screwed her eyes up small so that she could see better – the stage was bare other than the piano, but the backdrop was a deep blue with a beautiful thistle embroidered in silver. Mimi glanced around; the first six rows of the stalls were full, the noise of chatter bubbling softly, and two people were shaking hands, a man and a woman, their expressions business-like. Mimi snuggled back in her seat and inhaled memories of her early days as a teenager in the theatre, when she had first watched the chorus girls together and dreamed of being a dancer.

A spotlight appeared centre-stage, a sharp circle of yellow light, and Hamish was there, smart in a suit and tie. He raised a hand.

'Hello, and welcome. I'm sure you all know me, Hamish McKinlay. I'm the co-writer of this musical, *The Flower of the Highlands*, along with my partners Jomo Wairimu and Zane Diaz. And I'm sure you know why you're here this evening among an audience of specially invited guests, friends, family, sponsors.' Hamish gave a mischievous wriggle of his eyebrows. 'We're here to give you a tiny taste – some scenes, just a few songs and dances. Our musical tells the tragic tale of young Flora Fraser, a talented but unknown singer from the Highlands of Scotland, who is propelled to stardom by her ambitious manager. But when you've climbed to the dizzy heights of fame...' Hamish paused dramatically, '...there's a long way to fall.'

There was a small noise of agreement from the audience. Hamish continued. 'We were very lucky to cast Ruthie Morgan as the lovely Flora and Cornell Abayomi as Ethan Barrett, her manager, and we have some exceptional musicians from our orchestra here with us today. Anyway, enough from me – let's let the show do the talking. So, without further ado... welcome, all.'

Hamish gave a little bow as applause echoed around the theatre. The lights dimmed and Hamish walked over to the piano, sitting down and wiggling his fingers. Then the theatre was in blackout and a thunderous chord crashed, followed by a gentle tinkling like rain. Mimi held her breath.

The orchestra played a tender melody, soft as a breeze, as the stage was illuminated in luminous green and yellow. A young woman came on, her hair dark and curly, just as Mimi's had been when she was eighteen. Mimi held her breath as Flora, humble in a plain dress, sang a song about being a simple Highland girl who believed that one day she would sing for the world. Mimi's skin tingled; Flora's voice was pure, crystal clear, full of hope, ambition and yet tinged with vulnerability, the fear of failure. Mimi liked Flora immediately; she understood exactly how the character was feeling; she wanted to applaud and cheer before she had even finished her song.

Then the music changed, more dramatic. The manager, Ethan Barrett, sang to Flora with a smooth rich voice full of promises. He didn't look at all like Donald, but Mimi saw something in him, the confident gesture, the perfect fit of his clothes, the way he waved Flora's doubts to one side with a flick of his fingers, so reminiscent of her husband. Mimi knew immediately that Flora would be putty in his hands. She wanted to shriek warnings to Flora who quickly changed her hair colour to blonde and became Barrett's mistress, but she gripped Fin's hand on one side and Jess's on the other.

Mimi remained transfixed for thirty minutes as dancers dressed as roaming deer pirouetted gracefully through Highland forests. Then popping strobe lights revealed leaping shadows in Barrett's nightclub where he met women while Flora sobbed alone at home. Mimi watched the final scene as Flora sang a tragic song, 'Alone in a Crowd', a simple violin reaching the high notes for her as she faded to silence. She hadn't moved; her face was wet with tears.

The house lights were bright again: Mimi came back to reality as the theatre resonated with applause. Ruthie and Cornell held hands centre-stage and bowed; the space was suddenly filled with other cast members, dancers and the musicians from the orchestra stood up and bent their heads in acknowledgement. Hamish bounded from his piano; his face flushed with excitement.

'Thank you so much. I hope you've enjoyed a small soupçon of things to come from *The Flower of the Highlands*, which will open in this theatre next September after a run in Edinburgh and Manchester. But now we have arranged a small reception in the bar upstairs; if you would all like to go on through, the cast and I will join you shortly.'

The bar, shielded from public attention by closed doors and several vigilant attendants in uniforms, was a long room with a plush red carpet and chandeliers hanging from the ornate plaster ceilings. Mimi clutched the stem of a glass of white wine and gazed around the room full of guests. Fin was chatting to a tall man in a smart suit, as if they'd known each other for a long time. Jess was talking to Cornell Abayomi, who played the unscrupulous manager Barratt: he seemed to be telling the story of his life.

Mimi hadn't eaten any of the canapés constantly offered to her by young men and women in black and white attire. Her stomach felt as if it held a fluttering butterfly; she was nervous and yet strangely at home. She glowed with pride. Hamish was living the life she'd always hoped for him. She was sure this musical would be an outstanding success, propelling Hamish as a composer to greater heights.

Part of her still ached for young Flora Fraser who, by the end of the show, had been abandoned. Mimi stood stiffly; she knew how it felt to be alone. The hurt stayed under the skin like a spreading bruise she tried to forget, but the wound was tender. Mimi swallowed wine and for a moment, she felt better; the sharpness on her tongue seemed to pull her away from sad thoughts.

There was a voice at her elbow, a young woman with dark wavy hair who smiled and said, 'You must be Hamish's mother.'

Mimi gazed at Flora Fraser in sympathy, then she felt immediately foolish; it was Ruthie Morgan, the singer who had played the role. Mimi nodded. 'Hello, yes, I'm Mimi Solitaire.'

Ruthie was delighted. 'Hamish said he wrote the whole show for you. My character is based on you. I'm honoured to play Flora.'

Mimi was flushed with warmth. 'The honour is all mine.' She felt a familiar surge of empathy towards another performer. 'I loved the way you made Flora so innocent and at the end she was alone. I understood her completely. And the singing – oh, you have such a pure voice.'

'Thank you,' Ruthie said. 'So, you were a dancer in the forties?'

'The fifties,' Mimi corrected her. 'And I used to sing too.'

'Oh, which theatre did you perform in?'

Mimi put a hand to her head. 'I started off in Bermondsey –

my husband, of course I wasn't married to him then, partly owned it.' She took a breath. 'Then I went on to perform in the West End – all over.'

'Which musicals?' Ruthie's eyes widened. 'The fifties must have been such a wonderful time to be on stage.'

'Oh, yes.' Mimi waved a hand as if trying to remember. 'I was in *My Fair Lady* with Julie Andrews and *The King and I* with Yul Brynner. Oh, they were such good times, such lovely people.'

'Julie Andrews.' Ruthie was impressed. 'She did *My Fair Lady* on Broadway, didn't she?'

Mimi's voice was firm. 'She performed here first.' She continued quickly. 'We wore such lovely clothes in the chorus, flapper dresses, cloche hats...'

'It sounds wonderful,' Ruthie agreed. 'And Yul Brynner – did you actually meet him?'

'Oh, yes, a charming man – he was even more handsome close up. And he played the King of Thailand...'

'Siam, wasn't it, originally?'

'Didn't I say King of Siam?' Mimi was momentarily flustered then she gave a small shrug. 'Oh, but we wore gold harem pants and tall ornate helmets, sprayed gold, like a pagoda.' She pushed her shoulders back to demonstrate that she still had poise. 'It was so lovely to work with Yul.'

Then Hamish was at her side. 'Ruthie, has Mum been telling you all about her theatre days?'

'Yes, it's really interesting...'

'I'm so sorry to interrupt.' Hamish put up a hand. 'Er, Mum, there's a man at the door claiming he knows you and security are having a bit of a hard time with him. He's refusing to go away until he's spoken to you.'

Mimi waved a gracious hand. 'Is it the man from the Bellaire restaurant?' She offered an expression of complicity. 'I'm sure you understand, Ruthie – some men are obsessive...'

Hamish shook his head. 'It's someone called Charlie Gosling.'

Mimi froze. 'Charlie?'

Hamish put out a hand to steady her. 'He says you both go back a long way. He heard about the show on the radio and he was sure you'd invite him in. He's been outside for over an hour.' Hamish raised his eyebrows. 'Shall I tell security to kick him out?'

Mimi's eyes had become wild. 'Charlie? Are you sure? No, you must let him in.' She turned to Ruthie. 'Do I look nice? I mean...' She looked around, then called out, 'Jess – please, can you help me?'

Jess was by her side in a moment. 'Are you all right?'

'Oh, oh yes.' Mimi drank her wine in a gulp and fanned herself with one hand. Her heart was knocking hard. 'Yes, it's just – it's Charlie. He's outside and I haven't seen him in – in years.' She gripped Hamish's arm with talon-like fingers, her face feverish. 'Let him in, please, Hamish. It's Charlie. Oh, my goodness me. Charlie Gosling. You must let him come in at once.'

32

'Blimey, you haven't changed a bit...'

Mimi stared at Charlie Gosling, who had been waiting outside in the rain, his grey coat damp, darker on the shoulders, a flat cap on his head covering white hair. He was obviously much older than she remembered him, his smile was different, his stomach a little rounder and his face lined. But the crinkled mischievous eyes, the playful tone of his voice, his ready grin were still the same.

As he stepped towards her, the years melted away and she remembered the young man in his teens, smart in his uniform, who had greeted everyone with a joke at the theatre in Bermondsey. He'd been shy when they first met, gazing at Mimi with awe because she was a few years older and more sophisticated. Then she'd married the boss, but they stayed close. He spoke to the showgirls with respect and humour, and he'd share cigarettes and sweets and gossip. Mimi knew he secretly admired her. She'd catch him watching her and he'd blush with embarrassment. Later, when he was in his twenties and used to the sight of the girls running around in underclothes, when she'd married

Donald, and had the boys, he was a faithful friend. Charlie helped her out a few times when she felt low or rejected, when she'd broken the heel of a shoe, or when she'd needed advice or a square of chocolate, he'd never let her down.

Mimi gasped. 'Charlie, you've hardly changed either.'

He took both her hands and looked her up and down. 'You look a million dollars, Mimi. Is this a new fashion, ladies wearing men's jackets as dresses? It's very nice.'

'It's my son's. I stole it. Do you remember Hamish, my youngest? He's one of the composers.'

'He was just a baby...'

Charlie stopped, his eyes fixed on Mimi's, and they gazed at each other. Mimi recalled the rising notes of an orchestra, the girls dancing, legs kicking high, and Charlie peeping from behind the curtains, watching, his thumb up. She remembered just how nice he was.

Then she noticed the damp raincoat. 'Have you been outside long? You're soaked. And no one's offered you any refreshment.' Mimi lifted a hand and a waiter was by her side, holding out a tray of drinks. Another was at her elbow, offering canapés. 'Knock yourself out, Charlie,' she offered. 'It's all free.'

Charlie held a glass of wine in one hand and a finger roll in the other. Mimi took his elbow. 'Let's go downstairs into the theatre and sit in the stalls. It'll be just like old times. Then you can tell me everything you've been doing since 1964.'

* * *

Mimi and Charlie sat in the stalls, their heads close; people moved busily around the theatre, musicians packing instruments into cases, technicians rolling cables of wire. Someone had filmed the performance and was packing away camera gear into cases.

Mimi didn't notice the constant buzzing of voices; her eyes were on Charlie.

He sipped wine. 'I knew you'd moved away – I heard Donald had taken you back to his home in Scotland.'

'He did – he's gone now. I missed London so much.'

'But you were a busy mother – you were bringing your boys up. There can't have been much time for anything else.'

Mimi continued. 'I was miles away from all my friends. Yes, I had the boys. Don't get me wrong – I was so glad to be with them all the time, but I missed the theatre.'

'It was in your blood, the theatre – mine too,' Charlie said. 'When I left to become a window cleaner, the money was better and the hours regular – especially since the missus had the little ones – but I missed the life, the banter, the jokes.'

'Where is your wife now? And the children?'

'Jean passed away a few years ago,' Charlie said thoughtfully. 'David's a schoolteacher – I am so proud of my two – Lizzie designs silver jewellery, she's doing well. They both live nearby – they come over at weekends. I have grandchildren too...' He sighed. 'All flown the nest. Most of the time, it's just me.'

'I know how it feels to be by yourself, with only memories as friends.' Mimi shuddered.

Charlie patted her hand. 'It's been so good to catch up with you – when I heard your son on the radio talking about you, such pride in his voice, and about the musical he'd written, I had to find you.' His face was earnest. 'It took me an hour on two buses to get here – roadworks everywhere in London now. I spent most of the time staring out the window at traffic signs.'

'Finlay insists we go everywhere in a taxi when we're in London,' Mimi replied. 'And we're still always stuck in roadworks, gazing out of the window.'

'I say – what's your favourite traffic sign?'

'Favourite? I don't know – they are all the same.' Mimi was thoughtful. 'We get pretty crystal shapes on signs in Scotland, that means a high chance of snow...'

'I like the roadworks one, that poor chap in the triangle struggling to open the umbrella...'

Mimi thought for a moment, then the image came to her, and she let out a peal of laughter. 'Charlie, you're so funny...'

'Mind you,' he frowned. 'They should change that one they put up outside the old folks' home – the two bent banana people crossing the road, the man leaning on a stick and the woman hanging on behind him as if she can't stand up by herself. I don't like that one. It's disrespectful. It's as if we old codgers are all feeble.' His face was fierce. 'And we're not.'

Mimi patted his cheek. 'Still the same old Charlie, funny and sweet.'

Charlie was still scowling. 'I might be long in the tooth, Mimi, but I'm not senile. There's not enough respect for older people.' He wagged a finger. 'Or enough opportunities for the youngsters. Do you know, I used to run a club for kids when my two were little – just to give the less advantaged ones something to do at nights: we did dancing, boxing, keep fit. I even got someone in to produce a musical once. *Oliver!* it was. Not really my sort of thing. Too much wife-beating and glorification of poverty.' He clenched a fist. 'And anti-Semitism.'

Mimi was observing him carefully, her mouth open. 'Charlie – I love *Oliver!*'

'Oh, dear.' His face was anxious. 'I hope I haven't offended you.'

'Not at all – I can't imagine Donald ever saying such things,' she replied. 'You sound just like Angus.'

Charlie raised his eyebrows and said, 'The boy that wasn't Donald's.'

Mimi sighed. 'Yes.'

'That all went down very badly...'

'I never mention the whole story.' Tears appeared in Mimi's eye. 'Even Angus doesn't know what happened to his father. I hated Donald for what he did.'

'Donald was possessive.' Charlie took her hand. 'Some men in those days had a very peculiar way of showing love. He was all wallet where you were concerned. He bought you the very best, fought his way into your affection and thought that love meant ownership.'

'You're so right, Charlie. That's how it was then.'

'But not now. Not these days. I might be old, but I'm a man of today. I think women need to be treated right.' He brought her hand to his lips. 'I never forgot about you, Mimi. It's been a long time, but I always hoped we'd meet up one day...'

'So did I...' Mimi smiled. A small cough came from nearby. Fin had arrived, with Jess at his elbow. He spoke softly to Mimi as if they were sharing a secret. 'It's time we were going back to Islington now, Mother.'

'Finlay, Jess.' Mimi's face was serious. 'This is my friend, Charlie Gosling. We know each other from years ago, when I was in the theatre. Charlie was the door boy at Bermondsey, the theatre your father owned, Finlay.'

Jess was delighted. 'Pleased to meet you, Charlie.'

Fin shook Charlie's hand formally. 'Charlie.' He turned his gaze on Mimi. 'There's a taxi waiting for us outside.'

Mimi's expression was imperious. 'Will it seat four, Finlay?'

'Of course.'

'Then it's decided. Charlie is coming back.'

For a moment, Fin appeared flustered. 'I suppose he could stay for an hour or two...'

'He can stay as long as I say he can.' Mimi was insistent. 'And that's final.'

Fin was unsure. 'We've only three bedrooms...'

Charlie smiled. 'I don't want to intrude.' He stared hard at Fin, his mouth curving in recognition. 'I remember changing your nappy when you were a pup, young Finlay.' He turned back to Mimi. 'That was almost a lifetime ago. Your mother and I have some catching up to do.'

'Indeed we do,' Mimi said haughtily, standing slowly. Jess wrapped an arm around her, but Mimi held out her hand to the man in the cap and raincoat. 'Come on, Charlie – we'll go together.'

* * *

Fin walked up and down in the lounge, clutching a glass of whisky in his hand, his voice thick with anxiety. 'They've been in her room for hours, Jess – it's gone eleven.'

Jess said, 'She's enjoying herself, Fin.'

'But who is this man? She's only just met him again after, I don't know, fifty-something years? He might be anyone...'

'They're making up for lost time. She's happy,' Jess explained. 'Hamish's musical's going to be good...'

Fin flopped down next to her. 'It was a great afternoon. Hamish was very pleased – it was good publicity, all the right people there.'

'Where is Hamish now?'

'Out with friends – he won't be back until tomorrow, I'm sure. But it's not Hamish I'm bothered about right now.' He turned to Jess. 'Do you think I'm crazy, worrying about my mother in there with that man? We don't even know who he is.'

'He's Charlie.' Jess put gentle fingers on his hand. 'He's an old friend.'

'But is he?' Fin's face was strained. 'Shouldn't he go home now?'

'Do you want me to go in and check on her?'

'You think I'm being the overprotective son, don't you, Jess?' Fin sighed. 'But my mother is very trusting. I'd hate to see her hurt...'

'I think you're being thoughtful,' Jess soothed. 'And it would be very easy for me to knock on the door and pop my head round, ask if they'd like a coffee.'

'Would you do that?' Fin was relieved.

'Of course I will.' Jess nudged his arm playfully. 'I've no idea what you think I might find in there. Two old friends chatting...'

'Kissing?' Fin shook his head.

'If they are, then that's fine,' Jess told him. 'They deserve a bit of happiness. We all do.'

'I agree with that sentiment.' Fin was staring at her. 'Mother's not the only one whose life could be improved by finding that special someone to spend time with. When this is all over with Karen, I...' He paused.

Jess met his eyes. 'You'll what?'

'Ah, we'll see.' Fin finished the last of his whisky in one mouthful.

Jess stood up quickly. 'I'll go and check on Mimi, shall I?'

'Thanks, Jess – for everything.'

Jess padded through the lounge into the hallway, stopping outside Mimi's room to knock. There was no sound from inside, no talking. She knocked again. There was no reply.

'Mimi?'

Jess pushed the door open and stepped into the room, peering in the light of a softly glowing bedside lamp. She saw two figures lying on the bed, fully clothed. The scarf Mimi had borrowed from Hamish and Charlie's shoes were lying on the floor, abandoned. Mimi and Charlie were both breathing lightly, fast asleep.

Jess used both sides of the duvet to cover them, wrapping them warmly in turn. She turned off the lamp and, as she leaned forward, she noticed Mimi's face was utterly peaceful, the hint of a smile curving her lips.

33

Fin stared at his laptop: it hadn't exactly been the long weekend break in London he'd planned, that was for sure. And now on Monday evening, he was searching through the British Airways website, trying to buy another ticket, a frown on his face.

He'd wanted to spend Sunday with his mother but when he'd woken, Jess was in the kitchen drinking tea, telling him that his mother and Charlie had gone out on a sightseeing tour and wouldn't be back until late. To compound the problem, Hamish hadn't returned to the flat either: the trip to see *Hamilton* had been forgotten. Jess had gone to an art gallery, then met Hamish and his friends for lunch.

Fin had spent most of his day of rest on the phone, attempting to sort out a business deal. Mimi returned with Charlie on her arm and a sparkle in her eye, full of excitement: they'd shared breakfast with Isabella and Lionel in their hotel, spent the morning in the park reminiscing, then Charlie had somehow found four last-minute tickets to a matinee of *Singing in the Rain* at Sadler's Wells. They had all enjoyed themselves thoroughly; the fifteen-minute ride back to the flat hadn't been long enough for Mimi to enthuse about how delightful it had been. She'd talked about it non-stop for forty minutes before she and Charlie holed up in her room. Fin was astonished at his mother's newfound energy – and, as he'd said to Jess later, she hadn't even asked for a glass of Chardonnay.

Earlier that morning, Mimi had disappeared with Charlie, clutching credit cards with the intention of visiting Harvey Nichols and buying herself a completely new wardrobe. She intended to donate all the old evening wear in her suitcase to a charity shop. She announced boldly that she was a different woman now, then she and Charlie had left, chatting together, their heads close. They had arrived back at the flat, having enjoyed a long afternoon tea with Isabella and Lionel in the Savoy, courtesy of Hamish and his friends. Mimi was wearing a new red woollen dress, clutching bags of clothes and shoes and a CD that Hamish's friend Zane had made for her that contained all the songs from *The Flower of the Highlands*. She explained every detail of the cakes they had ordered and how smart the waiters' uniforms had been. Then, all of a sudden, Mimi cleared her throat, demanding attention. She had a special announcement: Charlie was coming back to Scotland to stay for a while. Fin would need to buy another ticket for the aeroplane journey to Inverness.

Fin immediately rang Angus for support but Angus was non-committal. He had said that Mimi was an adult and she could do as she liked; furthermore, he had to get off the phone soon as Mila was there and, given the amount Fin was paying her, he should probably let her get on with her work. Fin had then phoned Hamish, who said that he thought Charlie was a lovely bloke and he found the whole thing hilarious, that his mum was spending time with a man in a flat cap who was clearly a socialist, completely the opposite of their capitalist father. Hamish then reminded Fin that Jess was leaving in a couple of weeks so it would be quite sensible for Mimi to have Charlie to stay, especially since Angus would be off on his travels at the first opportunity. Besides which, Hamish suggested, if Mimi and Charlie were old friends, what was the problem?

Fin cautiously asked Hamish if he thought Charlie Gosling was after Mimi's money and Hamish said no, he seemed an honest sort, but did it matter if he was, as long as Mimi was happy? Fin shook his head, confused by Hamish's remark, and poured himself a whisky.

Fin searched the website for the flight they were due to catch the next day; there were two remaining seats and he bought one quickly. He had arranged the first booking so that he, Jess and Mimi could sit together, but he supposed he'd be sitting alone now: Mimi wouldn't allow herself to be parted from Charlie and he wouldn't ask Jess to take the solitary seat.

Fin closed down the website, reaching for his glass, taking a swig of sharp whisky. He was conscious of someone standing behind him. Jess put a light hand on his shoulder. He swivelled round. 'Is everything all right – with the lovebirds?'

'Mimi and Charlie are in their room.'

'*Their* room?' Fin's eyebrows shot up.

'Charlie has phoned for a takeaway meal: they are having fish and chips tonight. I promised to answer the door. The delivery will be here at seven.'

'Fish and chips? I'm not sure my mother has eaten fish and chips in her life. Whatever next?' Fin gazed at the clock on the wall. It was almost seven o'clock. He sighed. 'Shall I cook us something? An omelette, maybe? We could open a bottle...'

'I have an idea...' Jess said. 'Why don't I treat us to dinner? I like the look of the Turkish restaurant down the road. Do you think they'll have a table?'

Fin's expression brightened. 'I'll phone and check.'

By eight o'clock, Jess and Fin were sitting at a small cloth-covered table in the corner of a long room, sharing warm lavaş bread with cheese, oil and walnuts and a bottle of Lebanese red wine: halfway through the second glass, Jess was feeling mellow and relaxed. Fin seemed to have settled to the idea that his mother and her new beau were tucked up in bed with a glass of beer each and a tray of fish, chips and mushy peas. He shrugged. 'Well, the visit to London wasn't exactly as planned. I'm sorry, Jess – I had wanted to make it a real McKinlay family weekend.'

'I've enjoyed myself. I caught up with Saffy, which was really lovely – I've missed her. I've been to a gallery, had a great lunch with Hamish, Jomo and Zane, and the musical preview was fabulous.' Jess tore the hot bread in her fingers.

'I'm glad,' Fin said. 'You know we think of you as one of the family.'

'Thanks, Fin.' Jess exhaled. 'I've had a great time working with Mimi. She's lovely. I mean, I'm not really carer material, but it's worked out well...'

'You're very caring.' Fin's eyes glowed. 'We're all very fond of you.'

'All?' Jess couldn't help it. 'You and Hamish are really easy to get on with, but...'

'Angus? Has he been difficult?'

'No, not at all.' Jess hadn't meant to mention him, but he was never far from her thoughts. She tried an excuse. 'He's just not as... spontaneous as you and Hamish.' She recalled the kiss in the forest: that had certainly been spontaneous. She was smiling.

Fin said, 'Angus is independent. He was wild as a kid, always out in the woods while Hamish and I were at home, studying. And since his wife died, he's become even more reclusive.'

'It must have been hard.' Jess wanted to ask more about Angus's past, but she didn't want to sound too interested.

'It was tough. He's a good father to Fabrice, though – he visits him in Toulouse whenever he can, but I think he's still grieving,' Fin said sadly. 'I don't think Angus will ever find anyone he'd love like he loved Augustine.'

Jess suddenly felt awkward. She gulped wine, wondering what was happening to her, why she was suddenly feeling as if she had been rejected, as if an opportunity for something beyond friendship with Angus had been snatched away. She sighed. 'Well, I'll be going home soon.'

Fin met her eyes. 'We'll miss you, Jess.'

Jess stared down at her plate. 'I'll miss everyone too. Christmas will be dull...'

'You'll be with Saffy.'

'Oh – she's going to Dublin now. I'll be by myself,' Jess blurted and then placed a hand over her mouth. She wasn't used to drinking wine: she hadn't intended to tell Fin that she'd be alone. She made her face as happy as possible and took another gulp from her glass. 'I'll be enjoying my new cottage. It'll be great. And I'll probably invite Paul, my brother, and Jodie and Luke – I haven't seen them in ages.'

'Ah...' Fin seemed about to say something, then he changed his mind. 'Well, I wonder if we'll have Charlie with us this year? Isabella will be there, and she has this new antiques man. I might invite a few people round, some friends, maybe Alasdair and Faye. We'll have a houseful.'

Jess felt suddenly sad. The McKinlay Christmas sounded so joyously festive, so much more fun compared to being by herself in an empty house. She dipped her bread in oil. 'You'll have a great time.'

'Christmas in our family is always special,' Fin enthused. 'But

Hogmanay is the best time ever.' He met her eyes. 'I wish you could be there.'

'It sounds wonderful.' Jess was immediately irritated with herself. She had definitely drunk too much – she felt ridiculously emotional; she needed to get a grip on herself.

Jess finished the remains of her wine and Fin refilled her glass. She instantly swallowed another mouthful and, like the intoxicating hit of alcohol, she realised something she had been holding back. She had been pretending there wasn't a problem, but now reality had hit her full force, like the thunder of a passing train. She didn't want to leave Scotland; she would miss Mimi. The McKinlays had taken her into their lives, and she had taken them into her heart. She was fond of Fin and Hamish; they had treated her warmly, with respect, like family, and she would miss them too. But most of all, she would miss Angus: he was aloof, brooding, but he was also warm, affectionate, sweet and kind. She had a bond with him, more than a bond: she'd been struggling to admit it to herself, but she was in love with him. She would miss him most of all.

Fin was staring again, noticing the tears that shone in her eyes. He assumed Jess was embarrassed by his constant pressure on her to stay for Christmas; she was clearly a free spirit and ready to go home. Her lifted his glass. 'To new beginnings, Jess.'

Jess took a deep breath and raised her wine glass, making her voice confident and strong. She would not be held to ransom by her emotions. It was important to move on, to stay in control. 'To new beginnings, Fin.'

* * *

Hamish and Isabella, with Lionel in tow, chattered excitedly as they stood at the entrance to Heathrow airport. As Hamish hugged Jess, she wondered if she'd ever see him again, but he moved swiftly to Mimi, kissing his mother's cheek, promising to see her at Christmas time. Isabella had an announcement too: her face shone as she told everyone that she and Lionel were driving to Italy. They were going to stay in Palermo with her niece: they would enjoy the Italian sunshine – Scotland was far too cold in December – but she'd probably be back in time for Christmas. However, she laughed with a twinkle in her eye, if she felt like it, she would stay forever.

Charlie looked around as he boarded the plane, holding a new case, murmuring about how much air travel had changed; that he hadn't been on a plane since he and Jean had holidayed in Benidorm. Fin took the seat by himself further down the plane, and Mimi positioned herself between Charlie and Jess. She was excited, making plans with Charlie about what they would do in Drumnadrochit, then she told him all about the fun times, cream teas and the Hallowe'en ball where she had taught everyone to dance 'The Time Warp'. Charlie leaned over Mimi, his eyes shining. 'I can just imagine her doing that, Jess. She was always a one for leading the dancing.'

Jess enthused, 'You should see Mimi's apartment, Charlie. She has some wonderful costumes – feathers and silky dresses. She's a great dancer.'

Charlie's eyes shone. 'Perhaps you'll dance with me, Mimi Solitaire?'

'Perhaps I will, Charlie Gosling.' Mimi raised an eyebrow. 'My dancing days are certainly not over. But the first thing I'll do when we get home is to ask Finlay to get a television for you. I want you to be comfortable. You can stay as long as you wish.'

'We'll take things day by day. But I don't want you to change anything for me.' Charlie was insistent.

'What about your house, Charlie?' Jess asked. 'Will it be all right?

'Oh, it's just a little terrace. My son David will look after it for me while I'm away – and Sally, the neighbour, she's a good sort. They both have a key.' He glanced at Mimi. 'I won't miss it while I'm in Drumnadrochit. I'll miss David and Lizzie and the grand-children, though.'

'We can invite them up to visit us. That will be wonderful. You could stay until Christmas, into the New Year. We have plenty of time to decide what we'll do.' Mimi turned to Jess and smiled. 'I thought we could go on a cruise in January. Charlie has never been to the Caribbean. He has a bad chest in the winter; I thought the sunshine would do him good.'

Charlie said to Jess, 'Mimi says the air is purer in Scotland. She says it's wonderful, the view over the loch from the apartment.'

'It is,' Jess sighed. 'Especially in the morning when the mist is hanging low, or when the sun goes down and it's just like an orange ice lolly melting into the water... and the forests, the deer at night...' Jess stopped herself. 'You'll love it, Charlie.'

'As you love it, Jess,' Mimi pointed out. 'I'm a London girl and I'll always miss the city life, but Scotland steals your heart away.'

Jess sat back in her seat, closing her eyes. Images came flood-ing; the view from the house over the loch; the ride through the forest, clinging to Angus as the bike climbed uphill; the thunder of the waterfall in her ears as she was surrounded by darkness so intense that she couldn't see her hand. She realised that Mimi was talking to her and she opened her eyes. 'Sorry?'

'Jess...' Mimi had been worrying about Jess leaving before Christmas; the idea was making her fretful. 'You must come up to stay with us next year. We could all go to Skye in the spring.'

'That would be nice.'

'We could drive there, maybe stop somewhere nice for lunch – you could stay for the weekend in your flat. I'll keep it empty just for you...' Mimi threaded an arm though Charlie's and laid her head on his shoulder. 'There might even be snow on the mountains.'

'Snow in springtime, eh? That's romantic, Mimi, my dear.'

'Oh, it will be wonderful, Charlie. You'll stay on for spring, won't you? You'll love Scotland so much.'

Jess closed her eyes, visualising the trip to Skye: in her imagination, it was a cold winter's morning, the pine branches hung with snow, the mountain tops white as if dredged with too much sugar icing. But it wasn't Mimi and Charlie who were with her; she saw it all from the back of a motorbike. She imagined herself on the beach, her arms wrapped around Angus, her cheek against his chest. She recalled him saying he'd like to take her around the Highlands, the Orkneys, the Hebrides. They'd drive along an open road, craggy rocks and the ocean on either side; they'd share laughter and take photographs of the wildlife, and he'd hold her in his arms.

Jess exhaled; she was being foolish. In two weeks' time, she was going home. It had always been a temporary job; she'd known that from the start. She took another breath: she was fine.

They drove back to Drumnadrochit in Fin's Jaguar, which was in the airport car park, but now it had a layer of snow on the roof, sparkling in the light of the setting sun. Charlie peered through the window in the back seat, gazing at the scenery, muttering, 'This is just marvellous, Mimi.'

Mimi was glowing with pride. 'You wait until the morning. The view will be spectacular from our bedroom.'

Fin glanced at Jess in the passenger seat next to him and raised an eyebrow.

'I'm hungry,' Charlie said. 'I'll be glad when we get back for some grub.'

Fin's voice was smooth. 'I texted Angus earlier. He's pushed the boat out and made a family meal to welcome you, Charlie.'

'Oh, no.' Mimi put her hands to her face. 'Not rabbit food and that green sludge in a jug.'

'Angus can cook when he wants to,' Fin replied. He glanced at his mother through the driver's mirror. 'And there will be wine.'

He saw Mimi pull a face. 'I've gone off wine, Finlay. I shan't be drinking Chardonnay again.'

Fin glanced at Jess, his face flooding with relief.

'Charlie and I have decided that wine's not for us,' Mimi piped up from the back seat. 'We have beer now. It's a proper people's drink.'

Jess pressed her lips together to hide a smile.

Fin caught her expression. 'That's more wine for me and you tonight then, Jess.'

Jess pretended to yawn. 'I might pass on dinner, Fin,' she sighed. 'It's been a long day. I might just get an early night.'

34

Mimi and Charlie walked into the garden, their feet sinking into snow, and gazed up at the bright stars overhead. Charlie's heavy jacket was draped around Mimi's shoulders, the woollen dress warm beneath. He pointed at a glowing planet. 'That's Mars, look – it's bright tonight.'

'It is beautiful.' Mimi leaned her head against his shoulder. 'So... what do you think of Scotland so far?'

'It's very nice indeed.' Charlie paused for a moment, thinking. 'Dinner was delicious, the lasagne. Your Angus can cook all right. You have fine sons, Mimi. You must be proud of them.'

'Oh, I am.' Mimi's voice was soft. 'I don't tell them often enough. Especially Finlay – I'm too hard on him. He sometimes reminds me of Donald...'

'To look at, yes, he's got the same suave charm.' Charlie frowned. 'But they are chalk and cheese. Fin is warm, more in touch with his emotions.'

'He is. He's adorable. Hamish is more like me.'

Charlie shook his head. 'They are all like you, all three of them – more than you can see.'

'Angus looks like his father.'

'He does, very much.'

Mimi took a deep breath. 'Jess should stay on... I am really fond of her.'

'I wish she'd shared dinner with us. She's such lovely company. It's a shame she rushed off to her flat. Fin should make her his lady friend.' Charlie wrapped an arm around Mimi. 'I'm sure he likes her.'

'Who knows with Finlay and women? He never has much luck.' Mimi snuggled closer. 'I'm so glad I found you again, Charlie.'

'I had a soft spot for you, all those years ago; of course, you were Donald's wife. I couldn't say anything.'

'But not any more.' Mimi turned, gazing at him with sparkling eyes. 'I have been alone for so long now, it feels like I've had a magic wish granted, just meeting you again. Do you think we're being foolish, my dear?' Mimi squeezed Charlie's fingers. 'Hoping for happiness at our age?'

'Not at all.' Charlie reached for her fingers. 'Everyone wants the same thing, whether they are young or old – to mean something special to someone, to be the centre of somebody's world, like you're the centre of my world, Mimi.' He brought her hand to his mouth. 'You aren't getting cold out here, are you, my dear?'

'My heart is warm,' Mimi whispered. 'I'm here with you under the stars and I'll cherish it forever, the first time you told me how you feel.'

'I haven't told you yet,' Charlie protested. 'How did you know I was about to say I love you?'

'I just knew.' Mimi pressed a finger on his lips. 'We understand each other. We're the same, cut from the same cloth. And I know that, whatever happens to us, this moment is precious, and all our moments will be precious from now on because we have each other.'

Her eyes were glistening as she stared up at the skies, a black velvet canopy with diamond shards of stars. 'You told me that one's Mars.' She pointed a finger. 'And that one is Venus – there, the small and intensely bright one. Donald showed me that one years ago, but I didn't listen. I didn't really see the significance then. But now I know why it's important. Venus is the goddess of love. It's special.' Her face was calm. 'It'll be there for ever. It's beautiful.'

Charlie spoke softly. 'Beauty is truth, truth beauty – that is all ye know on earth, and all ye need to know.'

'What's that? Poetry? It's lovely.'

He kissed her. 'Keats, my dear. He could have written it about us, just standing together under the skies on a cold winter's night in Scotland.' He wrapped an arm around her, snuggled inside his jacket. 'We should go inside. I don't want you catching your death of cold.'

'Cold?' Mimi's eyes shone. 'I don't think I've ever felt so warm, Charlie – or so alive.'

* * *

Jess huddled on the bed in her room, her fingers massaging her temples, thinking. She should have joined the McKinlay family for dinner; she should have braved it out. She counted the days: today was the fourteenth – she'd leave on the twenty-third, so she had nine more days as Mimi's companion. She thought about asking Fin if it might be sensible for her to leave earlier, now Charlie was staying. Mimi wouldn't need her as much and it might be a good time to make a break. But she didn't want Mimi to take it personally. Jess could manage nine more days: she wouldn't see much of Angus, she'd spend a few evenings with Heather, and Amy too, if she could tear herself away from her new man.

Jess thought about the projects she could concentrate on once she returned home. Photography might be a nice hobby. She pulled out her phone and gazed at recent pictures she'd taken: the deer in the forest at night-time, the moon overhead.

She closed her eyes and sighed, then she threw her phone on the bed: all roads didn't have to lead to Angus!

There was a soft knock on the door. Jess was momentarily startled, then she called out, 'Who is it?'

A hushed voice came back. 'Room service.'

She knew the tone straight away. In a flash, she opened the door. Angus was there, smiling; he was carrying a tray, a plate of food and a bottle of wine.

'You missed dinner, Jess. I didn't want you to go hungry.'

Jess's eyes locked on his. She dragged them away, making her voice cheerful. 'Come in.'

Angus limped into the room, placing the tray by the bed, looking pleased with himself. 'I heard you were tired after the journey and Fin said you hadn't eaten much, so I saved you some lasagne.' He gazed around the room and back at Jess. 'How was London?'

'Fine, it was good fun...' Jess searched for something to say: she didn't want to tell him she'd missed him. 'How is Thor? How – how are you?'

'Thor's asleep in my room on his cushion. He's doing well, moving around now. Kelvin says he's about 98 per cent recovered in terms of his pelvis, which is as good as he'll get. That's a few per cent more than me,' Angus admitted. 'Mila's done a great job, but I think the limp will stay.'

Jess found herself hanging onto every word, enjoying the

sound of his voice. She searched for something to say. 'Do you want a glass of wine?' She immediately regretted her words: she hadn't intended to ask him to stay.

'That would be nice.' Angus moved slowly to a cupboard, brought out two glasses and sat down on the floor, leaning against the bed, pouring wine. Jess took in his easy movements; he was making himself comfortable in her room and she was suddenly edgy. He gazed at her. 'The lasagne's still hot.'

Jess sat down next to him, her shoulder inches from his, and picked at the food. She was determined she wouldn't drink much; it would make her thoughts muddy, and she mightn't be able to control her emotions as well as she'd like. 'This is lovely – thank you.'

'I didn't want you going hungry. I thought of you as I made it... I missed you this evening.'

Jess caught his soft gaze and turned away quickly, afraid she'd betray her own feelings. Angus sipped wine; the glass small in his large hands. 'Charlie seems a nice man. I like the way he thinks about the world.'

Jess agreed. 'Mimi likes him – that's the important thing.'

'He said he knew my father.'

Jess could hear the emotion in Angus's voice. 'Did he tell you anything about him?'

'I wouldn't ask him. That part of my history belongs to my mother. She's told me he was called Emile, from Louisiana, and that he was already married. I think he played the violin and they shared a night together.' Angus's eyes glowed and Jess looked away.

'You don't want to know more about him than that?'

'It's not important,' Angus said. 'Emile was my biological father. Donald McKinlay played the part of my dad throughout his life, and he did the best he could: there's nothing more to it.

My loyalty's to Mum: she'll tell me as much as she wants me to know.'

'It's good to see Mimi so happy.'

'It is,' Angus replied. 'She's waited long enough.'

'To be happy?'

'I don't think she's been truly happy since we left London as kids. She was lonely in the marriage – he didn't really spend quality time with her, with any of us. Loneliness is a bad place for everyone, whatever their situation.'

Jess sipped wine and watched him gaze around the room.

'Hamish had this flat as a teenager. He had some wild parties here.' Angus spoke softly. 'Hamish has always been a party animal. Mum loved it when he had friends round, his music turned up too loud. Dad used to shout and Mum would take Hamish's side. Like I said, she was a tigress and we were her cubs.'

'This house must have so many memories for you.'

'I stayed here for a while with Augustine, here in this flat.' He smiled. 'I can remember the look on her face when she came to Scotland for the first time, when she saw this house. It was so unlike anything she'd seen before. She liked this flat, though – it was quiet and we had the space to ourselves.' He met Jess's eyes. 'It was tough for her at first here because she didn't speak much English.'

'How did you communicate with each other?'

Angus raised an eyebrow. 'In French.'

'Did you meet her when you were working abroad?'

'Yes. Her father worked at the university in Yaoundé. I was doing some photographs for the faculty.' He was quiet for a moment. 'It's a long story, but at first it was difficult for some people to accept Augustine being with me. We had a few battles to fight in order to get married then we moved here, then to Paris and we had Fabrice. We spent a long time in Paris. Then she went back to visit Cameroon briefly while I was working in New Zealand. I received a call that she was ill and by the time I got to her...'

He shrugged. Jess was a little surprised to hear Angus being so open about his past. He turned to her, as if reading her thoughts. 'But what about you, Jess? What do you do in... Worcestershire?'

'Not much now. I was married, then I wasn't. I ran a hotel, then I sold it. Now I have my own place and I suppose the world is my oyster.'

'Do you have plans for when you get back?'

'No – not yet.'

Angus turned to her. 'So, you can go anywhere, do anything?' He touched her arm, resting his hand there, and Jess closed her eyes as he said, 'When you finish here at Christmas time, you can do whatever you like. That's a great position to be in.'

'What would you do?'

His eyes gleamed. 'I'd go to Canada and photograph the wildlife – lynx, moose – and the scenery is so special: Prince Edward Island, Abraham Lake, Yukon, New Brunswick, Alberta. After I've done the project in Sri Lanka next year, there's a chance I could go to Canada for a while and do some work for a magazine.'

'You'll be very busy.' Jess finished the last mouthful of wine, thinking that Angus had no time for a relationship in his life. She wondered if that was why he was here: perhaps he wanted to make sure she knew that he preferred to be independent and single, to be free to travel.

Angus poured more wine for her and Jess wondered why she didn't refuse it. She put her glass to one side; she needed to keep a clear head. He refilled his own. 'There's a possibility of a job in Borneo in the offing later in the year as well. I love travelling. It keeps me alive.' He sighed. 'I have Thor to think of – I make sure I spend quality time with him, and take him everywhere when I can. When I can't, there are lots of people prepared to make a fuss of him. It can be a lonely life though, when I'm away with just my own thoughts for company.'

'I'm sure it can.' Jess frowned, unsure of the signals: she had no idea if he was simply being honest and friendly, or if he had come to her room because he believed that there was something more to resolve between them, something special. Her thoughts moved quickly. She reminded herself to keep a check on her emotions, but it was too late: she was already ready to fall into his arms. 'So.' She tried to keep her tone light. 'You're off to Sri Lanka soon after the beginning of the New Year? You'll be ready to travel by then?'

Angus breathed out slowly and Jess knew something was wrong. His face was inches from hers. 'Jess...'

She caught her breath and waited. For a moment, she was sure he was going to kiss her again. She stretched out an arm for her glass, but she couldn't pull her gaze away.

'I came here to tell you something...'

Jess faced him. Whatever he was about to say, she was ready. 'All right.'

'When we kissed each other, the night when we were in the forest...'

'Mmm.' Jess remembered it well.

'I thought we might, you and I... You're very special...' Angus's voice trailed off. He stared around the room. 'I came to tell you that I'm going to Toulouse tomorrow. I'm going to spend Christmas with my son.'

'Oh.' Jess had expected him to say that he had feelings for her, or that he didn't have feelings for her: she hadn't expected him to say he'd be leaving. She wasn't sure how to react, so she stammered, 'What about Thor?'

'He'll be fine here for a while.' Angus leaned back against the bed and exhaled slowly. 'I came to say that we probably won't see each other again. I won't be back until well after Christmas and by then, you'll be gone.'

Jess couldn't find words, so she nodded.

'It's been very nice to meet you. Perhaps, you never know...' His eyes were dark, serious. 'Perhaps one day you'll be in your cottage in Worcestershire and you'll hear the sound of a motorcycle outside and I'll be there to take you for a ride...'

'I'd like that,' Jess said honestly.

He stood up slowly, a hand reaching to massage his thigh, then he picked up the tray. 'Well, I'd better be going. I'm up early tomorrow – Fin is giving me a lift to Inverness.'

Jess stood up, facing him. Their eyes caught and held for a moment, and she hoped he'd take her in his arms. Then she said, 'Have a good journey, Angus. Enjoy Christmas with your son.'

'I will,' he replied, limping towards the doorway. 'I'll think of you.'

Then he was gone. Jess stood where she was, frowning at the closed door. She wasn't sure what had happened: Angus seemed to have suggested that he cared for her, he'd almost kissed her and then he'd rushed away forever.

35

For the next few days, Mimi was queen of Glen Carrick House, fluttering around, organising everyone in preparation for the Christmas festivities. It was late afternoon, the sky already dark outside, the room filled with the soft glow of lamps. Mimi, wearing a warm jumper, stood in the centre of the lounge, ordering Fin where to place each decoration, helping Jess to tie baubles on the tall pine tree. Thor had started to follow Jess everywhere; he clearly missed Angus and had decided that Jess was the next best thing, even sleeping in the basement room at night.

Charlie stacked piles of logs in the hearth for a huge fire, his flat cap on his head and his overcoat on, damp where he'd been outside chopping wood for kindling. Fin protested that log chopping was his and Angus's job and, in the absence of Angus, he'd do it by himself. Then Heather arrived from the kitchen, tinsel woven in her hair, with a tray of mulled wine in glasses and they all sat round the long table, inhaling the sweet smell of cloves and cinnamon.

Mimi was in good spirits as she called for attention. 'Right.

Today's Monday. Christmas Day is on Saturday, so – Finlay, grab a pen and some paper – let's make sure we are organised.' She turned to Charlie and patted his hand. 'This will be the best Christmas ever.'

Fin gave a little cough. 'Food and drink are ordered – it will arrive mostly on Thursday. The tree is up, looking good – we can start putting presents around. Of course, I can't predict who'll get what this year but, just so you know, Mother, Angus and Hamish and I still haven't worn the socks you gave us last year.'

Heather laughed, and Jess smiled. Mimi stiffened as if a thought had just occurred to her. 'When's Hamish coming home?' Mimi grasped Charlie's fingers. 'Christmas won't be the same without Hamish.'

'He hasn't said yet,' Fin frowned. 'But he and his friends will be here for Hogmanay.'

'And Isabella is going to try to come for Christmas dinner.' Mimi waved a hand in triumph. 'She's hoping to be back from Italy on Christmas Eve.' Mimi's face was suddenly anxious. 'Will Angus be here in time for Hogmanay?'

'I'm not sure, Mother,' Fin said and Jess gazed at her fingers.

'I want everyone here.' Mimi folded her arms. 'I want this to be a spectacular Christmas.'

'It will be.' Fin met her gaze. 'I may invite a few extra people to dinner this year – leave it with me. I just have a few guests to finalise.'

'I've already said that I'll come,' Heather chirped. 'Thanks for asking me, Fin. I'd only be in the B & B by myself.'

'Make sure there's smoked salmon for Christmas breakfast please, Finlay.' Mimi pursed her lips. 'And extra cream: we have to make sure we have raspberries for the cranachan. It was always Hamish's favourite and I do want you to try it, Charlie.'

'I love cranachan,' Heather enthused. 'Have you sampled it, Jess?'

'Not yet.' Jess shook her head, smiling. 'But I think I'll make some for Christmas Day, so that I can remember you all.' Jess imagined herself in her cottage, everything pristine and unused, eating a creamy pudding by herself.

Mimi turned to Jess; her eyes sad. 'I can't imagine Christmas without you. I wish you could stay on.'

Jess smiled. 'You have Charlie. He'll be here.'

'Finlay, we need to talk about Jess's present – she's not leaving without something by way of a thank you.'

Jess hoped her face wouldn't give away her emotions. She made her voice bright. 'Oh, there's really no need.'

'And you must come up and visit us soon,' Heather added. Thor trooped across and plopped himself at Jess's feet beneath the table in agreement.

Fin met Jess's gaze. 'I wish you could be with us for Christmas. Aren't you going to be all by yourself now?'

'By yourself?' Mimi was horrified. 'You can't be alone at Christmas. You must stay here with us.'

Jess felt herself weakening: she took a breath. 'Saffy's going to Dublin, but I'll have my brother and his family – they'll probably come over.'

Charlie was looking at her levelly. 'When are you travelling back, Jess?'

'Thursday – the twenty-third. It means I won't be home until the twenty-fourth because I'll stay overnight somewhere on the drive down.'

'You're driving all that way?' Charlie looked concerned. 'Alone?'

'She's an independent woman, our Jess,' Heather smiled.

Mimi wasn't sure. 'It doesn't give you much time to get organised for the big day.'

'I'll take some things with me...' Jess suggested. 'There won't be a lot to organise.'

Mimi shook her head sadly. 'I'm not happy that you're leaving us.'

'I'll visit...' Jess said optimistically.

Heather suddenly stared at the ceiling and gasped. 'Mistletoe – oh, my goodness, there's no mistletoe, hen.'

Mimi looked around in horror. 'Oh, you're right. We've no mistletoe. And we'll need lots of it.' She turned to Charlie, offering him a sweet smile. 'We need to get some at once before it's all sold out. Finlay, can you go?'

'I'm going out tonight,' Fin said. 'I need to get ready.'

'Out again?' Mimi was shocked. 'You were out last night and the night before. Where are you going?'

'With friends.' Fin met her gaze. 'Alasdair and Faye.'

'Don't worry – I'll pop into Drumnadrochit and buy some now, before the shops shut,' Heather offered. 'Come with me, Jess. I'll drive – I haven't started on the mulled wine...'

Jess stood up, thankful not to be talking about her lack of plans for Christmas. 'All right.'

As they moved towards the door, Fin waved his wallet and called out, 'You'd best buy some more beer too – I think Mother and Charlie have drunk up our entire stock.'

* * *

Jess and Heather stood in front of a huge display of mistletoe, bright green leaves and shiny white berries, in the Co-op in Drumnadrochit. Heather lifted a handful. 'We'll need a lot –

Mimi will be kissing Charlie non-stop throughout the festive season.'

'I'm so pleased for her.' Jess filled her arms with a bunch. 'She's been a different woman since he came to stay.'

Heather agreed. 'Fin invited me for Christmas dinner – isn't that great?' She waved her arms full of mistletoe. 'Maybe I'll get a snog.'

'I thought you were off men?' Jess suggested.

'Yes, but Fin, though – any woman would.' Heather lowered her voice.

'Oh, I don't know...' Jess said.

'I get it – Angus is more your type.'

Jess felt her cheeks tingle, wondering if she had given her feelings away; she changed the subject quickly. 'I think that Mimi was very lonely in her marriage and quite dependent on Donald – after he died, she's found it hard.' They were carrying the bundles of mistletoe to the till. 'Charlie seems to have made her very happy.'

'I suppose love comes in all shapes and sizes at all ages,' Heather said and, as they turned the corner of the aisle, they almost ran into a woman in a smart coat, hair swishing around her shoulders. She was delighted to see them.

'Heather, Jess – I was just thinking about you.'

'Mila.' Heather tried to hug her, the mistletoe under one arm. 'We miss you up at Glen Carrick House.' She turned to Jess. 'Mila and I would often have a coffee in the kitchen when she'd finished Angus's treatment, while you were away.'

'Heather is very good at giving me all the inside information on the McKinlays,' Mila observed. 'While you were in London, we had some very interesting conversations...'

Jess knew that she'd be drawn into a discussion she'd prefer to avoid, so she waved the mistletoe and said, 'We're on an errand for Mimi.'

'I need to buy wine.' Mila frowned. 'I want something nice, a really good red. What does Fin drink, Jess? He has good taste.'

Jess thought for a moment. 'Burgundy – I remember when I first came, he opened a bottle of it.'

'Perfect. I'll buy that.' Mila's expression relaxed. 'By the way, has anyone else heard from Angus?'

Jess was suddenly anxious. 'Is he all right?'

'Oh, yes – he sent me some pictures today from Toulouse.' Mila waved her phone and flicked through some shots: the first picture was of Angus by a river with a handsome young man; the rest of the photos were of buildings: a domed structure, some sort of white palace. The sky was pale, and Jess wondered if it would snow there. Toulouse felt a long way away.

Mila pushed her phone in her pocket. 'I'd best be off – we must catch up for that coffee soon, Jess – you too, Heather.'

'That would be great,' Jess replied.

'Come for a quick one now, when you've bought your wine – we'll meet you at the door,' Heather suggested, pushing an arm though Jess's, dragging her towards the tills. She leaned towards Jess and put her mouth close to her ear, her voice low with conspiracy.

'So, Angus is messaging the lovely Mila?' She arched a brow. 'There's more going on between those two than meets the eye. Let's find out, shall we?'

Jess kept her expression calm; despite her heart thumping, she resolved that since she was going home soon, whatever might be between Angus and Mila was none of her business.

* * *

Mimi was sitting in the snug with Charlie, his cap firmly on his head, the CD of *The Flower of The Highlands* playing through speakers. Mimi was singing along: already she knew the words to the songs. She and Charlie huddled close together on the sofa, the laptop between them, gazing at photos: a white ship on the horizon of azure seas, a woman in an evening dress on deck watching a young man pour champagne into a glass. She clicked the mouse and sighed: the next picture was a luxury divan bed in a cabin, the windows open to reveal a distant island, crystal water, white sand, bowing coconut trees. She turned to Charlie. 'What do you think?'

'February in the Caribbean, cruising around St Lucia. It looks lovely, my dear.'

'Shall we book it?'

'I think we should, but not until I've spoken to Fin.'

Mimi frowned. 'What's Finlay got to do with it? I don't need his permission to go on holiday.'

Charlie's voice was soft. 'No, but I do. He's the oldest male of the family.'

'I'm the head of this family, Charlie.'

'I wasn't being sexist, my dear – I was being respectful.'

Mimi was still confused, more so by Charlie's soft laughter. She offered him a raised eyebrow. 'I don't understand why you need permission from Finlay to go on holiday with me. I mean, it's not as if he's my father and you're about to ask for my hand in...' She placed her fingers over her mouth, her eyes suddenly moist. 'Oh, Charlie.'

Charlie wrapped an arm around her, kissing her cheek. 'I ought to have asked you first...'

'You don't need to ask me. I'm yours.'

'Then let's make this a honeymoon cruise, Mimi – a February wedding.'

'Oh,' Mimi gasped. 'Oh, how wonderful.' She frowned again. 'You don't need to ask Finlay, though. I'm saying yes now.'

'It's about being honest, upfront. Fin's a man who sees things financially.' Charlie's voice was low. 'I've been frugal in my life – I'm not without savings, and I've been thinking it all out. I'll rent my house out in Southwark, cheap-like, to a young family who haven't got anywhere.' Charlie met Mimi's eyes. 'But I want to make it clear to your boys that I'm not out for profit. My feelings for you are genuine and I want to make sure they know that. There will come a time, Mimi, one day in the future...'

'Oh, don't talk about death, please, Charlie.'

'It's important to get it straight, though, especially if we're going to live here, in this house. In ten years, maybe – one of us will go first. Our kids are our beneficiaries. I don't want to take anything from your family and my will is already done, my two will get everything, the grandchildren...'

'Hugo made my will for me. I'll just ask him to go over everything for me once we're married. He'll update yours too, if you want. Hugo organises everything for the McKinlays. And I've told him I wanted my ashes scattered over the loch – I can't abide the thought of being buried next to Donald.' Mimi waved the thought away with her hand. 'Let's talk about weddings instead, shall we? Oh, Charlie – I can just see myself in an ivory gown, in a beautiful old church, my boys and your David in kilts. Angus will take photos. Your daughter will be matron of honour and Jess, too.'

'I think we should announce it in the New Year. We need to speak to your sons first, all three of them,' Charlie smiled.

Fin was in the doorway, smelling of aftershave. 'I'm off out now, Mother.'

'Blimey,' Charlie breathed. 'You're looking tidy, Fin.'

Fin was smart in a new jacket and jeans and a crisp shirt, a bottle of wine in his hand. 'Don't wait up.'

'Where did you say you were going, Finlay?'

'To dinner with Alasdair and Faye, Mother. I'm going by taxi so I can have a couple of drinks.'

'Well, don't do anything I wouldn't,' Charlie called with a laugh as Fin launched himself towards the front door.

Jess pushed the front door wide, her keys still in the lock, an arm full of mistletoe, and bumped straight into Fin, who was handsome and smelled of fresh pine. Fin seemed pleased to see her. 'I thought you'd have come back ages ago, Jess?'

'I went for a coffee with Heather and we met Mila...'

'Indeed?' Fin raised an eyebrow. 'And all this mistletoe? That's a good sign. Perhaps I'll get my Christmas kiss before you go?'

And he sauntered through the door, whistling, clearly in a fine mood. Jess watched him; her mouth open: the McKinlays were an unpredictable bunch.

36

On Wednesday evening, Jess packed her case and sat sadly in the basement, staring at it. She had accumulated far more luggage than she had brought and had to resort to filling carrier bags. She gazed for a long time at the photo Angus had taken of her by the bonfire, then she'd pressed it carefully between the pages of a large book and sighed. Mimi and Charlie had come down to the flat half an hour earlier, Mimi with a package wrapped in tissue paper, a Christmas present, and she and Jess both clutched each other and sobbed. Then Fin arrived, trying to persuade her to stay. Jess wasn't sure why she was still refusing: Christmas was going to be a non-event, but she had to drag herself away from the McKinlays and one McKinlay in particular who, although he was absent, filled her thoughts and her heart. Fin presented her with an envelope which he said she mustn't refuse: it contained a cheque, her Christmas present, and he said it wasn't nearly enough given the incredible job she'd done as Mimi's companion. Jess gave Fin a canvas bag bulging with presents for the family to put under the tree. There was one for Angus too, a scarf for him to wear when he was in the forest, or in Canada – she didn't want to draw attention by omitting him – and one for Thor, dog biscuits wrapped in brown paper.

That night Jess slept badly, Thor at her feet. When she woke, it was eight o'clock. She wondered if there would be anyone upstairs, or if she could simply slip away without any fuss. She knew she'd cry. But she was sure that once she was on her way with home in her sights, her new cottage and a new year on the horizon, she'd feel fine. Jess was nothing if she wasn't a survivor.

She climbed the stairs, reaching the kitchen, with her handbag, two cases and a laptop in her arms, Thor padding behind her. Fin was seated at the table, a mug of coffee in his hand, wearing a dressing gown, smiling broadly.

Jess put her luggage down. 'Fin?' Thor rubbed himself against her legs and Jess patted his head.

Fin left his seat and came over to her, standing behind her, placing his hands on her shoulders. He was cheerful. 'Are you sure you can't stay with us for Christmas? After all, you said your daughter is in Dublin – you don't *have* to go home, do you?'

'But I'm all packed...'

Fin propelled her towards the back door, heaving it open with some difficulty. Snow was banked up high, spilling soft powder onto the floor. An icy blast hit Jess in the face as she gazed out at thick twirling snowflakes. Fin shook his head. 'I'm not sure you're going anywhere today.'

Mimi and Charlie sauntered into the kitchen, all smiles. 'You were right, Finlay – I should have believed you when you said it would snow...' Mimi cooed, her face shining.

'I heard the weather warning last night, blizzards over Inverness, travelling ill-advised.' Charlie sounded pleased. 'So, I hope you'll stay for Christmas, Jess.'

Mimi threw her arms around Jess in a hug. Jess could smell the sweetness of jasmine. 'Stay for Christmas and Hogmanay, please. Say you'll stay, Jess – until after the piper has piped in the New Year. It'll be good luck for all of us...'

Jess nodded. 'All right. I'll have to phone Paul and talk it through with him but—' She was suddenly surprised how happy she felt. 'It looks like I'll be staying here after all.'

An hour later, Jess had replaced her clothes neatly in drawers in the flat. She rang Paul, a little anxious about what he would say. He answered immediately. 'Jessie?'

'Paul, I rang to say—'

'I've seen the pictures on TV of snow in the Highlands. Are the roads bad where you are?'

'Yes. It would be impossible to travel...' Jess took a breath. 'Paul, I'm going to stay on here until the New Year.'

'Ah.' Paul sounded relieved. 'So, you'll have Christmas in Scotland?'

'Yes, I'm sorry.'

'No, no, it's probably for the best: there have been some developments here.' She heard Paul take a breath. 'Cathy's turned up.'

'Luke's ex, Cathy?'

'Yes, she turned up yesterday afternoon all tears and apologies, and now she and Luke are back together up in his room, discussing their future.'

'That's good.'

'It's good that Luke's happy again, of course. But they want to stay here with us for Christmas and, quite honestly, Luke being here for so long in the doldrums drinking himself stupid every night has taken it out of me and Jodie – we've done nothing but argue – and we could do with some time for ourselves. He and Cathy are all loved-up now and, to be truthful, it's too much for us to put up with them for the entire Christmas break.'

'Oh.'

'Jessie.' Paul tried the wheedling voice he'd used as a child. 'I don't suppose that Luke and Cathy could stay in your cottage over Christmas, since you won't be using it? It would give me and Jodie a bit of time to be...'

'Of course.'

'The furniture's in place now, everything's wired up, and – well, they can come to us for Christmas lunch, but it would be nice just for me and Jodie to have some time to ourselves.'

'That makes sense...'

'Jessie, you're a star. I promise they'll keep the cottage pristine. You'll love the place when you're home – it looks really nice.'

'Brilliant.' Jess was thrilled. 'Happy Christmas, Paul. I'll put your presents in the post – and I'll send something for Cathy too.'

* * *

That evening the snow continued to tumble, the garden invisible beneath the crisp layer that glowed in the darkness beneath the moon. Fin reversed the Land Rover nicknamed the Big Beastie from the garage and he, Mimi, Charlie and Jess drove to Drumnadrochit for carol singing around the Christmas tree on the green, where groups of people were already congregating. Dressed in a thick woollen hat, scarf, coat, mittens and boots, Mimi was all smiles. There were damp snowflakes on her cheeks as she joined in 'O Come All Ye Faithful', hugging Charlie's arm for warmth. During the chorus of 'Ding Dong Merrily', Alasdair Harris arrived with his wife Faye, her hair tucked beneath a cloche hat. And when trays of mulled wine were handed around, with hot fruit punch for the drivers, Heather joined them, then Mila, smiling and shiny-faced as the snow made their cheeks glow under the lamplight.

Mimi gazed up at the tall pine tree, the baubles glittering, and said, 'This is how it feels to have friends. Life's so different now, compared to this time a year ago. Last Christmas, Angus was away somewhere, Thor had gone with him, Hamish was partying, and Fin was living in Inverness with Karen. I couldn't go carol singing by myself.' For a moment her face was sad. 'Ailsa wasn't keen to chat to me. I spent most of the time alone. My only company was music and dancing. I'd dress up in my costumes and drink wine all evening. I called it my Chardonnay Show Time.' She sighed. 'Loneliness is a disease, Charlie. And it's contagious – that's why people stay away from you, in case they catch it too.'

Charlie lifted a finger to her cheek, wiping away melting snow, a warm tear, both. 'You'll never be lonely again, my dear. Not while you've got me.'

* * *

Christmas morning was cold and bright, the sun gleaming on crisp snow. Jess took Thor out for a brisk walk by the loch while Mimi and Charlie made breakfast. The morning was spent in the kitchen, cooking. Mimi was bustling around organising everyone. Fin was in charge of the haggis-stuffed turkey and gravy, Jess would take care of the nut roast and sauces, Charlie would organise tatties, neeps, and other vegetables, and Mimi would lay the table, resplendent in a red plaid tablecloth and matching napkins, with place settings for ten people. Heather had already polished the candelabra, the cutlery and goblets. Mimi insisted on playing *The Flower of the Highlands* on repeat, although Charlie replaced it sneakily with a CD of Christmas hits.

Michael Bublé was singing 'It's Beginning to Look a Lot Like Christmas' just as Alasdair and Faye arrived, clutching wine and presents, explaining that the snow ploughs had been out in full force and cleared the main road to Inverness: the other guests should be able to get through, although cars were moving slowly. Mila turned up in a taxi fifteen minutes later, tinsel and mistletoe in her hair, and Heather made her arrival on foot just before three o'clock. Then, just as everyone was about to sit down to lunch, Isabella made her entrance, squealing with delight as she tugged Lionel behind her, hugging Mimi and showering everyone with panettone and Prosecco, trilling, 'I'm here! Happy Christmas! We flew in yesterday. I didn't think we'd make it, but the roads have been gritted. There was a tree down outside Beauly. Italy was wonderful! And guess what else? Lionel has persuaded me to give up smoking!'

'I have,' Lionel smiled. 'I want to keep her for as long as possible.'

Isabella laughed. 'Now I will probably die from all the alcohol I am going to drink this Christmas.'

Fin insisted on kissing all the women, shaking the men's hands firmly. Mimi served up sherry in delicate glasses and Charlie passed round a plate of nibbles. The fire in the hearth was blazing, red tinsel adorning the mantelpiece, as they all sat down for dinner at 3.30.

Fin carved the turkey; dishes were passed and plates were filled. Jess found herself sitting between Mimi and Fin. Mimi said, 'This is the most gorgeous Christmas, isn't it, Jess? I'm so glad you could be here with us.'

Charlie leaned over and winked. 'A proper family Christmas, eh? The only thing that would have made it better is Hamish and Angus being here, what do you say, Jess?'

'Of course...' Jess wondered momentarily if Charlie suspected her feelings. But after a glass of sherry, she felt warm and fuzzy and comfortable, among friends.

Fin cleared his throat and Mimi said, 'Go ahead, Finlay,' as he stood, holding up his glass. Everyone's eyes were on him as he paused, his face sombre.

'Thank you, Mother,' he began. 'As is traditional each Christmas, one of us makes a welcome speech before dinner. My father used to do it each year and as Hamish is in London, and Angus is in Toulouse, it falls to me to make the speech this year. Well...' His eyes shone as he gazed around the table. 'It's a pity my brothers aren't here, but it's a pleasure to see so many new faces at Glen Carrick House. First, Charlie, my mother's new...'

'Fiancé,' Mimi whispered to herself.

'New love. And that's my theme for Christmas today, new love, new friends. As you all know, this year has had its difficulties – Mother's illness...' Fin caught Alasdair's eye. 'Angus's accident, which gave us all a huge shock. My divorce, which probably didn't come as that big a surprise...' There was muted agreement. 'But there have been positives. New faces have joined us, new friends. Heather, we're so happy you're here with us – you keep the place spotless and all of us smiling.'

Heather winked in reply.

'And Mila...' Fin offered his charming smile and she gave him a dazzling one in return. 'You have completely transformed Angus. I thank you.'

'My pleasure,' Mila replied, glancing at Jess.

'Hear, hear,' Alasdair said.

'Ali – my dear friend, and lovely Faye...' Fin blew her a kiss. 'You've been so supportive since Mother's illness.'

'I'm much better now,' Mimi intervened, raising her glass. 'There's no need to fuss, Finlay.'

'Small steps, Mimi – you still need to take things easily,' Alasdair said as he watched her swallow half a glass of champagne.

'Dear Isabella.' Fin's voice was smooth. 'You always bring joy to this house.'

Isabella raised her glass. 'And so much Prosecco.' She leaned over, kissing Lionel's cheek. 'It's so good to be here with you, Mimi darling, and your wonderful Charlie.'

'And dear Jess, who came here as a companion to Mother and has become so much more.'

Jess smiled; her eyes gleaming.

Fin's glass was held high. 'To new love, new friends, and to family: who knows where the line is that distinguishes one from the other? I welcome you all into the McKinlay home. Merry Christmas.'

'Merry Christmas.' The chorus of voices paused to sip champagne, then there was silence except for the clatter of knives and forks against china.

* * *

It was late as the last guests left, Isabella shrieking with laughter, being helped into Lionel's Maserati having drunk too much, insisting that he drive extra slowly despite the main road being clear now. Mila took a lift home with Alasdair and Faye in their four-by-four as she had arrived in a taxi, and Heather too, delighted not to be walking home. Fin insisted on kissing the women twice. The guests took their leave quickly: snow was falling again in thick feathery flakes, and Mimi retired to her chair by the hearth next to Charlie, nursing a glass of Scotch. Fin poured a large drink for Jess, although she put up a hand in refusal, and then he held mistletoe over her head. 'Thanks for today, Jess. It's been special.'

'I had a wonderful time...' She pecked him lightly on the cheek.

They sat sipping whisky, the four of them in silence, watching sparks crackle up the chimney. Jess sighed. Christmas had been wonderful; she felt loved, among family. 'Today has been magical.'

'It has.' Mimi rested a hand on Charlie's. 'I wish Hamish and Angus had been here to share it with us, though.'

'You did a great job as host, Fin,' Charlie admitted. 'Will the boys be back for New Year?'

'Hamish wouldn't miss Hogmanay for the world,' Fin said. 'As for Angus, who knows? I expect he'll stay with Fabrice.'

Jess closed her eyes, imagining spending the New Year with Angus, walking in the snow, laughing, kisses beneath the mistletoe.

'I love Hogmanay.' Mimi sipped whisky and winked at Charlie. 'And next year, there will definitely be new beginnings for us. This Hogmanay will be one we'll all remember for a long time to come.'

Jess heard Fin say, 'You couldn't be more right, Mother.' She was almost falling asleep, bathed in the firelight, too warm. She was thinking how at home she felt in Scotland. The McKinlays had a special place in her heart now. Lunch had been perfect, everyone around the table had been happy, convivial and kind. She was looking forward to seeing Hamish again in the New Year – he was such good company. And Angus was the most wonderful of all. Jess sighed sadly.

'It's going to be special, this coming year.' Fin patted her hand and whispered; his voice confidential. 'Many of us have announcements to make this Hogmanay. I'm ready with mine. And what I have to say will take a few people by surprise, you can be sure of that.'

37

The days after Christmas passed in a whirl for everyone except Mimi, who stretched out on the sofa while Charlie fussed over her, ordering her to take it easy. Fin and Jess headed towards the hills with Thor. Mimi watched them through the window as they walked across the snow. The rattle of the new television came from behind her; Charlie had arranged for them to have one in the apartment and he was watching it now, a programme about politics, fists clenched, grumbling to himself about injustices.

Mimi glanced over her shoulder, glimpsing the top of his flat cap above the armchair. 'It's stopped snowing, Charlie.'

He looked up from the screen. 'That's good.'

'It's beautiful, all the trees full of snow. The roads are clear. You can drive west to Skye, or up to the Orkneys. The Highlands are beautiful, whatever the season. We must visit the islands in the spring.'

Charlie had moved to stand behind her. 'I'm in heaven, my dear – all I need is you and Scotland.'

'I've been thinking...' Mimi said.

Charlie pretended to be alarmed. 'That's always dangerous.'

'Shall we wait until New Year's Day to announce our engagement?'

'Not New Year's Eve?'

'Well, you haven't spoken to Finlay yet and I was wondering – I'm going to ask Hamish what he thinks but – I'd love it if I could perform as part of the Hogmanay celebrations.'

Charlie wrapped his arms around her, kissing her cheek. 'What mischief are you planning?'

'I just want to sing one of Hamish's songs from his musical... I know I can do it justice. What do you think, Charlie?'

'It's not too energetic, is it – kicking and twirling and suchlike?'

'Flora's song...' Mimi's eyes shone. 'I want to perform it on Friday evening. Then on Saturday at breakfast, we can tell the world we're engaged.'

'What about the ring?'

'We can go together to Inverness and choose one,' Mimi replied emphatically. She gazed out of the window. 'The skies are full. It will snow again.'

'Beautiful,' Charlie murmured, nuzzling her neck.

Mimi raised a finger as a thought popped into her head. 'Finlay was out again last night.'

'I saw him, dressed up like the dog's you know whats...' Charlie observed. 'He goes out – I think he sees the doctor and his wife most nights now.'

'He said he was going to the cinema, but he didn't come home until very late – I heard his car pull up outside after one o'clock.' Mimi frowned. 'Do you think he's back with Karen again?'

'No, Fin's had his fingers burned...' He sighed. 'I do wish he'd take Jess out, though. They'd make a nice couple.'

'Oh, yes.' Mimi closed her eyes. 'And I'd get the daughter I always wanted. Wouldn't that be perfect?'

* * *

Jess was standing at the top of a hill, looking down, Thor at her heels, thinking that the view was perfect: unspoiled snow stretching towards laden pine branches. She stared harder to see if there were any deer roaming in the dark depths.

Fin was a few feet away, talking to Faye. They had built a snow character together, hoops of packed ice to resemble the Loch Ness monster, and were admiring their handiwork. Alasdair was on a sledge, whooping and waving, surrounded by lots of other people towing toboggans to the summit and sliding down again. Jess was glad of her warm hat and gloves, although she wasn't sure about the bright cerise colour: it had been Heather's present. Mimi had given her another gold bangle – she had two bracelets on her wrist now. Fin had given her a huge card thanking her from the bottom of his heart and he had included a cheque for more money than he should have. Jess had bought everyone scarves, just to prove that she loved them all equally. Angus and Hamish's presents were still beneath the tree where she'd left them.

She stared at the blank skies overhead: it would probably snow again tomorrow, New Year's Eve. Then hopefully it would clear, the roads would be safe and she would go home.

Heather was at her side, tugging a sledge, her glasses misty, a huge hat pulled over her ears. 'This is fun, Jess – I feel just like a kid again. Have you seen Amy?'

Jess pointed to a ridge below the hill where two figures were play-fighting in the snow, Amy and Kyle. 'Everyone's here today.'

'Except Mila – she's spending time with her daughter.'

'I didn't know Mila had a child.' Jess shook her head. 'When we had coffee together, she spent the whole time asking about the trip to London.'

'Oh, she likes to keep up with the McKinlay family gossip – do you know Mila's fifty-two? You'd never believe it.' Heather's breath was a cloud in the cold air. 'Her daughter is at uni studying architecture – that's why she asked Angus to send all the photos of the buildings in Toulouse, for her daughter's research. She's called Livy – she spent Christmas with her father in Nairn this year and now she's back with Mila.'

'Oh – that's nice.' Jess was thoughtful. 'So, Mila's single now?'

'Very much so. She gets on well with her ex, just like you do, Jess. But I don't think she'll be single for long...'

'Oh?'

'Well, look at her – she's such an attractive personality.' Heather rubbed her hands together. 'I think she'll be at the festivities at Glen Carrick House tomorrow evening. Sadly, I won't be there.'

Jess was disappointed. 'Oh, please come.'

'The B & B's booked up for Hogmanay. I can't get away, hen.' She gazed across the snow to where Alasdair had arrived, tugging his sledge, then Faye plonked herself on it, screaming with delight as Fin pushed her along and Alasdair clapped his hands.

Heather nudged Jess gently with her elbow and pointed at Fin. 'It's a shame I'll miss the party – you'll have to let me know what happens. With those three, for instance... do you think it's a *ménage à trois*?' Her eyes widened. 'There's a tradition in these parts. Hogmanay always reveals a few interesting secrets by the time the piper brings in the New Year.'

* * *

On the evening of the party, a deep path of footprints had been trudged to and from the door to Glen Carrick House. Hamish and his friends, Zane and Jomo, arrived, speaking in excited voices and hugging everyone before Mimi whisked her youngest son away to rehearse her song for the evening performance. Caterers brought in boxes from Transit vans; the table was laden with glasses, food and drink. Fin and Jess were rearranging furniture, hanging up more twinkling lights and decorations, assisted by Thor, who was barking excitedly. Throughout the commotion, Charlie sat in the lounge in front of the fire oblivious, his cap on his head, avidly reading the newspaper.

Then, in the afternoon, as the skies darkened, Hamish and his friends left: they were going back to Hamish's house in Inverness and would return by eight o'clock. Fin retired to his room. Jess went for a shower. Mimi and Charlie sat by the fire, gazing at the sparks whirling up the chimney. Mimi took his hand. 'Will you help me choose what to wear tonight?'

'You'll look glamorous in anything, my dear.'

'Charlie, I want it to be special. It's a big thing for me, singing in public again as Mimi Solitaire. She's who I've been forever – even when I was the girl who sold tickets or when I was "Miriam" or "Mum" or "Mrs McKinlay", she was always the real essence of me. So I want to shine tonight. Gavin will pop in and do my hair. And tonight, I'm going to be the Flower of the Highlands: it's only one song, but it's important.'

Charlie squeezed her fingers gently. 'You'll look a million dollars.' He pushed a hand in his pocket. 'Here, wear this.'

Mimi gazed at the piece of red plastic in her palm. 'Whatever is it?'

'It's a ring, a silly gift from a cracker,' Charlie sighed. 'It will have to do until I can buy you a proper one. But you're my intended now – so I want you to have something to show for it, however small.'

'Thank you.' Mimi allowed him to slide the toy ring onto her finger. Her eyes shone in the firelight. 'Do you know, my dear, I think it's the nicest piece of jewellery I've ever been given.'

* * *

By 8.30, a throng of guests bustled into the house, dressed in their best. Most men wore kilts, tartans, sporrans and sashes, their expressions dignified. The women, in contrast, were bright peacocks in frothy dresses, jewellery sparkling. Jess had made the best effort she could, brushing her hair until it shone and hung loose around her shoulders, wearing a long dress in black velvet, Mimi's gold bangles shining at her wrist. She stood in the corner of the lounge, watching the guests mingle. There were so many people she didn't know, all speaking loudly, laughing, dressed in their finery.

She looked for Thor, but he was nowhere to be seen: he'd be either in the kitchen or in Angus's room. There were too many visitors in the lounge, and it was too noisy. In the corner, Hamish played jazz on the piano, a whisky nearby in a sturdy glass, half-finished. His fingers moved easily over the keyboard, a consummate performer. Next to him was a microphone, electric leads, and a small amplifier. He glanced up, brushing the keys with confident ease, and met Jess's eye; he winked and she winked back.

Mimi had arrived, glamorous in a pale ball gown, leaning on Charlie's arm. He was dapper in a dark suit and dicky bow; Jess noticed that he wasn't wearing his flat cap, his soft white hair sticking up. Mimi put her mouth close to Charlie's ear and whispered something, her face anxious and Charlie shook his head, smiling, reassuring her. Jess glanced around the room; Alasdair and Faye were standing near the long table; he was wearing a smart kilt, a plate of nibbles in his hand, and she was stunning in a sleek blue gown, her red hair shining like glass. Mila had arrived, elegant in an off-the-shoulder dress; she waved to Jess before moving towards the piano to talk to Hamish. Mimi caught Jess's eye and motioned that she should come over. Jess was about to move when a light hand rested on her shoulder.

'Mother and Charlie look well, don't they?' Fin was dashing in a dark tartan kilt and black jacket with brass buttons.

'They look fantastic.'

'So do you, as ever,' he said.

'Thanks, Fin.'

'You don't have a drink...' He raised his eyebrows. 'Let me get you one... and then there's someone I need to talk to. You remember a while ago I said I had a secret that I was keeping to myself?'

Jess leaned forwards, listening. 'Yes...'

'There's a special person that I've become close to, Jess... and she's here tonight.' Fin made a gesture, zipping his lips closed. 'I know I've found the right one this time. I want to make our relationship public, as long as she agrees. Let me get you that drink.'

Jess was joined by Mimi and Charlie, Mimi waving her hand in front of her face. 'Oh, Jess, I'm so nervous.'

Jess laid a hand on her arm. 'Are you all right?'

'I'm on stage at quarter to twelve. I'll sing just before midnight.'

'She's not usually worried about performing,' Charlie said. 'But it's Hamish's song, and in front of family and friends, it feels a bit different.'

'Don't sing if you don't want to,' Jess suggested. 'Just say you've changed your mind.'

Mimi was horrified. 'But I'm Mimi Solitaire – I have to sing. And it's for Hamish and for Charlie and for all of you.' She waved her hand again, using it as a fan in front of her face. 'My heart is going like the clappers and I'm breathless. I'll have to sit down. How about a Scotch, Charlie – just one, to steady my nerves.'

'A small one, my dear – you don't want to ruin your singing voice.' Charlie winked at Mimi.

'You will listen to me sing, won't you, Jess?'

Jess met her eyes. 'Of course.' She offered a reassuring smile. 'You'll be fabulous, Mimi.'

'She's always fabulous,' Charlie agreed.

Mimi glanced at the clock. 'It's almost 11.30. I need to get ready.'

Then Isabella arrived, in a flurry of frills, Lionel dapper in a kilt that he told everyone represented the McPherson clan. Isabella hugged Mimi. 'Oh, I can't wait for your beautiful song,' she trilled. 'And you look like heaven, darling. You will sing like an angel. *Che bella donna.*'

Hamish was playing another song on the piano, his fingers making the keys tinkle softly, and one of his friends, Zane, had stepped up to the microphone and was singing 'Falling in Love Again'. Jess knew the old song well, and Zane had the perfect voice, husky and low.

Jess listened to the soft lilt of his voice, the plaintive tone: she thought about Angus. Yes, she did love him; she'd go home in a few days' time, she'd think of him and miss him. Perhaps they'd meet one day in the future and perhaps they could carry on where they left off. She didn't know what would happen but, right now, at the Hogmanay party with twenty-five minutes to go until midnight, she was amongst friends, and that was enough.

Fin was talking to Alasdair and Faye, and Mila and Hamish's friend Jomo joined them. Jess studied the group. Fin was clearly in love with someone, but she had no idea who. The divorce between him and Karen was imminent and already he'd fallen for someone else: what had he said to her moments ago? 'I've found the right one.'

Jess glanced at Mimi and Charlie in the corner; they had found each other too. Mimi was smoothing her dress, gulping from a whisky glass as Charlie held her hand and spoke softly in her ear. She looked nervous. Jess adored Mimi; she loved all the McKinlays now: they were like family.

She wondered where Angus might be. She tried to picture him in a bar, his arm around a pretty French woman, or in a club with Fabrice, drinking champagne. She decided that was unlikely. He'd be somewhere quiet, thinking of her and their missed opportunity. The thought cheered her.

Fin was next to her, placing a glass of punch in her hand, kissing her cheek. Jess raised her glass and clinked it against his, murmuring, 'To new love and new beginnings. Whoever she is, Fin, I wish you the best.'

'Thanks, Jess,' Fin said. 'She's wonderful. I'm a bit edgy about it becoming public knowledge but...'

Then he paused as there was a clatter of applause. Mimi was clambering towards the microphone, Charlie next to her, helping her to arrange her dress, and as she faced the guests who gazed at her expectantly, she was Mimi Solitaire: ready to thrill everyone with her performance.

38

'Ladies and gentlemen...' Hamish spoke to the small audience, his eyes shining. 'For one night only, singing the finale song from our new musical, *The Flower of the Highlands*, I give you – Mimi Solitaire.'

Mimi stood in front of the microphone, gazing at the faces, all their attention on her. The years melted away, and she was on stage again, bright in a spotlight, illuminated beneath yellow lamps. Music tinkled from Hamish's piano and Mimi raised a hand graciously, imagining herself as Flora Fraser, young, alone, the Highland girl who had captured everyone's heart, telling her life story from the heart. Then Mimi began to sing, her voice throaty with emotion.

> I'm alone in a crowd
> I can't understand why
> Though I'm surrounded by laughter
> Inside I still cry
> In the Highlands, the glens

> I was happy and free
> But now up on stage
> I'm alone as can be
> The saddest of places
> Not by the loch all alone
> But here in the spotlight
> My heart heavy as stone
> I continue to dance
> I continue to sing
> But, with no one to love me
> I am worth not a thing.

Mimi paused while Hamish jangled the piano, a melody swelling with sadness. She waved a hand, a little swirl of her dress, and began again, her voice pure and strong, throwing all the emotion she had into Flora's plight.

> Alone, with no love
> How sadly will I live?
> With no heart in my song
> I have nothing to give.
> So again, I'll perform
> As I do, every night
> Up here on the stage
> Alone in the spotlight
> But when my song is all sung
> And the theatre is bare
> I'm alone by myself
> There's no one to care.

The sound of the piano rose and fell, a crescendo, a melodic moment of tragedy, then silence. Mimi bowed. The audience brought their hands together in rapturous applause, and her eyes shone with happiness. She clutched the microphone with a weak hand; she felt exhausted.

'Thank you.' Her voice was softer now, tired with the effort of singing. A thin film of sweat lay on her brow and she patted it away. 'Thank you. And thank you, Hamish, my pianist, and...' She glanced at him, her eyes dewy with affection. 'My youngest son, my baby...'

Hamish said, 'I'm fifty-eight, Mum.' Zane, who was next to him, turning over the pages of his sheet music, grinned and clapped him heartily on the back.

But Mimi hadn't finished. 'Finlay...' Her eyes caught sight of her eldest son, a glass in his hand, standing between Alasdair and Faye. Fin raised his drink in a toast.

'Finlay...' Mimi's voice was soft as tissue paper. 'My beloved son. I don't tell you enough how much you mean to me... how very much indeed...' She put a finger to her eye, wiping an invisible tear. 'And I want to say thank you to Charlie, my Charlie...' She turned to where he was standing, a few feet away. 'You have made my life wonderful again, my dear... And I won't forget Isabella, my dearest friend, and Jess, the daughter I always wanted.' Mimi extended a hand, then gasped as she caught sight of a figure in the doorway, a man in a dark jacket and kilt.

'Angus...' Mimi's voice caught in her throat. 'My own dear Angus. You're here too, you heard my song. That's so wonderful. Thank you.' Applause resounded from all corners. 'Thank you all.'

Charlie held out a hand and Mimi grasped his fingers, staggering towards him, away from the microphone. Charlie kissed her. 'You were incredible, Mimi.'

The Highland Hens 323

'Did I do Hamish's song justice?'

Charlie took her fingers in his. 'You were the Flower of the Highlands.'

The sound of bagpipes came from behind them; the distinguished, solemn drone that heralded midnight. Charlie held Mimi close. 'We'll see in the New Year, my dearest. This will be our year.'

'It will.' Mimi leaned against him. 'But would you mind – can we go upstairs to the apartment, you and me and a bottle of champagne? I'm feeling tired. Can we celebrate it together Charlie, just the two of us?'

'Anything you want, my dear.'

Mimi walked slowly to the door, Charlie's arm firmly around her; she was smiling, still stunned by her success, her eyes shining. Tonight, she had performed, she had proved to the world how talented she was; she was happy. All she wanted now was a cool glass of champagne and to be alone with the man she loved.

The piper finished playing, the last few notes a plaintive wail, and the clock began to chime. Suddenly the room was filled with a throng of people singing, their voices one roar, rushing forward, their arms crossed, smiles on their faces.

> Should auld acquaintance be forgot
> And never brought to mind?
> Should auld acquaintance be forgot
> And days of auld lang syne?
> For auld lang syne, my dear
> For auld lang syne
> We'll tak a cup o' kindness yet
> For days of auld lang syne.

Jess was propelled by the movement of so many people, the energy of the song and the bounteous good wishes of everyone in the room. The New Year had arrived and with it, hope and expectation and a surge of kindness. She gazed across the room as men shook hands, couples kissed, then she saw Fin, his arms around Mila, their lips glued together. She watched as Mila tangled her fingers in Fin's hair and he pulled her to him as if he'd never let go. Jess was pleased for them. They looked good together and she wished them every happiness. Alasdair was kissing Faye, Hamish seized Zane and kissed him, then he kissed Jomo, then he kissed everyone else in the vicinity.

Jess felt someone standing close to her: she turned and was in Angus's arms. He said, 'Happy New Year,' and they were kissing as they had in the forest, as if no one else was in the room, as if only they existed in the world.

Jess opened her eyes and gazed at him, tall, dark, impeccably dressed, and whispered, 'Angus.'

He wrapped an arm around her. 'Shall we take a walk?'

Jess nodded. In the hall, he took down his coat from a peg and wrapped it around her, then they stepped through the front door, an icy blast of cold air in their faces. Jess was conscious of something brushing around her heels and she put out a hand and rubbed the ears of a black Labrador.

'Thor's pleased to see you,' Angus said. 'But not as much as I am.'

Jess was puzzled. 'When did you come back?'

'Earlier this evening. I spent some time in my room with Thor – he's not missed me as much as I thought he would.'

'He's been sleeping downstairs in the flat with me.' They were in the garden, snow crunching beneath their feet. The whiteness of it glowed in the moonlight. As they walked, Jess was conscious of the unevenness of Angus's gait, his pronounced limp. She leaned against him, picking up the rhythm of his steps.

'Thor knows where he's best off,' Angus said. 'He knew to come to you. Just as I'm doing now.'

Jess caught her breath. 'How was Toulouse?'

'It was good to see Fabrice.' Angus spoke quietly. 'I did a lot of thinking, about me, about you, about what life holds for us both.'

Jess gazed up at him. 'And what did you decide?'

'I've spent a long time believing that being alone was right for me now. I'd never allowed the thought of someone else in my life.'

Jess nodded. 'Me too. It felt too risky.'

'It is risky. But there are risks in being alone. When I had the accident, when I was knocked off the bike, lying in hospital on morphine, hovering between this world and the next, I realised how totally insignificant my life was.'

Jess stared at him. 'How were you insignificant?'

'An arrogant man who ploughed his own furrow, whom nobody loved enough to care if I'd lived or died.'

'Your family would have cared, Angus.'

'Of course they'd have cared.' His eyes gleamed. 'But not like you care – not like I care for you now.' He pressed her arm. 'Am I right, Jess?'

'You're right.' Jess closed her eyes and leaned against him, hearing his voice whisper in her ear.

'I talked to Fabrice. I told him I'd met someone special. He said he was happy for me.' His fingers smoothed her hair. 'And I realised if I'd let you go away, I'd be a fool.'

Jess looked up. 'Fin persuaded me to stay. It snowed heavily...'

'Ah...' Angus's voice was soft. 'Fin knows how I feel about you. I spoke to him on the phone on Christmas Eve – he said he'd keep you here if he could. The rest was up to me.'

'So, now what?' Jess asked.

'Now I'll give you your Christmas present...'

'Christmas present?' Jess was confused.

'You gave me a warm scarf and I have something for you. Put your hand in the overcoat pocket.'

Jess felt a large, wrapped package stuffed inside his pocket. She tugged it out with some difficulty and held it in both hands.

'What is it, Angus?'

He raised his eyebrows. 'Open it.'

She ripped off the paper with eager fingers, revealing a black square box. For a moment, Jess was puzzled, then she gasped. 'A camera?'

His voice was low. 'Come with me to Sri Lanka. Then, later this year, we can maybe go to Canada.'

'I don't understand.'

'You have a good eye, Jess. And I've always needed a partner...'

She was still confused. 'You want me to take photos with you, to travel with you?'

'We'd be good together. And in between, when we're not travelling, you and I and Thor can stay here with Mum, or we can go to England, to your cottage...'

Jess was still astonished. 'Together?'

'Of course...' He pulled her into his arms, the camera pressed between them. 'You know I've fallen in love with you.'

She grinned. 'I do now you've told me.'

'You've given me the chance to smile again. It's been a long time. After Augustine, I thought I'd spend the rest of my days alone, and that was all right with me. But something's changed since I met you. I thought I was fine by myself, but I'm a better person with you. It takes courage to try again.'

'I know how that feels...' Jess said quietly.

'So, what do you say?' His eyes reflected the gleam of the snow. 'Am I worth the risk?'

Jess bit her lip. 'I chose a safe marriage rather than take the chance of being hurt, but now...' Her eyes met his. 'I know what I want. A new beginning – with you...' She was determined. 'Yes, that's what I want, Angus.'

She held the camera tightly in her hand and wrapped her arms around him, feeling the cold of his face and the warmth of his lips. She knew instantly that this was where she wanted to be. And Thor, not wanting to be left out, jumped up and barked with joy.

* * *

A light was on in Mimi's room, a lamp shedding a dim glow, shadows crowding in the corners. On the bedside table was an open bottle of champagne in an ice bucket. Charlie sat on the bed in his shirt and underpants, pulling off his socks, a glass of champagne on the floor next to him. Mimi sat up in bed in her white nightdress, smiling. Charlie found the pyjamas folded beneath the pillow and struggled into them, then positioned himself under the duvet next to her and picked up his glass, holding it towards her.

'Happy New Year, my dear.'

Mimi said. 'It's been a lovely evening. Did you see my boys? They were all there to hear me sing.'

'It was special,' Charlie replied. 'And tomorrow...' He lifted her hand to look at the plastic ring she wore on her finger. 'Tomorrow we can announce our engagement and book the honeymoon and...' He kissed her fingers. 'I'll have that talk with Fin and Hamish and Angus all together, tell them of my intentions.'

'And what intentions are those, Charlie?' Mimi's eyes gleamed with mischief.

'I've loved you all my life, from when I first saw you at the theatre, all silk stockings and red lips and too much to say for yourself. Now I've found you again...' His eyes shone. 'I don't want to let you go.'

Mimi met his gaze, her eyes misty. 'I won't let you go now, either. You've made me smile more than I smiled in all of my life with Donald.'

'I promise I'll never leave you.' Charlie's gaze was earnest. 'Never again, my dear Mimi.'

Mimi sighed. 'Oh, I have so much to look forward to, to be thankful for.' She leaned forward and kissed him. 'But I'm so, so thankful for you.'

'And you too.'

'I'm tired now – all the singing took it out of me.'

'Sleep well, my dear.' Charlie's lips met hers with a little smacking sound.

'Sleep well, Charlie.' Mimi snuggled down as Charlie flicked off the lamp and suddenly the room was dark. She closed her eyes, the sound of music, Hamish's tinkling piano still in her ears. She sighed. 'Goodnight, my love.' But Charlie was already asleep, the gentle rattle of his snore a soft purr in her ears.

Mimi burrowed into the warmth of the duvet and felt the chill leave her flesh; warmth from Charlie's sleeping body seeped into her skin and stayed. She closed her eyes, feeling a dream tugging her into its centre. Then she was on stage, illuminated by one spotlight, a single glimmer of light. She was waiting for the music to start, her cue, so that she could sing, but there was silence. The waiting unnerved her; the silence like stretching elastic, too long, her nerves tense and ready to snap.

She became aware of the audience, their eyes on her glowing

in the dark. There was stirring, muttering and Mimi was afraid; something was wrong, her music hadn't begun.

Then it started, the thumping, rhythmic pounding of a drum, each beat resonating. Mimi's breathing was ragged; she couldn't sing over a drumbeat. She rushed into the shadows and the audience were laughing, their faces distorted. The drum became the pounding of her own heart as she scurried away from ghoulish faces. She dashed for the blackout curtain at the far end of the stage and cannoned into a man who was standing in shadows, his face half hidden. She knew instantly who he was, the scent of his body, the warmth of his smile.

He held out a hand and she was reminded of Angus: they were so alike. She felt the man's fingers in hers, soft as cloud. For a second, Mimi couldn't remember his name; she'd referred to him as Emile for so long, but of course that wasn't right. He wasn't from Louisiana; he hadn't been married. She'd had to say all those things to hide who he was. Donald had treated him so badly, sent him away, but she had never forgotten him.

Mimi hesitated and her thoughts were only of Charlie; she was suddenly filled with a sadness that made her heart ache. Her Charlie. They had just started a life together and she had so much to look forward to. They were going to announce their engagement. She glanced down at her hand – the plastic ring was still on her finger. She'd believed they'd have more time, a Caribbean cruise, another year, another Christmas. She didn't want to let him go, not yet: she'd miss him, he'd miss her so badly. She wasn't ready to go. But wasn't it the truth: you thought you had all the time in the world for those plans and dreams, then it was too late? Time was over now. She couldn't look back.

In the distance, Mimi glimpsed a soft yellow haze that seemed to shimmer. The man pointed to it, and they stepped forward together. Mimi felt weightless, as if she was walking on a stage of air. She was filled with a sense of calm and peace unlike anything she'd known. He spoke softly and she remembered how much the resonant sound of his voice filled her heart with joy.

'Walk with me, Mimi. Just you and me, as I always promised.'

Mimi stared at him. 'And... what about my Charlie?'

'Charlie's turn will come too soon, as it does for us all...'

They took another pace forward, then everything else fell away.

39

A group of bleary-eyed, contented people sat around the breakfast table on New Year's morning. It was early, past six o'clock, but they were still awake, welcoming the new year. When the final guests had left at three o'clock, Hamish opened another bottle of champagne. Then everyone decided it would be fun to have a snowball fight in darkness and they tumbled in the garden until Thor's excited barking threatened to wake Mimi in the attic apartment.

Afterwards, they'd gazed at the moon over the loch glimmering on the water. Then they relocated into the warmth of the snug, sinking into soft chairs, leaving the vast lounge and all its party detritus, streamers, empty glasses, bowls of food, to drink black coffee and to chat until well after six. Fin declared he wasn't at all tired; Mila suggested they tidy the lounge before Mimi and Charlie woke, but Hamish installed himself at the piano and everyone began to sing.

By six thirty, everyone was hungry. Zane and Hamish cooked eggs and toast and Fin and Mila made more coffee. Angus was sitting with one arm around Jess, Thor's chin resting on his knee.

Jess wondered if it might be a nice gesture to take Mimi and Charlie breakfast in bed.

And now, while everyone else was discussing going outside to watch the sun rise on the first day of a new year, Thor pricked up his ears and lifted his head. Charlie was standing in the doorway in pyjamas, his eyes wide. He gasped, 'I got up and needed the bathroom...'

Zane gave a kind laugh. 'You made a wrong turn, mate...'

'No...' Charlie's face was haggard. 'It's Mimi. She won't wake up. I tried – I can't wake her...'

Chairs scraped and everyone was on their feet. Fin, Angus and Hamish rushed up the stairs, Charlie behind them, Jess's hand in his. They reached Mimi, who was lying in bed, perfectly still. Her eyes were half open, glassy beneath the lids, and her lips pursed as if she was singing a song. Her skin was the colour of wax. Fin reached for her hand. It was ice-cold. He tugged out his phone and pressed buttons, gasping, 'Ali – it's my mother – can you come over?'

Charlie stood back, unable to move, Jess's arm around him. Angus knelt uncomfortably by the side of the bed, gentle fingers at Mimi's throat, moving his hand once, twice, searching for the hint of a heartbeat. Hamish looked over his shoulder towards Jess, his face already wet with tears.

* * *

An hour later, Alasdair was talking quietly with Fin, Angus and Hamish. On his way out, he called into the snug and shook Charlie's hand, offering condolences. Once Charlie knew that nothing could be done, he asked Jess to fetch him a glass of Scotch. It was at this point that he began to sob as they sat on the sofa together, Jess folding him in her arms.

Mila, practical and sharp-witted, led Jomo and Zane into the lounge, declaring that they'd be most useful clearing up and giving the McKinlays some space. Charlie held on hard to Jess; he needed someone close and she was happy to stay.

'We were going to get married.' The whisky glass trembled in Charlie's hand as he turned hollow eyes on Jess. 'We were going to announce it today...'

'I didn't know.' Jess swallowed. Tears rolled down her cheeks.

'We'd found each other after so long.' Charlie wiped his nose. 'It was what we both wanted.'

'We all loved Mimi. She was wonderful.'

He smiled sadly. 'I loved her from the first day we met.'

Jess sighed. 'Of course...'

'I was a whippersnapper, a teenager, and she was a beautiful young woman, all stockings and red lips, and she married McKinlay. I felt protective towards her even then.'

Jess spoke softly. 'Did you see her perform often?'

'Oh, yes – she was on stage in Bermondsey with the rest of the girls. Even when she had her babies, she wanted to dance. That suited McKinlay – he could hire nannies and spend time with his mistresses.'

'And what about in the West End?' Jess squeezed his hand. 'With Yul Brynner and Julie Andrews on the big stage? Did you see her there?'

Charlie shook his head. 'I don't know, Jess – Mimi danced at the theatre in Bermondsey, but then I left. I don't know if she ever performed in the West End.'

'But she met Emile, the violinist, in the West End?'

'Who?' Charlie asked, sipping Scotch.

'Angus's father.'

Charlie sighed. 'You mean Tony?'

Jess nodded, encouraging him to go on. Charlie cleared his

throat. 'Tony was a lovely bloke – everyone liked him. He was Trinidadian. Donald employed him to do a bit of cleaning. He was talented, though: he could carve, paint. He helped out with scenery. He had a real soft spot for Mimi. She was fond of him too. Then one day, McKinlay had been out womanising and Mimi turned to Tony for support. They spent the night together, everyone knew it. McKinlay found out and sacked Tony, threatened him, told him he'd never work in London again. Tony left, went up north, and Mimi was pregnant with Angus.'

Jess sighed. 'So that's how the Emile story came to be.'

'Mimi was always one for romance,' Charlie said sadly. 'I suppose she just elevated Tony to where he was already in terms of her affections.' He shrugged. 'Donald kept a tight rein on her after that; he allowed her to work until after Hamish was born, then he brought her to live here.'

Jess squeezed his hand. 'That must've been hard, away from everything she knew.'

'She told me how lonely she was,' Charlie said.

'Then she met you again.'

'I couldn't keep her for long.' Charlie swallowed some whisky. 'There's nothing left for me here, Jess. Not without her. Scotland's beautiful but, without my Mimi, it would be a lonely place to live.'

* * *

Upstairs, three figures sat around Mimi's bed, their heads bowed. Fin sighed. 'It was exactly as Ali said – the fever she had weakened her heart. I shouldn't have let her do so much.'

Angus's voice was low. 'You couldn't have stopped her, Fin.'

'I never thought...' Fin put a thumb and forefinger to his eyes to stem the flow of tears. 'I never imagined she'd go... I mean, I thought there would be more time...'

Angus said quietly, 'We never imagined a day when she wouldn't be with us.'

Hamish snuffled. 'I feel so awful – the things I should have said, the things I ought to have done to make her life better, but I was living the life...'

'The life she wanted for you,' Angus said. A single tear made its way down his face.

'Charlie made her happy,' Fin replied. 'He must feel terrible.'

Angus agreed. 'Oh, he'll miss her.'

Hamish lifted Mimi's hand. 'What's this? A piece of plastic? A ring?' He snorted softly and was about to remove it from her finger.

'You should leave it,' Angus said quietly. 'It meant something to her. Leave it where it is.'

Fin wiped hands across his face. 'She still looks lovely, like she's sleeping.'

'We'll do right by her,' Fin said determinedly. 'We'll give her the best send-off, won't we?'

'Oh, we will.' Hamish wiped away more tears. The thought of Mimi's funeral filled him with more sorrow. 'I'll miss her.'

There was a soft knock on the door; a woman in her forties, wearing a black suit, her hair in one long dark plait, stood outside. She spoke softly. 'Mr McKinlay?'

The three men turned as one as she stepped into the room. 'I'm Rhona Wilson – from Wilson's Funeral Directors. Dr Harris phoned me and said you wanted me to call in.' She approached the bed and gazed at Mimi. 'So, this is the famous dancer? I've heard such wonderful things about her. I'm so sorry for your loss.'

* * *

Three hours later, Hamish was walking towards the Saab with Zane and Jomo. Charlie was with them, carrying a case. There was no reason for him to stay at Glen Carrick House now.

Hamish paused by the car, turning to Fin, Mila, Angus and Jess. He hugged them in turn and whispered, 'I'll put Charlie and the others on the plane, then I'll come back.'

Charlie raised his chin, his eyes glistening. 'I need to be home with my kids around me. I rang Lizzie – she'll pick me up in London. She and David will look after me...'

Jess wrapped him in her arms. 'You'll be back for the funeral in a fortnight though, won't you, Charlie? Will we see you then?'

Charlie nodded, swallowing hard. 'I will. I need to say goodbye to her properly...' Then he couldn't speak.

Jess took both of his hands in hers. 'I'm sorry...'

He inclined his head once then he turned away, sliding into the back seat, huddling inside the car. He looked small and frail.

Hamish leaped into the driver's seat and started the engine. As the car pulled away, Jess choked back a sob. Angus threaded his fingers through hers and she squeezed them gently.

They walked back to the house and Fin rang Isabella, who gasped that she'd always thought she would go first, then she began to weep. He pushed his phone in his pocket, pacing up and down, his head in his hands, muttering about organising the funeral, contacting people, sending invitations. He was clearly tired. Mila put her arms around his neck, urging him to have a hot bath, to try to relax: they would sort things out later. Fin kissed her and breathed out slowly, then padded dutifully towards the bathroom.

Jess met Angus's eyes and he wrapped his arms around her as she leaned against him. He kissed the top of her head. Jess gazed around the room where they had all spent New Year's Eve; her eyes fell on the piano where Hamish had played and Mimi had sung from her heart. The microphone was still standing. She touched the gold bangles on her arm, burying her head against Angus's chest, thinking that only hours ago she had hugged Mimi, not imagining that their time together would be so short. Her hands gripped Angus's arms, holding on tight. Then tears came in big gulps.

* * *

The pale winter sun gleamed on the loch as Jess and Angus trod across the snow, crisp and crunching underfoot, Thor padding behind them. A sharp icy wind blew in their faces. Angus held Jess's hand tightly in his and stared upwards. 'The sky's full of snow.'

'It is...' Jess followed his gaze and sighed. 'Charlie is heartbroken.'

'Hamish, too. He was still sobbing before we came out.' Angus took a breath. 'We're all grieving in our own ways – we all loved her more than we can say.'

'Everyone loved her...' Jess brought his hand to her lips. 'How can I help?'

'You're here with me – that helps.' He offered her a weak smile. 'We'll make sure Charlie's all right. He's on his way home. Hamish will fly back to London the day after tomorrow. They'll all come back on the fifteenth for the funeral.'

'Can I stay with you until then?'

'Stay, please,' Angus said quietly. Jess thought he looked tired. 'I don't want you to leave.'

'Fin's up at the house with Mila. She's been really good to him.'

'They'll be all right together.' Angus was thoughtful, then he gave a small grunt. 'Jess, my mother died last night and all I can think is that I want to hang on to you with everything I have.'

'That's understandable...'

'Life gives us opportunities. Mum fell in love with Charlie. They made the most of their time together, although it was too short.' He turned to her, his eyes glowing. 'Let's do the same.'

Jess exhaled. 'You're right, Angus. Each day is precious, each moment. Mimi would want that, wouldn't she? For every moment to be a chance to be the best we can, to live the dream?'

Angus made a low sound and gazed across the loch. The snow was a soft blue glare, blending into water and sky, gleaming beneath the pale sun. Thor ran ahead and started digging for something, his feet flicking up white clumps. A few snowflakes were twirling, held for a moment in the air.

Angus turned to Jess and kissed her lips. 'Next year, on New Year's Day, we'll come here to the loch with Fin and Hamish, perhaps we can all scatter Mum's ashes and remember.' Jess squeezed his hand. 'And who knows what we'll all have done by next year? Hamish and his music, Fin and Mila, me and you, the places we can go together, the good times we'll share. Who knows how brightly we can shine?'

'Who knows?' Jess took both of his hands. 'But Mimi will be there in our hearts, always.'

Angus wrapped an arm around her and gave a soft whistle. Thor was by his side in seconds, panting, his breath a circle of steam. The snow was falling faster now, thick flakes that stuck to Angus's coat and came to rest on his face. He exhaled. 'Shall we go back home, Jess?'

She glanced up at him. 'Are you tired?'

'Exhausted,' he said. They turned round, making their way steadily back towards the road, Glen Carrick House a blur in the distance. 'I need some sleep. You must be tired too.'

'Yes, I am.' Jess was conscious of the vapour her warm breath made on the air.

'Will you stay with me and sleep in my arms?'

Jess snuggled closer to him, sharing his warmth. 'I will. Isn't that how it's always going to be from now on?'

'I hope so – always is a very long time,' Angus said. 'All we have is now.'

'Now is good,' Jess agreed.

The air was filled with falling snow, a white, blinding blizzard of flakes that obliterated everything in the distance. They trudged back, one pace at a time, a woman and a man who limped slightly, a dog leaping and wagging its tail, leaving deep footprints behind them.

ACKNOWLEDGMENTS

Thanks to my agent, Kiran Kataria, for her wisdom, professionalism and integrity.

Thanks to Amanda Ridout, to Nia Beynon, Claire Fenby-Warren, Jenna Houston, Laura Kingston, Megan Townsend and the team at Boldwood Books.

Huge thanks to my editor Sarah Ritherdon for her support, insight and warmth.

So much appreciation to everyone who has made this book happen: designers, editors, technicians, magicians, voice actors, reviewers, bloggers – thanks to you all.

Thanks to Peter Blaker and Solitary Writers, Julie Mullen and Martin Seager, Radio Somerset, Planet Rock, Radio Iwoji.

Thanks to the generous and supportive community of Boldwood writers.

Much thanks to the talented Ivor Abiks at Deep Studios.

Thanks to so many supportive friends: Erika, Rich, Rog, Jan, Jan M, Bill, Ken, Trish, Lexy, Helen, Shaz, Frank, Ian, Susie, Chrissie, Kathy N, Nik R, Pete O', Sarah and Jim, Martin, Cath, Avril, Slawka, Beau, Zach, Matt B, Steve, Steve's Mum, Ruchi, Stephanie, Kay, Ingrid, Katie H, Jonno, Edward and Robin.

Thanks to my wonderful neighbours, the Wellington community and Books by the Blackdowns.

Special love to our Tony and Kim.

Love to my mum, who showed me the joy of reading, and to my dad, who proudly never read anything.

Love always to Liam, Maddie, Cait and to Big G for being my star.

Warmest thanks to my readers, wherever you are. You make this journey incredible.

MORE FROM JUDY LEIGH

We hope you enjoyed reading *The Highland Hens*. If you did, please leave a review.

If you'd like to gift a copy, this book is also available as an ebook, digital audio download and audiobook CD.

Sign up to Judy Leigh's mailing list for news, competitions and updates on future books:

http://bit.ly/JudyLeighNewsletter

Explore more fun, uplifting reads from Judy Leigh:

ABOUT THE AUTHOR

Judy Leigh is the bestselling author of *A Grand Old Time* and *Five French Hens* and the doyenne of the 'it's never too late' genre of women's fiction. She has lived all over the UK from Liverpool to Cornwall, but currently resides in Somerset.

Visit Judy's website: https://judyleigh.com

Follow Judy on social media:

f facebook.com/judyleighuk

𝕏 twitter.com/judyleighwriter

◎ instagram.com/judyrleigh

BB bookbub.com/authors/judy-leigh

Boldwd

Boldwood Books is an award-winning fiction publishing company seeking out the best stories from around the world.

Find out more at www.boldwoodbooks.com

Join our reader community for brilliant books, competitions and offers!

Follow us
@BoldwoodBooks
@BookandTonic

Sign up to our weekly
deals newsletter
https://bit.ly/BoldwoodBNewsletter